Praise for Ci

"An innovative and compassionate look at how knowledge shapes and changes humanity. Liu grounds his tales in contemporary Chinese life and society, using the sci-fi genre to tackle questions about humanity's place in the universe. . . . A must-have for readers of hard science fiction."

—*Publishers Weekly* on *To Hold Up the Sky*

"A well-rounded view of Liu's work, showing him both in the mode familiar to readers of the Remembrance of Earth's Past trilogy as well as in other, perhaps more unexpected, styles. Highly recommended for fans of Liu's work or for those interested in Chinese SF in general."

—*Booklist* (starred review) on *To Hold Up the Sky*

"These stories excel at linking hard science fiction with global humanism and quiet moments of emotion. Liu's writing maintains a calm, matter-of-fact demeanor, even as it conveys inventive cruelty and beautiful imagery. . . . Will appeal to readers of literary fiction and classic science fiction alike."

—Shelf Awareness on *To Hold Up the Sky*

"It is magic, this collection of short stories Liu wrote and published ten, twenty, thirty years ago. It is a time machine; a split-vision tunnel that lets you go back in time while staring forward, to see what 2003's or 1985's version of 2010 or 2020 or 3000 looked like from China. . . . *To Hold Up the Sky* gives us a window that looks out over a different sci-fi landscape than we've seen in decades."

—NPR on *To Hold Up the Sky*

"This audacious and ultimately optimistic early work will give Liu's English-reading fans a glimpse at his evolution as a writer and give any speculative fiction reader food for deep thought."

—Shelf Awareness on *Supernova Era*

TOR BOOKS BY CIXIN LIU

The Three-Body Problem

The Dark Forest

Death's End

Ball Lightning

Supernova Era

To Hold Up the Sky

The Wandering Earth

TO HOLD UP THE SKY

CIXIN LIU

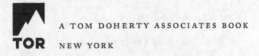

A TOM DOHERTY ASSOCIATES BOOK

NEW YORK

TO HOLD UP THE SKY

Copyright © 2020 by 刘慈欣 (Cixin Liu)

English translation © 2020 by China Educational Publications Import & Export Corp., Ltd.

This publication was arranged by Hunan Science & Technology Press.

"Ode to Joy" by Friedrich Schiller quoted in the story "Ode to Joy." English translation by William F. Wertz in *Friedrich Schiller Poet of Freedom Vol. 1*. Published by The Schiller Institute.

A Tor Book
Published by Tom Doherty Associates
120 Broadway
New York, NY 10271

www.tor-forge.com

Tor® is a registered trademark of Macmillan Publishing Group, LLC.

The Library of Congress Cataloging-in-Publication Data is available upon request.

ISBN 978-1-250-30606-7 (trade paperback)
ISBN 978-1-250-30607-4 (ebook)

Our books may be purchased in bulk for promotional, educational, or business use. Please contact your local bookseller or the Macmillan Corporate and Premium Sales Department at 1-800-221-7945, extension 5442, or by email at MacmillanSpecialMarkets@macmillan.com.

First Edition: October 2020
First Trade Paperback Edition: September 2021

Printed in the United States of America

0 9 8 7 6

TABLE OF CONTENTS

FOREWORD

TRANSLATED BY ADAM LANPHIER

This anthology includes more than ten of my short stories, most of which were published more than a decade ago. At that time, sci-fi was still a very marginal pursuit in China. The genre had few readers and was largely overlooked. In China, science fiction is seen as something foreign; its fundamental elements have never been a part of Chinese culture. Life has passed steadily, with few changes, from generation to generation over the course of China's long history, so people unconsciously believe that life will be ever thus. Historically, the term "future" itself appeared mostly in Buddhist texts, which are also foreign; people have seldom thought about or paid attention to the future in their daily lives.

But in recent years, things have changed drastically. China has entered wholesale into a process of rapid modernization, and every day, all around us, there are stupefying changes. Suddenly, the future stands before us in vivid detail, and it exerts a huge appeal. Old China has suddenly become a nation with an extremely keen sense of the future. It is understandable why people, under such circumstances, would pay unprecedented attention to science fiction.

In Europe and the US, the question I'm asked most often is: "What makes Chinese science fiction Chinese?" For my part, I have never consciously or deliberately tried to make my sci-fi more Chinese. The stories in this anthology touch on a variety of sci-fi themes, but they all have something in common: They are about things that concern all of humanity, and the challenges and crises they depict are all things humanity faces together. In fact, when you read or make science fiction, your sympathy automatically moves away from ideas of ethnicity and nation and toward a higher idea of humanity as a whole; from this vantage, humanity naturally becomes a collective unit, rather than an assembly of different parts divided by ethnicity and nation. Even if the sci-fi you read or write tells a distinctly trivial, mundane, or personal story, you'll still have this feeling. I believe this is one of the most valuable features of science fiction.

In China, the new generation's way of thinking is changing dramatically. They are gradually turning their eyes away from the reality of their immediate environment and the mundanities of life toward the distant, starry sky and the future. More and more, they are beginning to see themselves as members of humankind, not merely as Chinese people. They are also beginning to care about those ultimate questions that their forebears seldom considered: where humans and the universe came from, and where they're going. This change in their thinking will profoundly affect China's future and even the future of humanity. The science fiction stories in this book are a vivid expression of this new way of thinking.

Yet I am also Chinese, and, whether by design or not, these stories will inevitably have a strong Chinese flavor, imbued with the culture, history, and present reality of China.

In creating sci-fi, I always try hard to imagine and describe the relationship between the Great and the Small.

"The Small" refers here to human smallness. As individuals, we are small indeed, and collectively, humanity is small, too. Imagine a concert attended by all of humanity. How big a venue would you need? Not as big as I'd imagined—a space about as large as Shanghai's Pudong District would suffice. Here's another perverse thought experiment: If you were to make a meatball out of humankind, its diameter would be less than a kilometer.

"The Great" refers, of course, to the universe. Every person has a deep sense of its enormity. The most distant light we see was sent out over ten billion years ago. If you shrank the solar system to the size of a dinner plate, the diameter of a correspondingly shrunken Milky Way would still be one hundred thousand kilometers.

In my sci-fi, I challenge myself to imagine the relationship between Small people and the Great universe—not in the metaphysical sense of philosophy, nor as when someone looks up at the starry sky and feels such sentiment and pathos that their views on human life and the universe change. Stories about such relationships between people and the universe are not science fiction; they are realism. In my sci-fi, I work to imagine the direct, tangible relationship between people and the universe. In this relationship, the evolution and metamorphoses of the universe are inseparable from human life and human fate.

It's very difficult work, and it's the greatest challenge I face when writing science fiction. Common sense tells us that there is no such relationship. Whether the universe is expanding or contracting, or whether a star ten billion light-years away has gone supernova, truly has nothing to do with the mundane, insignificant events of my life. Yet I firmly believe that there is a relationship between humanity and the universe. When it was born, the universe was smaller than an atom, and everything within it was intermixed as a single whole; the natural connection between the universe's small parts and its great entirety was thus determined. Though the universe has expanded to whatever its current size, this connection still exists, and if we can't see it now, that doesn't mean we won't be able to in the future. I work hard to imagine all sorts of possibilities in the relationship between people and the universe, and I try to turn what I imagine into thrilling fiction. This anthology, just as its title suggests, contains a portion of my efforts.

Thank you all!

TO

HOLD

UP

THE

SKY

THE VILLAGE TEACHER

TRANSLATED BY ADAM LANPHIER

He knew he'd have to teach his final lesson early.

He felt another shot of pain in his liver, so strong he almost fainted. He didn't have the strength to get out of bed, and, with great difficulty, he pulled himself closer to the bedside window, whose paper panes glowed in the moonlight. The little window looked like a doorway leading into another world, one where everything shone with silver light, a diorama of silver and frostless snow. He shakily lifted his head and looked out through a hole in the paper window, and his fantasy of a silver world receded. He found himself looking into the distance, at the village where he had spent his life.

The village lay serenely in the moonlight, and it looked as if it had been abandoned for a hundred years. The small flat-roofed houses were almost indistinguishable from the mounds of soil surrounding them. In the muted colors of moonlight, it was as if the entire place had dissolved back into the hills. Only the old locust tree could be seen clearly, a few black crows' nests scattered among its withered branches, like stark drops of black ink on a silver page.

The village had its good times, like the harvest. When young men and women, who had left the village in droves to find work, came back, and the place was bustling and full of laughter. Ears of corn glistened on the rooftops, and children did somersaults in the piles of stalks on the floor of the threshing ground. The Spring Festival was another cheerful time, when the threshing ground was lit with gas lamps and decorated with red lanterns. The villagers gathered there to parade lucky paper boats and do lion dances. Now, only the clattering wooden frames of the lions' heads were left, stripped of paint. The village had no money to buy new trains for the heads, so they had been using bedsheets as the lions' bodies, which worked in a pinch. But as soon as the Spring Festival ended, all the youths of the village left again to look for work, and the place fell back into torpor.

At dusk every day, as thin wisps of smoke rose from the chimneys of the houses, one or two elderly villagers, their faces grooved like walnuts, would stand and gaze down the road that led beyond the mountains, until the last ray of gloaming light got caught in the locust tree and disappeared. People turned their lamps off and went to bed early in the village. Electricity was expensive, at ¥1.8 per kilowatt hour.

He could hear a dog softly whimpering somewhere in the village, whining in its sleep, perhaps. He looked out at the moonlit yellow soil surrounding the village, which suddenly seemed to him like a placid sheet of water. If only it *were* water—this year was the fifth consecutive year of drought, and they had had to carry water to the fields to irrigate them.

His gaze drifted into the distance, landing on the fields on the mountain, which looked in the moonlight like the footprints of a giant. Small, scattered plots were the only way to farm that rocky mountain, covered as it was with vines and brush. The terrain was too rough for agricultural equipment—even oxen would have had no good footing—so people were obliged to do all the labor by hand.

Last year, a manufacturer of agricultural machines had visited to sell a kind of miniature walking tractor, small enough to work those meager fields. It wasn't a bad little machine, but the villagers weren't having it. How much grain could those tiny plots produce? Planting them was detailed work, more like sewing than sowing, and a crop that could feed a man for a year was considered a success. In a year of drought, as it was, those fields might not even produce enough to recoup the cost of planting. A five-thousand-yuan tractor, and on top of that, diesel fuel at more than two yuan a liter—outsiders just didn't understand the difficulties of life in these mountains.

A few small silhouettes walked past the window. They formed a circle on a ridge between two fields and squatted down, inscrutable. He knew these were his students—as long as they were nearby, he could detect their presence even without seeing them. This intuition had developed in him over a lifetime, and it was particularly keen now that his life was drawing to a close.

He could even recognize the children in the moonlight. Liu Baozhu and Guo Cuihua were there. Those two were originally from the village and didn't have to live at school; nevertheless, he had taken them in.

Liu Baozhu's father had paid the dowry for a bride from Sichuan ten years before, and she had come and given birth to Baozhu. Five years after that, when Baozhu had grown a bit, his father began to neglect his wife, the small bit of closeness they'd had slipping away, and eventually she left him and returned to her family in Sichuan.

After that, Baozhu's father lost his way. He began gambling, just like the old bachelors of the village, and before long he had lost everything but four walls and a bed. Then he began drinking. Every night, he sold roasted sweet potatoes for eighty fen a kilogram and drank himself useless with the money. Useless and angry: he hit his son every day, and twice a week he hit him hard. One night the month before, he'd nearly beaten his son to death with a sweet potato skewer.

Guo Cuihua's home life was even worse. Her father had found a bride for himself through decent channels, a rare thing here, and he was proud. But good things seldom last, and right after the wedding, it became apparent that Cuihua's mother was unwell. No one could tell at the wedding—she'd likely been given a drug to calm her. Why would a respectable woman come to a village like this in the first place, so poor that even the birds wouldn't shit as they flew over? Nevertheless, Cuihua was born and grew up, and her mother got sicker and sicker. She attacked people with cooking knives in the daytime, and at night she would try to burn the house down. She spent most of her time laughing to herself like a ghoul, with a sound that would set your hair on end.

The rest of the children were from other villages, the closest of which was at least ten miles away on mountain roads, so they had to live at school. In a crude village school like this, they would spend the whole term there. The students brought their own bedding, and each hauled a sack of wheat or rice from home, which they cooked themselves on the school's big stove. As night fell in the winter, the children would gather around the stove and watch the cooking grain bubble and purl in the pot, their faces lit by straw-orange flames. It was the most tender sight he'd ever seen. He would take it with him into the next world.

On the ridge outside the window, within the ring of children, little stars of fire began to shine, bright in the moonlit night. They were burning incense and paper, and their faces were lit red in the firelight against the silver-gray night. He was reminded of the sight of the children by the stove. Another scene emerged from the pool of his memory. The electricity had gone out at school (due perhaps to a faulty circuit, or, as happened more often, a lack of funds) while he was teaching an evening class. He held a candle in his hand to illuminate the blackboard. "Can you see it?" he'd asked, and the children answered, as they always did, "Not yet!" It really was hard to read the blackboard with so little light, but they had a lot of material to cover, so night class was the only option. He lit a second candle and held them both up. "It's still too dark!" yelled the children, so he lit a third candle. It was still too dark to read the board, but the children stopped yelling. They knew their teacher wouldn't light another candle no matter how much they yelled. He couldn't afford to. He looked down at their faces flickering in the candlelight, those kids, who had fought off darkness with every fiber of their beings.

The children and firelight, the children and firelight. It was always the children and firelight, always the children at night, in the firelight. The image was forever embedded in his mind, though he never understood what it meant.

He knew the children were burning incense and paper for him, as they had done so many times before, but this time he didn't have the strength to criticize them for being superstitious. He had spent his whole life trying to ignite the flame of science and culture in the children's hearts, but he knew that, compared to the fog of ignorance and superstition that enshrouded this remote mountain village, it was a feeble flame indeed, like the flame of his candles in the classroom that night. Six months earlier, a few villagers had come to the school to scavenge rafters from the roof of the already-dilapidated dorm, with which they meant to renovate the temple at the entrance to the village. He asked where the children would sleep if the dorm had no roof, and they said they could sleep in the classroom.

"In the classroom? The wind blows right through the walls. How can the children sleep there in the winter?"

"Who cares? They're not from here."

He picked up a pole and fought them fiercely, and he wound up with two broken ribs. A kind villager propped him up and walked with him all the way to the nearest town hospital, fifteen miles or more on mountain roads.

While assessing his injuries, the doctor had discovered that he had esophageal cancer. There was a high incidence of this sort of cancer in the region, so it wasn't a rare diagnosis. The doctor congratulated him on his good fortune—he had come while the cancer was still in an early stage, before it had started to metastasize. It was curable with surgery; in fact, esophageal cancer was one of the types of cancer against which surgery was most effective. His broken ribs might well have saved his life.

After, he had gone to the province's main city, which had an oncology hospital, and asked a doctor there how much such a surgery would cost. The doctor told him that, considering his situation, he could stay in the hospital's welfare ward, and that his other expenses could also be reduced commensurately. The final amount wouldn't be too much—around twenty thousand yuan. Recalling that his patient came from such a remote place, the doctor proceeded to explain the details of hospitalization and surgery.

He listened silently and suddenly asked: "If I don't get the surgery, how long do I have?"

The doctor regarded him blankly for a long moment and said, "Maybe six months."

The teacher heaved a long sigh, as if greatly relieved, and the doctor was nonplussed. At least he could see this graduating class off.

He really had no way to pay twenty thousand yuan. Over his life, he could have saved up some money. Community teachers may not make much, but he had worked for so many years, and he had never married, nor did he have other financial obligations. But he had spent it all on the children. He couldn't remember how many children's tuition he had paid, how many of their incidental expenses he had covered. Recently, there were Liu Baozhu and Guo Cuihua, but more often, he would see that the school's big cooking pot had no oil in it, so he would buy meat and lard for the children. All the money he had left would cover perhaps a tenth of the surgery.

After the appointment with the doctor, he had walked along the city's wide avenue toward the train station. It was already dark out, and neon lights had come on in a dazzling blur of stripes and dots, bewildering him. At night, the tall buildings of the city were like rows of enormous lamps extending into the clouds, and snippets of music, alternately frenetic and gentle, filled the air along his way.

In that strange world of the city, he reflected on his own short life. He was feeling philosophical, calmly considering that each person has their own path in life, and that he had chosen his own path twenty years prior, when he had graduated from middle school and decided to return to the village. In fact, his destiny had been given to him by another village teacher.

He had spent his own childhood at the school where he now taught. His father and mother had died early, and the school had been his home. His teacher had raised him as a son, and while his childhood might have been poor, it was not lacking in love. When school had gone on winter break one year, his teacher decided to take him home for the season.

His teacher's home was far away, and snow had lain deep on the mountain road. It was the middle of the night by the time they laid eyes on the lights of his teacher's village. Not far behind them, they saw four glints of green, the eyes of two wolves. There were many wolves in the mountains back then, and you could find piles of wolf shit all around the school. Once, as a prank, he had taken a gray-white pile of the stuff, lit it on fire, and thrown it into the classroom, which filled with acrid smoke, choking his classmates. His teacher was furious.

The two wolves in the forest had slowly approached them. While his teacher had snapped a thick branch off a tree and brandished it in the wolves' path, yelling loudly, he had run off toward the village, scared out of his wits, running with all his might. He worried the wolves would go around his teacher and come after him; he worried he would run into another wolf on his way. He ran heaving into the village. Several men assembled with hunting rifles, and he went back with them to look for his teacher. They found him lying in a pool of blood and slush, half of his leg and most of his arm bitten off. His teacher took his final breath on the way to the town hospital, and he saw his teacher's eyes in a ray of torchlight. A large chunk of his cheek had been bitten off and he was unable to speak, but his eyes expressed an urgent plea, one that he'd understood and remembered.

After he graduated from middle school, he had turned down a promising opportunity to work in the town's municipal government. Instead, despite having no family or friends there, he returned directly to the mountain village, to the village primary school that his teacher had pleaded with him to save. By the time he returned, the school was abandoned, having had no teacher for several years.

Not long before that, the Board of Education had begun enforcing a policy that replaced community teachers with state-supported teachers. Some community teachers were able to obtain state support by taking a test. He passed that test and got his teaching certificate, and when he found out he was a licensed, state-supported teacher, he was happy, but that was the extent of his reaction. Other members of his cohort had been elated. But he didn't care whether he was a community teacher or a state-supported teacher; he only cared about the classes of children who would graduate from his primary school and go out into the world. Regardless of whether they left the mountains or stayed, their lives would be different in some way from the lives of children who had never gone to school.

Those mountains were one of the most impoverished areas in the country. But worse than the poverty was the apathy of the people there toward their condition. He remembered how, many years ago, when agricultural output quotas were set for each household, the village had divided and distributed its fields, and then its possessions. The village had one tractor, and the villagers couldn't come to a consensus on how to pay for its fuel or allot time to use it. The only solution everyone could accept was to divide the tractor itself. They literally disassembled it—you get a wheel, he gets an axle. And two months ago, a factory had sent poverty relief in the form of a submersible pump, and, electricity being expensive, they also sent a diesel generator along with plenty of fuel to operate it. They had barely left the village before the villagers sold the machines, the pump and the generator together, for just two hundred and fifty yuan. Everyone ate two good meals, more than in most years.

Another time, a leather manufacturer had bought some land in the village on which to build a tannery—who knew how it got sold to them in the first place. Once the tannery was up, lye and niter flowed into the river and seeped into the well water. The people who drank it broke out in red boils all over their bodies—but no one cared! They were just happy the land sold for a good price. It was a village of old, hopeless bachelors who spent all day gambling and drinking, never planting. They had it figured out—as long as they stayed poor, the county would receive small amounts of poverty relief every year, more than they could make plowing their tiny fields of rocks and dust. They had come to accept this sort of life because they knew nothing else. The village's fruitless ground and poison water were dispiriting, but what could truly make you lose hope was the dull eyes of the villagers.

He had reflected on all these things as he had walked from the doctor's office through the province's main city. His diagnosis still didn't feel real; the doctor's words felt far away. This walking had tired him, though, so he sat down next to the sidewalk. In front of him was a large, glamorous restaurant. Its façade was a single, transparent window, through which the restaurant's chandeliers cast their light onto the street. The restaurant looked like a huge aquarium, and the customers inside, in their fancy clothes, looked like a school of colorful fish. A heavyset man sat at a table by the window. His hair and face were slicked with oil, making him look like a painted wax sculpture. Two tall young women sat next to him, one on each side. The man turned and said something to one of the women, which made her burst out in laughter, and he started laughing, too. Who knew women could get so tall, he thought. Xiuxiu would have only come up to their waists. He sighed—he was thinking about Xiuxiu again.

Xiuxiu had been the only girl in the village who hadn't married out of the mountains. Maybe she was afraid of the outside world because she, like most of the villagers, had never left. Maybe she had a different reason. Either way, the two of them had spent more than two years together, and it had seemed things might work out—her family had asked for a reasonable birth-pain price,* only fifteen hundred yuan. But soon, some villagers who had left to find work came back with a bit of money. One of them, about the same age as him, was a clever guy, though illiterate. He had left for the city, where he'd gone door-to-door, cleaning people's kitchen exhaust hoods, and in a year he had made a bundle.

This cleaner had spent a month in the village two years ago, and Xiuxiu had somehow wound up with him. Her family turned a blind eye. The rough walls of her family's home were covered in melon seeds and scratched tallies of her father's debts over the years. Xiuxiu hadn't gone to school, but she had an affinity for people who could read. He knew that was the main reason she had initially been attracted to him. But the village boy gave her bottles of perfume, gold-plated necklaces, and eventually won her over.

"Being able to read won't put food on the table," she told him. He knew it could, but with his job, it wasn't *good* food, especially compared to what the cleaner could give her. So, he'd had no response. Xiuxiu had walked out the door and left only the smell of her perfume, which made him scrunch up his nose.

A year after marrying the village boy, Xiuxiu died in childbirth. He still remembered the midwife holding her rusty forceps over a flame for a second before poking them inside her. Xiuxiu's blood filled the copper basin beneath her. She died on the way to the town hospital. The village boy had spent thirty thousand yuan on the wedding, and it had been a spectacle like nothing the village had seen. Why wasn't he willing to part with a little more money so Xiuxiu could give birth in the hospital? He had asked around about the cost of delivering a child in the hospital. It was only two or three hundred yuan. But the village had its ways, and no villager had ever gone to the hospital to give birth. No one blamed the boy. They threw up their hands and said it was her fate. He heard later that compared to the cleaner's mother, Xiuxiu had been lucky. His mother had gone into obstructed labor. When

---

* A form of dowry payment in some rural areas of northwestern China, meant to compensate the bride's mother for the pain of having borne her.

the cleaner's father heard from the midwife that the child was a boy, he'd chosen to save the child. His mother was placed on the back of a donkey and driven around in circles, in order to spin the baby out. People who were there said that there was a ring of her blood in the dust.

The teacher took a deep breath and felt the ignorance and despair of the village sitting heavily on his chest. It was an ever-present sensation, and even here in the city he felt it just as strongly.

There was still hope for the children, he told himself, even as they sat in the freezing classroom in the winter and looked at the blackboard by candlelight. He was the candle. For as long as he could, with as much brightness as he could muster, he would burn, body and soul, for those children.

Eventually, he had risen from the city sidewalk and continued walking for a while, before stepping into a bookstore. The city was a good place—it even had bookstores that were open at night. There he spent all the money he had brought on books for the school's tiny library, saving for himself only enough to cover the fare home. In the middle of the night, clutching two heavy bundles of books, he had boarded the train.

In the center of the Milky Way, fifty thousand light-years from Earth, an interstellar war that had lasted for twenty thousand years was nearing its resolution.

A square-shaped, starless region was visible there, as distinctly as if it had been cut from the background of shining stars with a pair of scissors. Its sides were six thousand miles long, and its interior was blacker even than the blackness of space—a void within a void. Several objects began to emerge from within the square. They were of various shapes, but each was as large as Earth's moon, and their color was a dazzling silver. As more appeared, they took on a regular, cube-shaped formation. The cube of objects continued to emerge from the square, a mosaic set into the eternal wall of the universe itself, whose base was the complete, velvet blackness of the square and whose tiles were the luminescent silver objects. They were like a cosmic symphony given physical form. Slowly, the black square dissolved back into the stars, leaving only the cube-shaped array of silver objects floating ominously.

The interstellar fleet of the Galactic Federation of Carbon-Based Life had completed the first space-time warp of its journey.

The High Archon of the Carbon Federation looked out from the fleet's flagship onto a metallic, silver landscape. An intricate network of paths snaked across the land like circuits etched into an infinitely wide, silver circuit board. Teardrop-shaped craft appeared occasionally on the surface of the land; they shot at blinding speed along the paths, and after a few seconds, noiselessly disappeared into ports that suddenly opened in the surface to receive them. Cosmic dust had clung to the fleet during its warp travel; it formed clouds over the landscape that glowed faintly red as they ionized.

The High Archon was known for his cool demeanor. The endlessly tranquil, azure smart field that usually surrounded him was like a symbol of his personality. At this moment, however, traces of yellow light emerged from his smart field, as they did from the fields of the people around him.

"It's finally over." The High Archon's smart field vibrated, transmitting his message to the senator and the fleet commander, who stood on either side of him.

"Yes, it's over. This war went on too long—so long that we have forgotten its beginning," the senator replied.

The fleet began to cruise at sub-light speed. The ships' sub-light engines engaged simultaneously, and thousands of blue suns suddenly appeared around the flagship. The silver land below them reflected the engines' lights like an edgeless, infinite mirror, and each blue sun was doubled in the reflection.

The beginning of the war was a distant, ancient memory, and though it seemed to have been burned away in the fighting, no one had truly forgotten it. It was a memory that had passed through hundreds of generations, but to the trillion citizens of the Carbon Federation, it was still vivid, engraved into their hearts and minds.

Twenty thousand years earlier, the Silicon-Based Empire had launched a full-scale attack against the Carbon Federation from the periphery of the galaxy. The Empire's five million warships leapt from star to star along the ten-thousand-light-year-long battlefront. Each ship first drew power from its star to open a wormhole through space-time, then traveled through the wormhole to another star, which it likewise harnessed to create another wormhole and continue its travel.

Opening a wormhole depleted a large amount of a star's energy and shifted its light toward the red end of the spectrum. After the ship had jumped, the star's light would gradually return to its original state. The collective effect of millions of ships traveling in this way was terrifying. A band of red light ten thousand light-years long appeared at the edge of the galaxy and began moving toward its center, invisible to light-speed observations but clearly visible on hyperspace monitors. The band, created by the red-shifted light of stars, rushed toward the borders of Carbon Federation space, a tide of blood ten thousand light-years across.

The first Carbon Federation planet to be hit by the vanguard of the Silicon Empire forces was Greensea. It was a beautiful planet that orbited a pair of binary stars. Its surface was covered completely by ocean, on which floated great forests of soft, long, vine-like plants. These forests were home to the temperate, beautiful inhabitants of Greensea, who, swimming lithely among the plants with their crystal-clear bodies, had created an Edenic civilization. Tens of thousands of harsh beams of light suddenly pierced the sky of the planet— the lasers of the Silicon Empire fleet—and began evaporating the ocean. In a short time, Greensea's surface became a boiling cauldron, and all life on the planet, including its five billion inhabitants, died in agony in the boiling water. The ocean was completely evaporated in the end, and Greensea, which had once been so beautiful, was left a hellish, gray planet, shrouded in thick steam.

There was virtually nowhere in the galaxy untouched by the war. It was a ruinous fight for survival between carbon-based and silicon-based civilization. Yet neither side had expected the war to last twenty thousand galactic years!

Except for historians, no one remembers how many battles were waged between forces of a million or more ships. The largest-scale battle was the Battle of the Second Arm, which took place in the second spiral arm of the Milky Way Galaxy. In total, more than ten million warships from both fleets participated as combatants. Historical records tell that more than two thousand stars went supernova in the huge battle zone, like fireworks in the black void. They turned the whole spiral arm into an ocean of super-strong radiation, with groups of black holes floating like ghosts in its midst.

By the end of the battle, both sides had lost nearly their entire fleets. Fifteen thousand years had elapsed, and the story of the battle sounded like an ancient myth, except for the fact that the battle zone itself still existed. Ships rarely entered the zone. It was the most terrifying region of the galaxy, and not just because of the radiation and black holes.

During the battle, squadrons of ships from both unthinkably huge fleets made short-distance space-time jumps as a tactical maneuver. It was thought that in dogfights, some interstellar fighters made almost incredible jumps of a few miles at most! These jumps left space-time in the battle zone riddled with holes, more like rags than fabric. Any ship unfortunate enough to stray into the region risked hitting a patch of distorted space. A patch like that could twist a ship into a long, thin, metal pole, or press it into a sheet hundreds of millions of square miles in area and a few atoms thick, which the gale of radiation would immediately shred to pieces. More often, a ship that hit a patch of distorted space-time would regress into the pieces of steel it was made of, or immediately age into a broken husk, everything inside the ship decaying into ancient dust. Anyone aboard would revert in an instant to an embryonic state, or collapse into a pile of bones. . . .

The war's decisive battle was not a myth. It took place a year ago. The Silicon Empire assembled its remaining forces, a fleet of 1.5 million warships, in the desolate space between the galaxy's first and second spiral arms. They set up an antimatter cloud barrier around their location, with a radius of one thousand light-years.

The first Carbon Federation squadron to attack jumped directly to the edge of the cloud and entered it. The cloud was very thin, but it was lethal against warships, and it turned those ships into brilliant fireballs. Dragging long tails of flame from their hulls, the ships bravely continued to advance on their target, streaks of fluorescence in their wakes. An array of thirty thousand or more shooting stars, rushing bravely forward—it was the most magnificent, tragic image from the Carbon-Silicon War.

But these shooting stars thinned out as they passed through the anti-matter cloud, and at a location very close to the battle array of the Silicon Empire fleet, they disappeared. They had sacrificed themselves to open a tunnel through the cloud for the rest of the attack fleet. In the battle, the last fleet of the Silicon Empire was driven back to the most desolate region in the Milky Way: the tip of the first spiral arm.

Now, the Carbon Federation fleet was about to complete its final mission: constructing a five-hundred-light-year-wide isolation belt in the middle of the spiral arm. They would destroy most of the stars in the belt to prevent the Silicon Empire from making interstellar jumps. Interstellar jumps were the only way in the Milky Way system for large battleships to carry out fast, long-range attacks, and the greatest distance a ship could jump was two hundred light-years. Once the belt was built, the heavy warships of the Silicon Empire would have to cross five hundred light-years of space at sub-light speeds to get to the central region of the galaxy. In effect, the Silicon Empire would be imprisoned at the tip of the first spiral arm, unable to pose any serious threat to carbon-based civilization in the center of the galaxy.

The senator used his vibrating smart field to speak to the High Archon. "The will of the Senate is as follows: We maintain our strong recommendation to conduct a life-level protective screening in the belt before commencing stellar destruction."

"I understand the Senate's caution," said the High Archon. "In this long war, the blood of all forms of life has flowed, enough to fill the oceans of thousands of planets. Now that the war has ended, the most pressing concern for the galaxy is to reestablish respect for life—all forms of life, not only carbon-based life, but silicon-based life, as well. The Federation stopped short of completely annihilating silicon-based civilization on the basis of this ideal. Yet the Silicon Empire has no such qualms. They have an instinctual love for warfare and conquest. It has always been so, even before the Carbon-Silicon War. Now, these inclinations are embedded in each of their genes and in each line of their code. They are the ultimate goals of the Empire. Silicon-based life is far superior to us at storing and processing information. Even here, at the tip of the first spiral arm, their civilization will recover and develop quickly. It is therefore imperative that we construct a sufficiently wide isolation belt between the Federation and the Empire. Given the circumstances, a life scan on each of the hundred million stars in the belt is unrealistic. The first spiral arm may be the most barren region of the galaxy, but there are likely enough stars with inhabited planets to achieve leap density. Medium warships could use them to cross the belt, and just one Silicon Empire medium warship could cause immense damage if it managed to enter Federation space. We cannot conduct a life-level protective screening for each planet, only civilization-level. We must sacrifice the primitive life-forms in the belt, in order to save the advanced *and* primitive life-forms in the rest of the galaxy. I have explained this to the Senate."

"The Senate recognizes this imperative, sir. You have explained it, as has the Federal Defense Committee. The Senate's statement is a recommendation, not a piece of legislation. However, stars in the belt with life-forms that have reached 3C-civilization status and above must be protected."

"Rest assured," said the High Archon, his smart field flashing a determined red. "We will be extremely thorough in conducting civilization tests for each planetary system in the isolation belt!"

For the first time, the fleet commander's smart field emitted a message. "I think you are worried over nothing. The first spiral arm is the most barren wasteland in the galaxy. There won't be any 3Cs or above."

"I hope you are right," said the High Archon and the senator simultaneously. Their smart fields vibrated in resonance and sent a solitary ripple of plasma into the sky above the metallic land below.

The fleet began its second space-time leap, traveling at near-infinite speed toward the first spiral arm of the galaxy.

It was late at night. The children had gathered by candlelight at the foot of their teacher's sickbed.

"Teacher, you should rest. You can teach us the lesson tomorrow," said a boy.

The teacher managed a pained smile. "Tomorrow we have tomorrow's lesson."

If he could make it to tomorrow, then he would teach tomorrow's lesson. But his gut told him he wouldn't last the night.

He made a gesture, and one of the children placed a small blackboard on the sheet covering his chest. This was how he had been teaching them for a month. The children passed him a half-worn piece of chalk; he grabbed it weakly and put its tip to the blackboard with great effort. A sharp, strong pain shot through him. His hand trembled, knocking the chalk against the blackboard and leaving white dots.

He had not gone to the hospital since he returned from the city. His liver had begun to ache two months later—the cancer had spread.

The pain got worse with time until it overwhelmed everything. He groped under his pillow for a pain pill, the common, over-the-counter kind, packaged in plastic. They were completely ineffective at relieving the agony of late-stage cancer, but they had a bit of value as a placebo. Demerol wasn't expensive, but patients weren't allowed to take it out of the hospital, and even if they were, there was no one to administer the shot. As usual, he pushed two pills out of the plastic strip. He thought for a moment, then pushed out the remaining twelve pills and swallowed them all. He knew he would have no use for them later.

Again, he turned his attention to the blackboard and struggled to write out the lesson, but a cough overcame him. He turned his head to the side, where a child had rushed to hold up a bowl next to his mouth. He spit out a mouthful of red and black blood, then reclined on his pillow to catch his breath.

Several of the children stifled sobs.

He abandoned his effort to write on the blackboard. He waved his hand, and a child came over to remove it from his chest. In a small voice, almost a whisper, he began to speak.

"Like our lessons yesterday and the day before, today's lesson is meant for middle schoolers. It is not on your syllabus. Most of you will never have a chance to attend middle school, so I thought I would give you a taste of what it's like to study a subject in greater depth. Yesterday, we read Lu Xun's

Diary of a Madman. You probably didn't understand much of it, but I want you to read it a few more times, or, better yet, learn to recite it from memory. You'll understand it when you're older. Lu Xun was a remarkable man. Every Chinese person should read his books. I know all of you will in the future."

He stopped speaking to rest for a moment and catch his breath. He looked at the flickering candle flame. Another passage of Lu Xun came to him. It wasn't from *Diary of a Madman,* and it hadn't been in his textbook. He had encountered it many years before, in his own incomplete, thumbed-through set of Lu Xun's collected works. Since the first time he read it, he hadn't forgotten a single word.

> Imagine a windowless, iron room. Many people lie asleep inside. They will soon suffocate and die in their sleep. You shout, and a few hopeless sleepers awaken to a wretched fate that you are powerless to prevent. Have you done them a favor?
>
> Unless you wake them up, what hope do they have of escape?

With the last of his strength, he continued his lecture.

"Today's class is middle school physics. You may not have heard of physics before. It is the study of the principles of the physical world. It's an extremely rich, deep field of knowledge.

"We will learn about Newton's three laws. Newton was an important English scientist who lived a long time ago. He came up with three remarkable rules. These rules apply to everything in heaven and on Earth, from the sun and moon in the sky down to the water and air of our own planet. Nothing can escape Newton's three truths. With them, we can calculate to the second when solar eclipses—when the 'sun dog eats the sun,' as our village elders say—will happen. Humans can fly to the moon using Newton's three laws.

"The first law is as follows: A body at rest or moving in a straight line at a constant speed will maintain its velocity unless an outside force acts upon it."

The children watched him silently in the candlelight. No one stirred.

"This means that if you took the grindstone from the mill and gave it a good push, it should keep rolling, all the way to the horizon. What are you laughing at, Baozhu? You're right, that wouldn't actually happen. That's because a force called friction will bring the stone to a halt. There is nowhere in the world without friction."

That's right, nowhere in the world without friction—his life, especially. He didn't have the village surname,* so his words carried no weight. And he was so stubborn! Over the years he had offended practically everyone in the village in one way or another. He had gone door-to-door persuading each family to put their kids in school, and he had gotten some kids to stop following their parents to work by swearing he'd cover their tuition himself. None of this endeared him to the villagers. The plain truth was that his ideas about how to live were just too different from theirs. He talked all day about things that were meaningless to them, and it annoyed them.

Before he'd learned of his cancer, he had gone once to town and brought back some funds from the Education Bureau to repair the school. The villagers took a bit of the money to hire an opera troupe to perform for two days in an upcoming festival. This bothered the teacher deeply. He went to town again, and this time he brought back a vice county head, who made the villagers return the money. They had already built a stage for the singers. The school was repaired, but that was the end of what little goodwill there was for him in the village, and his life was even more difficult from then on.

First, the village electrician, the village head's nephew, cut off the school's electricity. Then they stopped giving the school cornstalks for heating and cooking, forcing him to abandon planting and spend his time in the hills instead, looking for kindling. Then there was the incident with the rafters in the dorm. Friction was omnipresent, exhausting his body and soul, making him unable to move in a straight line at a constant speed. He had to come to a stop.

Maybe the place he was heading was a frictionless world where everything was smooth and lovely. But what was there for him in a place like that? His heart would still be in this world of dust and friction, in the primary school he had devoted his whole life to. After he left, the two remaining teachers would leave, too, and the school would grind to a halt, like the

*In many Chinese villages, residents share a common, ancestral surname.

village millstone. He fell into a deep sorrow—in this world or the next, he had no hope of finding peace.

"Newton's second law is a little tricky, so we'll leave it for last. His third law is as follows: When a body exerts force on a second body, the second body will exert an equal force on the first body in the opposite direction."

The children were silent for a long time.

"Do you understand? Who can explain it back to me?"

Zhao Labao, his best student, stood and spoke. "I get the idea, but it doesn't make sense. This morning I got into a fight with Li Quangui and he hit me right in the face. It really hurt, and I've got a lump, right here. Those aren't equal forces!"

The teacher took a while to catch his breath, then explained, "The reason you hurt is that your cheek is softer than Quangui's fist. They exerted equal forces against each other."

He wanted to make a gesture to illustrate his point, but he couldn't lift his hand anymore. His limbs felt as heavy as iron, and soon his whole body felt heavy enough to collapse the bed and sink into the ground.

There wasn't much time.

```
Target Number: 1033715
Absolute Magnitude: 3.5
Evolutionary Stage: Upper Main Sequence
Two planets found, average orbital radii 1.3 and 4.7
Distance Units
Life discovered on Planet One
This is Vessel Red 69012 reporting
```

The hundred thousand warships of the Carbon Federation's interstellar fleet had spread out across a ten-thousand-light-year-long band of space to begin construction of the isolation belt. The first stage of the project was the trial destruction of five thousand stars. Only 137 of those star systems had planets; this was the first planet they had found with life.

"The first spiral arm is truly a barren place," said the High Archon, sighing.

His smart field vibrated, initiating a holographic projection that concealed the floor of the flagship and the stars overhead. The High Archon, the fleet commander, and the senator all appeared to be floating in a limitless void. Then, the High Archon switched the hologram feed to display the information sent back by the probe, and a glowing, blue fireball appeared in the middle of the void. The High Archon's smart field produced a white, square box; it adjusted its shape and moved to enclose the image of the star, plunging the space into near-darkness again. This time, however, a small point of yellow light remained. The focal length of the image adjusted rapidly, and in an instant, the yellow dot zoomed into the foreground, fully occupying half of the void. The three of them were bathed in its reflected, orange radiance.

It was a planet covered in a thick, tempestuous atmosphere, like an orange ocean. The motion of the gas produced an extremely complex, ever-changing lattice of lines. The image of the planet continued to grow until it seemed to occupy the whole universe, and they were swallowed by its orange, gaseous ocean. The probe took them through the thick clouds to a place where the fog was slightly thinner, enabling them to see the planet's life-forms.

In the upper part of the thick atmosphere floated a school of balloon-shaped animals. Their bodies were covered in kaleidoscopic patterns that changed from stripes to spots to all sorts of wonderful designs—perhaps a sort of visual language. Each balloon had a long tail whose tip occasionally produced a flash of light that traveled up the tail and into the balloon's body, where it became a diffuse fluorescence.

"Commence the four-dimensional scan!" said the pilot in command of Vessel Red 69012.

An extremely thin beam swept quickly across the balloons from top to bottom. Though the beam was only a few atoms thick, the interior of the beam had one more spatial dimension than normal space. It transmitted data from the scan back to the ship, and in the storage of the ship's main computer, the balloon creatures were cut into hundreds of billions of thin slices. Each slice was an atom-thick cross section that recorded everything with near-perfect accuracy, down to the state of each quark.

"Commence data mirror assembly!"

The ship's computer rearranged the hundreds of billions of cross-sectional images in its storage in their original order, superimposing them. Soon, a hollow balloon took shape—a perfect replica of the life-form they had found on the planet, re-created in the computer's vast digital universe.

"Commence 3C Civilization Test!"

The computer quickly identified the being's thinking organ, an elliptical structure that hung at the center of an intricate plexus of nerves. The computer analyzed the structure of the brain in an instant and established a direct, high-speed information interface with it, bypassing all of the creature's lower sensory organs.

The civilization test consisted of a set of questions selected at random from an enormous database. Three correct answers were considered a pass. If a life-form failed to answer the first three questions correctly, the tester had two options: He could end the test and declare a failure, or he could provide more questions. Three correct answers were considered a pass, regardless of how many questions the tester asked.

"3C Civilization Test, Question One: Please describe the smallest unit of matter you have discovered."

"Dee-dee, doo-doo-doo, dee-dee-dee-dee," answered the balloon.

"Incorrect. 3C Civilization Test, Question Two: According to your observations, in what direction does thermal energy flow through matter? Can its flow be reversed?"

"Doo-doo-doo, dee-dee, dee-dee-doo-doo," answered the balloon.

"Incorrect. 3C Civilization Test, Question Three: What is the ratio of a circle's circumference to its diameter?"

"Dee-dee-dee-dee-doo-doo-doo-doo-doo," answered the balloon.

"Incorrect. 3C Civilization Test, Question Four . . ."

"That's enough," said the High Archon, after the tenth question. "We don't have much time." He turned and signaled to the fleet commander.

"Fire the singularity bomb!" ordered the commander.

Strictly speaking, a singularity bomb was a sizeless object, a point in space, infinitely smaller than an atom. It had mass, though: the largest singularity bombs were billions of tons, and the smallest were more than ten million tons. When the bomb slid out of the arsenal of Vessel Red 69012, it appeared as a sphere, several thousand feet in diameter, that glowed with a faint fluorescence—radiation generated as the miniature black hole consumed the space dust in its path.

Unlike black holes formed by the collapse of stars, these miniature black holes were formed at the beginning of the universe, tiny models of the universal singularity that preceded the big bang. Both the Carbon Federation and the Silicon Empire maintained fleets of ships that cruised the empty space beyond the galactic equator collecting these primordial black holes. Inhabitants of some marine planets called these fleets "deep-sea trawlers." The "catches" that these fleets brought back were one of the most potent weapons in the galaxy, and the only weapon that could annihilate a star.

The singularity bomb left its guide rail and accelerated along a force-field beam from the ship toward its target star. It arrived in short order, a dusty black hole that quickly plunged into the star's fiery exterior. Stellar matter rushed from all directions in a turbulent arc toward the center of the black hole, where it disappeared. Copious radiation poured from the black hole, which appeared now as a blinding ball of light on the surface of the star, a diamond on the ring of the star's circumference.

As the black hole sank into the star's interior, the radiant orb grew dimmer, revealing the enormous, hundred-million-mile-wide vortex that encircled the orb. The rotating vortex scattered the orb's light in a kaleidoscopic display that looked, from the vantage of the ship, like a hideous, prismatic face. A moment later, the orb disappeared, as did the vortex, though more slowly; the star appeared to have returned to its original color and luminosity. This was the eye of the storm, the final moment of silence before annihilation.

The voracious black hole sank toward the dense center of the star, devouring everything in its path. In less than a second, it swallowed a mass of stellar material greater than the mass of a hundred medium-sized planets. Super-strong radiation spread out from the black hole toward the surface of the star. Some of it escaped, but most of it was blocked by stellar material, adding enough energy to the star to disrupt its convection and knock it out of equilibrium. The star's color began to shift, first from red to bright yellow, then to bright green, then to a deep, sapphire blue, and then to a forbidding violet. The radiation from the black hole by now was orders of magnitude more intense than the radiation from the star itself, and as more energy flowed out of the star in the form of nonvisible light, its violet color intensified—a spirit in agony, floating in the vastness of space. Within an hour, the star's billion-year journey had come to a close.

There was a flash of light that seemed to swallow the whole universe, then faded slowly away. Where the star had been, there was now a thin, spherical layer of material expanding rapidly, like a balloon being blown up. This was the surface of the star, swept outward in the explosion. As it expanded, it became transparent, and a second hollow sphere grew in its center, followed by a third. These waves of material were like exquisitely painted glass orbs, one inside another, and even the smallest of them had a surface area tens of thousands times larger than the original surface area of the star. The first wave vaporized the orange planet in an instant, though it was impossible to see its destruction against such a magnificent background. Compared to the size of the expanding stellar layer, the planet was a speck of dust, not even a dot on the surface of the orb.

The smart fields of the High Archon and the senator darkened. "Do you find this work distressing?" asked the fleet commander.

"Another species gone, like dew in the sun."

"Think of the Battle of the Second Arm, Your Excellency—more than two thousand supernovas detonated, one hundred and twenty thousand planets with life vaporized. We do not have the luxury to be sentimental."

The senator ignored the fleet commander. He addressed the High Archon directly. "Random planetary spot checks are unreliable. There may be signs of civilization elsewhere on a planet's surface. We should implement area scans, as well."

The High Archon said, "I have discussed that possibility with the Senate. We must destroy hundreds of millions of stars in the isolation belt. We estimate the belt contains ten million planetary systems and fifty million planets. Our time is limited; we will not be able to conduct a full area scan on each planet. All we can feasibly do is widen the detection beam to scan larger random samples . . . and pray the civilizations that might exist here have spread uniformly across their planets' surfaces."

"Next, we'll learn Newton's second law."

He spoke as quickly as he could, to teach the children as much as possible in the short time he had left.

"An object's acceleration is directly proportional to the force acting on it, and inversely proportional to its mass. To understand that, you need to know what acceleration is. Acceleration is the rate at which an object's speed changes over time. It's different from speed—an object that's moving fast isn't necessarily *accelerating* rapidly, and a quickly accelerating object may not be moving fast. For example, say there's an object moving at 110 meters per second. Two seconds later, it is moving at 120 meters per second. Its acceleration is 120 minus 110, divided by two . . . that's five meters per second—no, five meters per second squared. Another object is moving at ten meters per second, but two seconds later, it's moving at thirty meters per second. Its acceleration is thirty minus ten, divided by two—ten meters per second squared. The second object may not be as fast as the first, but its acceleration is greater! I mentioned squares—a square is just a number multiplied by itself . . ."

He was surprised that his thinking was suddenly so clear. He knew what this meant: If life is a candle, his had burned to its base, and its wick had fallen and ignited the last bit of wax there, with a flame ten times brighter than before. His pain was gone and his body no longer felt heavy; in fact, he was barely aware of his body at all. The life he had left seemed to be in his brain, which worked furiously to convey all its knowledge to the children gathered around him. Language was a bottleneck—he knew he didn't have enough time. He fantasized that the knowledge he had spent his life accumulating—not much, but dear to him—was lodged in his brain like small pearls, and that as he spoke, a crystal ax chopped the pearls out of his brain onto the floor, where the children scrambled to gather them like sweets at New Year's. It was a happy fantasy.

"Do you understand?" he asked restlessly. He could no longer see the children around him, but he could still hear them.

"We understand! Now please rest, teacher!"

He felt his flame begin to sputter. "I know you don't understand, but memorize it anyway. Someday, it will make sense to you. *The acceleration of an object is directly proportional to the force acting on it, and inversely proportional to the object's mass.*"

"We really do understand, teacher! Please, please rest!"

With his last ounce of strength, he gave the children a command. "Recite it!"

Through tears, the children began to chant. "The acceleration of an object is directly proportional to the force acting on it, and inversely proportional to the object's mass. The acceleration of an object is directly proportional to the force acting on it, and inversely proportional to the object's mass. . . ."

Hundreds of years ago, one of the world's great minds emerged in Europe, wrote down these words. Now, in the twentieth century, they filled the air of China's most remote mountain village, recited by a chorus of children in a thick, rural accent. In the sound of that sweet hymn, his candle burned out.

The children gathered around his body and wept.

Target Number: 500921473
Absolute Magnitude: 4.71
Evolutionary Stage: Middle Main Sequence
Nine planets found
This is Vessel Blue 84210 reporting

"What an exquisite planetary system," the fleet commander exclaimed.

The High Archon agreed. "Indeed. Its small, rocky planets and gas giants are spaced with wonderful harmony, and its asteroid belt is in a beautiful location, like a necklace. And its farthest planet, a little dwarf covered in methane ice, suggesting the end of one thing and the beginning of another, like the final note of a musical cadence . . ."

"This is Vessel Blue 84210. We are commencing a life scan on Planet

One. This planet has no atmosphere, a slow rotation, and a huge temperature differential. Scan beam is firing. First random site: white. Second random site: white. . . . Tenth random site: white. Vessel Blue 84210 reports
that this planet has no life."

"You could smelt iron on the surface of that planet. We shouldn't waste
time," said the fleet commander.

"We are commencing a life scan on Planet Two. This planet has a thick
atmosphere; a high, uniform temperature; and substantial acidic cloud cover.
Scan beam is firing. First random site: white. Second random site: white. . . .
Tenth random site: white. Vessel Blue 84210 reporting—this planet has no life."

"I have a strong feeling that Planet Three harbors life. Scan thirty random sites," said the High Archon, his message traveling instantly over the
four-dimensional communicator to the duty officer of Vessel Blue 84210,
over one thousand light-years away.

"Excellency, our schedule is very tight," said the fleet commander.

"You have your orders," said the High Archon resolutely.

"Yes, Your Excellency."

"We are commencing a life scan on Planet Three. This planet has a
medium-density atmosphere, and most of its surface is covered by ocean . . ."

The first shot of the life-scan beam struck a circle of land in Asia around
three miles across. In the light of day, the effect of the beam would have
been visible to the naked eye—it turned every nonliving object in its field
transparent. The scan hit the mountains of northwest China; in daylight, an
observer would have seen a spectacular sight as sunlight refracted through
the mountain range and the ground under her feet seemed to disappear,
revealing an abyss into the depths of the planet. Living things—people,
trees, grass—remained opaque, and their forms would have stood out clearly
against the crystal background. However, this effect only lasted for the half
a second it took the beam to initialize, and onlookers would likely assume
they had imagined it. Besides, it was nighttime.

In the direct center of the beam's field was the village school.

"First random site . . . we've got green! Vessel Blue 84210 reporting—we
have discovered life on target number 500921473, Planet Three!"

The beam began automatically to sort the many life-forms it had hit, entering them into its database in order of complexity and according to an initial intelligence estimate. At the top of the list was a group of life-forms inside a square shelter. The beam narrowed and focused on the shelter.

The High Archon's smart field received an image transmission from Vessel Blue 84210. He projected it onto the black background, and in an instant, he was standing within a projection of the village school. The image-processing system had removed the shelter from view, but the life-forms inside were still hard to make out, as their bodies were so similar to the silicon-based planetary surface around them. The computer eliminated all nonliving objects in the image, including the larger, lifeless body the other beings encircled, and the beings now appeared suspended in a void. Even so, they were still dull and colorless, like a bunch of plants. This was clearly not a species with any remarkable phenotypic features.

Vessel Blue 84210 was an interstellar warship as large as Earth's moon, and in its position outside Jupiter's orbit, it was like an extra planet in the solar system. It fired a four-dimensional beam that moved through three-dimensional space nearly instantaneously. In a moment, the beam had arrived at Earth and pierced the roof of the village school's dorm. It scanned the eighteen children inside down to their elementary particles and transmitted the enormous amount of data back into space at an unimaginable rate. The main computer of Vessel Blue 84210 had a storage capacity larger than the universe itself; in an instant, digital copies of the children were constructed and stored there.

The eighteen children floated in an endless void whose color was indescribable. In fact, it didn't strictly have a color. It was a limitless field of perfect transparency. The children instinctively tried to grab hold of nearby classmates, but their hands passed through their bodies without resistance. They were terrified. The computer detected their fear and judged that they required some familiar objects for comfort, so it altered the color of the simulation's background to match their home planet's sky. Immediately, the children saw a cloudless, sunless, deep blue sky. There was no ground beneath them, just endless blue, the same as above, and they were the only things in it.

The computer reassessed the digital children and found they were still panicking. In a hundred-millionth of a second, it understood why: Whereas most life in the galaxy had no fear of floating, these creatures were different in that they lived on land. The computer added Earth-like gravity and a ground to the simulation. The children were astonished to find under their feet a pure white plain, extending into infinity in all directions and crossed by a neat, regular black grid, like a huge piece of writing paper. A few children crouched down to touch the ground, and it was the smoothest surface they had ever touched; they tried taking a few steps, but the ground was completely frictionless and didn't move beneath them. They wondered why they didn't fall down. One child took off a shoe and threw it level with the ground. It slid along at a regular speed, and the children watched it glide off into the distance, never decelerating.

They had seen Newton's first law.

A melodious, ethereal voice permeated the digital universe.

"Commencing 3C Civilization Test. Question One: Please describe the basic principles of biological evolution on your planet. Is it driven by natural selection or spontaneous mutations?"

The children had no idea. They stayed silent.

"3C Civilization Test, Question Two: Please briefly describe the source of a star's power."

Silence.

. . .

"3C Civilization Test, Question Ten: Please describe the chemical composition of the liquid in your planet's oceans."

The children still did not speak.

The shoe had slid off into the horizon, where it became a black point and disappeared.

"That's enough!" said the fleet commander to the High Archon, one thousand light-years distant. "We won't be able to complete the first phase of the project on time if we keep on like this."

The High Archon's smart field vibrated slightly, signaling his consent.

"Fire the singularity bomb!"

The beam containing the command shot through four-dimensional space and arrived immediately at Vessel Blue 84210, which was holding its position in the solar system. A faintly glowing ball left the long track at the front of the ship and accelerated along an invisible force field toward the sun.

The High Archon, the senator, and the fleet commander turned their attention to another region of the isolation belt, where several planetary systems with life had been discovered, the most advanced of which was a brainless, mud-dwelling worm. Exploding stars filled the region, like galactic fireworks. They all thought of the Battle of the Second Arm.

A while later, a small portion of the High Archon's smart field split off from the rest and turned its attention back to the solar system. He heard the captain of Vessel Blue 84210.

"Prepare to exit the blast radius. T minus thirty to warp. Commence countdown!"

"A moment, please. How long until the singularity bomb reaches its target?" asked the High Archon, attracting the attention of the fleet commander and the senator.

"It's passing the orbit of the system's first planet. Approximately ten minutes to impact."

"We will take five minutes to continue the test."

"Yes, Your Excellency."

The duty officer of Vessel Blue 84210 continued administering the test. "3C Civilization Test, Question Eleven: What is the relationship between the three sides of a right triangle on a flat plane in three-dimensional space?"

Silence.

"3C Civilization Test, Question Twelve: Where is your planet's position relative to the other planets in your star system?"

Silence.

"This is pointless, Your Excellency," said the fleet commander.

"3C Civilization Test, Question Thirteen: How does an object move when it is not subjected to any external forces?"

Beneath the endless blue sky of the simulated universe, the children recited, "A body at rest or moving in a straight line at a constant speed will maintain its velocity unless an outside force acts upon it."

"Correct! 3C Civilization Test, Question Fourteen . . ."

"Wait!" called out the senator, interrupting the duty officer administering the test. "The next question is also about heuristics in low-speed mechanics. Doesn't that violate the test guidelines?" he asked the High Archon.

"Of course not, as long as the question is in the database," interjected the fleet commander. He was shocked that these unassuming life-forms had answered a question correctly, and all his attention was now on them.

"3C Civilization Test, Question Fourteen: Please describe how two objects exerting force on each other interact."

"When a body exerts force on a second body, the second body will exert an equal force on the first body in the opposite direction!" said the children.

"Correct! 3C Civilization Test, Question Fifteen: Please describe the relationship between an object's mass and acceleration when an external force acts upon it."

In unison, the children said, "The acceleration of an object is directly proportional to the force acting on it, and inversely proportional to the object's mass!"

"Correct! You have passed the Civilization Test! Confirming that there is a 3C-level civilization on Planet Three of Target Star 500921473."

"Reverse the singularity bomb! Disengage!!" The High Archon's smart field flashed and vibrated frantically as he sent his order through hyperspace to Vessel Blue 84210.

The force-field beam began to bend. Its hundred-million-mile path through the solar system curved away from the sun, like a tree branch that had been weighed down. As the force-field engine on board Vessel Blue 84210 worked at maximum power, its enormous heat sink glowed, first dark red, then with a bright white incandescence. The beam's new thrust vector began to affect the trajectory of the singularity bomb, which curved away from its target. However, it was already inside the orbit of Mercury, very close to the sun, and no one was confident that the force-field engine could bend its course enough to prevent impact.

The whole galaxy watched over hyperspace as the fuzzy, dark ball veered and grew substantially brighter, a worrisome sign that it had already entered the particle-rich space around the sun. The captain's hand rested on the red hyperspace button, ready to leap away from the solar system the moment before impact.

In the end, the bomb shot by the very edge of the sun, only a few dozen miles from its surface, sucking in huge amounts of material from the sun's atmosphere as it brushed past. It glowed intensely with a blue-white light, and for a moment, the sun appeared to have a brighter twin star locked in close, binary orbit, a phenomenon that was to become an enduring mystery to the inhabitants of Earth. The sun's fiery surface darkened beneath the bomb, like the wake of a speedboat in calm water, and as the black hole swept past the solar surface, its gravity consumed the sun's light, scratching a dark, crescent scar into the sun's surface which grew to eclipse the whole solar hemisphere. As the bomb left the sun, it dragged an enormous solar prominence behind it, a beautiful string of flame one million miles long. The tip of the prominence flared violently outward, blossoming into a mass of whirling plasma vortices.

After the singularity bomb brushed past the sun, it grew dark again. Soon, it disappeared into the infinite night of space.

"We almost destroyed a carbon-based civilization," said the senator, heaving a sigh of relief.

"A 3C-level civilization here, in this desert—unbelievable!" exclaimed the fleet commander.

"Yes. Neither the Carbon Federation nor the Silicon Empire has included this region in its plans for expansion and cultivation. If this civilization were to have evolved entirely on its own, that would be a rare thing indeed," said the High Archon.

"Vessel Blue 84210, you are to hold your position in that star system and commence a full-surface civilization test on Planet Three. Another ship will take over your prior mission," ordered the fleet commander.

The children in the village didn't notice anything amiss, unlike their digital replicas outside of Jupiter's orbit. They were still crying over their teacher's body in their candlelit dormitory. After a long time, they quieted down.

"We should go tell a grown-up," said Guo Cuihua, stifling a sob.

"What for?" asked Liu Baozhu, his eyes on the floor. "No one in this village cared about him when he was alive. I bet they won't even pay for a coffin!"

In the end, the children decided to bury their teacher themselves. With pickaxes and shovels, they dug a grave in a hill next to the school, and the brilliant stars above silently watched them work.

The senator watched Vessel Blue 84210's test results as they streamed instantly across a thousand light-years of space. "The civilization on this planet isn't 3C—it's 5B!" he exclaimed, astonished.

The skyscrapers of human cities appeared as holograms aboard the flagship.

"They have already begun using nuclear energy, and they can fly into space using chemical propellants. They've even landed on their moon."

"What are their basic features?" asked the fleet commander.

"You'll have to be more specific," said the duty officer of Vessel Blue 84210.

"Well, how advanced is their heritable memory?"

"They don't inherit memories. They acquire all their memories during their lives."

"What method do they use to communicate information to each other?"

"It's very primitive, and very rare. There is a thin organ in their bodies that vibrates, producing waves in their planet's atmosphere, which is primarily composed of nitrogen and oxygen. By modulating the vibrations, they encode information into the waves. They have separate organs—thin membranes—that receive the waves."

"What's the transmission rate of that method?"

"Approximately one to ten bits per second."

"What?!" Everyone on the flagship laughed out loud.

"It's true. We were incredulous at first, but it's been verified repeatedly."

"Captain, this is lunacy!" yelled the fleet commander. "You are telling us that an organism without *any* hereditary memory that transmits information using sound waves at *one to ten bits per second* can form a 5B-level civilization?!

And that they developed this civilization entirely on their own, without any external assistance from an advanced civilization?!"

"Sir, that is the case."

"If that's so, they have no way to pass knowledge between generations. Accumulated knowledge across generations is necessary for civilization to evolve!"

"There is a class of individuals, a certain proportion of the population spread evenly among their civilization. They act as mediums for the transmission of knowledge between generations."

"That sounds like a myth."

"It's not," said the senator. "Such a concept existed in the galaxy in prehistoric times, but even then, it was extremely rare. No one would know about it except historians of the evolution of civilization in the star systems where the idea had currency."

"By 'concept,' you mean individuals that transmit knowledge between generations of a species?"

"Yes. They're called 'teachers.'"

"Tea—cher?"

"An ancient word that was once in currency among a few long-lost civilizations. It's rare enough that it does not appear in most ancient vocabulary databases."

The holographic feed from the solar system zoomed out to display the blue orb of Earth rotating slowly in space.

The High Archon said, "A civilization evolving independently is rare enough, but I know of no other civilization in the Milky Way that has attained 5B level on its own, at least in the era of the Carbon Federation. We should let this civilization continue its evolution without interference, observing it as it does, not only to further our understanding of ancient civilizations, but also, perhaps, to gain insight into our broader galactic civilization."

"I'll have Vessel Blue 84210 leave the star system immediately and designate a hundred-light-year no-fly zone around it," said the fleet commander.

Insomniacs in the northern hemisphere might have seen a small group of stars begin to flutter slightly, then the stars around those, and so on across the whole sky, as if a finger had been dipped into the still water of the night sky.

The space-time shock wave caused by Vessel Blue 84210's hyperspace leap was considerably attenuated by the time it hit Earth. Every clock jumped three seconds ahead. Humans, confined as we are to three-dimensional space, were unaware of the disturbance.

"It's a pity," said the High Archon. "They'll be confined to sub-light speeds and three-dimensional space for another two thousand years without the intervention of a more advanced civilization. It will be at least a thousand years before they can harness the energy of matter-antimatter annihilation. Two thousand more years before they can transmit and receive multidimensional communications . . . and as for hyperspace galactic travel, that will take them at least five thousand years. It will be at least ten thousand years before they attain the minimum conditions for entry into the galactic family of carbon-based life-forms."

The senator said, "Independent evolution of this sort happened only in the prehistoric era of the galaxy. If our records of those times are correct, my distant ancestors lived in the deep ocean of a marine planet. They lived and died there in darkness, their governments rose and fell, and then, at some point, they felt adventurous. They launched a craft toward space—a buoyant, transparent ball that rose slowly to the surface of the ocean. It was the dead of night when they reached the surface. The people inside the craft were the first of my ancestors to see the stars. Can you imagine how they felt? Can you imagine how glorious and mysterious that sight was to them?"

The High Archon said, "It was an era full of passion and yearning. A terrestrial planet was a complete, limitless world to our ancestors. From their home in a planet's green waters or on its purple grasslands, they looked up at the stars with awe. We have not known such a feeling for tens of millions of years."

"I feel it now!" said the senator, pointing at the holographic image of Earth. It was a lustrous, blue ball, with white clouds floating above its surface, streaking and billowing. The senator felt as if he had found a pearl in the depths of his ancestors' ocean home. "Such a small planet, populated by organisms living their lives, dreaming their dreams, completely oblivious to us and to the strife and destruction in their galaxy. To them, the universe must seem like a bottomless well of hopes and dreams. It's like an ancient song."

And he began to sing. The smart fields of the three became as one, rippling with rose-colored waves. The song he sang was old, passed down from the forgotten beginnings of civilization itself. It sounded distant, mysterious, forlorn, and as it propagated through hyperspace to the hundreds of billions of stars in the galaxy, countless beings heard its sound and felt a long-forgotten kind of comfort and peace.

"The most incomprehensible thing about the universe is that it is comprehensible,"* said the High Archon.

"The most comprehensible thing about the universe is that it is incomprehensible," said the senator.

There was light in the east by the time the children had finished digging the grave. They tore the door off the classroom and put their teacher's body on it, and they buried him with two boxes of chalk and a used textbook. They stood a stone slab on top of the mound, and wrote on it in chalk: *Mister Li's Grave.*

The faint letters would wash off in the first rainfall, and not long after that, the grave and the person it contained would be forgotten completely.

The tip of the sun rose above the hills, casting a golden ray into the sleeping village. The grass of the valley was still in shadow, but its dew glowed with the light of dawn. A bird or two began timidly to sing.

The children walked along the narrow road back into the village. Their little shadows soon disappeared into the pale blue morning mist of the valley.

They were going to live their lives on that ancient, barren land, and though their harvests would be meager, they would always have hope.

---

* Albert Einstein, *Physics and Reality.*

THE TIME MIGRATION

TRANSLATED BY JOEL MARTINSEN

Where, before me, are the ages that have gone?
And where, behind me, are the coming generations?
I think of heaven and earth, without limit, without end,
And I am all alone and my tears fall down.

Chen Zi'ang (661–702), "On the Gate Tower at Yuzhou"*

MIGRATION

An Open Letter to All People
Due to insupportable environmental and population pressures, the gov-
ernment has been forced to undertake a time migration. A first group of
80 million time-migrants will migrate 120 years.

The ambassador was the last to leave. She stood on empty ground before an enormous cold-storage warehouse that held four hundred thousand frozen people, as did another two hundred like it throughout the world. They resembled, the ambassador thought with a shudder, nothing so much as tombs.

Hua was not going with her. Although he met all of the conditions for migration and possessed a coveted migration card, he felt an attachment to the present world, unlike those headed toward a new life in the future.

---

*Verse translated by Witter Bynner (1881–1968).

He would stay behind and leave the ambassador to travel 120 years on her own.

The ambassador set off an hour later, drowned by liquid helium that froze her life at near absolute zero, leading eighty million people on a flight along the road of time.

THE TREK

Outside of perception time slipped past, the sun swept through the sky like a shooting star, and birth, love, death, joy, sorrow, loss, pursuit, struggle, failure, and everything else from the outside world screamed past like a freight train . . .

. . . 10 years . . . 20 years . . . 40 years . . . 60 years . . . 80 years . . . 100 years . . . 120 years.

STOP 1: THE DARK AGE

Consciousness froze along with the body during zero-degree supersleep, leaving time's very existence imperceptible until the ambassador awoke with the impression that the cooling system had malfunctioned and she had thawed out shortly after departure. But the atomic clock's giant plasma display informed her that 120 years had passed, a lifetime and a half, rendering them time's exiles.

An advance team of one hundred had awakened the previous week to establish contact. Its captain now stood next to the ambassador, whose body had not yet recovered enough for speech. Her inquiring gaze, however, drew only a head shake and forced smile from the captain.

The head of state had come to the freezer hall to welcome them. He looked weatherworn, as did his entourage, which came as a bit of a surprise 120 years into the future. The ambassador handed over the letter from the government of her time and passed on her people's greetings. The head said little, but clasped the ambassador's hand tightly. It was as rough as his face, and gave the ambassador the sense that things had not changed as much as she had imagined. It warmed her.

But the feeling vanished the moment she left the freezer. Outside was all black: black land, black trees, a black river, black clouds. The hovercar they rode in swirled up black dust. A column of oncoming tanks formed a line of black patches moving along the road, and low-flying clusters of helicopters passing overhead were groups of black ghosts, all the more so since they flew silently. The earth seemed scorched by fire from heaven. They passed a huge hole as large as an open-pit mine from the ambassador's time.

"A crater."

"From a . . . bomb?" the ambassador said, unable to say the word.

"Yes. Around fifteen kilotons," the head of state said lightly, as if the misery was unremarkable for him.

The atmosphere of the cross-time meeting grew weighty.

"When did the war start?"

"This one? Two years ago."

"This one?"

"There've been a few since you left."

Then he changed the subject. He seemed less like a younger man from the future than an elder of the ambassador's own time, someone to show up at work sites or farms and gather up every hardship in his embrace, letting none slip by. "We will accept all immigrants, and will ensure they live in peace."

"Is that even possible, given the present circumstances?" The question was put by someone accompanying the ambassador, who herself remained silent.

"The current administration and the entire public will do all they can to accomplish it. That's our duty," he said. "Of course, the immigrants must do their best to adapt. That might be hard, given the substantial changes over one hundred and twenty years."

"What kind of changes?" the ambassador asked. "There's still war, there's still slaughter . . ."

"You're only seeing the surface," a general in fatigues said. "Take war for example. Here's how two countries fight these days. First, they declare the type and quantity of all of their tactical and strategic weapons. Then a computer can determine the outcome of the war according to their mutual rates of destruction. Weapons are purely for deterrence and are never used. Warfare is a computer execution of a mathematical model, the results of which decide the victor and loser."

"And the mutual destruction rates are obtained how?"

"From the World Weapons Test Organization. Like in your time there was a . . . World Trade Organization."

"War is as regular and ordered as economics?"

"War is economics."

The ambassador looked through the car window at the black world. "But the world doesn't look like war is only a calculation."

The head of state looked at the ambassador with heavy eyes. "We did the calculations but didn't believe the results."

"So we started one of your wars. With bloodshed. A 'real' war," the general said.

The head changed the subject again. "We're going to the capital now to study the issues involved with immigrant unfreezing."

"Take us back," the ambassador said.

"What?"

"Go back. You can't take on any additional burdens, and this isn't a suitable age for immigrants. We'll go on a little further."

The hovercar returned to Freezer No. 1. Before leaving, the head handed the ambassador a hardbound book. "A chronicle of the past hundred and twenty years," he said.

Then an official led over a 123-year-old man, the only known individual who had lived alongside the immigrants, and who had insisted on seeing the ambassador. "So many things happened after you left. So many things!" The old man brought out two bowls from the ambassador's time and filled them to the brim with alcohol. "My parents were migrants. They left me this when I was three to drink with them when they were thawed out. But now I won't see them. And I'm the last person from your time you'll see."

After they had drunk, the ambassador looked into the man's dry eyes, and just as she was wondering why the people of this era seemed not to cry, the old man began to shed tears. He knelt down and clasped the ambassador's hands.

"Take care, ma'am. 'West of Yang Pass, there are no more old friends!'"*

Before the ambassador felt the supercooled freezing of the liquid helium, her husband suddenly appeared in her fragmented consciousness. Hua stood on a fallen leaf in autumn, and then the leaf turned black, and then a tombstone appeared. Was it his?

THE TREK

Outside of perception, the sun swept through the sky like a shooting star, and time slipped past in the outside world.

. . . 120 years . . . 130 years . . . 150 years . . . 180 years . . . 200 years . . . 250 years . . . 300 years . . . 350 years . . . 400 years . . . 500 years . . . 620 years.

STOP 2: THE LOBBY AGE

"Why did you wait so long to wake me up?" the ambassador asked, looking in surprise at the atomic clock.

"The advance team has mobilized five times at century intervals and even spent a decade awake in one age, but we didn't wake you because immigration was never possible. You yourself set that rule," the advance-team captain said. He was noticeably older than at their last meeting, the ambassador realized.

"More war?"

"No. War is over forever. And although the environment continued to

---

* A quotation from "Seeing Off Yuan Er on a Mission to Anxi" by Tang Dynasty poet Wang Wei (699–759).

deteriorate over the first three centuries, it began to rebound two hundred years ago. The last two ages refused immigrants, but this one has agreed to accept them. The ultimate decision is up to you and the commission."

There was no one in the freezer lobby. When the giant door rumbled open, the captain whispered to the ambassador, "The changes are far greater than you imagine. Prepare yourself."

When the ambassador took her first step into the new age, a note sounded, haunting, like some ancient wind chime. Deep within the crystalline ground beneath her feet she saw the play of light and shadows. The crystal looked rigid, but it was as soft as carpet underfoot, and every step produced that wind-chime tone and sent concentric halos of color expanding from the point of contact, like ripples on still water. The ground was a crystalline plane as far as the eye could see.

"All the land on Earth is covered in this material. The whole world looks artificial," the captain said, and laughed at the ambassador's flabbergasted expression, as if to say, *This surprise is only the beginning!* The ambassador also saw her own shadow in the crystal—or rather, shadows—spreading out from her in all directions. She looked up . . .

Six suns.

"It's the middle of the night, but night was gotten rid of two hundred years ago. What you see are six mirrors, each several hundred square kilometers in area, in synchronous orbit to reflect sunlight onto the dark side of the Earth."

"And the mountains?" The ambassador realized that the line of mountains on the horizon was nowhere to be seen. The separation between ground and sky was ruler-straight.

"There aren't any. They've been leveled. All the continents are flat plains now."

"Why?"

"I don't know."

To the ambassador, the six suns were like six welcoming lamps in a bright hotel lobby. *A lobby!* The idea glimmered in her mind. This was, she realized, a peculiarly clean age. No dust anywhere, not even a speck. It beggared belief. The ground was as bare as an enormous table. And the sky was similarly clean, shining with a pure blue, although the presence of the six suns detracted from its former breadth and depth, so that it more resembled the dome of a lobby. *A lobby!* Her vague idea crystallized: The entire world had been turned into a lobby. One carpeted in tinkling crystal and lit by six hanging lamps. This was an immaculate, exquisite age, contrasting starkly with the previous darkness. In the time immigrants' chronicles, it would be known as the Lobby Age.

"They didn't come to greet us?" the ambassador asked, gazing upon the broad plain.

"We have to visit them in person in the capital. Despite its refined appearance, this is an inconsiderate age, lacking even in basic curiosity."

"What's their stance on immigration?"

"They agree to accept migrants, but they can only live in reservations separated from society. Whether these reservations are to be located on Earth or on other planets, or if we should build a space city, is up to us."

"This is absolutely unacceptable!" the ambassador said angrily. "All migrants must be integrated into society and into modern life. Migrants cannot be second-class citizens. This is the fundamental tenet of time migration!"

"Impossible," the captain said.

"That's their position?"

"Mine as well. But let me finish. You've just been thawed out, but I've been living in this age for more than half a year. Please believe me, life is far stranger than you think. Even in your wildest imagination you'd never dream up even a tenth of life in this age. Primitive Stone Age humans would have an easier time understanding the era we are from!"

"This issue was taken into consideration before immigration began, which is why migrants were capped at age twenty-five. We'll do our best to study and to adapt to everything!"

"Study?" The captain shook his head with a smile. "Got a book?" He pointed at the ambassador's luggage. "Any will do." Baffled, the ambassador took out a copy of Ivan Aleksandrovich Goncharov's *Frigate Pallada,* which she had gotten halfway through before migration. The captain glanced at the title and said, "Open at random and tell me the page number." The ambassador complied, and opened to page 239. Without looking, the captain rattled off what the navigator saw in Africa, accurate to the letter.

"Do you see? There's no need for learning whatsoever. They import knowledge directly into the brain, like how we used to copy data onto hard drives. Human memory has been brought to its apex. And if that's not enough, take a look at this—" He took an object the size of a hearing aid from behind his ear. "This quantum memory unit can store all of the books in human history—down to every last scrap of notepaper, if you'd like. The brain can retrieve information like a computer, and it's far faster than the brain's own memory. Don't you see? I'm a vessel for all human knowledge. If you so desire, in under an hour you can have it too. To them, learning is a mysterious, incomprehensible ancient ritual."

"So their children gain all knowledge the moment they're born?"

"Children?" The captain laughed again. "They don't have any children."

"So where are the kids?"

"Did I mention that families vanished long ago?"

"You mean, they're the last generation?"

"'Generation' doesn't exist as a concept anymore."

The ambassador's amazement turned to befuddlement, but she strove to understand. And she did, a little. "You mean they live forever?"

"When a bodily organ fails, it's replaced with a new one. When the brain fails, its information is copied out and into a transplant. After several centuries of these replacements, memory is all that's left of an individual. Who's to say whether they're young or elderly? Maybe they think of themselves as old, and that's why they haven't come to meet us. Of course, they can have children if they desire, by cloning or in the old-fashioned way. But few do. This generation's survived for more than three hundred years and will continue to do so. Can you imagine how this determines the form of their society? The knowledge, beauty, and longevity we dreamed of is easily attainable in this age."

"It sounds like the ideal society. What else do they desire but can't attain?"

"Nothing. But precisely because they have it all they have lost everything. It's hard for us to understand, but to them it's a real concern. This is far from an ideal society."

The ambassador's confusion turned to contemplation. The six suns were heading west and soon dipped below the horizon. When only two remained, Venus rose, and then rays of the true sun's dawn spread from the east. Its gentle light gave the ambassador a smidgen of comfort; some things, at least, were unchanging in the universe.

"Five hundred years isn't all that long. Why have things changed so much?" she asked, as much to the whole world as to the captain.

"The acceleration of human progress. Compare our fifty years of progress to the previous five centuries. It's been another five centuries, which might as well be fifty millennia. Do you still think migrants can adapt?"

"And what's the end point of this acceleration?" the ambassador asked, eyes narrowed.

"I don't know."

"There's no answer to that question in the sum total of human knowledge you possess?"

"The strongest feeling I've gotten from my time in this age is that we're beyond the time when knowledge can explain everything."

"We'll continue onward!" the ambassador decided. "Take that chip with you, as well as their device for importing knowledge into the brain."

The ambassador saw Hua again before entering the haze of supersleep, only a glance after 620 years, a captivating, heartbreaking glance, but it anchored her to home within the lonely flow of time. She dreamed of a cloud of dust drifting over the crystal ground—was this the form his bones now took?

THE TREK

Outside of perception, the sun swept through the sky like a shooting star, and time slipped past in the outside world.

. . . 620 years . . . 650 years . . . 700 years . . . 750 years . . . 800 years . . . 850 years . . . 900 years . . . 950 years . . . 1,000 years.

STOP 3: THE INVISIBLE AGE

The sealed door to the freezer rumbled open and for a third time the ambassador approached the threshold of an unknown age. This time she had mentally prepared herself for a brand-new era, but she discovered that the changes weren't as great as she had imagined.

The crystal carpet that blanketed the ground was still present and six suns still shone in the sky. But the impression given by this world was entirely different from the Lobby Age. First of all, the crystal carpet seemed dead; although there was still light in the depths, it was far dimmer, and footsteps no longer tinkled on its surface, nor did gorgeous patterns appear. Four of the six suns had gone dim, the dull red they emitted serving only to mark their position but doing nothing to light the world below. The most conspicuous change was the dust. A thin layer covered all the crystal. The sky wasn't spotless, but held gray clouds, and the horizon was no longer a ruled line. It all contributed to a feeling that the previous age's lobby had gone vacant, and the natural world outside had begun to invade.

"Both worlds refuse to take migrants," the advance-team captain said.

"Both worlds?"

"The visible and invisible worlds. The visible world is the one we know, different though it may be. People like us, even if most of them are no longer primarily formed of organic material."

"There's no one to be seen on the plain, just like last time," the ambassador said, straining to look.

"People haven't needed to walk on the ground for several hundred years. See—" The captain pointed at a place in the air, where, through the dust and clouds, the ambassador saw indistinct flying objects, little more than a cluster of black dots at this distance. "—those could be planes or people. Any machine might be someone's body. A ship in the ocean, for instance, could be a body, and the computer memory directing it might be a copy of a human brain. People generally have several bodies, one of which is like ours. And that one, although it's the most fragile, is the most important, perhaps due to a sort of nostalgia."

"Are we dreaming?" the ambassador murmured.

"Compared to this visible world, the invisible world is the real dream."

"I've got an idea of what that might be. People don't even use machines for bodies."

"Right. The invisible world is stored in a supercomputer, and each individual is a program."

The captain pointed ahead to a peak, glittering metallic blue in the sunlight, that stood alone on the horizon. "That's a continent in the invisible world. Do you remember those little quantum memory chips from last time? It's an entire mountain of them. You can imagine, or maybe you can't, the capacity of that computer."

"What sort of life is it on the inside, when people are nothing more than a collection of quantum impulses?"

"That's why you can do whatever you please, and create whatever you desire. You can build an empire of a hundred billion people and reign as king, or you could experience a thousand different romances, or fight in ten thousand wars and die a hundred thousand times. Everyone is master of their personal world, and more powerful than a god. You could even create your own universe with billions of galaxies containing billions of planets, each that can be whatever different world you desire, or that you dare not desire. Don't worry about not having the time to experience it all. At the computer's speed, centuries pass every second. On the inside, the only limit is your imagination. In the invisible world, imagination and reality are the same thing. When something appears in your imagination, it becomes reality. Of course, as you said, reality in quantum memory is a collection of impulses. The people of this age are gradually transitioning to the invisible world, and more of them now live there than in the visible world. Even though a copy of the brain can be in both worlds, the invisible world is like a drug. No one wants to come back once they've experienced life there. Our world with its cares is like hell for them. The invisible world has the upper hand and is gradually assuming control of the whole world."

As if sleepwalking across a millennium, they stared at the quantum memory mountain and forgot about time, and only when the true sun lit up the east as it had for billions of years did they return to reality.

"What's going to come next?" the ambassador asked.

"As a program in the invisible world, it's simple to make lots of copies of yourself, and whatever parts of your personality you dislike—being too tormented by emotions and responsibility, for example—you can get rid of, or off-load for use the next time you need them. And you can split yourself into multiple parts representing various aspects of your personality. And then you can join with someone else to form a new self out of two minds and memories. And then you can join with several or dozens or hundreds of people. . . . I'll stop before I drive you mad. Anything can happen at any time in the invisible world."

"And then?"

"Only conjecture. The clearest signs point to the disappearance of the individual; everyone in the invisible world will combine into a single program."

"And then?"

"I don't know. This is a philosophical question, but after so many times thawing out I'm afraid of philosophy."

"I'm the opposite. I've become a philosopher now. You're right that it's a philosophical question and needs to be studied from that standpoint. We really should have done that thinking long ago, but it's not yet too late. Philosophy is a layer of gauze, but at least for me, it's been punctured, and in an instant, or practically an instant, I know what lies on the road ahead."

"We need to terminate our migration in this age," the captain said. "If we continue onward, migrants will have an even harder time adapting to the target environment. We can rise up and fight for our own rights."

"That's impossible. And unnecessary."

"Do we have any other choice?"

"Of course we do. And it's a choice as clear and bright as the sun rising in front of us. Call out the engineer."

The engineer had been thawed out together with the ambassador and was now inspecting and repairing the equipment. His frequent thaws had turned him from a young man to an old one. When the confused captain called him out, the ambassador asked, "How long can the freezer last?"

"The insulation is in excellent condition, and the fusion reactor is operating normally. In the Lobby Age, we replaced the entire refrigeration equipment with their technology and topped up the fusion fuel. Without any equipment replacement or other maintenance, all two hundred freezer rooms will last twelve thousand years."

"Excellent. Then set a final destination on the atomic clock and put everyone into supersleep. No one is to wake up until that destination is reached."

"And that destination is . . ."

"Eleven thousand years."

Again, Hua entered the ambassador's fragmented consciousness, more real than ever: his dark hair floated about in the chill wind, his eyes wet with tears, and he called out to her. Before she entered the void of unconsciousness, she said to him, "Hua, we're coming home! We're coming home!"

THE TREK

Outside of perception, the sun swept through the sky like a shooting star, and time slipped past in the outside world.

. . . 1,000 years . . . 2,000 years . . . 3,500 years . . . 5,500 years . . . 7,000 years . . . 9,000 years . . . 10,000 years . . . 11,000 years.

STOP 4: BACK HOME

This time, even in supersleep time felt endless. Over the long ten-thousand-year night, the hundred-century wait, even the computer steadfastly controlling the world's two hundred superfreezers went to sleep.

During the final millennium, parts began to fail, and one by one its myr-

iad sensor-eyes closed, its integrated circuit nerves paralyzed, its fusion reactor energy petered out, leaving the freezers holding at zero through the
final decades only by virtue of their insulation. Then the temperature began
to rise, quickly reaching dangerous levels, and the liquid helium began to
evaporate. Pressure rose dramatically inside the supersleep chambers, and it
seemed as if the eleven-thousand-year trek would terminate unconsciously
in an explosion.

But then, the computer's last remaining set of open eyes noticed the time
on the atomic clock, and the tick of the final second called its ancient memory to send out a weak signal to boot up the wake-up system. A nuclear
magnetic resonance pulse melted the cellular liquid within the bodies of the
advance-team captain and a hundred squad members from near absolute
zero in a fraction of a second, and then elevated it to normal body temperature. A day later they emerged from the freezer. A week later, the ambassador and the entire migration commission were awakened.

When the huge freezer door was open just a crack, a breath of wind
came in from the outside. The ambassador inhaled the outside air; unlike that
of the previous three ages, it carried the scent of flowers. It was the smell of
springtime, of home. She was practically certain that the decision she made ten
thousand years ago was the correct one.

The ambassador and the commissioners crossed into the age of their final
destination.

The ground beneath their feet was covered in green grass as far as the eye
could see. Just outside the freezer door was a brook of clear water in which
beautiful, colored stones were visible on the riverbed and fish swam leisurely.
A few young advance-team members washed their faces in the brook, where
mud covered their bare feet and a light breeze carried off their laughter. A
blue sky held snow-white clouds and just one sun. An eagle circled languidly
and smaller birds called. In the distance, the mountain range that had vanished ten thousand years ago during the Lobby Age was back again against
the sky, topped with a thick forest. . . .

To the ambassador, the world before them seemed rather bland after the
previous three ages, but she wept hot tears for its blandness. Adrift for eleven

thousand years, she—and all of them—needed this, a world soft and warm as goose down into which they could lay their fractured, exhausted minds.

The plain held no signs of human life.

The advance-team captain came over to face the focused attention of the ambassador and the commissioners, the stare of the day of judgment for humanity.

"It's all over," he said.

Everyone knew the significance of his words. They stood silent between the sacred blue sky and green grass as they accepted this reality.

"Do you know why?" the ambassador asked.

The captain shook his head.

"Because of the environment?"

"No, not the environment. It wasn't war, either. Nor any other reason we can think of."

"Are there any remains?"

"No. They left nothing behind."

The commissioners gathered round and launched into an urgent interrogation:

"Any signs of an off-world migration?"

"No. All nearby planets have returned to an undeveloped state, and there are no signs of interstellar migration."

"There's really nothing left behind? No ruins or records of any kind?"

"That's right. There's nothing. The mountains were restored using stone and dirt extracted from the ocean. Vegetation and the ecology have returned nicely, but there's no sign of any work by human hands. Ancient sites are present up to one century before the Common Era, but there's nothing more recent. The ecosystem has been running on its own for around five thousand years, and the natural environment now resembles the Neolithic period, although with far fewer species."

"How could there be nothing left?"

"There's nothing they wanted to say."

At this, they all fell silent.

Then the captain said to the ambassador, "You anticipated this, didn't you? You must have thought of the reason."

"We can know the reason, but we'll never understand it. It's a reason rooted deeply in philosophy. When their contemplation of existence reached its highest point, they concluded that nonexistence was the most rational choice."

"I told you that philosophy scares me."

"Fine. Let's drop philosophy for the moment." The ambassador took a few steps forward and turned to face the commission.

"The migrants have arrived. Thaw them all out!"

A last burst of powerful energy from the two hundred fusion reactors produced an NMR pulse to thaw out eighty million people. The next day, humanity emerged from the freezers and spread out onto continents that had been unpeopled for thousands of years. Tens of thousands gathered on the plain outside Freezer No. 1 as the ambassador stood facing them on a huge platform before the entrance. Few of them were listening, but they spread her words to the rest like ripples through water.

"Citizens, we had planned to travel one hundred and twenty years but have arrived here at last after eleven thousand. You have now seen everything. They're gone, and we're the only surviving humans. They left nothing behind, but they left everything behind. We've been searching for even a few words from them since awaking, but we've found nothing. There's nothing at all. Did they really have nothing to say? No! They did, and they said it. The blue sky, the green earth, the mountains and forests, all of this re-creation of nature is what they wanted to say. Look at the green of the land: This is our mother. The source of our strength! The foundation of our existence and our eternal resting place! Humanity will still make mistakes in the future, and will still trek through the desert of misery and despair, but so long as we remain rooted in Mother Earth we won't disappear like they did. No matter the difficulty, life and humanity will endure. Citizens, this is our world now, and we embark on a new round for humanity. We begin with nothing except all that humanity has to offer."

The ambassador took out the quantum chip from the Lobby Age, and held that sum total of human knowledge up for everyone to see. Then, she froze as her eyes were drawn to a tiny black dot flying swiftly over the crowd. As it drew near, she saw the black hair she'd glimpsed countless times in her dreams, and the eyes that had turned to dust a hundred centuries ago. Hua had not remained eleven thousand years in the past, but had come after her in the end, crossing the ceaseless desert of time in her wake. When they embraced, sky, earth, and human became one.

"Long live the new life!" someone shouted.

"Long live the new life!" resounded the plain. A flock of birds flew overhead, singing joyously.

At the close of everything, everything began.

2018-04-01

TRANSLATED BY JOHN CHU

It's yet another day when I can't make up my mind. I've been dragging my feet for a couple of months already, as though I were walking through a pool of thick, heavy sludge. I feel my life being used up dozens of times faster than before—where "before" is before the Gene Extension program was commercialized. And before I came up with my plan.

I gaze into the distance from a window on the top floor of an office building. The city spreads below me like an exposed silicon die, and me no more than an electron running along its dense nanometer-thick routes. In the scheme of things, that's how small I am. The decisions I make are no big deal. If I could only make a decision . . . But as so many times before, I can't decide. The waffling continues.

Hadron shows up late, again, bringing a gust of wind with him into the office. He has a bruise on his face. A bandage is stuck on his forehead, but he seems very self-possessed. He holds his head high, as though a medal were stuck there. His desk is opposite mine. He sits down, turns on his computer, then stares at me, clearly waiting for me to ask a question. However, I'm not interested.

"Did you see it on TV last night?" Hadron finally asks.

He's talking about the "Fair Life" attack on a hospital downtown, also the biggest Gene Extension Center in the country. Two long, black burn scars mar the hospital's snow-white exterior as though dirty hands had fondled the face of a jade-like beauty. Frightening. "Fair Life" is the largest and also most extreme of the many groups opposed to Gene Extension. Hadron is a member, but I didn't see him on TV. The crowd outside the hospital had roiled like the tide.

"We just had an all-hands," I say in response. "You know the company policy. Keep this up and you won't have a way to feed yourself."

Gene Extension is short for Gene Reforming Life-Extension Technology. By removing those gene segments that produce the aging clock, humanity's typical life span can be extended to as long as three hundred years. This technology was first commercialized five years ago, and it quickly became a disaster that's spread to every society and government in the world. Though it's widely coveted, almost no one can afford it. Gene Extension for one person costs as much as a mansion, and the already widening gap between the rich and the poor suddenly feels even more insurmountable.

"I don't care," Hadron says. "I'm not going to live even a hundred years. What do I have to care about?"

Smoking is strictly prohibited in the office, but Hadron lights a cigarette now. Like he's trying to show just how little he cares.

"Envy. Envy is hazardous to your health." I wave away the smoke from my eyes. "The past also had lots of people who died too early because they couldn't afford to pay the medical bills."

"That's not the same thing. Practically everyone can afford health care. Now, though, the ninety-nine percent look helplessly at the one percent who have all the money and will live to be three hundred. I'm not afraid to admit I'm envious. It's envy that's keeping society fair." He leans in toward me from the table. "Are you so sure you're not envious? Join us."

Hadron's gaze makes me shiver. For a moment, I wonder if he's looking through me. Yes, I want to become who he envies. I want to become a Gene Extended person.

But the fact is, I don't have much money. I'm in my thirties and still have an entry-level job. It's in the finance department, though. Plenty of opportunities to embezzle funds. After years of planning, it's all done. Now, I only have to click my mouse, and the five million I need for Gene Extension will go into my secret bank account. From there, it'll be transferred to the Gene Extension Center's account. I've installed layers upon layers of camouflage into the labyrinthian financial system. It'll be at least half a year before they discover the money is missing. When they do, I'll lose my job, I'll be sentenced, I'll lose everything I own, I'll suffer the disapproving gazes of countless people . . .

But, by then, I'll be someone who can live for three hundred years.

And yet I'm still hesitating.

I've researched the statutes carefully. The penalties for corruption are five million yuan and at most twenty years. After twenty years, I'll still have over two hundred years of useful life ahead of me. The question now is, given that the math is so simple, can I really be the only one planning something like that? In fact, besides crimes that get the death penalty, once you've become one of Gene Extended, they're all worth committing. So, how many people are there like me, who've planned it but are hesitating? This thought makes me want to act right now and, at the same time, makes me flinch.

What makes me waver the most, though, is Jian Jian. Before I met her, I didn't believe there was any love in the world. After I met her, I didn't believe that there was anything but love in the world. If I leave her, what would be the point in living even two thousand years? On the scales of life, two and a half centuries sits on one side and the pain of leaving Jian Jian sits on the other. The scales are practically balanced.

The head of our department calls a meeting, and I can guess from the look on his face that it isn't to discuss work. Rather, it's directed at a specific person. Sure enough, the chief says, today, he wants to talk about the "intolerable" conduct of some of the staff. I don't look at Hadron, but I know he's in trouble. The chief, however, says someone else's name.

"Liu Wei, according to reliable sources, you joined the IT Republic?"

Liu Wei nods, as self-assured as Louis XVI walking to the guillotine. "This has nothing to do with work. I don't want work interfering with my personal freedoms."

The chief sternly shakes his head. He thrusts a finger at Liu Wei. "Very few things have nothing to do with work. Don't bring your cherished university ideals into the workplace. If a country can condemn its president on

Main Street, that's called democracy. However, if everyone disobeys their boss, then this country will collapse."

"The virtual nation is about to be recognized."

"Recognized by whom? The United Nations? Or a world power? Stop dreaming."

The chief doesn't seem to have much faith in his last utterance. The territory human society owns is divided into two parts. One part is every continent and island on Earth. The other part is cyberspace.

The latter recapitulated human history at a hundred times the speed. In cyberspace, after tens of years of a disorganized Stone Age, nations emerged as a matter of course. Virtual nations chiefly stem from two sources. The first is every sort of bulletin-board system aggregated together. The second is massively multiplayer online games. Virtual nations have heads of state and legislatures similar to those of physical nations. They even have online armed forces. Their borders and citizenships are not like those of physical nations. Virtual nations chiefly take belief, virtue, and occupation as their organizing principles. Citizens of every virtual nation are spread all over the world. Virtual nations, with a combined population of over two billion, established a virtual United Nations comparable to the physical one. It's a huge political entity that overlaps the traditional nations.

The IT Republic is a superpower in the virtual world. Its population is eighty million and still rapidly growing. The country is composed mostly of IT professionals, and makes aggressive political demands. It also has formidable power against the physical world. I don't know what Liu Wei's citizenship is. They say that the head of the IT Republic is an ordinary employee of some IT company. Conversely, more than one head of a physical nation has been exposed as an ordinary citizen of a virtual nation.

The chief gives everyone on our team a stern warning. No one can have a second nationality. He allows Liu Wei to go to the president's office, then he ends the meeting. We haven't even risen from our seats when Zheng Lili, who had stayed at her desk during the meeting, lets out a head-splitting scream. Something horrible has happened. We rush to turn on the news.

Back at my desk I pull up a news site. A broadcast is streaming on the homepage; the newsreader is in a daze. He announces that the United Nations has voted down Resolution 3617. That was the IT Republic's request for diplomatic recognition. It had passed the Security Council. In response, the IT Republic has declared war against the physical world. It began attacking the world's financial systems half an hour ago.

I look at Liu Wei. This seems to have surprised him, too.

The picture changes to that of a large city, a bird's-eye view of a street of tall buildings, and a traffic jam. People stream out of cars and buildings. It's like the aftermath of an earthquake. The shot cuts to a large supermarket. A crowd pushes in like the tide. Madly, they scramble for cans and packages of food. Row after row of shelves shake and crash into each other, like sandbars broken up by a tidal wave. . . .

"What's happening?" I ask, terrified.

"You still don't understand?" Zheng Lili asks. "There's no rich or poor anymore. Everyone is penniless. Steal or you won't eat!"

Of course, I understand, but I don't dare to believe this nightmare is real. Coins and paper money stopped circulating three years ago. Even buying a pack of cigarettes from a kiosk on the side of the street requires a card reader. In this total information age, what is wealth? Ultimately, it's no more than strands of pulses and magnetic marks inside computer storage. As far as this grand office building is concerned, if the electronic records in relevant departments are deleted, even though a company holds title deeds, no one will recognize its property rights. What is money? Money isn't worth shit. Money is just a strand of electromagnetic marks even smaller than bacteria and pulses that disappear in a flash. As far as the IT Republic is concerned, close to half the IT workers in the physical world are its citizens. Erasing those marks is extremely easy.

Programmers, network engineers, and database managers form the main body of the IT Republic. They are a twenty-first-century revival of the nineteenth-century industrial army, except physical labor is now mental labor, and gets more and more difficult. They work with code as indistinct as thick fog and labyrinthine network hardware and software. Like dockworkers from two hundred years ago, they bear a heavy load on their backs.

Information technology advances in great strides. Except for those lucky enough to climb into management, everyone's knowledge and skills grow obsolete quickly. New IT graduates pour in like hungry termites. The old workers (not actually old, most are just over thirty) are forced to the side, replaced and abandoned. The newcomers, though, don't last long either. The vast majority of them don't have long-term prospects. . . . This class is known as the technology proletariat.

Do not say that we own not a thing. We're about to reformat the world! This is a corrupt version of "The Internationale."

A thought strikes me like lightning. Oh, no. My money, which doesn't belong to me but will buy me over two hundred years of life, will it be deleted? But if everything will be reformatted, won't the result be the same? My money, my Gene Extension, my dreams . . . It grows dark before my eyes. My chest grows tight and I stumble away from my desk.

Zheng Lili laughs then, and I stop. She stands near me.

"Happy April Fool's Day," a sober Liu Wei says, glancing at the network switch at a corner of the office.

The office network isn't connected to the outside world. Zheng Lili's laptop is sitting on the switch, acting as a server. That bitch! She must have gone to a lot of trouble to pull off this April Fool's joke, most of it to produce that news footage. An in-house designer, though, could have used 3-D software to produce that footage. It wouldn't have been that hard.

Others obviously don't think Zheng Lili's joke went too far. "Oh, come on," Hadron says to me. "Practical jokes are supposed to raise the hair on your neck if they're being done right. What's there to be afraid of?" He points at the executives upstairs.

I break into a cold sweat, wondering whether he suspects anything because of my reaction to Zheng Lili's prank. Can he see through me? But even that's not my biggest worry.

Reformatting the world, is that really just the mad ravings of IT Republic extremists? Is this really just an April Fool's joke? How long can the hair that suspends the sword last?

In an instant, like a bright light driving away the dark, my doubt is gone. I have decided.

I ask Jian Jian to meet me this evening. When I see her against the backdrop of a sea of the city's streetlamps, my hard heart softens again. She seems so delicate, like a candle flame that can be snuffed out by the slightest breeze. How can I hurt her? As she comes closer and I can see her eyes, the scales in my heart have already tilted completely to the other side. Without her, what do I even want those two-hundred-plus years for? Will time truly heal all wounds? It could simply be two centuries of nonstop punishment. Love elevates me, an extremely selfish man, to lofty heights.

Jian Jian speaks first, though. Unexpectedly, she says what I prepared to say to her, word for word: "I've been turning this over in my head for a long time now. I think we should break up."

Lost, I ask her why.

"Many years from now, I'll still be young. You'll already be old."

It takes a long moment for me to understand what she's saying. Then I realize what the look on her face as she was walking toward me meant. I mistook her solemn expression as her having guessed what I was about to do. Laughter bubbles through me. It grows until it is loud and pitched at the sky. I am such an idiot. I never considered what era this is, what temptations appear before us. When I stop laughing, I feel relieved. My body is so light, I might float away. At the same time, though, I'm genuinely happy for Jian Jian.

"Where did you get so much money?" I ask her.

"It's just enough for me." Her voice is low. She avoids my gaze.

"I know. It doesn't matter. I mean, it takes a lot of money for just you, too."

"My dad gave me some. One hundred years is enough. I saved some money. By then, the interest ought to be sizable."

I guessed wrong. She doesn't want Gene Extension. She wants hibernation, another achievement of life science that's been commercialized. At about fifty degrees below zero, drugs and an extracorporeal circulation system reduce the metabolism down to 1 percent of normal. Someone hibernating for one hundred years will only age one.

"Life is tiring, and tedious. I just want to escape," Jian Jian says.

"Can you escape after a century? By then, no one will recognize your academic credentials. You won't be used to what society will have become. Will you be able to cope?"

"The times always get better, don't they? In the future, maybe I can do Gene Extension. By then, it will surely be more affordable."

Jian Jian and I leave without saying anything else. Perhaps, one century later, we can meet again, but I didn't promise her anything. Then, she will still be her, but I'll be someone who has experienced another hundred years of change.

Once she is gone, I don't hesitate. I take out my cell phone, log into the online banking system, and transfer five million into the Gene Extension Center's bank account. Although it's close to midnight, I still receive a call from the center's director right away. He says that the manipulations to improve my genes can start tomorrow. If all goes smoothly, it will be over in a week. He earnestly repeats the center's promise of secrecy. Out of the Gene Extended whose identities have been revealed, three have already been murdered.

"You'll be happy with your decision," the director says. "Because you will receive not just over two centuries but possibly eternal life."

I understand what he's getting at. Who knows what technologies may arise over the next two centuries? Perhaps, by then, it'll be possible to copy consciousness and memory, create permanent backups that can be poured into a new body whenever we want. Perhaps we won't even need bodies. Our consciousnesses will drift on the network like gods, passing through countless sensors to experience the world and the universe. This truly is eternal life.

The director continues: "In fact, if you have time, you have everything. Given enough time, a monkey randomly hitting keys on a typewriter can type out the complete works of Shakespeare. And what you have is time."

"Me? Not us?"

"I didn't go under Gene Extension."

"Why?"

After a long silence, he says, "This world changes too quickly. Too many opportunities, too many temptations, too many desires, too many dangers. I get dizzy thinking about it. When all is said and done, you're still old. But don't worry." He then says the same thing Jian Jian says. "The times always get better."

Now, I'm sitting in my cramped apartment writing in this diary. This is the first diary I've ever kept. I'll keep diaries from now on because I should leave something behind. Time also allows someone to lose everything. I know. I'm not just a long lifetime. The me of two centuries from now will surely be a stranger. In fact, considering it carefully, what I thought at first is very dubious. The union of my body, memory, and consciousness is always changing. The me before I broke up with Jian Jian, the me before I paid the embezzled money, the me before I spoke with the director, even up to the me before I typed out "even," they are all already different people. Having realized this, I'm relieved.

But I should leave something behind.

In the dark sky outside the window, predawn stars send out their last, pallid light. Compared to the brilliant sea of streetlamps in the city, the stars are dim. I can just make them out. They are, however, symbols of the eternal. Just tonight, I don't know how many are like me, a new generation setting off on a journey. No matter good or bad, we will be the first generation to truly touch eternity.

FIRE IN THE EARTH

TRANSLATED BY JOEL MARTINSEN

Father had reached the end of his life. He breathed with difficulty, using far more effort than when he used to hoist hundred-kilo iron struts in the mine. His face was pale, his eyes bulged, and his lips were purple from lack of oxygen. An invisible rope seemed to be slowly tightening around his neck, drowning all of the simple hopes and dreams of his hard life in the all-consuming desire for air. But his father's lungs, like those of all miners with stage-three silicosis, were a tangle of dusty black chunks; reticular fibers that could no longer pull oxygen from the air he inhaled into his bloodstream. Bit by bit, through twenty-five years in the mine, his father had inhaled the coal dust that made up those chunks, a tiny part of a lifetime's worth of coal.

Liu Xin knelt by the bed, his heart torn by his father's labored breaths. Suddenly, he sensed another sound in the rasping, and realized his father was trying to speak.

"What is it, Dad? Are you trying to say something?"

His father's eyes locked on him. The noise came again, indecipherable through his father's scratchy gasps, but even more urgent-sounding this time.

Liu Xin repeated his question again, desperate to understand what his father was trying to say.

The noise stopped, and his father's breathing became a light wheeze, then halted altogether. Lifeless eyes stared back at Liu Xin, as if pleading with him to heed his father's last words.

Liu Xin felt frozen; he couldn't look away from his father's eyes. He didn't see his mother fainting at the bedside or the nurse removing the oxygen tube from his father's nose. All he heard, echoing in his brain, was that noise, every syllable engraved on his memory as if etched on a record. He remained in that trance for months, the noise tormenting him day after day, until at last it began to strangle him, too. If he wanted to breathe, to keep on living, he had to figure out what it meant. Then one day, his mother, in the midst of her own long illness, said to him, "You're grown up. You need to support the family. Drop out of high school and take over your father's job at the mine." Liu Xin absently picked up his father's lunch box and headed out through the winter of 1979 toward the mine—Shaft No. 2, where his father had been. The black opening of the pit gazed at him like an eye, its pupil the row of explosion-proof lights that stretched off into the depths. It was his father's eye. The noise replayed in his head, urgently, and in a flash he understood his father's dying words:

"Don't go into the pit . . ."

TWENTY YEARS LATER

The Mercedes was a little out of place, Liu Xin felt. Too conspicuous. A handful of tall buildings had been erected, and hotels and shops had multiplied along the road, but everything at the mine was still shrouded in dismal gray.

When he reached the Mine Bureau, he saw a throng of people in the square outside the main office. He felt even more out of place in his suit and dress shoes as he made his way through the work-issued coveralls and sweat-stained T-shirts. The crowd watched him silently as he passed. He felt himself blushing, and looked at the ground to avoid the gaze of so many eyes on his two-thousand-dollar suit.

Inside, on the stairs, he ran into Li Minsheng, a high school classmate of his who now worked as chief engineer in the geology department. Li Minsheng was still as wiry as he had been two decades before, though he now had worry lines on his face, and the rolls of paper he carried seemed like a huge weight in his hands.

After greeting him, Li Minsheng said, "The mine hasn't paid salaries in ages. The workers are demonstrating." As he spoke, he gestured at the crowd, and also looked Liu Xin over curiously.

"There hasn't been any improvement? Even with the Daqin Railway Company and two years of state coal restrictions?"

"There was for a time, but then things went bad again. I don't think anyone can do anything about this industry." Li Minsheng gave a long sigh, looking anxious to move past Liu Xin. He seemed uncomfortable talking to him. But as the engineer turned to go, Liu Xin stopped him.

"Can you do me a favor?"

Li Minsheng forced a smile. "In high school, you were always hungry," he said, "but you never accepted the ration tickets we snuck into your book bag. You're the last person who needs help from anyone these days."

"No, I really do. Can you find me a small coal seam? Just a tiny one. No more than thirty thousand tons. It has to be independent though, that's key. The fewer connections to other seams, the better."

"That . . . should be doable."

"I need information on the seam and its surrounding geology. The more detailed the better."

"That's fine, too."

"Shall we talk over dinner?" Liu Xin asked. Li Minsheng shook his head and turned to leave, but Liu Xin caught him again. "Don't you want to know what I'm planning?"

"I'm only interested in surviving, just like the rest," he said, inclining his head toward the crowd. Then he left.

Taking the weathered stairs, Liu Xin looked at the high walls, the coal dust coated on them appearing for a moment like massive ink wash paintings of dark clouds over dark mountains. A huge painting, *Chairman Mao En Route to Anyuan*, still hung there, the painting itself free of dust but the frame and surface showing their age. When the solemn gaze of the figure in the painting fell upon him after an absence of more than ten years, Liu Xin finally felt at home.

On the second floor, the director's office was still where it had been two decades earlier. A leather covering had been applied to the doors, but it had since split. He pushed through and saw the director, graying head facing the door, bent over a large blueprint on the desk, which he realized was a mine-tunneling chart as he drew closer. The director seemed not to have noticed the crowd outside.

"You're in charge of that project from the ministry?"* the director asked, looking up only briefly before returning to the chart.

"Yes. It's a very long-term project."

"I see. We'll do our best to cooperate. But you've noticed our current situation." The director looked up and extended a hand. Liu Xin saw the same weariness he'd seen on Li Minsheng's face, and when he shook the director's hand, he felt two misshapen fingers, the result of an old mining injury.

"Go look up Deputy Director Zhang, who's in charge of scientific research, or Chief Engineer Zhao. I have no time. I'm very sorry. We can talk once you've got results." The director returned his attention to the blueprint.

"You knew my father. You were a technician on his team," Liu Xin said, then gave his father's name.

The director nodded. "A fine worker. A good team leader."

"What's your opinion of the mining industry now?" Liu Xin asked.

"Opinion about what?" the director asked without looking up. *The only way to get this man's attention is to be blunt,* Liu Xin thought, then said, "Coal is a traditional, backward, and declining industry. It's labor-intensive, it has wretched work conditions and low production efficiency, and requires enormous transport capacity. . . . Coal used to be a backbone industry in the UK, but that country closed all of its mines a decade ago!"

"We can't shut down," the director said, head still down.

"That's right. But we can change! A complete transformation of the industry's production methods! Otherwise, we'll never be free of those difficulties," Liu Xin said, taking quick steps over to the window. He pointed outside. "Mine workers, millions upon millions of them, with no chance of a fundamental change to their way of life. I've come today—"

The director cut him off. "Have you been down below?"

"No." After a moment, he added, "Before he died, my father forbade me."

---

*The Ministry of Coal Industries was abolished in 1998, some of its functions replaced by the State Administration for Coal Industries.

"And you achieved that," the director said. Bent over the chart as he was, his expression was unreadable, but Liu Xin felt color flooding his cheeks again. He felt hot. In this season, his suit and tie were appropriate only in air-conditioned rooms, but here there was no air-conditioning.

"Look. I've got a goal, a dream, one my father had before he died. I went to college to realize it, and I did a doctorate overseas. . . . I want to transform coal mining. Transform the lives of the mine workers."

"Get to the point. I don't have time for childhood dreams and flights of fancy." The director pointed behind him, but Liu Xin wasn't certain whether he was pointing at the crowd outside or not.

"I'll be as brief as I can. As it stands, the present state of coal production is: Under extremely poor conditions, coal is transported to its point of use, and then put into coal gas generators to produce coal gas, or into electric plants where it's pulverized and burnt . . ."

"I'm well aware of the coal production process."

"Yes, of course." Liu Xin faltered momentarily before continuing. "Well, here's my idea: Turn the mine itself into a massive gas generator. Turn the coal into coal gas underground, in the seam, and then use petroleum or natural gas extraction techniques to extract the combustible gas, and then transport it to its points of use in dedicated pipes. Furnaces in power stations, the largest consumers of coal, can burn coal gas. Mines could disappear, and the coal industry could become a brand-new, totally modern industry, completely different from what it is today!"

"You think your idea is a new one?"

Liu Xin did not think his idea was new. He also knew that the director, who had been a talented student at the Mining Institute in the 1960s and was now one of the country's leading authorities on coal extraction, did not think it was new either. The director was certainly aware that subterranean gasification of coal had been studied throughout the world for decades, during which time no small number of gasification catalysts had been developed by countless labs and multinational companies. But it had remained a pipe dream for the better part of a century for one simple reason: The cost of the catalysts far outstripped the value of the coal gas they produced.

"Listen to this: I can achieve subterranean gasification of coal without using a catalyst!"

"And how would you do that?" the director said, pushing aside his blueprint and giving Liu Xin his full attention. An encouraging sign, Liu Xin thought, and revealed his plan:

"Ignite the coal."

The director was silent for a moment, then lit a cigarette and motioned for Liu Xin to continue. But Liu Xin felt his enthusiasm drain as he realized the nature of the director's excitement: Here, after days of constant drudgery, he had at last found a brief opportunity to relax. A free performance by an idiot. But Liu Xin pressed stubbornly onward.

"Extraction is accomplished through a series of holes drilled from the surface to the seam, using existing oil drills. These holes have the following effects: First, they distribute a large number of sensors into the seam. Second, they ignite the subterranean coal. Third, they inject water or steam into the seam. Fourth, they introduce combustion air into the seam. Fifth, they remove the gasified coal.

"Once the coal is ignited and comes into contact with the steam, the following reactions occur: Carbon reacts with water to produce carbon monoxide and gaseous hydrogen, and carbon dioxide and hydrogen; then carbon and carbon dioxide react to form carbon monoxide; and carbon monoxide and water react to form more carbon dioxide and hydrogen. The ultimate result is a combustible gas akin to water gas, with a combustible portion consisting of fifty percent hydrogen and thirty percent carbon monoxide. This is the coal gas we will obtain.

"Sensors transmit burn and production conditions of all combustible gases at every point in the seam to the surface by ultrasound. These signals are aggregated by a computer to build a model of the coal-seam furnace, enabling us to control, through the holes, the scale and depth of the subterranean fire as well as the burn rate. Specifically, we can inject water into the holes to arrest the burn, or pressurized air or steam to intensify it. All of this proceeds automatically in response to changes in the computer's burn model so that the fire is kept at an optimum state of incompletely combusted water and coal, to ensure maximum production. You'd be most concerned, of course, with controlling the fire's range. We can drill a series of holes ahead of its advance and inject pressurized water to form a fire barrier. Where the burning is fierce, we can also employ a pressurized cement curtain, the kind used in dam building, to block the fire." He trailed off. "Are you listening to me?"

A noise outside had attracted the director's attention. Liu Xin knew that the image his plan evoked in the director's mind was different from his own vision. The director surely knew what igniting subterranean coal meant: right now, coal mines were burning all over the world, including several in China.

The previous year, Liu Xin had seen ground fire for the first time in Xinjiang. Not a stitch of grass on the ground or hillsides as far as the eye could see, and the air churned in hot waves of sulfur, shimmering his vision as if he were underwater or as if the entire world were roasting on a spit. At night, Liu Xin saw ribbons of ghostly red where light seeped through countless cracks in the earth. He had approached one to peer inside, and immediately gulped a nervous breath. It was like the entrance to hell. The light shone dimly from deep within, but he could still sense its ferocious heat. Looking out at the glowing lines beneath the night sky, he'd felt as if the Earth were a burning ember wrapped in a thin layer of crust. Aygul, the brawny Uighur man who had accompanied him, was the leader of China's sole coal-seam fire brigade, and Liu Xin's aim in making the trip there had been to recruit him for his lab.

"It'll be hard to pull myself away," Aygul had said in accented Chinese. "I grew up watching these ground fires, so to me they're an integral part of the world, like the sun or the stars."

"You mean the fire started burning when you were born?"

"No, Dr. Liu. This fire has been burning since the Qing Dynasty."

Liu Xin stood rooted in place and shivered as the heat waves rolled over him in the night.

Aygul had continued, "I'd do better to stand in your way than agree to help you. Listen to me, Dr. Liu. This isn't a game. You're working with devilry!"

Now, in the director's office, the noise outside the window had grown louder. As the director stood up and went over to it, he said to Liu Xin,

"Young man, I really hope that the sixty million the bureau is investing in this project could be put to better use. You can see there's much that needs to be done. Until next time."

Liu Xin followed the director out of the building, where the workers' sit-in protest had grown larger, and a leader was shouting something he couldn't make out to the crowd. His attention was drawn to a corner of the crowd, where he saw a group of people in wheelchairs. More were filing in, each one a miner who had lost a limb in a work accident.

Liu Xin felt like he couldn't breathe. He loosened his tie, lowered his head, and passed quickly through the crowd before ducking into his car. He drove aimlessly, his mind blank, and after a while slammed on the brakes at the top of a hill. He used to come here as a kid. From here, there was a bird's-eye view of the whole mine. He got out and stood motionless for a long time.

"What are you looking at?" a voice said. Liu Xin looked back and saw Li Minsheng, who had come up at some point to stand behind him.

"That's our school," Liu Xin said, pointing off at a large mining school that housed both primary and secondary classes. The athletic field on the campus was conspicuously large. It was there they had lain to rest their childhood and youth.

"Do you think you remember everything?" Li Minsheng said tiredly as he sat down on a nearby rock.

"I do."

"That afternoon in late autumn, when the sun was hazy. We were playing football on the field, when the building's loudspeaker came on . . . do you remember?"

"It was playing a dirge, and then Zhang Jianjun came running over barefoot to say that Chairman Mao had died . . ."

"We called him a counterrevolutionary, and walloped him, even as he was crying out that it was true, honest to Chairman Mao it was true. We didn't believe him, though, and dragged him off to the police . . ."

"But we slowed down at the school gate, since the dirge was playing outside too, as if that dark music was filling the whole world . . ."

"That dirge has been playing in my mind for more than two decades. These days, when the music plays it's Nietzsche who runs over barefoot and says, 'God is dead.'" Li Minsheng barked out a laugh. "I believe it."

Liu Xin stared at his childhood friend. "When did you turn into this? I hardly even recognize you."

Li Minsheng jumped up and glared back at him, jabbing a finger at the gray world at the foot of the hill. "When did the mine turn into that? Do you still recognize it?" Then he sat down heavily again. "Our fathers were such a proud group. Such a proud, grand group of miners. Take my dad. He was a level-eight worker* and earned a hundred and twenty yuan a month. A hundred and twenty yuan in the Chairman Mao era, no less."

Liu Xin was silent for a moment, then tried to change the subject. "How's your family? Your wife . . . uh, something Shan, is it?"

Li Minsheng smiled thinly. "Last year she told me she was taking a work trip, told her work unit she was taking annual leave, and took our daughter and left me and vanished. Two months later she sent a letter, posted from Canada, in which she said she had no wish to waste her life with a dirty coalman."

"You've got to be kidding. You're a senior engineer!"

"Same difference." Li Minsheng swept his hand about them. "To those who've never been below, it's all the same. We're all dirty coalmen. Do you remember how badly we wanted to become engineers?"

"Those were the days of record-chasing production," Liu Xin said. "We brought our fathers lunch. It was the first time we'd been down the shaft, and it was so dark down there. I asked my father and those standing near him, 'How do you know where the coal seam is? How do you know where to dig the tunnels? And how are you able to get two tunnels dug from different directions to meet so precisely so far down?' And your father answered, 'Child, no one knows except for the engineers.' And when we got to the surface, he pointed out a few men carrying hard hats and clipboards, and said, 'Look, those are engineers.' Do you remember that, Minsheng? Even we could see that they were different. The towels around their necks, at least, were a bit

---

* The highest of eight working-class wage levels adopted nationwide in the 1950s.

whiter. We've achieved that childhood dream now. Of course, it's not all that glorious, but we have to at least fulfill our duty and accomplish something. Otherwise, won't we be betraying ourselves?"

"That's enough," Li Minsheng said, standing up with a sudden anger. "I've been doing my duty this whole time. I've been accomplishing things. But you? You're living in a dream! Do you really believe you can bring miners up from the mines? Turn this mine into a gas field? Say all that theory is correct and your test succeeds. So what? Have you calculated the cost of the thing? Also, how are you going to lay tens of thousands of kilometers of pipe? You realize that we can't even pay rail shipping fees these days?"

"Can't you take the long view? In a few years, or a few decades . . ."

"The hell with the long view! The people here aren't certain about the next few days, much less the next few decades. I've said before that you live on dreams. You've always been that way. Sure, back in your quiet old institute headquarters in Beijing you can have that dream, but I can't. I live in the real world."

Li Minsheng turned to leave, then added, "Oh, I came to tell you that the director has arranged for us to cooperate with your experiment. Work is work, and I'll do it." Then he set off down the hill without looking back.

Liu Xin silently surveyed the mine where he had been born and spent his childhood. Its towering headframes and their enormous top wheels spinning, lowering large cages down the shaft out of sight; rows of electric trams going in and out of the entrance to the shaft where his father had worked; a train outside the coal-separator building easing past more piles of coal than he could count; the cinema and soccer field where he had spent the best moments of his youth; the huge bathhouse—only miners had ones so large—where he had learned how to swim in water stained black from coal dust. Yes, he had learned to swim in a place so far from rivers and oceans.

Turning his gaze toward the distance, he saw the spoil tip, the accumulation of more than a century's worth of shale dug out of the mine. It seemed taller than the surrounding hills, with smoke rising where the sulfur heated the rain. . . . All of it black, blanketed over time in a layer of coal dust. It was the color of Liu Xin's childhood, the color of his life. He closed his eyes, and as he listened to the sounds of the mine below, time seemed to stop.

Dad's mine. My mine . . .

The valley was not far from the mine, whose smoke and steam were visible beyond the ridge during the day, whose glow projected into the sky at night, and whose steam whistles were always audible. Liu Xin, Li Minsheng, and Aygul stood in the center of the desolate valley. In the distance, a herder was driving a flock of scrawny goats slowly along the foot of the mountain. Beneath the valley lay the small isolated coal seam that Liu Xin wanted to use for his subterranean gasified coal extraction experiment, found by Li Minsheng and the engineers in the geology department after a month of combing through mountains of materials in the archives.

"We're pretty far from the main mining area, so we've got fewer geological details on it," Li Minsheng said.

"I've read the materials, and from what we have now, the experimental seam is at least two hundred meters from the main seam. That's acceptable. We should get to work," Liu Xin said excitedly.

"You're not an expert in mining geology, and you're even less familiar with the actual conditions here. I advise you to be more cautious. Think about it some more."

"There's nothing to think about. The experiment can't proceed," Aygul said. "I've read the materials too. They're too sketchy. The separation between exploratory boreholes is too large, and they were made in the sixties. They need to be redone, to prove conclusively that the seam is independent, before the experiment can begin. Li and I have drawn up an exploratory plan."

"How long until exploration is complete, according to your plan? And how much more investment is needed?"

Li Minsheng said, "At the geology department's current capacity, at least a month. We didn't run the investment numbers. To estimate . . . at least two million or so."

"We have neither the time nor the money for that!"

"Then put in a request to the ministry."

"The ministry? A bunch of bastards in the ministry want to kill this project! The higher-ups are anxious for results, so I'm dooming the entire project if I go back and ask for more time and a bigger budget. Instinct tells me there won't be major problems, so why not take a little risk?"

"Instinct? Risk? Not on a project like this! Dr. Liu, do you realize where we're starting this fire? You call that a small risk?"

"I've made my decision!" Liu Xin cut him off with a wave of his hand and walked off alone.

"Engineer Li, why aren't you stopping that madman? The two of us are on the same side," Aygul said.

"I'm going to do what I'm required to," Li Minsheng said.

Three hundred men were at work in the valley. Besides physicists, chemists, geologists, and mining engineers, there were a few unexpected experts. Aygul led a coal-seam fire brigade of more than ten members, and there were two entire drilling squads from Renqiu Oil Field in Hebei Province, as well as a number of hydraulic-construction engineers and workers who would erect subterranean firebreaks. On the work site, in addition to tall rigs and piles of drilling poles, there were piles of cement bags and a mixer, a high-pressure slurry pump whining as it injected liquid cement into the ground, rows of high-pressure water and air pumps, and a spiderweb of crisscrossing multicolored pipes.

Work had been progressing for two months, and an underground cement curtain more than two thousand meters long had been constructed surrounding the seam. Liu Xin had thought of adapting hydraulic engineering technology used in waterproofing the foundation of dams to the subterranean firewall: high-pressure cement was injected underground, where it hardened into a tight fireproof barrier. Within the curtain, the drills had sunk nearly a hundred boreholes, each directly into the seam. The holes were connected by pipes that split into three prongs attached to different high-pressure pumps that could inject water, steam, or compressed air.

The final bit of work was the release of the "ground rats," as they called the fire sensors. The curious gizmos, Liu Xin's own design, resembled not rats but bombs. Each was twenty centimeters long with a bit at one end and a drive wheel at the other, and once released into the borehole, it could drill nearly a hundred meters farther into the seam and reach its designated location autonomously. Operable even under high temperatures and pressures, it would transmit the parameters at its location back to the master computer once the seam was ignited via seam-penetrating infrasound. More than a thousand of these ground rats had been released into the seam, half of which were positioned outside of the fire curtain to detect potential breaches.

Liu Xin stood in a large tent in front of a projection screen showing the fire curtain, with flashing lights that indicated the position of each ground rat according to the signals. They were densely distributed, giving the screen the look of an astronomical chart.

Everything was ready. Two bulky ignition electrodes had been lowered down a borehole at the center of the enclosure and were directly wired to a red button switch in the tent where Liu Xin was standing. All of the workers were in place and waiting.

"There's still time to change your mind, Dr. Liu," Aygul said quietly. "Or to take more time to think on it."

"Aygul, that's enough. You've been spreading fear and uncertainty from day one, and you've complained about me all the way to the ministry. To be fair, you've contributed immensely to this project, and without your work this past year, I wouldn't be so quick to conduct the experiment."

"Dr. Liu . . ." Aygul was pleading now. Liu Xin had never seen him like this. "We don't have to do this. Don't release the demon from the depths!"

"You think we can quit now?" Liu Xin smiled and shook his head, then turned toward Li Minsheng.

Li Minsheng said, "As you instructed, we reviewed all of the geological materials a sixth time. We found no problems. Last night we added an additional curtain layer to a few sensitive spots." He pointed out several short lines on the screen, outside the enclosure.

Liu Xin went up to the ignition switch, and when his hand made contact with the red button he paused and closed his eyes as if in prayer. His lips moved, but only Li Minsheng, standing closest to him, heard the word he said—

"Dad . . ."

The button made no sound or flash. The valley remained the same as ever. But somewhere deep underground, a glittering high-temperature electric arc was created by more than ten thousand volts of electricity in the seam. On the screen, at the location of the electrodes, a small red dot appeared and quickly expanded like a blot of red ink on rice paper. Liu Xin moved the mouse, and the screen switched to a burn model produced from the data returned by the ground rats, a continuously growing, onion-like sphere, where each layer was an isotherm. High-pressure pumps roared, pouring combustion air into the seam through the boreholes, and the fire expanded like a blown-up balloon. . . . An hour later, when the control computer switched on the high-pressure water pumps, the fire onscreen twisted and distorted like a punctured balloon, although its volume remained the same.

Liu Xin exited the tent. The sun had set behind the hill, and the thunder of machines echoed in the darkening valley. More than three hundred people were assembled outside, surrounding a vertical jet the diameter of an oil barrel. They made way for him, and he approached the small platform at the foot of the jet. Two people were standing on the platform, one of whom twisted the knob when he saw Liu Xin coming; the other struck a lighter to light a torch, which he passed to Liu Xin. The turning of the knob produced a hiss of gas from the jet that rose dramatically in volume until it roared throughout the valley like a hoarse giant. On all sides, three hundred nervous faces watched in the faint torchlight. Liu Xin closed his eyes and spoke silently to himself again. Then he brought the torch to the mouth of the jet and ignited the world's first gasified coal well.

With a bang, a huge pillar of fire leapt into the air, shooting up almost twenty meters. Closest to the mouth of the jet, the column was a clear, pure blue, but just above that it turned a blinding yellow before gradually turning red. It whistled in the air, and those closest to it could feel its surge of heat.

Its radiance lit the surrounding hills, and from a distance it would look as if a sky lantern were shining over the plateau.

A white-haired man, the director, emerged from the crowd and shook Liu Xin's hand. He said, "Please accept the congratulations of a closed-minded relic. You've succeeded! But I hope you'll extinguish it as soon as possible."

"Even now you don't trust me? It won't be extinguished. I want it to keep burning, for the whole country and the whole world to see."

"They've already seen it." The director pointed to the throng of TV reporters behind him. "But as you well know, the test seam is no more than two hundred meters from the surrounding main seam at its closest point."

"But we've laid three firebreaks at those spots. And we have high-speed drills on standby. There won't be any problems."

"You're engineers from the ministry, so I have no authority to interfere. But there's potential danger in any new technology, no matter how successful it may seem. I've seen my share of dangers in my decades in coal. Maybe that's the reason for my rigid thinking. I'm truly worried. . . . However," and the director again extended a hand to Liu Xin, "I'd still like to thank you. You've shown me hope for the coal industry." He gazed at the pillar of fire again. "Your father would be pleased."

Two more jets were ignited in the next two days, so there were now three pillars of fire. The production volume of the test seam, calculated at a standard supply pressure, had reached five hundred thousand cubic meters per hour, equivalent to more than a hundred large coal gas furnaces.

The underground coal fire was moderated entirely by computer, with the scale controlled to a stable-bounded area no larger than two-thirds of the total area within the curtain. At the mine's request, multiple fire-control tests had been conducted. On the computer, Liu Xin described a ring around the fire with the mouse, and then clicked to constrict it. The whining of the high-pressure pumps outside changed, and within an hour the fire had been contained within that ring. Meanwhile, two more fire curtains, each two hundred meters long, had been added in the risky direction of the main seam.

There was little for him to do. Most of his time he devoted to taking media interviews. Major companies inside and outside of China, including the likes of DuPont and Exxon, were swarming to propose investment and collaboration projects.

On the third day, a coal-seam firefighter came to Liu Xin to say that their chief was about to collapse from fatigue. Aygul had for the past two days led the firefighting squad in a mad series of subterranean firefighting exercises. He had also, on his own initiative, rented satellite time from the National Remote Sensing Center to survey the region's crust temperature. He hadn't slept in three days, spending his time instead doing rounds outside the curtain ring, each circuit taking all night.

When Liu Xin found Aygul, he saw that the stocky man had gotten much thinner, and his eyes were red. "I can't sleep," he said. "The nightmares start as soon as I shut my eyes. I see those fire columns erupting all around me, like a forest of fire . . ."

"Renting a sensor satellite is a huge expense," Liu Xin said gently. "And although I don't see the need, you've done it and I respect your decision. I'll be needing you in the future, Aygul. I don't think your firefighting squad will have much to do, but even the safest place still needs a fire team. You're exhausted. Go back to Beijing for a few days' rest."

"Leave now? You're insane!"

"You grew up above ground fire. That's why your fear of it goes so deep. Right now we may not be able to control a massive fire like the one in the Xinjiang mines, but we soon will be. I want to set up the first gasified coalfield for commercial use in Xinjiang. When that time comes, the underground fires will be under our control, and the land of your hometown will be covered in glorious vineyards."

"Dr. Liu, I respect you. That's why I'm working with you. But you overestimate yourself. Where ground fire is concerned, you're still just a child." Aygul smiled bitterly and walked away, shaking his head.

Disaster struck on the fifth day. The sun had just come up when Liu Xin was shaken awake by Aygul, who was out of breath, wild-eyed, and almost feverish. His trouser legs were soaked through with dew. He held a laser-printed photograph in front of Liu Xin's face, so close it blocked his vision entirely. It was a false-color infrared sensor image returned from the satellite, a vibrant abstract painting he couldn't understand, so he just stared in confusion. "Come!" Aygul shouted, and dragged Liu Xin out of the tent by the hand.

Liu Xin followed him up a hill on the north side of the valley, his confusion growing all the while. First, this was the safest direction, separated from the main seam by more than a kilometer. Second, Aygul had led him nearly to the top of the hill, but the curtain ring was far, far beneath them. What was there to go wrong here? When they reached the top, Liu Xin was about to gasp out a question when Aygul pointed in a different direction, to a place even farther off. Liu Xin laughed in relief—there was no disaster. The mine was directly ahead of where Aygul pointed, and between that hill and the one beneath their feet was an even slope that led to a meadow at the bottom. That was Aygul's target. The mine and the meadow seemed peaceful at this distance, but after a longer look Liu Xin saw something strange about the meadow: in one circular spot, the grass appeared darker than the surrounding area, a difference only noticeable upon careful observation. He felt his heart seize, then he and Aygul raced down the hill to that patch of darker green.

When they got there, Liu Xin examined the round patch of grass, which had wilted to the ground as if it had been scalded. He put his hand on it and felt heat emanating from the ground. In the center of the circle a puff of steam rose in the light of the rising sun. . . .

After a morning of emergency drilling and the dispatch of another thousand-odd ground rats, Liu Xin confirmed the nightmarish fact: the main seam had caught fire. The scope of the fire was unknown for the time being, since the ground rats had a maximum below-ground speed of around ten meters per hour. However, with the fire so much deeper than the test seam, the fact that its heat was radiating above ground meant it had been burning for quite some time. It was a big fire.

The strange thing was that the thousand meters of earth and stone between the main seam and the test seam was whole and unbroken. The ground fire had ignited on either side of the thousand-meter buffer zone, leading someone to suggest that it was unrelated to the experiment. But that was no more than self-delusion; even the person who had said it didn't really believe the two weren't in some way connected. Deeper exploration cleared up the matter late that night.

Eight narrow coal belts extended from the test seam. Only half a meter at their narrowest point, they were hard to detect. Five of them were bisected by the fire curtain, but the other three led downward and just skirted the curtain's bottom edge. Two of these terminated, but the last one led directly to the main seam a kilometer away. All of them were actually ground fissures that had been filled up by coal; their connection to the surface provided them with an excellent supply of oxygen. The one linking the test seam and the main seam thus acted as a fuse.

None of the three was marked on the materials Li Minsheng had provided, and in fact, such long and narrow belts were extremely rare in the field of coal geology. Mother Nature had played a cruel joke.

"I had no choice. My kid's got uremia and needs continual dialysis. The money from this project was too important to me, so I didn't fight you as strongly as I could have. . . ." Li Minsheng's face was pale, and he avoided Liu Xin's eyes.

The three of them stood atop the hill between the two ground fires. It was another early morning. The entire meadow between the mine and the peak was now dark green, apart from the previous day's circular area, which was now a burnt yellow. Steam wafted from the ground, obscuring their view of the mine.

Aygul said to Liu Xin, "My fire brigade from Xinjiang has landed in Taiyuan with equipment, and they'll be here soon. Teams from elsewhere in the country are headed here too. The fire looks to be spreading fast."

Liu Xin looked silently at Aygul for a long moment before he asked in a low voice, "Can you tame it?"

Aygul shook his head.

"Then tell me: How much hope is there? If we seal off the vents, or inject water to quell the fire . . ."

Again, Aygul shook his head. "I've been doing this my whole life, but ground fire still consumed my hometown. I told you that where ground fire is concerned, you're still just a child. You don't know what it is. That far underground it's slipperier than a viper, wilier than a ghost. Mortals can't stop it from going where it wants. Under our feet is a huge quantity of high-quality anthracite, and this devil's been coveting it for millions of years. Now you've released it, and given it limitless energy and power. The ground fire here will be a hundred times worse than in Xinjiang."

Liu Xin shook the Uighur man by the shoulders in desperation. "Tell me how much hope we have! Tell me the truth, I beg you!"

"Zero," Aygul said with a slow shake of his head. "Dr. Liu, you can't atone for your sins in this lifetime."

An emergency meeting was held in the main bureau building attended by the bureau leadership and the heads of the five mines, as well as a group of alarmed officials from the city government, including the mayor. The meeting's first act was to establish an emergency command center headed up by the director, with Liu Xin and Li Minsheng as members of the leading group.

"Engineer Li and I will do our utmost, but I'd like to remind you all that we're now criminals," Liu Xin said, as Li Minsheng sat silently, head bowed.

"Now's not the time for recrimination," the director said. "Act, and think of nothing else. Do you know who said that? Your father. Once, back when I was a technician on his squad, I ignored his warning and enlarged the extraction range so I could meet production targets. As a result, a huge quantity of water entered the works, trapping more than twenty squad members in the corner of a passageway. Our lamps had gone out, and we didn't dare strike a lighter, afraid of gas on the one hand and of using up the oxygen on the other, since the water had sealed us off completely. You couldn't see your hand in front of your face, it was so dark. Then your father told me he remembered there was another passageway above us, and our ceiling was probably not all that thick. Next thing I heard was him scratching at the ceiling with a pick. The rest of us felt around for our picks and joined him, digging in the darkness. As the oxygen level dropped, we began to feel woozy and tight-chested. And on top of that there was the darkness, an absolute blackness no one on the surface is able to imagine, but for the glint of picks striking the ceiling. Staying alive was sheer torture, but it was your father who kept me going. Over and over he said to me in the darkness, 'Act, and think of nothing else.' I don't know how long we dug, but just when I was about to faint from lack of breath, a chunk of the ceiling fell in and the glare of the explosion-proof lamps from the overhead passageway shone through the hole. . . . Later your father told me that he had no idea how thick the roof was, but it was the only thing we could do: act, and think of nothing else. Your father's words have been etched ever deeper on my brain over the years, and now I pass them on to you."

Experts who had rushed from all over the country to attend the meeting soon drafted a plan for fighting the fire. The options at hand were limited to just three. First, cut off the underground fire's oxygen. Second, use a grout curtain to cut the path of the fire. Third, inject massive quantities of water underground to quench the fire. These three techniques were to proceed simultaneously, but the first had been demonstrated ineffective long ago. Air vents supplying oxygen to the fire were difficult to pinpoint, and they would be hard to seal off even if located. The second method was effective only against shallow coal-seam fires and was much slower than the pace of the underground fire's advance. The third method was most promising.

News was still embargoed, and the firefighting proceeded quietly. High-power drilling rigs, emergency transfers from Renqiu Oil Field, passed through the mining city under the eyes of curious onlookers; the army entered the hills; whirling choppers appeared in the sky . . . a cloud of uncertainty descended over the mine, and rumors spread like wildfire.

The drills were lined up at the head of the subterranean fire, and once drilling was complete, more than a hundred high-pressure pumps began injecting water into the hot, smoking boreholes. The sheer quantity of water meant that the water supply to both the mine and the city was cut off, which only increased uncertainty and unrest among the public. But initial results were encouraging: On the big screen in the command center, dark spots appeared surrounding the position of the boreholes at the head of the red-colored fire, indicating that the water had dramatically dropped the fire temperature. If the line of dots connected, then there was hope for stopping the fire's spread.

But this slightly comforting situation did not last long. The leader of the oil field drilling crew found Liu Xin at the foot of the enormous rig.

"Dr. Liu, no more drilling can be done at two-thirds of the well positions!" he shouted over the roar of the drills and pumps.

"Are you joking? We've got to add more water-injection holes to the fire."

"No. Well pressure at those positions is growing too quickly. Any more drilling and there'll be a blowout!"

"Bullshit. This isn't an oil field. There's no high-pressure gas reservoir. What's going to blow?"

"You know nothing! I'm shutting down the drills and pulling out."

Enraged, Liu Xin grabbed his collar. "You will not. I order you to continue drilling. There will not be a blowout. You hear me? There won't!"

Even before he finished speaking, they heard a loud crash from the direction of the rig, and they turned in time to witness the well's heavy seal fly off in two pieces as a yellowish-black mud spurted into the air together with pieces of broken drill pipe. Bystanders shouted in alarm, and the mud gradually lightened in color as its particulate content reduced. Then it turned snow-white, and they realized that the ground fire had heated the injected water into pressurized steam. High up on the rig they saw the body of the drill driver, suspended and twisting slowly in the roiling steam. There was no trace of the other three engineers who had been on the platform.

What happened next was even more terrifying. The head of the white dragon broke free from the ground and gradually took flight, until finally the white steam had risen above the rig like a white-haired demon in the sky. There was nothing in the space between the demon and the mouth of the well apart from the wreckage of the rig. Nothing but that terrifying hiss. A few young engineers, under the impression that the blowout had stopped, took hesitant steps forward, but Liu Xin grabbed two of them and shouted, "That's suicide! It's superheated steam!"

They watched in terror as the damp headframe was blasted dry in the steam's heat, and the thick rubber pipes strung from it liquefied like wax. The infernal steam assaulted the frame with a hair-curling thunder. . . .

Further water injection was impossible, and even if it weren't, it would act more to combust than to quench the fire.

All emergency command center personnel assembled at the third mine, by Shaft No. 4, the nearest to the fire line.

"The fire is nearing the mine's extraction zone," Aygul said. "If it gets there, then the mine passages will supply it with oxygen and multiply its strength considerably. . . . That's the present situation." He broke off, and glanced at the bureau director and the heads of the five mines uncomfortably, unwilling to violate the greatest taboo in mining.

"And conditions in the shafts?" the director asked without emotion.

"Excavation and extraction are proceeding as normal in eight shafts, primarily for stability's sake," the head of one mine said.

"Shut down production altogether. Evacuate all staff in the shafts. Then . . ." The director paused and remained silent for a few seconds.

Those few seconds felt immeasurably long.

"Seal the shafts," the director said at last, uttering the heartbreaking words.

"No! You can't!" The cry burst from Li Minsheng before he could stop himself. "What I mean is . . ." He grasped for counterlogic to present the director. "Sealing the shafts . . . sealing the shafts . . . will throw everything into chaos. And . . ."

"Enough," the director said with a gentle wave of his hand. His expression said everything: *I know how you feel. I feel the same way. We all do.*

Li Minsheng crouched on the ground, head in hands, shoulders shaking with silent sobs. The mining leadership and engineers stood silently before the shaft. The cavernous entrance stared back at them like a giant eye, just as Shaft No. 2 had stared at Liu Xin two decades before.

They shared a moment of silence for the century-old mine.

After a while, the bureau's chief engineer broke the silence with a low voice: "Let's take up as much equipment as we can from down below."

"Then," the mine chief said, "we ought to get together demolition squads."

The director nodded. "Time is of the essence. You get to work. I'll file a request with the ministry."

The bureau party secretary said, "Can't we use military engineers? If we use miners for the demolition squad, and anything happens . . ."

"I've considered it," said the director. "But we only have one detachment of military engineers at the moment, far too few even for one shaft. Besides, they're not familiar with subterranean demolitions."

Shaft No. 4, closest to the fire, was the first to shut down. When the tramloads of miners reached the entrance, they found a hundred-strong demolition squad waiting around a pile of drills. They inquired, but the demolition squad members didn't know what they were expected to do; their orders were only to assemble beside the drilling equipment. Suddenly, their attention was seized by a convoy heading toward the entrance. The first truck bristled with armed police, who jumped down to secure a perimeter around a parking area for the vehicles that followed. When the eleven trucks stopped, the canvas was pulled back to reveal neat stacks of yellow wooden crates. The miners were stunned. They knew what was in these crates.

Each crate held twenty-four kilos of ammonium nitrate fuel oil, fifty tons of it altogether in the ten trucks. The final, somewhat smaller truck carried a few bundles of bamboo strips for lashing the explosives together, and a pile of black plastic bags, which the miners knew held electronic detonators.

Liu Xin and Li Minsheng hopped down from the cab of one of the trucks and saw the newly appointed captain of the demolition squad, a muscular, bearded man, coming their way with a roll of charts.

"What are you making us do, Engineer Li?" the captain asked as he unrolled the paper.

Li Minsheng pointed to a spot on the chart, his finger trembling slightly. "Three blast lines, each thirty-five meters long. Detailed positions are on the chart underneath. One-hundred-fifty-millimeter and seventy-five-millimeter boreholes, filled with twenty-eight kilos and fourteen kilos of explosives, respectively, at a density of . . ."

"I'm asking, what are you trying to make us do?"

Li Minsheng went silent and bowed his head under the captain's fiery stare.

The captain turned toward the crowd. "Brothers, they want us to blow up the tunnels!" he shouted. There was a moment of commotion among the miners, but a wall of armed police came forward in a semicircle to block the crowd from reaching the trucks. But the police line distorted under the pressure of the surging black human sea, until it was at the breaking point. All of this took place in a heavy silence, with the scuffle of footsteps and clack of gun bolts the only sounds. At the last moment, the crowd ceased its tumult as the director and mine head stepped up onto the bed of one of the trucks.

"I started work in this mine when I was fifteen. Are you just going to destroy it?" shouted one old miner. The wrinkles carved into his face were visible even beneath the thick cover of coal dust.

"What are we going to live on after it's closed?"

"Why are you blowing it up?"

"Life in the mine was difficult enough without you all messing around."

The crowd exploded, waves of anger surging ever fiercer over the sea of coal-blackened faces flashing white teeth. The director waited silently until the crowd's anger turned to restless movement, then, when it was just about to get out of control, he spoke.

"Take a look in that direction," he said, pointing to a small rise near the mine entrance. His voice was not loud, but it quieted the angry storm, and everyone looked where he was pointing.

"We all call that the old coal column, but do you realize that when it was erected, it wasn't a column, but a huge cube of coal? That was in the Qing Dynasty, more than a hundred years ago, when Governor Zhang Zhidong erected it at the founding of the mine. A century of wind and rain have weathered it into a column. Our mine has weathered so much wind and rain during that century, so many difficulties and disasters, more than anyone can remember. That's more than a brief moment, comrades. That's four or five generations! If there's nothing else we've learned or remembered over the past century, then we must remember this—"

The director raised his hands toward the sea of faces.

"The sky won't fall!"

The crowd stood frozen. It seemed as if even their breathing had ceased.

"Out of all of China's industrial workers, all of its proletariat, none has a longer history than us. None has a history with more hardship and tumult than ours. Has the sky fallen for miners? No! That all of us can stand here and look at that old coal column is proof of that. Our sky won't fall. It never did, and it never will!

"Hardship? There's nothing new about that, comrades. When have we miners ever had it easy? From the time of our ancestors, when have miners ever had an easy day in their lives? Rack your brains: Of all the industries and all the professions in China and the rest of the world, are any of them harder than ours? None. None at all. What's new about hardship? If it were easy, now that would be surprising. We're holding up both the sky and the earth! If we feared hardship, we'd have died out long ago.

"But talented people have been thinking of solutions for us as society and science have advanced. Now we have a solution, one that has the hope of totally transforming our lives, bringing us out of the dark mines and into the sun to mine coal beneath blue skies! Miners will have the world's most enviable job. This hope has now arrived. Don't take my word for it, but look at the pillars of fire shooting skyward in the south valley. But these efforts have caused a catastrophe. We will explain all of this in detail later. Right now all you need to understand is that this may be the very last hardship for miners. This is the price for our wonderful tomorrow. So let's stand together and face it. As so many generations have before—again, the sky hasn't fallen!"

The crowd dispersed in silence. Liu Xin said to the director, "I've known you and my father, and I can die without regret."

"Act, and think of nothing else," the director said, clapping Liu Xin on the shoulder, then gripped him in an embrace.

The day after demolition work commenced on Shaft No. 4, Liu Xin and Li Minsheng walked side by side through the main tunnel, their footsteps echoing emptily. They were passing the first blast area, and in the dim light of their headlamps, they could see the boreholes densely distributed in the high ceiling, and the colorful waterfall of detonation wires streaming toward a pile on the floor.

Li Minsheng said, "I used to hate the mine. Hate it, because it consumed my youth. But now I realize that I've become one with it. Hate it or love it, it's what my youth was."

"We shouldn't torture ourselves," Liu Xin said. "We've done something with our lives, at least. If we're not heroes, then at least we've gone down fighting."

They fell silent, realizing that they were talking about death.

Then Aygul ran up, breathing hard. "Engineer Li, look at that," he said, pointing at the ceiling. A few thick canvas hoses, used for ventilating the mine, were now limp and slack.

Li Minsheng blanched. "Shit! When was ventilation cut off?"

"Two hours ago."

Li Minsheng barked into his radio, and soon the chief of ventilation and two ventilation engineers showed up.

"There's no way to restore ventilation, Engineer Li. All of the equipment from down below—blowers, motors, anti-explosion switches, and even some pipes—have been taken out!" the ventilation chief said.

"You fucking idiot! Who told you to take them out? Are you fucking suicidal?" Li Minsheng shouted, far past caring about decorum or professionalism.

"Engineer Li, watch your language. Do you know who told us? The director expressly said for us to take out as much equipment as possible before the shaft is sealed. We all were at the meeting. We've been working day and night for two days and have taken out more than a million yuan worth of equipment. And now you're cursing at us? What's the point of ventilation anyway when the shaft's going to be sealed?"

Li Minsheng let out a long sigh. The truth of the situation had still not been disclosed, leading to this kind of coordination issue.

"What's the problem?" Liu Xin asked after the ventilation staff had left. "Shouldn't the ventilation be stopped? Won't that reduce the supply of oxygen to the mine?"

"Dr. Liu, you're a theoretical giant but a practical dwarf. You're clueless in the face of reality. Like Engineer Li said, you only know how to dream!" Aygul said. He had not spoken courteously to Liu Xin since the fire had started.

Li Minsheng explained, "This coal seam has a high incidence of gas. Once ventilation is shut off, the gas will quickly accumulate at the bottom of the shaft, and when the fire gets here, it may touch off an explosion powerful enough to blow out the seal. At the very least it will blow out new channels for oxygen. There's no choice but to add another blast area."

"But Engineer Li, the two areas above us are only half done, and the third hasn't even started. The fire is nearing the southern mining zone; there might not even be enough time to complete three zones."

"I . . ." Liu Xin said carefully. "I have an idea that may or may not work."

"Ha!" Aygul laughed coldly. "This is unprecedented. When has Dr. Liu ever been uncertain? When has Dr. Liu ever had to ask someone else before making a decision?"

"What I mean is that we've got a blast zone already set up at this deep point. Can we detonate it first? That way, if there's an explosion farther down the shaft, there will be one obstacle, at least."

"If that worked we would have done it already," Li Minsheng said. "The blast will be large enough to fill the tunnels with toxic gas and dust that won't disperse for a long time, impeding further work in the tunnels."

The ground fire's advance was faster than anticipated. The construction group decided to detonate with only two blast zones in place, and ordered all personnel evacuated from the shaft as quickly as possible. It was near dark. They were standing around a chart in a production building not far off from the entrance, considering how to detonate at the shortest possible distance using a spur tunnel, when Li Minsheng suddenly said, "Listen!"

A deep rumble was coming from somewhere below ground, as if the earth were belching. A few seconds later they heard it again.

"Methane explosions. The fire has reached the mine," Aygul said nervously.

"Wasn't it supposed to still be farther away?"

No one answered. Liu Xin's ground rats had been used up, and with the only sensing techniques now at their disposal it was difficult to precisely determine the fire's position and speed.

"Evacuate at once!"

Li Minsheng snatched up his radio, but no matter how he shouted, there was no answer.

"Before I came up, Chief Zhang was worried he'd smash a radio while working," a miner from the demolition squad told him. "So he put them with the detonation wires. There are a dozen drills working simultaneously down there. It's pretty loud!"

Li Minsheng jumped up and dashed out of the building without even grabbing a helmet. He called a tram, then headed down the shaft at top speed. The moment the tram vanished into the shaft entrance, Liu Xin could see Li Minsheng waving at him, and there was a smile on his face. It had been a long time since he'd smiled.

The ground belched a few more times, but then silence descended.

"Did that series of explosions consume all of the methane in the mine?" Liu Xin asked an engineer standing beside him, who looked back at him in wonder.

"Consume it all? You've got to be kidding. It will just release more methane from the seam."

A sky-spitting thunder rolled, as if the Earth itself were exploding under their feet. The mouth of the mine was engulfed in flames. The blast lifted Liu Xin up into the air, and the world spun madly about him. A mess of stones and crossties were thrown by the blast, and he saw a tramcar hurtle out of the flames, spit out of the entrance like an apple core. He landed heavily on the ground as rock rained down on him, and it felt as if each was coated in blood. He heard more deep rumbles, the sound of the explosives detonating in the mine. Before he lost consciousness, he saw the fire at the entrance disappear, replaced by thick clouds of smoke. . . .

ONE YEAR LATER

He walked as if through hell. Clouds of black smoke covered the sky, rendering the sun a barely visible disk of dark red. Static electricity from dust friction meant the smoke flickered with lightning, which lit up the hills above the ground fire with a blue light, exposing the image indelibly onto Liu Xin's mind. Smoke issued from shaft openings that dotted the hills, the bottom of each column glowing a savage dark red from the ground fire before gradually blackening farther up the columns that swirled snakelike into the heavens.

The road was bumpy, and the blacktop surface was melted enough that with every few steps it almost peeled the soles off his shoes. Refugees and their vehicles packed the roadway, all of them in masks against the stifling sulfurous air and the snowflake-like ash that fell endlessly and turned their bodies white. Fully-armed soldiers kept order on the crowded road, and a helicopter cut through the smoke overhead, calling through a loudspeaker for no one to panic. . . . The exodus had begun in the winter and was initially planned to be completed in one year, but a sudden intensification of the ground fire meant they had to proceed more urgently. Chaos reigned. The court had repeatedly delayed Liu Xin's hearing, but this morning he had been left unguarded in the detention center and had made his way uncertainly outside.

The land around the road was parched and fractured into fissures filled with the same thick dust that billowed around him. A small pond steamed, its surface crammed with floating corpses of fish and frogs. It was the height of summer, but no stitch of green was visible. Grass was withered yellow and buried under dust. The trees were dead as well, and some were even smoking, their charcoal branches reaching toward the evening sky like grotesque hands. Smoke wafted from some of the windows of the empty buildings. He saw an astonishing number of rats, driven from their nests by the fire's heat, crossing the road in waves.

As he went farther into the hills, the heat became even more palpable, rising up around his ankles, and the air more choked and dirty.

Even through his mask it was hard to breathe. The fire's heat was not evenly distributed, and he instinctively skirted the most scorching places. It left him few paths. Where the fire was particularly fierce, the buildings had caught flame, and there were periodic crashes as structures collapsed.

He had reached the mine entrances. He walked past a vertical shaft, now more of a chimney, its enormous rig red-hot under the heat and emitting a sharp hiss that made his skin crawl. He had to detour around its surging heat. The separator building was enveloped in smoke, and the piles of coal behind it had been burning for days. They had melted into a single enormous chunk of glowing coal flickering with flames. . . .

There was no one here. The soles of his feet were burning, the sweat had almost dried off his body, his difficulty breathing pushed him to the edge of shock, but his mind was clear. With his last ounce of strength he walked toward his destination. The mouth of the shaft, glowing red from the fire within, beckoned to him. He had made it. He smiled.

He turned in the direction of the production building. The roof might be smoking but it was not on fire, at least. He walked through the open door and entered the long changing room. Light from the shaft fire shining through the window filled the room with a hazy red glow and caused everything to shimmer, including the line of lockers. He walked along the long row, inspecting the numbers until he found the one he wanted.

He remembered it from his childhood: His father had just been appointed head of extraction, the wildest team, well-known for being hard to handle. Those rough young workers had been dismissive of his father at first, because of the way he had timidly asked for a detached locker door to be nailed back in place before their first prework meeting. The crew had mostly ignored him, apart from a few insults, but his father had said only, "Then give me some nails and I'll put it up myself." Someone tossed him a few nails, and he said, "And a hammer too." This time they really ignored him. But then they suddenly fell quiet, and watched in awe as his father pressed the nails into the wood with a bare thumb. At once the atmosphere changed, and the workers lined up and listened respectfully to his father's prework talk. . . .

The locker wasn't locked, and upon opening it, Liu Xin found it still contained clothes. He smiled again, at the thought of the miners who had used his father's locker over the past two decades. He took out the clothes and put them on, first the thick work trousers, then the equally thick jacket. The

uniform smeared with layers of mud and coal dust had a sharp odor of sweat
and oil that was surprisingly familiar, and a sense of peace came over him.

He put on the boots, picked up the helmet, took the lantern out of the
locker, wiped the dust off of it with his sleeve, and clipped it to the helmet.
There were no batteries, so he looked in the next locker, which had one.
He strapped the bulky lantern battery to his waist, then realized that it
was drained: work had been halted for a year, after all. But he remembered
where the lamp shop was, directly opposite the changing room, where in his
youth female workers would spray the batteries with smoking sulfuric acid
to charge them. That was impossible now; the lamp shop was shrouded in
yellow sulfuric acid smoke. He solemnly put on the lamp-equipped helmet
and walked over to a dust-covered mirror. There, in the flickering red light,
he saw his father.

"Dad, I'll go down below in your place," he said with a smile, then strode
out toward the smoking mouth of the shaft.

A helicopter pilot recalled later that during a low-altitude flyby of Shaft
No. 2, a final sweep of the area, he thought he saw someone near the opening, a black silhouette against the red glow of the ground fire. The figure
seemed to be heading down the shaft, but in the next instant there was only
red light, and nothing else.

120 YEARS LATER
(A MIDDLE-SCHOOL STUDENT'S JOURNAL)

People really were dumb in the past, and they really had a tough time.

Do you know how I know? Today we visited the Mining Museum. What
impressed me the most was this:

They had solid coal!

First, we had to put on weird clothing: there was a helmet, which had a
light on it, connected by a wire to a rectangular object that we hung at our
waists. I thought it was a computer at first (even if it was a little large), but
it turned out to be a battery for the light. A battery that big could power a
racing car, but they used it for a tiny light. We also put on tall rain boots.

The teacher told us this was the uniform that early coal miners used for going down the mines. Someone asked what "down the mines" meant, and the teacher said we'd find out soon enough.

We boarded a metallic, small-gauge segmented vehicle, like an early train, only much smaller and powered by an overhead wire. The vehicle started up and soon we entered the black mouth of a cave. It was very dark inside, with only an occasional dim lamp above us. Our headlamps were weak as well, only enough to make out the faces right beside us. The wind was strong and whistled in our ears; it felt like we were dropping into an abyss.

"We're going down the mine now, students!" the teacher said.

After a long while, the vehicle stopped. We passed from this relatively wide tunnel into a considerably thinner and smaller spur, and if not for my helmet, I would have knocked a few lumps in my head. Our headlamps created small patches of light but we couldn't see anything clearly. Students shouted that they were scared.

After a while, the space opened up in front of us. Here the ceiling was supported by lots of columns. Opposite us, there were many points of light shining from lamps like the ones on our helmets. As we drew closer, I saw lots of people were at work, some of them making holes in the cave wall with a long-bore drill. The drills were powered by some sort of engine whose sound made my skin crawl. Other people with metal shovels were shoveling some sort of black material into railcars and leather satchels. Clouds of dust occasionally blocked them, and lanterns cast shafts of light through the dust.

"Students, we're now in what's called the ore zone. What you see is a scene of early mining work."

A few miners came toward us. I knew they were holograms, so I didn't move out of the way. Some of them passed through me, so I could see them very clearly, and I was astonished.

"Did China hire black people to mine coal?"

"To answer that question," the teacher said, "we'll have a real experience of the air of the ore zone. Please take out your breathing masks from your bags."

We put on our masks, and heard the teacher say, "Please remember that this is real, not a hologram."

A cloud of black dust came toward us. In the beams from our headlamps I was shocked to see the thick cloud of particles sparkling. Then someone started to scream, and like a chorus, a lot of other kids screamed as well. I turned to laugh at them, but I, too, yelped when I got a look: Everyone was completely black, apart from the portion the masks covered. Then I heard another shout that turned my hair on end: It was the teacher's voice!

"My god, Seya! You don't have your mask on!"

Seya hadn't put on his mask, and now he was as completely black as the holographic miners. "You said over and over in history class that the key goal was to get a feel for the past. I wanted a real feel!" he said, his teeth flashing white on his black face.

An alarm sounded somewhere, and within a minute, a teardrop-shaped micro-hovercar stopped soundlessly in front of us, an unpleasant intrusion of something modern. Two doctors got out. By now, all of the real coal dust had been sucked away, leaving only the holographic dust floating around us, so their white coats stayed spotless as they passed through it. They pulled Seya off to the car.

"Child," one doctor said, looking straight into his eyes. "Your lungs have been seriously harmed. You'll have to be hospitalized for at least a week. We'll notify your parents."

"Wait!" Seya shouted, his hands fumbling with the rebreather. "Did miners a hundred years ago wear these?"

"Shut your mouth and go to the hospital," the teacher said. "Why can't you ever just follow the rules?"

"We're human, just like our ancestors. Why . . ."

Seya was shoved into the car before he could finish. "This is the first time the museum has had this kind of accident," a doctor said severely, pointing at the teacher and adding, before getting into the hovercar, "This falls on you!" The hovercar left as silently as it had come.

We continued our tour. The chastened teacher said, "Every kind of work in the mine was fraught with danger, and required enormous physical energy. For example, these iron supports had to be retrieved after extraction in this zone was completed, in a process called support removal."

We saw a miner with an iron hammer striking an iron pin in one of the supports, buckling it in two. Then he carried it off. Me and a boy tried to pick up another support that was lying on the ground, but it was ridiculously heavy. "Support removal was a dangerous job, since the roof overhead could collapse at any time . . ."

Above our heads came scraping sounds, and I looked up and saw, in the light of the mining lanterns, a fissure open up in the rock where the support had just been removed. Before I had time to react, it fell in, and huge chunks of holographic stone fell through me to the ground with a loud crash. Everything vanished in a cloud of dust.

"This accident is called a cave-in," the teacher's voice sounded beside me. "Be careful. Harmful stones don't always come from up above."

Before she even finished, a section of rock wall next to us toppled over, falling a fair distance in a single piece, as if a giant hand from the ground had pushed it over, before finally breaking up and raining down as individual stones. We were buried under holographic rocks with a crash, and our headlamps went out. Through the darkness and screams, I heard the teacher's voice again.

"That was a methane outburst. Methane is a gas that builds to immense pressure when sealed in a coal seam. What we saw just now was what happens when the rock walls of the work zone can't hold back that pressure and are blown out."

The lights came back on, and we all exhaled. Then I heard a strange sound, at times as loud as galloping horses, sometimes soft and deep, like giants whispering.

"Look out, children! A flood is coming!"

We were still processing what she said when a broad surge of water erupted from a tunnel not far away. It quickly swamped the entire work zone. The murky water reached our knees, and then was waist-high. It reflected the light of our headlamps to shine indistinct patterns on the rocky ceiling. Wooden beams stained black with coal dust floated by, and miners' helmets and lunch boxes. . . . When the water reached my chin, I instinctively held my breath. Then I was entirely underwater, and all I could see was a murky brown where my headlamp shone, and air bubbles that sometimes floated up.

"Mine floods have many causes. Whether it's groundwater, or if the mine has dug into a surface water source, it's far more life-threatening than a flood above ground," the teacher said over the sound of the water.

The holographic water vanished and our surroundings returned to normal. Then I noticed an odd-looking object, like a big metal toad puffing out its stomach. It was huge and heavy. I pointed it out to the teacher.

"That's an anti-explosion switch. Since methane is a highly flammable gas, the switch suppresses the electric sparks that ordinary switches create. That's related to what we'll see next, the most terrifying mining danger of all . . ."

There was another loud crash, but unlike the previous two times, it seemed to come from within us, bursting through our eardrums to the outside, as huge waves contracted our every cell, and in the searing waves of heat, we were plunged into a red glow emitted from the air around us that filled every inch of space in the mine. Then the glow disappeared, and everything plunged into darkness.

"Few people have actually seen a methane explosion, since it's hard to survive one in the mines." The teacher's disembodied voice echoed in the darkness.

"Why did people used to come to such a terrible place?" a student asked.

"For this," the teacher said, holding a chunk of black rock into the light from our headlamps, where its innumerable facets sparkled. That was the first time I saw solid coal.

"Children, what we just saw was a mid-twentieth-century coal mine. There were a few new machines and technologies after that, such as hydraulic struts and huge shearers, which went into use in the last two decades of the century and improved conditions somewhat for the workers, but coal mines remained an incredibly dangerous, awful working environment. Until . . ."

It turned dull after that. The teacher lectured us on the history of gasified coal, which was put to use eighty years ago, when oil was nearly exhausted and major powers mobilized troops to seize the remaining oil fields. The Earth was on the brink of war, but it was gasified coal that saved the world. . . . We all knew this, so it was boring.

Then we toured a modern mine. Nothing special, just all those pipes we see every day, leading out from underground into the distance, although it was the first time I went inside a central control building and saw a hologram of the burn. It was huge. And we saw the neutrino sensors and gravity-wave radar monitoring the underground fire, and laser drills . . . all pretty boring, too.

The teacher recounted the history of the mine, and said that over a century ago, it had been destroyed in an uncontrolled fire that burned for eighteen years before going out. In those days our beautiful city was a wasteland where smoke blotted out the sky, and all the people had left. There were many stories of the cause of the fire; some people said it had been started by an underground weapons test, and others said it was connected to Greenpeace.

We don't have to be nostalgic for the so-called good old days. Life in those days was dangerous and confusing. But we shouldn't be depressed about today, either. Because today will one day be referred to as the good old days.

People really were stupid in the past, and they really had a tough time.

CONTRACTION

TRANSLATED BY JOHN CHU

The contraction will start one hour, twenty-four minutes, seventeen seconds before sunrise.

It will be observed in the auditorium of the country's largest astronomical observatory. The auditorium will receive images sent back from a space telescope in geosynchronous orbit, then project them onto a gigantic screen about the size of a basketball court. Right now, the screen is still blank. There aren't many people here, but they are all authorities in theoretical physics, astrophysics, and cosmology, the few people in the world who can truly understand the implications of the moment to come. Waiting for that moment, they sit still, like Adam and Eve, having just been created from mud, waiting for the breath of life from God. The exception is the observatory head, impatiently pacing back and forth.

The gigantic screen isn't working and the engineer responsible for maintaining it hasn't shown up yet. If she doesn't show up in time, the image coming from the space telescope can be projected only on the small screen. The historic sense of the moment will be ruined.

Professor Ding Yi walks into the hall.

The scientists all come to life. They stand in unison. Aside from the universe itself, only he can hold them all in awe.

As usual, Ding Yi holds everyone beneath his notice. He doesn't greet anyone and he doesn't sit in the large, comfortable chair prepared for him. Instead, he strolls aimlessly until he reaches a corner of the auditorium, where there's a large glass cabinet. He admires the large clay plate, one of the observatory head's local treasures, propped up inside. It's a priceless relic of the Western Zhou era. Carved onto its surface is a star atlas as seen by the naked eye on a summer night several thousand years ago. Having suffered the ravages of time, the star atlas is now faint and blurred. The starry sky outside the hall, though, is still bright and clear.

Ding Yi digs out a pipe and tobacco from his jacket pocket. Self-assured, he lights the pipe, then takes a puff. This surprises everyone, because he has severe tracheitis. He's never smoked before and no one has ever dared to smoke around him. Furthermore, smoking is strictly prohibited in the auditorium, and that pipe produces more smoke than ten cigarettes.

However, Professor Ding is entitled to do anything he wants. He founded the unified field theory, realizing Albert Einstein's dream. The series of predictions his theory has made about space over a vast scale have all been confirmed by actual observations. For three years, as many as a hundred supercomputers ran a mathematical model of the unified field theory nonstop and obtained a result that was hard to believe: The universe that had been expanding for about fourteen billion years would, in two years, start collapsing. Now, out of those two years, there's only one hour left.

White smoke lingers around his head. It forms a dreamlike pattern, as if his incredible ideas are floating out of his mind. . . .

Cautiously, the observatory head approaches Ding Yi. "Professor Ding, the governor will be here. Persuading her to accept the invitation wasn't easy. Please, I beg you, use the influence you have so that she'll increase our funding. Originally, we weren't going to bother you with this, but the observatory is out of funds. The national government can't give us any more money this year. We can only ask the province. We are the main observatory for the country. You can see what we've been reduced to. We can't even afford the electric bill for our radio telescope. We're already trying now to figure out what to do about this." The observatory head points to the ancient star atlas plate Ding Yi has been admiring. "If selling antiquities weren't illegal, we would have sold it long ago."

At that moment, the governor and her entourage of two enter the auditorium. The exhaustion on their faces drags a thread of the mundane into this otherworldly place.

"My apologies. Oh. Hello, Professor Ding. Everyone. So sorry for being late. This is the first time it hasn't been pouring outside in days. We're still worried about flooding. The Yangtze River is close to its 1998 record high."

Excitedly, the observatory head welcomes the governor and brings her to Ding Yi. "Why don't we have Professor Ding introduce you to the idea of universal contraction. . . ." He winks at Ding Yi.

"Why don't I first explain what I understand, then Professor Ding and everyone else can correct me. First, Hubble discovered redshifts. I don't remember when. The electromagnetic radiation that we measure from a galaxy is shifted toward the red end of the spectrum. This means, according to the Doppler effect, galaxies are receding from us. From that, we can draw this conclusion: The universe is expanding. We can also draw another conclusion: About fourteen billion years ago, the big bang brought the universe into being. If the total mass of the universe is less than some value, the universe will continue to expand forever; if it is greater than that value, then gravity will gradually slow the expansion until it stops and, eventually, gravity will cause it to contract. Previous measurements of the amount of mass in the universe suggested the first alternative. Then we discovered that neutrinos have mass. Moreover, we discovered a vast amount of previously undetected dark matter in the universe. This greatly increased the amount of mass in the universe and people changed their minds in favor of the other alternative, that the universe will expand ever more slowly until it finally starts to contract. All the galaxies in the universe will begin to gather at the gravitational center. At the same time, due to the same Doppler effect, we will see a shift in stars' electromagnetic radiation toward the blue end of the spectrum, namely a blueshift. Now, Professor Ding's unified field theory has calculated the exact moment the universe will switch from expansion to contraction."

"Brilliant!" The observatory head claps his hands a few times flatteringly. "So few leaders have such an understanding of fundamental theory. I bet even Professor Ding thinks so." He winks again at Ding Yi.

"What she said is basically correct." Ding Yi slowly knocks the ash from his pipe onto the carpet.

"Right, right. If Professor Ding thinks so—" The observatory head beams with happiness.

"Just enough to show her superficiality." Ding Yi digs more tobacco out of his coat pocket.

The observatory head freezes. The scientists around him titter.

The governor smiles tolerantly. "I also majored in physics, but the last thirty years, I've forgotten practically all of it. Compared to you all here, my knowledge of physics and cosmology, I'm afraid, isn't even superficial. Hell, I only remember Newton's three laws."

"But that's a long way from understanding it." Ding Yi lights his newly filled pipe.

The observatory head shakes his head, not knowing whether to laugh or cry.

"Professor Ding, we live in two completely different worlds." The governor sighs. "My world is a practical one. No poetry. Bogged down with details. We spend our days bustling around like ants, and like ants, our view is just as limited. Sometimes, when I leave my office at night, I stop to look up at the stars. A luxury that's hard to come by. Your world is brimming with wonder and mystery. Your thoughts stretch across hundreds of light-years of space and billions of years of time. To you, the Earth is just a speck of dust in the universe. To you, this era is just an instant in time too short to measure. The entire universe seems to exist to satisfy your curiosity and fulfill your existence. To be frank, Professor Ding, I truly envy you. I dreamed of this when I was young, but to enter your world was too difficult."

"But it's not too difficult tonight. You can at least stay in Professor Ding's world for a while. See the world's greatest moment together," the observatory head says.

"I'm not so lucky. Everyone, I'm extremely sorry. The Yangtze dykes are ready to burst. I must go right away to make sure that doesn't happen. Before I go, though, I still have some questions I'd like to ask Professor Ding. You'll probably find these questions childish, but I've thought hard about them and I still don't understand. First question: The sign of contraction is the universe changing from redshift to blueshift. We will see light from all the galaxies shift toward blue at the same time. However, right now, the farthest galaxies we can observe are about fourteen billion light-years away. According to your calculations, the entire universe will contract at the same moment. If that's the case, it should be about fourteen billion years before we can see the blueshift from them. Even the closest star system, Alpha Centauri, should still need four years."

Ding Yi slowly lets out a puff of smoke. It floats in the air like a shrinking spiral galaxy.

"Very good. You can understand a little. It makes you seem like a physics student, albeit still a superficial one. Yes, we will see all the stars in the universe blueshift at the same time, not one at a time from four years to fourteen billion years from now. This is due to quantum effects over a cosmic scale. Its mathematical model is extremely complex. It's the most difficult idea in physics and cosmology to explain. I have no hope of making you understand it. From this, though, you've already received the first revelation. It warns you that the effects produced from the universe contracting will be more complex than what people imagine. Do you still have questions? Oh, you don't have to go right away. What you have to take care of is not as urgent as you think."

"Compared to your entire universe, the flooding of the Yangtze River is obviously not worth mentioning. But while the mysterious universe admittedly has its appeal, the real world still takes priority. I have other questions, but I really must go. Thank you, Professor Ding, for the physics lesson. I hope everyone sees what they want to see tonight."

"You don't understand what I mean," Ding Yi says. "There must be many workers battling the flood right now."

"I have my responsibilities, Professor Ding. I must go."

"You still don't understand what I mean. I'm saying those workers must be extremely tired. You can let them go."

Everyone is dumbstruck.

"What . . . let them go? To do what? Watch the universe contract?"

"If they aren't interested, they can go home and sleep."

"Professor Ding, surely you're joking!"

"I'm serious. There's no point to what they're doing."

"Why?"

"Because of the contraction."

After a long silence, the governor points at the ancient star atlas plate displayed in the corner of the auditorium: "Professor Ding, the universe has been expanding all along, but from ancient times until today, the universe that we can see hasn't changed much. Contracting is the same. The extent of humanity in space-time, compared to that of the universe, is negligible. Besides the importance to pure theory, I don't believe the contraction will have any effect on human life. In fact, after one hundred million years, we still won't observe even a tiny shift caused by contraction, assuming we're still around."

"One and a half billion years," Ding Yi says. "Even with our most accurate instruments, it will be one and a half billion years before we can observe the shift. By then, the sun will already have gone out. We probably won't be around."

"And the complete contraction of the universe needs about fourteen billion years. Humanity is a dewdrop on the great tree of the universe. During its brief life span, it absolutely cannot perceive the maturing of the great tree. You surely don't believe the ridiculous rumors from the internet that the contraction will squash the Earth flat!"

A young woman enters, her face pale and her gaze gloomy. She's the engineer responsible for the gigantic screen.

"Miss Zhang, this is inexcusable! Do you know what time it is?" The flustered observatory head rushes to her as he shouts.

"My father just died at the hospital."

The observatory head's anger dissipates instantly. "I'm so sorry. I didn't know. Can you take a look . . ."

The engineer doesn't say any more. She just walks silently over to the computer that controls the screen and sinks herself into diagnosing the problem. Ding Yi, biting his pipe, walks over to her slowly.

"If you truly understood the meaning of the universe contracting, your father's death wouldn't grieve you so much."

Ding Yi's words infuriate everyone there. The engineer stands suddenly. Her face grows red with fury. Tears fill her eyes.

"You're not from this world! Perhaps compared to your universe, fathers aren't much, but mine's important to me. They're important to us ordinary people! And your contraction, that's just the frequency of light that can't possibly be weaker in the night sky changing a little. Without precise instruments to amplify it over ten thousand times, no one can see even the change, not to mention the light in the first place. What is the contraction? As far as ordinary people are concerned, it's nothing! The universe expanding or contracting, what's the difference? But fathers are important to us. Do you understand?"

When the engineer realizes who she lost her temper to, she masters herself, then turns back to her work.

Ding Yi sighs, shaking his head. He says to the governor, "Yes, like you said, two worlds. Our world." He waves his hand, drawing a circle around the physicists and cosmologists in the room, then points at the physicists. "Small scale is ten-quadrillionths of a millimeter." He points at the cosmologists. "Large scale is ten billion light-years. This is a world that you can grasp only through imagination. Your world has the floods of the Yangtze River, tight budgets, dead and living fathers . . . a practical world. But what's lamentable is people always want to separate the two worlds."

"But you can see that they're separate," the governor says.

"No! Although elementary particles are tiny, we are made of them. Although the universe is vast, we are inside it. Every change in the microscopic and macroscopic world affects everything."

"But what is the coming contraction going to affect?"

Ding Yi starts to laugh loudly. It's not a nervous laugh. It seems to embody something mystical. It scares the hell out of everyone.

"Okay, physics student. Please recite what you remember about the relationship between space-time and matter."

The governor, like a pupil, recites: "As proved by the theories of relativity and quantum physics that form modern physics, time and space cannot be separated from matter. They have no independent existence. There is no absolute space-time. Time, space, and the material world are all inextricably linked together."

"Very good. But who truly understands this? You?" Ding Yi first asks the governor, then turns to the observatory head. "You?" Then to the engineer buried in her work. "You?" Then to the technicians in the auditorium. "You?" Then, finally, to the scientists. "Not even you? No, none of you understand. You still think of the universe in terms of absolute space-time as naturally as you stamp your feet on the ground. Absolute space-time is your ground. You have no way to leave it. Speaking of expansion and contraction, you believe that's just the stars in space scattering and gathering in absolute space-time."

As he speaks, he strolls to the glass display case, opens its door, then takes out the irreplaceable star atlas plate. He runs a hand lightly over its surface, admiring it. The observatory head nervously holds his hands beneath the plate to protect it. This treasure has been here for over twenty years and no hand has dared to touch it until now. The observatory head waits anxiously for Ding Yi to put the star atlas plate back, but he doesn't. Instead, he flings the plate away.

The priceless ancient treasure lies on the carpet, smashed into too many pieces to count.

The air freezes. Everyone stares dumbstruck. Ding Yi continues his leisurely stroll, the only moving element in this deadlocked world. He continues to speak.

"Space-time and matter are not separable. The expansion and contraction of the universe comprises the whole of space-time. Yes, my friends, they comprise all of time and space!"

Another cracking sound rings through the room. It's a glass cup that fell out of a physicist's grasp. What shocks the physicists isn't what shocks everyone else. It isn't the star atlas plate. It's what Ding Yi's words imply.

"What you're saying . . ." A cosmologist fixes his gaze on Ding Yi. His words catch in his throat.

"Yes." Ding Yi nods, then says to the governor, "They understand now."

"So, this is the meaning of the negative time parameter in the calculated result of the unified mathematical model?" a physicist blurts. Ding Yi nods.

"Why didn't you announce this to the world earlier? You have no sense of responsibility!" another physicist shouts.

"What would be the point? It could have only caused global chaos. What can we do about space-time?"

"What are you all talking about?" the governor asks, bewildered.

"The contraction . . ." the observatory head, also an astrophysicist, mumbles as if he were dreaming. "The contraction of the universe will influence humanity?"

"Influence? No, it will change it completely."

"What can it change?"

The scientists are scrambling to recalibrate their thoughts. No one answers him.

"Tell me, all of you, when the universe contracts or when the blueshift starts, what will happen?" the governor, now worried, asks.

"Time will play back," Ding Yi answers.

". . . Play back?" The governor looks at the observatory head, puzzled, then at Ding Yi.

"Time will flow backward," the observatory head says.

The gigantic screen has been repaired. The magnificent universe appears on it. To better observe the contraction, computers process the image the space telescope returns to exaggerate the effect of the frequency shift in the visual range. Right now, the light all the stars and galaxies emit appears red on the screen to represent the redshift of the still-expanding universe. Once the contraction starts, they will all turn blue at once. A countdown appears on a corner of the screen: 150 seconds.

"Time has followed the expansion of the universe for about fourteen billion years, but now, there isn't even three minutes of expansion left. Afterward, time will follow the contraction of the universe. Time will flow backward." Ding Yi walks over to the stupefied observatory head, pointing at the smashed star atlas plate. "Don't worry about this relic. Not long after the blueshift, its shattered pieces will fuse back together like new. It will return to the display case. After many years, it will return to the ground where it was buried. After thousands of years, it will return to a burning kiln, then become a ball of moist clay in the hands of an ancient astronomer. . . ."

He walks to the young engineer. "And you don't need to grieve your father. He will come back to life and you two will reunite soon. If your father is so important to you, then you should take comfort from this because, in the contracting universe, he will live longer than you. He will see you, his daughter, leave the world. Yes, we old folk will have all just started life's journey and you young folk will have already entered your declining years. Or maybe your childhood."

He returns to the governor. "If there is no past, the Yangtze River will never overflow its dykes during your term of office because there's only one hundred seconds left to this universe. The contracting universe's future is the expanding universe's past. The greatest danger won't occur until 1998. By then, though, you will be a child. It won't be your responsibility. There's still a minute. It doesn't matter what you do now. There won't be any consequences in the future. Everyone can do what they like and not worry about the future. There is no future now. As for me, I now just do what I wanted to do but couldn't because of my tracheitis." He digs out a bowl of tobacco from a pocket with his pipe. He lights the pipe, then smokes contentedly.

The blueshift countdown: fifty seconds.

"This can't be!" the governor shouts. "It's illogical. Time playing back? If everything will go in reverse, are you saying that we'll speak backward? That's inconceivable!"

"You'll get used to it."

The blueshift countdown: forty seconds.

"In other words, afterward, everything will be repeated. History and life will become boring and predictable."

"No, it won't. You will be in another time. The current past will become your future. We are now in the future of that time. You can't remember the future. Once the blueshift starts, your future will become blank. You won't remember any of it. You won't know any of it."

The blueshift countdown: twenty seconds.

"This can't be!"

"As you will discover, going from old age to youth, from maturity to naïveté, is quite rational, quite natural. If anyone speaks about time going in another direction, you will think he's a fool. There's about ten seconds left.

Soon, in about ten seconds, the universe will pass through a strange point. Time won't exist in that moment. After that, we will enter the contracting universe."

The blueshift countdown: eight seconds.

"This can't be! This really can't be!!"

"No matter. You'll know soon."

The blueshift countdown: five, four, three, two, one, zero.

The starlight in the universe changes from a troublesome red to an empty white . . .

. . . time reaches a strange point . . .

. . . starlight changes from white to a beautiful, tranquil blue. The blueshift has begun. The contraction has begun.

. . .

. . .

.nugeb sah noitcartnoc ehT .nugeb sah tfihseulb ehT .eulb liuqnart ,lufi-tuaeb a ot etihw morf segnahc thgilrats . . .

. . . tniop egnarts a sehcaer emit . . .

. . . etihw ytpme na ot der emoselbuort a morf segnahc esrevinu eht ni thgilrats ehT

.orez ,eno ,owt ,eerht ,ruof ,evif :nwodtnuoc tfihseulb ehT

".noos wonk ll'uoY .rettam oN"

"!!eb t'nac yllaer sihT !eb t'nac sihT"

.sdnoces thgie :nwodtnuoc tfihseulb ehT

".esrevinu gnitcartnoc eht retne lliw ew ,taht retfA .tnemom taht ni tsixe t'now emiT .tniop egnarts a hguorht ssap lliw esrevinu eht ,sdnoces net tuoba ni ,nooS .tfel sdnoces net tuoba s'erehT .loof a s'eh kniht lliw uoy ,noitcerid rehtona ni gniog emit tuoba skaeps enoyna fI .larutan etiuq . . .

. . .

MIRROR

TRANSLATED BY CARMEN YILING YAN

As research delves deeper, humanity is discovering that quantum effects are nothing more than surface ripples in the ocean of existence, shadows of the disturbances arising from the deeper laws governing the workings of matter. With these laws beginning to reveal themselves, quantum mechanics' ever-shifting picture of reality is once again stabilizing, deterministic variables once again replacing probabilities. In this new model of the universe, the chains of causality that were thought eliminated have surfaced once more, and clearer than before.

PURSUIT

In the office were the flags of China and the CCP. There were also two men, one on either side of the broad desk.

"I know you're very busy, sir, but I must report this. I've honestly never seen anything like it," said the man in front of the desk. He wore the uniform of a police superintendent second class. He was near fifty, but he stood ramrod-straight, and the lines of his face were hard and vigorous.

"I know the weight of that last sentence coming from you, Xufeng, veteran investigator of thirty years." The Senior Official looked at the red and blue pencil slowly twirling between his fingers as he spoke, as if all his attention were focused on assessing the merit of its sharpening. He tucked away his gaze like this much of the time. In the years Chen Xufeng had known him, the Senior Official had looked him in the eyes no more than three times. Each time had come at a turning point in Chen's life.

"Every time we take action, the target escapes one step ahead of us. They know what we're going to do."

"Surely you've seen similar things before," the Senior Official said.

"If it were simply that, it wouldn't be a big deal, of course. We considered the possibility of an inside job right off."

"Knowing your subordinates, I find that rather improbable."

"We found that out for ourselves," Chen said. "Like you instructed, we've reduced the participants in this case as much as possible. There are only four people in the task force, and only two know the full story. But just in case, I planned to call a meeting of all the members and question them one by one. I told Chenbing to handle it—you know him, the one from the Eleventh Department, very reliable, took care of the business with Song Cheng—and that's when it happened.

"Don't take this for a joke, sir. What I'm going to say next is the honest truth." Chen Xufeng laughed a little, as if embarrassed by his own defensiveness. "Right then, they called. Our target called me on the phone! I heard them say on my cell phone, *You don't need this meeting, there's no traitor among you.* Less than thirty seconds after I told Chenbing I wanted to call a meeting!"

The Senior Official's pencil stilled between his fingers.

"You might be thinking that we were bugged, but that's impossible. I chose the location for the conversation at random to be the middle of a government agency auditorium while it was being used for chorus rehearsals for National Day. We had to talk right into each other's ears to hear.

"And similar funny business kept happening after that. They called us eight times in total, each time about things we had just said or done. The scariest part is, not only do they hear everything, they see everything. One time, Chenbing decided to search the target's parents' home. He and the other task force member were just standing up, not even out of the department office, when they got the target's call. *You guys have the wrong search warrant,* they told them. *My parents are careful people. They might think you guys are frauds.* Chenbing took out the warrant to check, and sir, he really had taken the wrong one."

The Senior Official set the pencil lightly on his desk, waiting in silence for Chen Xufeng to continue, but the latter seemed to have run out of steam. The Senior Official took out a cigarette. Chen Xufeng hurriedly patted at his coat pockets for a lighter, but couldn't find one.

One of the two phones on the desk began to ring.

Chen Xufeng swept his gaze over the caller ID. "It's them," he said quietly.

Unperturbed, the Senior Official motioned at him. Chen pressed the speaker button. A voice immediately sounded, worn and very young. "Your lighter is in the briefcase."

Chen Xufeng glanced at the Senior Official, then began to rummage through the briefcase on the desk. He couldn't find anything at first.

"It's wedged in a document, the one on urban household registration reform."

Chen Xufeng took out the document. The lighter fell onto the desk with a clatter.

"That's one fine lighter there. French-made S. T. Dupont brand, solid palladium-gold alloy, thirty diamonds set in each side, worth . . . let me look it up . . . 39,960 yuan."

The Senior Official didn't move, but Chen Xufeng raised his head to study the office. This wasn't the Senior Official's personal office; rather, it had been selected at random from the rooms in this office building.

The target continued the demonstration of their powers. "Senior Official, there are five cigarettes left in your box of Chunghwas. There's only one Mevacor cholesterol tablet left in your coat pocket—better have your secretary get some more."

Chen Xufeng picked up the box of cigarettes on the desk; the Senior Official took out the blister pack of pills from his pocket. The target was correct on both counts.

"Stop coming after me. I'm in a tricky situation just like you. I'm not sure what to do now," the target continued.

"Can we discuss this in person?" asked the Senior Official.

"Believe me, it would be a disaster for both sides." With that, the phone went dead.

Chen Xufeng exhaled. Now he had the proof to back up his story—the thought of disbelief from the Senior Official unsettled him more than his opponent's antics. "It's like seeing a ghost," he said, shaking his head.

"I don't believe in ghosts, but I do see danger," said the Senior Official. For the fourth time in his life, Chen Xufeng saw that pair of eyes bore into his.

THE INMATE AND THE PURSUED

In the No. 2 Detention Center at the city outskirts, Song Cheng walked under escort into the cell. There were already six other prisoners inside, mostly other inmates serving extended terms.

Cold looks greeted Song Cheng from all directions. Once the guard left, shutting the door behind him, a small, thin man came up.

"Hey, you, Pig Grease!" he yelled. Seeing Song Cheng's confusion, he continued, "The law of the land here ranks us Big Grease, Second Grease, Third Grease . . . Pig Grease at the bottom, that's you. Hey, don't think we're taking advantage of the latecomer." He pointed his thumb at a heavily bearded man leaning in the corner. "Brother Bao's only been here three days, and he's already Big Grease. Trash like you may have held a pretty government rank before, but here you're lowest of the low!" He turned toward the other man and asked respectfully, "How will you receive him, Brother Bao?"

"Stereo sound," came the careless reply.

Two other inmates sprang up from the bunks and grabbed Song Cheng by the ankles, dangling him upside down. They held him over the toilet and slowly lowered him until his head was largely inside.

"Sing a song," Skinny Guy commanded. "That's what stereo sound means. Give us a comrade song like 'Left Hand, Right Hand'!"

Song Cheng didn't sing. The inmates let go, and his head pitched all the way into the toilet.

Struggling, Song Cheng pulled his head out. He immediately began to vomit. Now he realized that the story designed by those who had framed him would make him the target of all his fellow inmates' contempt.

The delighted prisoners around him suddenly scattered and dashed back to their bunks. The door opened; the police guard from earlier came in. He looked with disgust at Song Cheng, still crouched in front of the toilet. "Wash off your head at the tap. You have a visitor."

Once Song Cheng rinsed off, he followed the guard into a spacious office where his visitor awaited. He was very young, thin-faced with messy hair and thick glasses. He carried an enormous briefcase.

Song Cheng sat down coldly without looking at the visitor. He had been permitted a visit at this time, and here, not in a visitation room with a glass partition; from that, Song Cheng had a good guess as to who sent him. But the first words out of his visitor's mouth made Song lift his head in surprise.

"My name's Bai Bing. I'm an engineer at the Center for Meteorological Modeling. They're coming after me for the same reason they came after you."

Song Cheng looked at the visitor. His tone of voice seemed odd: this was a subject that should have been discussed in whispers, but Bai Bing spoke at a normal volume, as if he wasn't talking about anything that needed hiding.

Bai Bing seemed to have noticed his confusion. "I called the Senior Official two hours ago. He wanted to talk face-to-face with me, but I turned him down. After that, they got on my trail, followed me all the way to the detention center doors. They haven't seized me because they're curious about our meeting. They want to know what I'll tell you. They're listening in to our conversation right now."

Song Cheng shifted his gaze from Bai Bing to the ceiling. He found it hard to trust this person, and regardless, he wasn't interested in the matter. The law might have spared him the death penalty, but it had sentenced and executed his spirit all the same. His heart was dead. He could no longer muster interest in anything.

"I know the truth, all of it," Bai Bing said.

A smirk flickered at the corner of Song Cheng's mouth. *No one knows the truth but them,* but he didn't bother to say that out loud.

"You began working for the provincial-level Commission for Discipline Inspection seven years ago. You were promoted to this rank just last year."

Song Cheng remained silent. He was angry now. Bai Bing's words had dragged him back into the memories he'd worked so hard to escape.

THE BIG CASE

At the beginning of the century, the Zhengzhou Municipal Government began a policy of setting aside a number of deputy-level positions for holders of Ph.D.s. Many other cities followed its example, and later, provincial governments began to adopt the same practice, even removing graduation-year requirements and offering higher starting positions. It was an excellent way to demonstrate the recruiters' magnanimity and vision to the world, but in reality, the attractive concept amounted to little more than political record engineering. The recruiters were farsighted indeed—they knew perfectly well that these book-smart, well-educated young people lacked any sort of political experience. When they entered the unfamiliar and vicious political sphere, they found themselves swallowed whole in labyrinthine bureaucracy, unable to gain any foothold. The whole business was no big loss in job vacancies, while substantially padding the recruiters' political résumés.

An opportunity like this led Song Cheng, already a law professor at the time, to leave his peaceful campus study for the world of politics. His peers who chose the same road didn't last a year before they left in utter despair, beaten men and women, their only achievement being the destruction of their dreams. But Song Cheng was an exception. He not only stayed in politics, but did exceptionally well.

The credit belonged to two people. One was his college classmate Lu Wenming. In their last year as undergraduates, he'd placed in the civil service even as Song Cheng tested into grad school. With his advantageous family background and his own dedicated effort, ten years later he'd become the youngest provincial secretary of discipline inspection in the nation, head of the organization in charge of maintaining discipline within the provincial-level Party. He was the one who'd advised Song Cheng to give up his books for governance.

When the simple scholar first began, Lu didn't lead him by the hand so much as he toddled him along by the feet, hand-placing Song's every step as he taught him how to walk. He'd steered Song Cheng around traps and treachery that the latter could never have spotted himself, allowing him to progress up the road that had led to today. The other person he should thank was the Senior Official . . . on that thought, Song Cheng's heart gave a spasm.

"You have to admit, you chose this for yourself. You can't say they didn't give you a way out."

Song Cheng nodded. Yes, they'd given him a way out, a boulevard with his name in lights at that.

Bai Bing continued, "The Senior Official met with you a few months ago. I'm sure you remember it well. It was in a villa out in the exurbs, by the Yang River. The Senior Official doesn't normally see outsiders there.

"Once you were out of the car, you found him waiting for you at the gate, a very high honor. He clasped your hand warmly and led you into the drawing room.

"The décor would've given off a first impression of unassuming simplicity, but you'd be wrong there. That aged-looking mahogany furniture is worth millions. The one plain scroll painting hanging on the wall looks even older, and there's insect damage if you look closely, but that's *Dangheqizi* by the Ming Dynasty painter Wu Bin, bought at a Christie's auction in Hong Kong for eight million HKD. And the cup of tea the Senior Official personally steeped for you? The leaves were ranked five stars at the International Tea Competition. It goes for nine hundred thousand yuan per half kilo."

Song Cheng really could recall the tea Bai Bing spoke of. The liquid had sparkled the green of a jewel, a few delicate leaves drifting in its clarity like the languid notes from a mountain saint's zither. . . . He even recalled how he'd felt: *If only the outside world could be this lovely and pure.* The tarp of apathy was torn from Song Cheng's stifled thoughts, his blurred mind snapping back into focus. He stared at Bai Bing, eyes wide with shock.

How could he know all this? The whole affair had been dispatched to the deepest oubliettes, a secret among secrets. No more than four people in all the world knew, and that was counting himself.

"Who are you?!" He opened his mouth for the first time.

Bai Bing smiled. "I introduced myself earlier. I'm an ordinary person. But I'll tell you straight off, not only do I know a lot, I know everything, or at least have the means to know everything. That's why they want to get rid of me like they got rid of you."

Bai Bing continued his account. "The Senior Official sat close, one hand on your shoulder. That benevolent gaze he turned on you would have moved anyone from the junior ranks. From what I know (and remember, I know everything), he'd never shown anyone else the same intimacy. He told you, *Don't worry, young man, we're all comrades here. Whatever the matter, just speak honestly and trust that you'll get honesty in return. We can always come to a solution . . . you have ideas, you're capable, you have a sense of duty and a sense of mission. Those last two in particular are as precious as an oasis in a desert among young cadres nowadays. This is why I think so highly of you. In you, I see the reflection of what I was once like.*

"I should mention that the Senior Official may have been telling the truth. Your official work didn't give you many chances to interact with him, but quite a few times, you'd run into him in the hallways of the government building or coming out of a meeting, and he'd always be the one to come up to you to chat. He very rarely did that with lower-ranking officials, especially the younger ones. People took notice. He might not have said anything to help you at organizational meetings, but those gestures did a lot for your career."

Song Cheng nodded again. He'd known all this, and had been immensely grateful. All that time, Song had wanted the opportunity to repay him.

"Then the Senior Official raised his hand and gestured behind him. Immediately, someone entered and quietly set a big stack of documents and materials on the table. You must have noticed that he wasn't the Senior Official's normal secretary.

"The Senior Official passed a hand over the documents and said, *The project you just completed fully demonstrates those priceless assets of yours. It required such an immense and difficult investigation to collect evidence, but these documents are ample, detailed, and reliable, the conclusions drawn profound. It's hard to believe you did it all in half a year. It would be the Party's great fortune to have more outstanding Discipline Inspection officials like you.* . . . I don't need to tell you how you felt at that moment, I think."

Of course he didn't. Song Cheng had never been so horrified in his life. That stack of documents first sent him shaking as if electrocuted, then froze him into stone.

Bai Bing continued: "It all started with the investigation into the illegal apportionment of state-owned land you undertook on behalf of the Central Commission, yes. . . .

"I recall that when you were a child, you and two of your friends went exploring in a cave, called Old Man Cavern by the locals. The entrance was only half a meter high, and you had to crouch down to enter. But inside was an enormous, dark vault, its ceiling too high for your flashlights to reach. All you could see were endless bats swishing past the beams of light. Every little sound provoked a rumbling echo from the distance. The dank cold seeped into your bones. . . . It's a lively metaphor for the investigation: walking along, following that seemingly run-of-the-mill trail of clues, only to find yourself led toward places that made you afraid to believe your own eyes. As you deepened your investigation, a grand network of corruption spanning the entire province unfolded before you, and every strand of the web led in one direction, to one person. And now, the top-secret Discipline Inspection report you'd prepared for the Central Commission was in his hands! In this investigation, you'd considered all sorts of worst-case scenarios, but you never dreamed of the one that you faced now. You were thrown into total panic. You stammered, *H-how did this end up in your hands, sir?* The Senior Official smiled indulgently and lifted his hand to gesture lightly again. You immediately got your answer: The secretary of discipline inspection, Lu Wenming, walked into the room.

"You stood and glared at Lu Wenming. *How—how could you do this? How could you go against our organization's rules and principles like this?* Lu Wenming cut you off with a wave of his hand and asked in the same furious tone of voice as you, *How could you go ahead with something like this without telling me?*

"*I've taken over your duties as secretary for the year you're undergoing training at the Central Party School,* you shot back. *Of course I couldn't tell you, it was against the rules of the organization!*

"Lu Wenming shook his head sorrowfully, looking as if he wanted to weep in despair. *If I hadn't caught this report in time . . . can you even imagine the consequences? Song Cheng, your fatal flaw is that insistence on dividing the world into black and white, when reality is nothing more than gray!*"

Song Cheng exhaled long and slow. He remembered how he'd stared dumbly at his classmate, unable to believe that he could say something like that. He'd never revealed thoughts in that vein before. Was the hatred of internal corruption he'd shown in their many late-night conversations, the steadfast courage he displayed as they tackled sensitive cases that drew pressure from all directions, the deeply personal concern for the Party and the nation he'd expressed at so many dawns, after grueling all-nighters at work—was all that nothing but pretense?

"It's not that Lu Wenming was lying before. It's more that he never delved *that* deeply into his soul in front of you. He's like that famous dessert, Baked Alaska, flash-cooked ice cream. The hot parts and the cold parts are both real. But the Senior Official didn't look at Lu Wenming. Instead, he slammed a hand onto the table. *What gray? Wenming, I really can't stand this side of you! What Song Cheng did was outstanding, faultless. In that respect he's better than you!* He turned to you and said, *Young man, you did exactly as you should have done. A person, especially a young person, is gone forever if they lose that faith and sense of mission. I look down on people like that.*"

The part that had struck Song Cheng the deepest was that, although he and Lu Wenming were the same age, the Senior Official only called him "young," and emphasized it repeatedly at that. The unspoken implication was clear: *With me as an opponent, you're still nothing but a child.* In the present, Song Cheng could only concede that he was right.

"The Senior Official continued on. *Nonetheless, young man, we still need to mature a little. Let's take an example from your report. There really are problems with the Hengyu Aluminum Electrolysis Base, and they're even worse than you discovered in your investigations. Not only are domestic officials implicated, foreign investors have collaborated with them in serious legal trespasses. Once the matter is dealt with, the foreigners will withdraw their investments. The largest aluminum-electrolysis enterprise in the country will be put out of business. Tongshan Bauxite Mines, which provides the aluminum ore for Hengyu, will be in deep trouble too. Next comes the Chenglin nuclear power plant. It was built too big due to the energy crisis the last few years, and with the severe domestic overproduction of electricity now, most of this brand-new power plant's output goes to the aluminum-electrolysis base. Once Hengyu collapses, Chenglin Nuclear Facility will face bankruptcy as well. And then Zhaoxikou Chemical Plant, which provides the enriched uranium for Chenglin, will be in trouble. . . . With that, nearly seventy billion yuan in government investment will be gone without a trace, and thirty to forty thousand people will lose their jobs. These corporations are all located within the provincial capital's outskirts—this vital city will be instantly thrown into turmoil. . . . And the Hengyu issue I went into is only a small part of this investigation. The case implicates one provincial-level official, three sub-provincial-level officials, two hundred and fifteen prefectural-level officials, six hundred and fourteen county-level officials, and countless more in lower ranks. Nearly half of the most successful large-scale enterprises and the most promising investment projects in the province will be impacted in some way. Once the secrets are out, the province's entire economy and political structure will be dead in the water! And we don't know, and have no way of predicting, what even worse consequences might arise from so large-scale and severe a disturbance. The political stability and economic growth our province has worked so hard to attain will be gone without a trace. Is that really to the benefit of the Party and the country? Young man, you can't think like a legal scholar anymore, demanding justice by the law come hell or high water. It's irresponsible. We've progressed along the road of history to today because of balance, arising from the happy medium between various elements. To abandon balance and seek an extreme is a sign of immaturity in politics.*

"When the Senior Official finished, Lu Wenming began. *I'll take care of things with the Central Commission. You just make sure you take over properly from the cadres in that project group. I'll break off training at the Central Party School next week and come back to help you—*

"*Scoundrel!* The Senior Official once again slammed the table. Lu Wenming jumped in fright. *Is that how you took my words? You thought I was trying to get this young man to abandon his principles and duty?! Wenming, you've known me for years. From the depths of your heart, do you really think I have so little sense of Party and principle? When did you become so oily? It saddens me.* Then he turned to you. *Young man, you've done a truly exceptional job so far on your work. You must stand fast in the face of interference and pressure, and hand the corrupt elements their comeuppance! This case hurts the eyes and heart to look upon. You must not spare them, in the name of the people, in the name of justice! Don't let what I just said burden you. I was just reminding you as an old Party member to be careful, to avoid serious consequences beyond your prediction. But there's one thing I know—you must get to the bottom of this terrible corruption case.* The Senior Official took out a piece of paper as he spoke, handing it to you solemnly. *Is this wide enough in scope for you?*"

Song Cheng had known right then that they'd set up a sacrificial altar and were ready to lay out the offerings. He looked at the list of names. It was wide enough in scope, truly enough, enough in both rank and quantity. It would be a corruption case to astound the entire nation, and with the case's triumphant conclusion, Song Cheng would become known throughout the country as an anti-corruption hero, revered by the people as a paragon of justice and virtue.

But he was clear in his heart that this was nothing more than a lizard severing its own tail in a crisis. The lizard would escape; the tail would grow back in no time. He saw the Senior Official watching him, and in that moment he really did think of a lizard, and he shivered. But Song Cheng knew, too, that the Senior Official was afraid, that he'd made him afraid, and it made Song Cheng proud. The pride made him vastly overestimate his own capabilities at that moment, but more vitally, there was that ineffable thing running in the blood of every scholar-idealist. He made the fatal choice.

"You stood and took up the pile of documents with both hands. You said to the Senior Official, *By the Internal Supervision Regulations of the CCP, the secretary of discipline inspection has the authority to conduct inspections upon Party officials of the same rank. According to the rules, sir, these documents can't stay with you. I'll take them.*

"Lu Wenming went to stop you, but the Senior Official gently tugged him back. At the door, you heard your classmate say in a low voice behind you, *You've gone too far, Song Cheng.*

"The Senior Official walked you to your car. As you were about to leave, he took your hand and said slowly, *Come again soon, young man.*"

Only later did Song Cheng fully realize the deeper meaning to his words: *Come again soon. You don't have much time left.*

THE BIG BANG

"Who the hell are you?" Song Cheng stared at Bai Bing fearfully. How could he know this much? No one could know this much!

"Okay, we'll end the reminiscing here." Bai Bing cut off his narrative with a wave of his hand. "Let me go into the whys and wherefores, to clear up the questions you have. Hmm . . . do you know what the big bang is?"

Song Cheng stared blankly at Bai Bing, his brain unable to immediately process Bai's words. At last he managed the response of a normal human and laughed.

"Okay, okay," Bai Bing said. "I know that was sudden. But please trust that I'm all there in the head. To go through everything clearly, we really do need to start with the big bang. This . . . Damn, how do I even explain it to you? Let's return to the big bang. You probably know at least a little.

"Our universe was created in a massive explosion twenty billion years ago. Most people picture the big bang like some ball of fire bursting forth in the darkness of space, but that's incorrect. Before the big bang, there was nothing, not even time and space. There was only a singularity, a single point of undefined size that rapidly expanded to form our universe today. Anything and everything, including us, originated from the singularity's expansion. It is the seed from which all living things grew! The theory behind it all is really deep, and I don't fully understand it myself, but the relevant part is this: With the advancement of physics and the appearance of 'theories of everything' like string theory, physicists are starting to figure out the structure of that singularity and create a mathematical model for it. This is different from the quantum-theory models they had before. If we can determine the fundamental parameters of the singularity before the big bang, we can determine everything in the universe it forms too. An uninterrupted chain of cause and effect running through the entire history of the universe . . ." He sighed. "Seriously, how am I supposed to explain it all?"

Bai Bing saw Song Cheng shake his head, as if he didn't understand, or as if he didn't even want to keep listening.

Bai Bing said, "Take my advice and stop thinking about the suffering you've gone through. Honestly, I haven't been much luckier. Like I said, I'm just an ordinary person, but now they're hunting me, and I may end up even worse than you, all because I know everything. You can hold on to the fact that you were martyred for your sense of duty and faith, but I'm . . . I just have really shitty luck. Enough shit luck for eight reincarnations. I've been screwed over even worse than you."

Song Cheng only continued to look at him, silently, as if to say: *No one can be screwed over worse than me.*

FRAMED

A week after he met with the Senior Official, Song Cheng was arrested for murder.

To be fair, Song Cheng had already known they'd take extraordinary measures against him. The usual administrative and political methods were too risky to use on someone who knew so much and was already in the process of taking action. But he hadn't imagined his opponent would move so quickly, or strike so viciously.

The victim was a nightclub dancer called LuoLuo, and he'd died in Song Cheng's car. The doors were locked from the outside. Two canisters of propane, the type used to refill cigarette lighters, had been tossed into the car, both slit open. The liquid inside had completely evaporated, and the high concentration of propane vapor in the car had fatally poisoned the victim. When the body was discovered, it was clutching a battered, broken cell phone in one hand, clearly used in an attempt to smash the car windows.

The police produced ample evidence. They had two hours of recordings to prove that Song Cheng had been in most irregular association with LuoLuo for the last three months. The most incriminating piece of evidence was the 110 call LuoLuo had made to the police shortly before his death.

> LuoLuo
> ...Hurry. Hurry! I can't open the car doors! I can't
> breathe, my head hurts ...
> 110
> Where are you? Can you clarify your situation?!
> LuoLuo
> ...Song ... Song Cheng wants to kill me ...
> (End of transmission)

Afterward, the police found a short phone-call recording on the victim's cell, preserving an exchange between Song Cheng and the victim.

> Song Cheng
> Now that we've gone this far, how about you break
> things off with Xu Xueping?
> LuoLuo
> Why the need, Brother Song? Me and Sister Xu just have
> the usual man-woman relations. It won't affect our
> thing. Hell, it might help.

Song Cheng

It makes me uncomfortable. Don't make me take action.

LuoLuo

Brother Song, let me live my life.

(End of transmission)

This was a highly professional frame-up. Its brilliance lay in that the evidence the police held was just about 100 percent real.

Song Cheng really had been associating with LuoLuo for a while, in secret, and it could indeed be called irregular. The two recordings weren't faked, although the second had been distorted.

Song Cheng met LuoLuo because of Xu Xueping, director general of Changtong Group, who held intimate financial ties to many nodes of the network of corruption and no doubt considerable knowledge of its background and inner workings. Of course, Song Cheng couldn't get any information directly from her, but with LuoLuo he had an in.

LuoLuo didn't provide Song Cheng information out of any inner sense of righteousness. In his eyes, the world was already good for nothing but wiping his ass on. He was in it for revenge.

This hinterland city shrouded in industrial smog and dust might have been ranked at the bottom of the list of similar-sized Chinese cities for average income, but it had some of the most opulent nightclubs in the nation. The young scions of Beijing's political families had to watch their image in the capital city, unable to indulge their desires like the rich without Party affiliations. Instead, they got in their cars every weekend and zipped four or five hours along the highway to this city, spent two days and one night in hedonistic extravagance, and zipped back to Beijing on Sunday night.

LuoLuo's Blue Wave was the highest-end of all the nightclubs. Requesting a song cost at least three thousand yuan, and bottles of Martell and Hennessy priced at thousands each sold multiple cases every night. But Blue Wave's real claim to fame was that it catered exclusively to female guests.

Unlike his fellow dancers, LuoLuo didn't care about how much his clients paid, but how much that money meant to them. A white-collar foreign worker making just two or three hundred thousand yuan a year (rare paupers in Blue Wave) could give him a few hundred and he'd accept. But Sister Xu wasn't one. Her fortune of billions had made waves south of the Yangtze the last few years, and likewise she was smashing the opposition in her expansion northward. But after several months spent together, she'd sent LuoLuo off with a mere four hundred thousand.

It had taken a lot to catch Sister Xu's eye; after she had broken it off, any other dancer would have, in LuoLuo's words, swigged enough champagne to make his liver hurt. But not LuoLuo, who was now filled with hatred for Xu Xueping. The arrival of a high-ranking Discipline Inspection official gave him hope of revenge, and he used his talents to entangle himself with Sister Xu once more. Normally, Xu Xueping was closemouthed even with LuoLuo, but once they had too many drinks or snorted too many lines, it was a different story. LuoLuo knew how to take the initiative, too; in the darkest hours before dawn, while Sister Xu slept soundly beside him, he'd silently climb out of bed and search her briefcase and drawers, snapping pictures of documents that he and Song Cheng needed.

Most of the video recordings the police used to prove Song Cheng's association with LuoLuo had been taken in the main dance hall in Blue Wave. The camera liked to start with the pretty young boys dancing enthusiastically on the stage, before shifting to the expensively dressed female guests gathered in the dim areas, pointing at the stage, now and then smiling confidentially. The final shot always captured Song Cheng and LuoLuo, often sitting in some corner in the back, seeming very intimate as they conversed quietly with heads bent close. As the only male guest in the club, Song Cheng was instantly recognizable. . . .

Song Cheng didn't have anything to say to that. Most of the time, he could only find LuoLuo at Blue Wave. The lighting in the dance hall was always dim, but these recordings were high resolution and clear. They could only have been taken with a high-end low-light camera, not the sort of equipment normal people would have. That meant they'd noticed him from the very beginning, showing Song Cheng how very amateur he had been compared to his opponent.

That day, LuoLuo wanted to report his latest findings. When Song Cheng met him at the nightclub, LuoLuo uncharacteristically asked to talk in the car. Once they were done, he'd told Song that he felt unwell. If he went back to the club now, his boss would make him get on stage for sure. He wanted to rest for a while in Song Cheng's car.

Song Cheng had thought that LuoLuo's addiction might have been acting up again, but he didn't have a choice. He could only drive back to his office to take care of the work he hadn't finished during the day, parking in front of the department building with LuoLuo waiting in the car. Forty minutes later, when he came back out, someone had already found LuoLuo dead in a car full of propane fumes. Song Cheng had to open the car door from the outside.

Later, a close friend in the police force who'd participated in the investigation told Song that the lock on his car door didn't show any signs of sabotage, and the evidence elsewhere really was enough to rule out the possibility of another killer. Logically enough, everyone assumed that Song Cheng had killed LuoLuo. But Song Cheng knew the only possible explanation: LuoLuo had brought the two propane canisters into the car himself.

This was too much for Song Cheng to fight against. He gave up his attempts to clear his name: if someone had used his own life and death as a weapon to frame him, he didn't have a chance of escape.

Really, LuoLuo committing suicide didn't surprise Song Cheng; his HIV test had returned positive. But someone else must have prompted him to use his death to frame Song Cheng. What would have been in it for him? What would money be worth to him now? Was the money for someone else? Or maybe his recompense wasn't money. But what was it, then? Was there some temptation or fear even stronger than his hatred of Xu Xueping? Song Cheng would never know now, but here he could see even more clearly his opponent's capabilities, and his own naïveté.

This was his life as the world knew it: a high-ranked Discipline Inspection cadre living a secret life of corruption and affairs, arrested for murdering his paramour in a lover's spat. The temperance he'd previously displayed in his heterosexual relationship only became further proof in the public mind. Like a trampled stinkbug, everything he had possessed disappeared without a trace.

Now Song Cheng realized that he'd been so prepared to sacrifice everything for faith and duty only because he hadn't even understood what sacrificing everything entailed. He'd of course imagined that death would be the bottom line. Only later did he realize that sacrifice could be far, far crueler. The police took him home one time when they searched his house. His wife and daughter were both there. He reached toward his daughter, but the child shrieked in disgust and buried her face in her mother's arms, shrinking into a corner. He'd seen the look they gave him only once before, one morning when he'd found a mouse in the trap under the wardrobe, and showed it to them. . . .

"Okay, let's set aside the big bang and the singularity and all the abstract stuff for now." Bai Bing broke off Song Cheng's painful reminiscences and hauled the large briefcase onto the table. "Take a look at this."

SUPERSTRING COMPUTER, ULTIMATE CAPACITY, DIGITAL MIRROR

"This is a superstring computer," Bai Bing said, patting the briefcase. "I brought it over, or, if you prefer, stole it from the Center for Meteorological Modeling. I'll depend on it to escape pursuit."

Song Cheng shifted his gaze to the briefcase, clearly confused.

"These are expensive. There are only two in the province as of now. According to superstring theory, the fundamental particles of matter aren't point-like objects, but an infinitely thin one-dimensional string vibrating in eleven dimensions. Nowadays, we can manipulate this string to store and process information along the dimension of its length. That's the theory behind a superstring computer.

"A CPU or piece of internal storage in a traditional electronic computer is just an atom in a superstring computer! The circuits are formed by the particles' eleven-dimensional microscale structure. This higher-dimensional subatomic array has given humanity practically infinite storage and operational capacity. Comparing the supercomputers of the past to superstring computers is like comparing our ten fingers to those supercomputers. A superstring computer has ultimate capacity, that is to say, it has the capacity to store the current status of every fundamental particle existing in the known universe and perform operations with them. In other words, if we only look at three dimensions of space and one of time, a superstring computer can model the entire universe on the atomic level. . . ."

Song Cheng alternately looked at the briefcase and Bai Bing. Unlike before, he seemed to be listening to Bai Bing's words with full attention. In truth, he was desperately seeking any kind of relief, letting this mysterious visitor's rambling extricate him from his painful memories.

"Sorry for going on and on like this—big bang this and superstring that. It must seem completely unrelated to the reality we're facing, but to give a proper explanation I can't sidestep it. Let's talk about my career next. I'm a software engineer specializing in simulation software. That is, you create a mathematical model and run it in a computer to simulate some object or process in the real world. I studied mathematics, so I do both the model-creating and the programming. In the past I've simulated sandstorms, soil erosion on the Loess Plateau, energy generation and economic development trends in the Northeast, so on. Now I'm working on large-scale weather models. I love my work. Watching a piece of the real world running and evolving inside a computer is honestly fascinating."

Bai Bing looked at Song Cheng, who was staring at him unblinkingly. He seemed to be listening attentively, so Bai Bing continued.

"You know, the field of physics has had huge breakthroughs one after another in recent years, a lot like at the beginning of the last century. Now, if you give us the boundary conditions, we can lift the fog of quantum effects to accurately predict the behavior of fundamental particles, either singly or in a group.

"Notice I mentioned groups. A group of enough particles means a macroscopic body. In other words, we can now create a mathematical model of a macroscopic object on the atomic level. This sort of simulation is called a digital mirror. I'll give an example. If we used digital mirroring to create a mathematical model of an egg—as in, we input the status of every atom in the egg into the model's database—and run it in the computer, given suitable boundary conditions, the virtual egg in memory will hatch into a chick. And the virtual chick in memory would be perfectly identical to the chick hatched from the egg in real life, down to the tips of every feather! And think further, what if the object being modeled were bigger than an egg? As big as a tree, a person, many people. As big as a city, a country, or even all of Earth?" Bai Bing was getting worked up, gesturing wildly as he spoke.

"I like to think this way, pushing every idea to its limit. This led me to wonder, what if the object being digitally mirrored were the entire universe?" Bai Bing could no longer control his passion. "Imagine, the entire universe! My god, an entire universe running in RAM! From creation to destruction—"

Bai Bing broke off his enthusiastic account and stood up, suddenly on guard. The door swung open soundlessly. Two grim-faced men entered. The slightly older one turned to Bai Bing and raised his hands to show that he should do the same. Bai Bing and Song Cheng saw the leather handgun holster under his open jacket; Bai Bing obediently put his hands up. The younger man patted Bai Bing down carefully, then shook his head at the older man. He picked up the large briefcase as well, setting it down farther from Bai Bing.

The older man walked to the door and made a welcoming gesture outward. Three more people entered. The first was the city's chief of police, Chen Xufeng. The second was the province's secretary of discipline inspection, his old classmate, Lu Wenming. Last came the Senior Official.

The younger cop took out a pair of handcuffs, but Lu Wenming shook his head at him. Chen Xufeng turned his head minutely toward the door, and the two plainclothes police left. One of them removed a small object from the table leg as he left, clearly a listening device.

INITIAL STATE

Bai Bing's face didn't show any sign of surprise. He smiled placidly. "You've finally caught me."

"More accurately, you flew into our net on purpose. I have to admit, if you really wanted to escape, we would've had a hard time catching you," said Chen Xufeng.

Lu Wenming glanced at Song Cheng, his expression complicated. He seemed to want to say something, but stopped himself.

The Senior Official slowly shook his head. He intoned solemnly, "Oh, Song Cheng, how did you fall so low . . ." He stood silent for a long time, hands resting on the table's edge, his eyes a little damp. No onlooker could have doubted that his grief was real.

"Senior Official, I don't think you need to playact here," Bai Bing said, coldly watching the proceedings.

The Senior Official didn't move.

"You were the one who arranged to frame him."

"Proof?" the Senior Official asked indulgently, still unmoving.

"After that meeting, you only said one thing about Song Cheng, to him." Bai Bing pointed at Chen Xufeng. *"Xufeng, you know what that whole business with Song Cheng means, of course. Let's put a little effort into it."*

"What does that prove?"

"It won't count for anything in court, of course. With your cleverness and experience, you didn't let anything slip, even in a secret conversation. But he," Bai Bing pointed again at Chen Xufeng, "got the message loud and clear. He's always understood you perfectly. He ordered one of the two people earlier to carry out the framing. His name is Chenbing, and he's his most competent subordinate. The whole process was one formidable engineering project. I don't think I need to go into detail here."

The Senior Official slowly turned around and sat down in a chair by the office table. He looked at the ground as he said, "Young man, I have to admit, your sudden appearance has been astonishing in many ways. To use Chief Chen's words, it's like seeing a ghost." He was silent for a while, and then his voice rang out with sincerity. "How about you tell us your real identity? If you really were sent by the central officials, please trust that we'll assist you however we can."

"I wasn't. I've said again and again that I'm an ordinary guy. My identity is nothing more than what you've already looked up."

The Senior Official nodded. It was impossible to tell whether Bai Bing's words had reassured him, or added to his concern.

"Sit, let's all sit." The Senior Official waved a hand at Lu and Chen, both still standing, and drew closer to Bai Bing. "Young man," he said solemnly. "Let's get to the bottom of all this today, okay?"

Bai Bing nodded. "That's my plan too. I'll start from the beginning."

"No, that won't be necessary. We heard everything you said to Song Cheng earlier. Just continue where you left off."

Bai Bing was momentarily at a loss for words, unable to remember where he'd stopped.

"Atomic-level model of the entire universe," the Senior Official reminded him, but seeing that Bai Bing still couldn't figure out how to start talking again, he added his own input. "Young man, I don't think your idea is feasible. Superstring computers have ultimate capacity, yes, providing the hardware basis for running this sort of simulation. But have you considered the problem of the initial state? To make a digital mirror of the universe, you must start the simulation from some initial state—in other words, to construct a model that represents the universe on an atomic level, for the instant the model starts at, you'll have to input the status at that instant of every atom in the universe into the computer, one by one. Is this possible? It wouldn't be possible with the egg you mentioned, let alone the universe. The number of atoms in that egg outnumber the number of eggs ever laid since the beginning of time by orders of magnitude. It wouldn't even be possible with a bacterium, which still contains an astonishing number of atoms. Taking a step back, even if we put forth the near unimaginable manpower and computing power needed to find the initial state of a small object like the bacterium or the egg on an atomic level, what about the boundary conditions for when the model runs? For example, the outside temperature, humidity, and so on needed for a chicken egg to hatch. Taken on the atomic level, these boundary conditions will require unimaginable quantities of data too, perhaps even more than the modeled object itself."

"You've laid out the technical problems beautifully. I admire that," Bai Bing said sincerely.

"The Senior Official was once a star student in the field of high-energy physics. After Deng Xiaoping's reforms restored university degrees, his was one of the first classes to receive master's degrees in physics in China," said Lu Wenming.

Bai Bing nodded in Lu Wenming's direction, then turned toward the Senior Official. "But you forget, there's a moment in time in which the universe was extremely simple, even simpler than eggs and bacteria, simpler than anything in existence today. The number of atoms in it at the time was zero, see. It had no size and no composition."

"The big bang singularity?" the Senior Official said immediately, almost no delay between Bai Bing's words and his. It was a glimpse at the quick, agile mind beneath his slow and steady exterior.

"Yes, the big bang singularity. Superstring theory has already established a perfect model of the singularity. We just need to represent the model digitally and run it on the computer."

"That's right, young man. That really is the case." The Senior Official stood and walked to Bai Bing's side to pat his shoulder, revealing rare excitement. Chen Xufeng and Lu Wenming, who hadn't understood the exchange that had just taken place, looked at them with puzzled expressions.

"Is this the superstring computer you brought out of the research center?" the Senior Official asked, pointing at the briefcase.

"Stole," said Bai Bing.

"Ha, no matter. The software for the digital mirror of the big bang is on it, I expect?"

"Yes."

"Run it for us."

CREATION GAME

Bai Bing nodded, hauled the briefcase onto the desk, and opened it. Beside the display equipment, the briefcase also contained a cylindrical vessel. The superstring computer's processor was in fact only the size of a pack of cigarettes, but the atomic circuitry required ultralow temperatures to operate, so the processor had to be kept submerged in the insulated vessel of liquid nitrogen. Bai Bing set the LCD screen upright and moved the mouse, and the superstring computer awoke from sleep mode. The screen brightened, like a dozing eye blinking open, displaying a simple interface composed of just a drop-down text box and a header reading:

Please Select Parameters to Initiate Creation of the Universe

Bai Bing clicked the arrow beside the drop-down text box. Row upon row of data sets, each composed of a sizable number of elements, appeared below. Each row seemed to differ considerably from the others. "The properties of the singularity are determined by eighteen parameters. Technically, there's an infinite number of possible parameter combinations, but we can determine from superstring theory that the number of parameter combinations that could have resulted in the big bang is finite, although their exact number is still a mystery. Here we have a small selection of them. Let's select one at random."

Bai Bing selected a group of parameters, and the screen immediately went white. Two big buttons appeared in striking contrast at the center of the screen.

Initiate Cancel

Bai Bing clicked Initiate. Now only the white background was left. "The white represents nothingness. Space doesn't exist at this time, and time itself hasn't begun. There really is nothing."

A red number "0" appeared in the lower left corner of the screen.

"This number indicates how long the universe has been evolving. The zero appearing means that the singularity has been generated. Its size is undefined, so we can't see it."

The red number began to increment rapidly.

"Notice, the big bang has begun."

A small blue dot appeared in the middle of the screen, quickly growing into a sphere emitting brilliant blue light. The sphere rapidly expanded, filling the entire screen. The software zoomed out, and the sphere once again shrank into a distant dot, but the ballooning universe quickly filled the screen once more. The cycle repeated again and again in rapid frequency, as if marking the beats to some swelling symphony.

"The universe is currently in the inflationary epoch. It's expanding at a rate far exceeding the speed of light."

As the sphere slowed in its growth, the field of view began to zoom out less frequently, too. With the decrease in energy density, the sphere turned from blue to yellow, then red, before the color of the universe stabilized at red and began to darken. The field of view no longer zoomed out, and the now-black sphere expanded very slowly now on the screen.

"Okay, it's ten billion years after the big bang. At this point, this universe is in a stable stage of evolution. Let's take a closer look." Bai Bing moved the mouse, and the sphere rushed forward, filling the whole screen with black. "Right, we're in this universe's outer space."

"There's nothing here?" said Lu Wenming.

"Let's see. . . ." As Bai Bing spoke, he right-clicked and pulled up a complicated window. A script began to calculate the total matter present in the universe. "Ha, there are only eleven fundamental particles in this universe." He pulled up another massive data report and read it carefully. "Ten of the particles are arranged in five mutually orbiting pairs. However, in each pair, the two particles are tens of millions of light-years apart. They take millions of years to move one millimeter with respect to each other. The last particle is free."

"Eleven fundamental particles? But after all that talk, there's still nothing here," said Lu Wenming.

"There's space, nearly a hundred billion light-years in diameter! And time, ten billion years of it! Time and space are the true measures of existence! This particular universe is actually one of the more successful ones. In a lot of the universes I created before, even the dimensions of space quickly disappeared, leaving only time."

"Dull," harrumphed Chen Xufeng, turning away from the screen.

"No, this is very interesting," said the Senior Official delightedly. "Do it again."

Bai Bing returned to the starting interface, selected a new set of parameters, and initiated another big bang. The formation process of the new universe looked to be about the same as the earlier one, an expanding and dimming sphere. Fifteen billion years after creation, the sphere became fully black: the evolution of the universe had stabilized. Bai Bing moved the viewpoint into the universe. Even Chen Xufeng, least interested out of all of them, exclaimed. Beneath the vast darkness of space, a silvery surface extended endlessly in all directions. Small, colorful spheres decorated the membrane like multicolored dewdrops tumbling on the broad surface of a mirror.

Bai Bing brought up the analysis window again. He looked at it for a while and said, "We were lucky. This is a universe rich in variety, about forty billion light-years in radius. Half of its volume is liquid, while the other half is empty space. In other words, this universe is a massive ocean, forty billion light-years in depth and radius, with the solid celestial bodies floating on its surface!" Bai Bing pushed the field of view closer to the ocean's surface, allowing them to see that the silvery ocean surface was gently rippling. A celestial body appeared in their close-up view. "This floating object is . . . let me see, about the size of Jupiter. Whoa, it's rotating by itself! The mountain ranges look amazing when they're coming in and out of—let's just call this liquid water! See the water being flung up by the mountain ranges, along its orbit. It forms a rainbow arc above the surface!"

"It's beautiful, indeed, but this universe goes against the basic laws of physics," the Senior Official said, looking at the screen. "Never mind an ocean forty billion light-years deep, a body of liquid four light-years deep would have collapsed into a black hole due to gravity long ago."

Bai Bing shook his head. "You've forgotten a fundamental point: This isn't our universe. This universe has its own set of laws of physics, completely different from ours. In this universe, the gravitational constant, Planck's constant, the speed of light, and other basic physical constants are all different. In this universe, one plus one might not even equal two."

Encouraged by the Senior Official, Bai Bing continued the demonstration, creating a third universe. When they entered for a closer look, a chaotic jumble of colors and shapes appeared on the screen. Bai Bing immediately exited. "This is a six-dimensional universe, so we have no way of observing it. In fact, this is the most common case, and we were lucky to get two three-dimensional universes on our first two tries. Once the universe cools down from its high-energy state, the odds of having three available dimensions on the macroscopic scale is only three out of eleven."

A fourth universe manifested. To the bafflement of everyone: the universe appeared as an endless black plane, with countless bright, silvery lines intersecting it perpendicularly. After reading the analysis profile, Bai Bing said, "This universe is the opposite of the previous one—it has fewer dimensions than our own. This is a two-and-a-half-dimensional universe."

"Two and a half dimensions?" The Senior Official was astonished.

"See, the black two-dimensional plane with no thickness is this universe's outer space. Its diameter is around five hundred billion light-years. The bright lines perpendicular to the plane are the stars in space. They're hundreds of millions of light-years long, but infinitely thin, because they're one-dimensional. Universes with fractional dimensions are rare. I'm going to make note of the parameters that produced this one."

"A question," said the Senior Official. "If you use these parameters to initialize a second big bang, would it produce a universe exactly the same as this one?"

"Yes, and the evolution process would be identical too. Everything was predetermined at the time of the big bang. See, after physics got past the obfuscation of quantum effects, the universe once again displayed an inherently causal and deterministic nature." Bai Bing looked at the others one by one. He said seriously, "Please keep this point in mind. This will be key to understanding the terrifying things we'll be seeing later."

"This really is fascinating." The Senior Official sighed. "Playing God, aloof and ethereal. It's been a long time since I've felt this way."

"I felt the same," Bai Bing said as he stood up from the computer to pace back and forth, "so I played the creation game again and again. By now, I've initiated more than a thousand big bangs. The awe-inspiring wonder of those thousand-plus universes is impossible to describe with words. I felt like an addict . . . I could have kept going like that, never coming into contact with you, never getting involved. Our lives would have continued along our orbits. But . . . ah, hell . . . It was a snowy night at the beginning of the year, nearly two in the morning, really quiet. I ran the last big bang of the day. The superstring computer gave birth to the one thousand two hundred and seventh universe—this one. . . ."

Bai Bing returned to the computer, scrolled to the bottom of the drop-down list, and selected the last set of parameters. He initiated the big bang. The new universe rapidly expanded in a glow of blue light before extinguishing to black. Bai Bing moved the mouse and entered his Universe No. 1207 at nineteen billion years after creation.

This time, the screen displayed a radiant sea of stars.

"1207 has a radius of twenty billion light-years and three dimensions. In this universe, the gravitational constant is 6.67 times 10^{-11}, and the speed of light in a vacuum is three hundred thousand kilometers per second. In this universe, an electron has a charge of 1.602 times 10^{-19} coulombs. In this universe, Planck's constant is 6.62 . . ." Bai Bing leaned in toward the Senior Official, watching him with a chilling gaze. "In this universe, one plus one equals two."

"This is our own universe." The Senior Official nodded, still steady, but his forehead was now damp.

SEARCHING HISTORY

"Once I found Universe No. 1207, I spent more than a month building a search engine based on shape and pattern recognition. Then I looked through astronomy resources to find diagrams of the geometrical placement of the Milky Way with respect to the nearby Andromeda Galaxy, Large and

Small Magellanic Clouds, and so on. Searching for the arrangement within the entire universe gave me more than eighty thousand matches. Next I searched those results for matches for the internal arrangement of the galaxies themselves. It didn't take long to locate the Milky Way in the universe." Onscreen, a silver spiral appeared against a backdrop of pitch-black space.

"Locating the sun was even easier. We already know its approximate location in the Milky Way—" Bai Bing used his mouse to click and drag a small rectangle over the tip of one arm of the spiral.

"Using the same pattern-recognition method, it didn't take long to locate the sun in this area." A brilliant sphere of light appeared onscreen, surrounded by a large disk of haze.

"Oh, the planets in the solar system haven't formed yet right now. This disk of interstellar debris is the raw material they're made up of." Bai Bing pulled up a slider bar at the bottom of the window. "See, this lets you move through time." He slowly dragged the slider forward. Two hundred million years passed before them; the disk of dust around the sun disappeared. "Now the nine planets have formed. The video window shows real distances and proportions, unlike your planetarium displays, so finding Earth is going to take more work. I'll use the coordinates I saved earlier instead." With that, the nascent planet Earth appeared on the screen as a hazy gray sphere.

Bai Bing scrolled the mouse wheel. "Let's go down . . . good. We're about ten kilometers above the surface now." The land below was still shrouded in haze, but crisscrossing glowing red lines had appeared in it, a network like the blood vessels in an embryo.

"These are rivers of lava," Bai Bing said, pointing. He kept scrolling down, past the thick acidic fog. The brown surface of the ocean appeared, and the point of view plunged lower, into the ocean. In the murky water were a few specks. Most were round, but a few were more complicated in shape, most obviously different from the other suspended particles in that they were moving on their own, not just floating with the current.

"Life, brand new," Bai Bing said, pointing out the tiny things with the mouse.

He rapidly scrolled the mouse wheel in the other direction, raising their point of view back into space to once again show the young Earth in full. Then he moved the time slider. Countless years flew past; the thick haze covering Earth's surface disappeared, the ocean began to turn blue, and the land began to turn green. Then the enormous supercontinent Pangaea split and broke apart like ice in spring. "If you want, we can watch the entire evolution of life, all the major extinctions and the explosions of life that followed them. But let's skip them and save some time. We're about to see what this all has to do with our lives."

The fragmented ancient continents continued to drift until, at last, a familiar map of the world appeared. Bai Bing changed the slider-bar settings, advancing in smaller increments through time before coming to a stop. "Right, humans appear here." He carefully shifted the slider a little further forward. "Now civilization appears.

"You can only see most of distant history on a macro scale. Finding specific events isn't easy, and finding specific people is even harder. Searching history mainly relies on two parameters: location and time. It's rare that historical records give them accurately this far back. But let's try it out. We're going down now!" Bai Bing double-clicked a location near the Mediterranean Sea as he spoke. The point of view hurtled downward with dizzying speed. At last, a deserted beach appeared. At the far side of the yellow sand was an unbroken grove of olive trees.

"The coast of Troy in the time of the ancient Greeks," said Bai Bing.

"Then . . . can you move the time to the Trojan Horse and the Sack of Troy?" Lu Wenming asked excitedly.

"The Trojan Horse never existed," Bai Bing said coolly.

Chen Xufeng nodded. "That sort of thing belongs in children's stories. It would be impossible in a real war."

"The Trojan War never happened," said Bai Bing.

"If that's the case, did Troy fall due to other reasons?" The Senior Official sounded surprised.

"The city of Troy never existed."

The other three exchanged looks of astonishment.

Bai Bing pointed at the screen. "The video window is now displaying the real coast of Troy at the time the war supposedly happened. We can look five hundred years forward and back. . . ." Bai Bing carefully shifted the mouse. The beach onscreen flashed rapidly as night and day alternated, and the shape of the trees changed quickly, too. A few shacks appeared at the far end of the beach, human silhouettes occasionally flickering past them. The shacks grew and fell in number, but even at their greatest they formed no more than a village. "See, the magnificent city of Troy only ever existed in the imaginations of the poet-storytellers."

"How is that possible?" Lu Wenming cried. "We have archaeological evidence from the beginning of the last century! They even dug up Agamemnon's gold mask."

"Agamemnon's gold mask? Fuck that!" Bai Bing laughed harshly. "Well, as the historical records improve in quality and quantity, later searches get increasingly easy. Let's do it again."

Bai Bing returned their point of view to Earth's orbit. This time, he didn't use the mouse, but entered the time and geographical coordinates by hand. The view descended toward western Asia. Soon, the screen displayed a stretch of desert, and a few people lying under the shade of a cluster of red willows. They wore ragged robes of rough cloth, their skin baked dark, their hair long and matted into strands by sweat and dust. From a distance, they looked like heaps of discarded rubbish.

"They aren't far from a Muslim village, but the bubonic plague has been going around and they're afraid to go there," Bai Bing said.

A tall, thin man sat up and looked around. After checking that the others were soundly asleep, he picked up a neighbor's sheepskin canteen and took a swig. Then he reached into another neighbor's battered pack and took out a piece of traveler's bread, broke off a third, and put it in his own bag. Satisfied, he lay back down.

"I've run this at normal speed for two days and seen him steal other people's water five times and other people's food three times," Bai Bing said, gesturing with his mouse at the man who'd just lain down.

"Who is he?"

"Marco Polo. It wasn't easy to search him up. The Genoan prison where he was imprisoned gave me fairly precise times and coordinates. I located him there, then backtraced to that naval battle he was in to extract some identifying traits. Then I jumped much earlier and followed him here. This is in what used to be Persia, near the city of Bam in modern Iran, but I could have saved myself the effort."

"That means he's on his way to China. You should be able to follow him into Kublai Khan's palace," said Lu Wenming.

"He never entered any palace."

"You mean, he spent his time in China as just a regular commoner?"

"Marco Polo never went to China. The long and even more dangerous road ahead scared him off. He wandered around West Asia for a few years, and later told the rumors he heard along the way to his friend in prison, who wrote the famous travelogue."

His three listeners once again exchanged looks of astonishment.

"It's even easier to look up specific people and events later on. Let's do it one more time with modern history."

The room was large and very dim. A map—a naval map?—had been spread out on the broad wooden table, surrounded by several men in Qing Dynasty military uniforms. The room was too dark to see their faces.

"We're in the headquarters of the Beiyang Fleet, quite a ways to go before the First Sino-Japanese War. We're in the middle of a meeting."

Someone was talking, but the heavy southlands accent and the poor sound quality made the words unintelligible. Bai Bing explained, "They're saying that for coastal defense purposes, given their limited funds, purchasing heavy-tonnage ironclads from the West is less worthwhile than buying a large number of fast, steam-powered torpedo boats. Each vessel could hold four to six gas torpedoes, forming a large, fast attack force, maneuverable enough to evade Japanese cannon fire and strike at close range. I asked a number of naval experts and military historians about this. They unanimously believe that if this idea had been implemented, the Beiyang Fleet would have won their battles in the First Sino-Japanese War. He's brilliantly ahead of his time, the first in naval history to discover the weaknesses of the traditional big-cannons-and-big-ships policy with the new innovations in armaments."

"Who is it?" Chen Xufeng asked. "Deng Shichang?"

Bai Bing shook his head. "Fang Boqian."

"What, that coward who ran away halfway through the Battle of the Yellow Sea?"

"The very one."

"Instinct tells me that all this is what history was really like," the Senior Official mused.

Bai Bing nodded. "That's right. I didn't feel so aloof and ethereal after this stage. I started to despair. I had discovered that practically all the history we know is a lie. Of all the noble, vaunted heroes we hear about, at least half were contemptible liars and schemers who used their influence to claim achievements and write the histories, and managed to succeed. Of those who really did give everything for truth and justice, two-thirds choked to death horribly and quietly in the dust of history, forgotten by everyone, and the remaining one-third had their reputations smeared into eternal infamy, just like Song Cheng. Only a tiny percentage were remembered as they were by history, less than the exposed corner of the iceberg."

Only then did everyone notice Song Cheng, who'd remained silent throughout. They saw him quietly stir, his eyes alight. He looked like a felled warrior rising to stand once more, taking up his weapon astride a fresh warhorse.

SEARCHING THE PRESENT

"Then you came to Universe No. 1207's present day, am I correct?" asked the Senior Official.

"That's right, I set the digital mirror to our time." As he spoke, Bai Bing moved the time slider to the far end. The point of view once again returned to space. The blue Earth below didn't look particularly different from how it had appeared in ancient times.

"This is our present day shown through the mirror of Universe No. 1207: after decades of continuous exporting of natural resources and energy, our hinterland province still doesn't have a presentable industry to its name aside from mining and power generation. All we have is pollution, most of the rural areas still below the poverty line, severe unemployment in the cities, deteriorating law and order . . . naturally, I wanted to see how our leaders and planners did their jobs. What I saw, well, I don't need to tell you that."

"What were you after?" asked the Senior Official.

Bai Bing smiled bitterly, shaking his head. "Don't think I had some lofty goal like him," he said, pointing at Song Cheng. "I was just an ordinary person, happy to mind my own business and live out my days in peace. What do your antics have to do with me? I wasn't planning to mess with you, but . . . I put so much work into this supersimulation software, and naturally I wanted to get some material benefits out of it. So I called a couple of your people, hoping they'd give me a bit of cash for keeping quiet. . . ." He abruptly swelled with indignation.

"Why did you have to overreact? Why did I have to be eliminated? If you'd just given me the money, we'd all be done here! . . . Anyway, I've finished explaining everything."

The five people sank into a long silence, all of them watching the image of Earth on the screen. This was the digital mirror of the current Earth. They were in there, too.

"Can you really use this computer to observe everything in the world that's ever happened?" Chen Xufeng said, breaking the silence.

"Yes, every detail of history and the present day is data in the computer, and that data can be freely analyzed. Anything, no matter how secret, can be observed by extracting the corresponding information from the database and processing it. The database holds an atomic-level digital replica of the entire world, and any part of it can be extracted at will."

"Can you prove it?"

"That's easy. You leave the room, go anywhere you want, do anything you want, and come back."

Chen Xufeng looked at the Senior Official and Lu Wenming in turn, then left the room. He returned two minutes later and looked at Bai Bing wordlessly.

Bai Bing moved the mouse so that the point of view rapidly descended from space to hover above the city, which seamlessly filled the screen. He panned around, searching carefully, and quickly found the No. 2 Detention Center at the city outskirts, then the three-story building they were in. The point of view entered the building, gliding along the empty hallway on the second floor. The two plainclothes detectives sitting on the bench outside appeared onscreen, Chenbing lighting a cigarette. At last, the screen displayed the door of the office they were in.

"Right now, the simulation only lags behind reality as it happens by 0.1 seconds. Let's go back a few minutes." Bai Bing nudged the time slider left.

Onscreen, the door swung open and Chen Xufeng walked out. The two police on the bench immediately stood; Chen waved them an all's-well and walked in the opposite direction. The point of view followed closely, as if someone were filming from right behind him with a camera. In the digital mirror, Chen Xufeng entered the restroom, took a handgun from his trouser pocket, pulled the trigger, and returned it to his pocket. Bai Bing paused the simulation here and rotated the view around to different angles as if it were a 3-D cartoon. Chen Xufeng walked out of the restroom, and the point of view followed him back to the office, revealing the four people waiting for him.

The Senior Official watched the screen expressionlessly. Lu Wenming raised his head warily and eyed Chen Xufeng. "That thing really is impressive," Lu Wenming said with a dark expression.

"Next I'll demonstrate an even more impressive feature," said Bai Bing, pausing the simulation. "Since the universe is stored in the digital mirror on the atomic level, we can search up any and every detail in the universe. Next, let's see what's in Chief Chen's coat pocket."

On the paused screen, Bai Bing clicked and dragged a rectangle over the area of Chen Xufeng's coat pocket, then opened an interface to process it. With a series of actions, he removed the cloth on the outside of the pocket, revealing a small piece of folded-up paper inside. Bai Bing pressed Ctrl+C to copy the piece of paper, then started up a 3-D model-processing program and pasted in the copied data. A few more actions unfolded the piece of paper. It was a foreign exchange check for 250,000 USD.

"Next, we'll track this check to its origin." Bai Bing closed the model-processing software and returned to the paused video window. Bai Bing right-clicked the already-selected check in Chen Xufeng's coat pocket, then chose Trace from the list of options. The check flashed, and the still screen jumped to life. Time was flowing backward, showing the Senior Official and his retinue backing out of the office, then out of the building, then into a car. Chen Xufeng and Lu Wenming put on earphones, clearly listening in on Bai Bing and Song Cheng's conversation. The trace search continued, the surroundings continuing to change, but the flashing check remained at the center of the screen as the subject of the search, seeming to tug Chen Xufeng with it through scene after scene. Finally, the check jumped out of Chen's coat pocket and slipped into a small basket, which then jumped from Chen's hand into another person's. At that moment, Bai Bing paused the simulation.

"I'll resume playing here," said Bai Bing, selecting normal playback speed. They seemed to be looking at Chen Xufeng's living room. Onscreen, a middle-aged woman in a black suit stood with the fruit basket in her hand, as if she'd just entered. Chen Xufeng was sitting on the sofa.

"Chief Chen, Director Wen sent me to visit you, and to express his gratitude for last time. He wanted to come in person, but thought it was best not to show up here too often to prevent idle gossip."

Chen Xufeng said, "When you go back, tell Wen Xiong that he'd better stay on the straight and narrow, now that he's in good shape. Going too far all the time doesn't do anyone good. He'd better not blame me for losing patience!"

"Yes, of course, how could Brother Wen forget your advice? Nowadays, he's been actively contributing to society—he's built four elementary schools in impoverished districts. He's also dedicated to making progress in politics. The city has already elected him as its delegate to the National People's Congress!" As she spoke, the visitor set the fruit basket onto the coffee table.

"Take that with you," Chen Xufeng said, waving a hand.

"We would never bring anything too fancy, Chief Chen. We know how you'd hate it. This is just some fruit as a token of our gratitude. I suppose you haven't seen the way Chief Wen tears up whenever he mentions you. He calls you our loving parents reborn, you know."

Once the visitor left, Chen Xufeng shut the door and returned to the coffee table. He tipped all the fruit out of the basket, picked up the check at the bottom, and slid it in his pocket.

The Senior Official and Lu Wenming eyed Chen Xufeng coldly. Clearly they hadn't known any of this. Wen Xiong was the director general of Licheng Group, an enormous corporation spanning dining, long-distance travel, and many other services. Its start-up money had come from drug profits from Wen Xiong's crime syndicate, which had made this city into a crucial hub in the Yunnan-Russia drug-trafficking route. With Wen Xiong's successful expansion into aboveboard commerce, his underground business, drawing nourishment from the former, grew even more rapidly. The result in the hinterland city was the proliferation of drugs and the decline of public safety. And Chen Xufeng, the backstage supporter, was a powerful safeguard for its continued survival.

"You took payment in dollars? It must have gone to your son," Bai Bing said cheerfully. "The money that's paying for his American college education all came from Wen Xiong, after all. . . . Speaking of which, don't you want to see what he's doing right now, on the other side of the planet? That's easy enough. It's midnight in Boston right now, but the last two times I saw him, he wasn't sleeping yet." Bai Bing sent the point of view up into space, twirled the Earth 180 degrees, then zoomed in on North America. He found the city splendid with lights on the Atlantic coast, then located the apartment building so quickly it was clear he must have searched it before. The point of view entered an apartment bedroom, exposing an awkward scene: the boy in his room with two prostitutes, one white and one black.

"See how your son's spending your money, Chief Chen?"

Furious, Chen Xufeng tipped the monitor screen-side down onto the briefcase.

The deeply stunned group once again sank into a long silence. At last Lu Wenming asked, "Why did you spend all this time just running away? Didn't you consider using more . . . conventional means to free yourself from this predicament?"

"You mean, report to Discipline Inspection? Excellent idea, yes. I had the same idea at first, so I used the digital mirror to run a search on the Discipline Inspection leadership." Bai Bing raised his head to look at Lu Wenming. "You can guess what I saw. I didn't want to end up like your old college buddy here. In that case, could I go to the public prosecutors or the Anti-Corruption Bureau? I'm sure Director Guo and Chief Chang process the vast majority of serious accusations strictly by the law, and very carefully tiptoe around a small portion. For what I'd report, they'd join you in hunting me down the moment I told them. Where else could I go? Could I get the press to run an exposé? I think you're all familiar with those certain key figures in the provincial news media groups. After all, weren't they the ones who came up with the Senior Official's shining résumé? The only difference between those reporters and prostitutes is that they sell a different body part. It's all tied together in one big web, not a strand safe to touch. I didn't have anywhere to go."

"You could go to the Central Commission," the Senior Official said neutrally, closely observing Bai Bing for a reaction.

Bai Bing nodded. "It's the only choice left. But I'm a nobody. I don't know anyone. I came to see Song Cheng first to find reliable connections, pursuit or no." Bai Bing paused, then continued, "But this decision wasn't an easy one. You're all smart people. You know the ultimate consequences of doing this."

"It means that this technology will be revealed to the world."

"That's right. Every bit of the fog that covers history and reality will be swept away. Anything and everything, in light and darkness, past and present, will be stripped naked and paraded before the light of day. At that time, light and dark will be forced into a deciding battle for supremacy unlike anything in history. The world's going to descend into chaos—"

"But the end result will be the victory of the light," said Song Cheng, who'd been silent until then. He walked in front of Bai Bing and looked straight at him. "Do you know how shadows derive their power? It comes from their very nature of secrecy. Once they're exposed to the light, their power is gone. You see that with most cases of corruption. And your digital mirror is the burning brand that will tear the darkness open."

The Senior Official exchanged looks with Chen and Lu.

Silence fell. On the superstring computer screen, the atomic-level digital mirror of Earth hovered placidly in space.

The Senior Official put a hand on Bai Bing's shoulder. "Why don't you move the time slider in the simulation farther forward?"

Bai Bing, Chen Xufeng, and Lu Wenming looked uncomprehendingly at the Senior Official.

"If we can accurately predict the future, we can change the present and control the course the future will take. We'd control everything—young man, don't you think this is possible? Perhaps, together, we can shoulder the great duty of shaping the history to come."

Bai Bing realized what he was saying and gave a pained smile, shaking his head. He stood and walked over to the computer. He clicked and dragged the time slider bar, extending its length beyond Now into the future. Then he said to the Senior Official, "Try it for yourself."

INFINITE RECURSION

The Senior Official leapt toward the computer, quicker than anyone had ever seen him move, bringing to mind the dark image of a hungry eagle spotting a baby chick on the ground. He moved the mouse with practiced motions, sliding the time past the Now. In the instant that the slider entered the future, an error window popped up.

Stack Overflow

Bai Bing took the mouse from the Senior Official's hand. "Let's run a debugging program and trace that step by step."

The simulation software returned to the state it had been in before the error and began to run line by line. When the real Bai Bing moved the slider past the present, the simulation Bai Bing in the digital mirror did the same. The debugging program immediately zoomed in on the digital mirror's superstring computer display, allowing them to see that, on the simulated screen, the simulated simulated Bai Bing two layers down was also moving the slider past the present. Then the debugging program zoomed in on the superstring computer display in the third layer. . . . In this way the debugger progressed layer after layer deeper, each layer's Bai Bing in the process of moving the slider past the present time, an infinite Droste image.

"This is recursion, a programming approach where a piece of code calls itself. Under normal circumstances, it finds its answer a finite number of layers down, after which the answer follows the chain of calls back to the surface. But here we see a function calling itself without end, forever unable to find an answer, in infinite recursion. Because it needs to store resources used by the previous layer on the stack at every call, it created the stack over-flow we saw earlier. With infinite recursion, even a superstring computer's ultimate capacity can be used up."

"Ah." The Senior Official nodded.

"As a result, even though the course of the universe was decided at the big bang, we still can't know the future. For people who hate the determinist idea that everything comes from a chain of cause and effect, this probably provides some consolation."

"Ah . . ." The Senior Official nodded again. He dragged out the sound for a long, long time.

THE AGE OF THE MIRROR

Bai Bing discovered that a strange change had overcome the Senior Official, as if something had been sucked out of him. His whole body seemed to be withering, swaying as if it had lost the strength to keep itself upright. His face was pale, his breathing rapid. He put both hands on the chair's arms and lowered himself into the seat, the movement difficult and painstaking, as if he were afraid his bones would snap.

"Young man, you have destroyed my life's work," the Senior Official said eventually. "You win."

Bai Bing looked at Chen Xufeng and Lu Wenming, finding that they were at a loss like himself. But Song Cheng stood straight-backed and un-afraid among them, his face alight with victory.

Chen Xufeng slowly stood, drawing his gun from his trouser pocket.

"Stop," said the Senior Official, not loudly, but with unsurpassed authority in his voice. The gun in Chen Xufeng's hand stilled in midair. "Put the gun down," the Senior Official commanded, but Chen didn't move.

"Sir, at this stage, we have to act decisively. We can explain away their deaths, shot and killed while resisting arrest and attempting escape—"

"Put the gun down, you mad dog!" the Senior Official roared.

The hand holding the gun fell to Chen Xufeng's side. He slowly turned toward the Senior Official. "I'm no mad dog. I'm a loyal dog, a dog who understands gratitude! A dog who will never betray you, sir! You can trust someone like me, who's crawled step by step up from the bottom, to know right and wrong like a good dog toward the superior who made him into who he is today. I don't think the slick thoughts of intelligentsia."

"What are you trying to say?" Lu Wenming, who had long been silent, got to his feet.

"Everyone knows what I mean. I'm not like some people, taking a step only after making sure there's two or three steps of retreat open. Where's my road out? At a time like this, if I don't protect myself, who will do it for me?!"

Bai Bing said calmly, "It's useless to kill me. That's the fastest way to expose the digital mirror technology to the public."

"Even an idiot would have realized he'd take precautionary measures. You've really lost all reason," Lu Wenming said quietly to Chen Xufeng.

Chen Xufeng said, "Of course I know the bastard wouldn't be that stupid, but we have our own technological resources. If we put in everything we have, we might be able to completely wipe out the digital mirror technology."

Bai Bing shook his head. "That's impossible. Chief Chen, this is the era of the internet. Concealing and distributing information is easy, and I have the defender's advantage. You can't beat me at my game, not even if you put in your best tech experts. I could tell you where I've hidden the digital mirror software backups and how I plan to release them after my death, and you wouldn't be able to do a thing. The initialization parameters are even easier to hide and distribute. Forget about that idea."

Chen Xufeng slowly put the gun back into his pocket and sat down.

"You think you're already standing on the summit of history, yes?" the Senior Official said tiredly to Song Cheng.

"Justice stands on the summit of history," Song Cheng said solemnly.

"Indeed, the digital mirror has destroyed us all. But its power to destroy far exceeds this."

"Yes, it will destroy all evil."

The Senior Official nodded slowly.

"Then it will destroy all the corruption and immorality that comes short of evil."

The Senior Official nodded again. "In the end, it will destroy all of human civilization."

His words made the others take pause. Song Cheng said, "Human civilization has never beheld such a bright future. This battle between good and evil will wash away all its grime."

"And then?" the Senior Official asked softly.

"And then, the great age of the mirror will arrive. All of humanity will face a mirror in which every action can be perfectly seen and no crime can be hidden. Every sinner will inevitably meet their judgment. It will be an era without darkness, where the sun shines into every crevice. Human society will become as pure as crystal."

"In other words, society will be dead," the Senior Official said. He raised his head to look Song Cheng in the eyes.

"Care to explain?" Song Cheng said, with the mocking note of a victor looking at a loser.

"Imagine if DNA never made mistakes, always replicating and inheriting with perfect fidelity. What would life on Earth become?"

While Song Cheng considered this, Bai Bing answered for him. "In that case, life would no longer exist on Earth. The basis of the evolution of life is mutation, caused by mistakes in DNA."

The Senior Official nodded at Bai Bing. "Society is the same way. Its evolution and vitality is rooted in the myriad urges and desires departing from the morality laid out by the majority. A fish can't live in perfectly clear water. A society where no one ever makes mistakes in ethics is, in reality, dead."

"Your attempt to defend your crimes is laughable," Song Cheng said contemptuously.

"Not completely," Bai Bing said immediately, surprising the others. He hesitated for a few seconds, as if to steel his resolve. "To be honest, there was another reason I didn't want to make the mirror simulation software public. I . . . I don't much like the idea of a world armed with the digital mirror either."

"Are you afraid of the light like them?" Song Cheng demanded.

"I'm an ordinary guy. I'm not involved in any shady business, but there are different kinds of the light you're talking about. If someone beams a searchlight through your bedroom window in the middle of the night, that's called light pollution. . . . I'll give an example. I've only been married two years, but I've already experienced that . . . wearying of the aesthetics, so to speak. So I got . . . uh, *involved* with a coworker. My wife doesn't know, of course. Everyone's lives are good—better this way even I suspect. I wouldn't be able to live this kind of life in the age of the mirror."

"It's an immoral and irresponsible life to begin with!" Song Cheng said, anger entering his voice.

"But doesn't everyone live like that? Who doesn't have some sort of secret? If you want to be happy these days, sometimes, you have to bend a little. How many people can be shining spotless saints like you? If the digital mirror makes everyone into perfect people who can't take a step out of line, then—then what's even fucking left?"

The Senior Official laughed, and even Lu and Chen, who'd been grim-faced all this time, cracked a smile. The Senior Official patted Bai Bing on the shoulder. "Young man, your argument might not be particularly high-minded, but you've thought far deeper than our scholar over here." He turned toward Song Cheng as he spoke. "There's no way we can extricate ourselves now, so you can put aside your hatred and thirst for vengeance toward us. As one so well-learned on the subject of social philosophy, surely you're not so shallow-minded as to think that history is made from virtue and justice?"

The Senior Official's words were a potent tranquilizer for Song Cheng. He recovered from the fever of victory. "My duty is to punish the evil, protect the virtuous, and uphold justice," he said after a moment of hesitation, his tone much calmer.

The Senior Official nodded, satisfied. "You didn't give a straight answer. Very good, it shows that you're not quite that narrow-minded yet."

Here, the Senior Official suddenly shuddered all over, as if someone had dumped cold water over him. He broke out of his daze. The weakness was gone; whatever vitality had deserted him earlier seemed to have returned. He stood, gravely buttoned his collar, and meticulously smoothed the wrinkles from his clothes. Then he said with utmost solemnity to Lu Wenming and Chen Xufeng, "Comrades, from now on, everything can be seen in the digital mirror. Please take care with your behavior and image."

Lu Wenming stood, his expression heavy. He attended to his appearance as the Senior Official had, then gave a long sigh. "Yes, from now on, Heaven watches from above."

Chen Xufeng stood unmoving with his head hanging.

The Senior Official looked at everyone in turn. "Very well, I'll be leaving now. I have a busy day at work tomorrow." He turned toward Bai Bing. "Young man, come to my office tomorrow at six in the evening. Bring the superstring computer." Then he turned toward Chen and Lu. "As for you two, do your best. Xufeng, keep your chin up. We may have committed sins beyond pardon, but we don't need to feel so ashamed. Compared to them," he pointed to Song Cheng and Bai Bing, "what we've done really doesn't amount to much."

He opened the door and left with his head held high.

BIRTHDAY

The next day really was a busy day for the Senior Official.

As soon as he entered the office, he summoned key officials in charge of industry, agriculture, finance, environmental protection, and more, one by one, to debrief them on their next orders of business. Though each meeting was short, the Senior Official drew on his ample experience to zero in on important aspects of the work and problems requiring attention. With his well-honed conversational skills, too, each official left thinking that this was only another typical work debriefing. They noticed nothing unusual.

At ten thirty in the morning, after sending away the last official, the Senior Official settled down to document his views on the province's economic development, and problems he foresaw with large- and medium-scale province-owned enterprises. The compilation wasn't long, less than two thousand characters, but it distilled decades of reflection and work experience. Anyone familiar with the Senior Official's philosophies would be astonished reading this document—it differed considerably from his previous views. In his long years at the apex of power, this was the first time he expressed views unadulterated by personal considerations, solely coming from concern for the Party and the country's best interests.

It was past noon by the time the Senior Official finished writing. He didn't eat, only drank a cup of tea, and continued work.

The first indication of the age of the mirror occurred then. The Senior Official was informed that Chen Xufeng had shot himself in his office; meanwhile, Lu Wenming seemed to be in a trance, compulsively reaching for his collar button and straightening his clothes, as if someone could be snapping a picture of him at any instant. The Senior Official met the two pieces of news with only a smile.

The age of the mirror had not yet arrived, but the darkness was already breaking.

The Senior Official ordered the Anti-Corruption Bureau to immediately assemble a task force; with the cooperation of the police and the related Departments of Finance and Commerce, they were to immediately seize all records and accounts belonging to his son's Daxi Trade and Commerce Group and his daughter-in-law's Beiyuan Corporation, and contain the legal entities according to the law. He took care of his other relatives' and cronies' various financial bodies in the same manner.

At four thirty, the Senior Official began to draft a list of names. He knew that, upon the arrival of the age of the mirror, thousands of officials at or above the county rank throughout the province would be sacked. The immediate concern was to seek suitable successors for key roles within each organization, and the list, meant for the provincial and central leadership, presented his suggestions. In reality, this list had existed in his mind long before the appearance of the digital mirror. These were the people he'd planned to eliminate, supplant, and retaliate against.

It was already five thirty, time to leave work. He felt a gratification he had never experienced before: he had spent at least today as a human being.

Song Cheng entered the office, and the Senior Official handed him a thick stack of documents. "This is the evidence you obtained on me. You should report to the Central Commission as soon as possible. I wrote a confession last night complete with supporting evidence and added them here. Aside from looking through and checking the results of your investigations, I also supplemented some material to fill in the gaps."

Song Cheng accepted the documents, nodding solemnly. He didn't say anything.

"In a moment, Bai Bing will arrive with the superstring computer. You should tell him that you're about to inform your superiors of the digital mirror software. The central officials, after considering the matter from all directions, will use it conservatively to begin with. He should therefore make sure the software doesn't leak to the public beforehand. That would pose serious dangers and adverse effects. Therefore, you will have him delete all the backup copies, whether online or elsewhere, that he made to protect himself. As for the initialization parameters, if he told them to anyone else, have him make a list of names. He trusts you. He'll do as you say. You must make sure all the backups are gone."

"We already plan to," said Song Cheng.

"Then," the Senior Official looked Song Cheng in the eye, "kill him, and destroy his superstring computer. At this point, you can hardly think I'm plotting for my own sake."

Once Song Cheng recovered from his surprise, he shook his head, smiling.

The Senior Official smiled, too. "Very well, I've said everything I have to say. Whatever happens next has nothing to do with me. The mirror has recorded these words of mine; perhaps one day, in the distant future, some-one will listen."

The Senior Official waved away Song Cheng, then leaned against the back of the chair. He exhaled, slowly, subsumed in a sense of relief and release.

After Song Cheng left, the clock struck six. Bai Bing entered the office on the dot, carrying the briefcase that contained the digital mirror of history and reality.

The Senior Official invited him to sit. Looking at the superstring computer resting on the table, he said, "Young man, I have something to ask of you: May I see my own life in the digital mirror?"

"Of course you can, no problem!" Bai Bing said, opening the briefcase and booting up the computer. He opened the digital mirror software, then set the time to the present and the location to the office. The two occupants appeared in real time on the screen. Bai Bing selected the Senior Official, right-clicked, and activated the tracking capability.

The image onscreen began to change rapidly, so rapidly that the whole image window filled with a blur. But the Senior Official, as the subject of the search, remained in the middle of the screen the entire time, steady like the center of the world. He was flickering rapidly, too, but the figure was discernibly becoming younger. "This is a reverse chronology tracking search. The image recognition software can't use your current form to iden-tify younger versions of you, so it has to track you step by step through your age-related changes to find the beginning."

Several minutes later, the screen stopped flashing through time, now dis-playing a newborn baby's slick, wet face. The maternity ward nurse had just removed him from the scale. The little creature didn't laugh or scream; his eyes were open and charming, taking stock of the new world around him.

The Senior Official chuckled. "That's me, all right. My mother always told me that I opened my eyes as soon as I was born," the Senior Official said, smiling. He was clearly feigning lightheartedness to conceal the breach in his calm; this time, unlike many other times, he wasn't particularly successful.

"Look here, sir," Bai Bing said, pointing to a menu bar below the image. "These buttons let you zoom and change angles. This is the time slider bar. The digital mirror program will continue to move forward in time following you as the search object. If you want to find a particular time or event, it's not that different from how you'd use the scrollbar to look up things in a large document in a word processor. First find the approximate location with large steps through time, then make smaller adjustments, moving the slider left or right based on scenes you recognize. You should be able to find it. It's also similar to the fast-forward and rewind functions on a DVD player, although, of course, this disk playing at normal speed would take—"

"I believe nearly five hundred thousand hours," said the Senior Official, doing the mental math for Bai Bing. He accepted the mouse and zoomed out, revealing the young mother on the maternity bed, and the rest of the hospital room. There were a bedside table and lamp in the plain style of that era, and a window with a wooden frame. What caught his attention was a spot of red-orange light on the wall. "I was born in the evening, about the same time as now. Perhaps this is the last ray of the setting sun."

The Senior Official shifted the time slider, and the image again began to jump rapidly. Time flew past. When he stopped, the screen showed a small circular table lit by a bare bulb hanging from the ceiling. At the table, his plainly dressed, bespectacled mother was tutoring four children. An even younger child of three or four, clearly the Senior Official himself, was clumsily feeding himself from a small wooden bowl. "My mother was an elementary school teacher. She liked to bring the students having trouble with schoolwork back home for tutoring. That way, she could pick me up from nursery school on time." The Senior Official watched for a while. His child self accidentally spilled the bowl of porridge all over himself. His mother hurriedly got up, reaching for a towel. Only then did the Senior Official move the time slider.

Time skipped forward a few years. The screen suddenly lit up in a blaze of red, apparently the mouth of a blast furnace. Several workers in dirty asbestos work suits were moving, their silhouettes flickering in and out of the furnace flames. The Senior Official pointed to one of the figures. "That's my father, a furnace worker."

"You can change the angle to the front," said Bai Bing. He tried to take the mouse from the Senior Official, who refused him politely.

"Oh, no. This year, the factory worked everyone overtime to increase production. The workers had to be brought meals by family members, and I went. This was the first time I saw my father at work, from this exact angle. His silhouette against the furnace fire impressed itself into my mind very deeply."

Once more, years passed in the wake of the time slider, stopping on a clear, sunny day. The bright red flag of the Young Pioneers of China waved against the azure sky. A boy in a white shirt and blue trousers gazed up at it as other hands fastened a red scarf around his neck. The boy's right hand flew above his head in a salute, passionately announcing to the world that he would always be prepared to struggle for the cause of Communism. His eyes were as clear as the cloudless blue sky.

"I joined the Young Pioneers in second grade of elementary school."

Time jumped forward, and a different flag appeared: that of the Communist Youth League, against the backdrop of a memorial to the fallen. A small group of older children were swearing their oaths to the flag. He stood in the back row, his eyes as bright as before, but tinged with new fervor and longing.

"I joined the Youth League first year of secondary school."

The slider moved. The third red flag of his life appeared, the flag of the Communist Party this time, in what appeared to be an enormous lecture hall. The Senior Official zoomed in on one of the six teenagers taking their oaths, letting his face fill the screen.

"I joined the Party sophomore year of college." The Senior Official pointed at the screen. "Look at my eyes. What do you see in them?"

In that pair of young eyes could still be seen the spark of childhood, the fervor and longing of youth, but there was a new and yet immature wisdom, too.

"I feel you were . . . sincere," Bai Bing said, looking at those eyes.

"You'd be right. Until then, I still meant every word of the oath." The

Senior Official wiped at his eye, the motion minute enough that Bai Bing didn't notice it.

The slider moved forward another few years. This time it sped too far, but after a few small adjustments, a tree-shaded path appeared on the screen. He stood there, looking at a young woman turning to leave. She turned her head to look at him one last time, her eyes bright with tears. She gave a powerful impression, solemn but resolute. Then she left, disappearing into the distance between the two rows of tall poplars. Tactfully, Bai Bing got up and prepared to leave some space, but the Senior Official stopped him.

"Don't worry, this is the last time I saw her." He put down the mouse, his gaze leaving the screen. "Very well, thank you. You may turn off the computer."

"Don't you want to keep watching?"

"That's all I have worth reminiscing."

"We can find where she is right now, no problem!"

"That won't be necessary. It's getting late; you should leave. Thank you, truly."

Once Bai Bing left, the Senior Official telephoned the security station, requesting that the building guard come up to his office for a moment. Soon after, the armed police guard entered and saluted.

"You're . . . Yang, yes?"

"You have an excellent memory, sir."

"I didn't call you up here for anything important. I just wanted to tell you that today is my birthday."

Taken by surprise, the guard was momentarily lost for words.

The Senior Official smiled indulgently. "Send my regards to the ranks. You may go." The guard saluted, but just as he turned to leave, the Senior Official seemed to think of something. "Oh, leave the gun behind."

The guard hesitated, but pulled out his handgun. He walked over and carefully set it on one end of the broad office desk, before saluting again and leaving.

The Senior Official picked up the gun, detached the magazine, and took out the bullets, one by one, until there was only the last. Then he pushed the magazine back in. The next person to handle this gun could be his secretary, or the janitor who came in at night. An empty gun was always safer.

He put down the gun, then stood the removed bullets on the table in a circle, like the candles on a birthday cake. After that he strode to the window, looking across the city to the sun on the verge of setting. Behind the outer city's industrial air pollution, it appeared as a deep red disk. He thought it looked like a mirror.

The last thing he did was to take the small "Serve the People" pin from his lapel and set it on the flag stand on the desk, beneath the miniature flags of China and the CCP.

Then he sat at his desk, calmly awaiting the last ray of the setting sun.

THE FUTURE

That night, Song Cheng entered the main computer room of the Center for Meteorological Modeling. He found Bai Bing alone, looking quietly at the screen of the booting superstring computer.

Song Cheng came over and patted his shoulder. "Hey, Bai, I've already notified your manager. A special car will arrive shortly to take you to Beijing. You'll give the superstring computer to a central official. Some other experts in the field might listen to your report too. With such an extraordinary technology, it won't be easy to get people to understand and believe it all. You'll have to be patient when you explain and give the demonstrations . . . Bai Bing, what's wrong?"

Bai Bing remained quiet, not turning from his seat. In the mirrored universe on the screen, the Earth floated suspended in space. The ice caps had altered in shape, and the ocean was a grayer shade of blue, but the changes weren't obvious. Song Cheng didn't notice them.

"He was right," Bai Bing said.

"What?"

"The Senior Official was right." Bai Bing turned slowly toward Song Cheng. His eyes were bloodshot.

"Did you spend an entire day and night coming up with that conclusion?"

"No, I got the future-time recursion to work."

"You mean . . . the digital mirror can simulate the future now?"

Bai Bing nodded listlessly. "Just the very distant future. I thought of a completely new algorithm last night. It avoids the relatively near future, which allows it to sidestep the disruption in the causal chain resulting from knowledge of the future changing the present. I jumped the mirror directly into the far future."

"How far?"

"Thirty-five thousand years later."

"What's society like, then?" Song Cheng asked cautiously. "Is the mirror having its effect?"

Bai Bing shook his head. "The digital mirror won't exist by that time. Society won't either. Human civilization already disappeared."

Song Cheng was speechless.

On the screen, the viewing angle descended rapidly, coming to a stop above a city surrounded by desert.

"This is our city. It's empty, already dead for two thousand years."

The first impression the dead city gave was of a world of squares. All the buildings were perfect cubes, arrayed in neat columns and rows to form a perfectly square city. Only the clouds of sandy dust that rose at times in the square grid streets prevented one from mistaking the city for an abstract geometrical figure in a textbook.

Bai Bing maneuvered the viewing angle to enter a room in one of the cube-shaped edifices. Everything in it had been buried by countless years of sand and dust. On the side with the window, the accumulated sand rose in a slope, already high enough to touch the windowsill. The surface of the sand bulged in places, perhaps indicating buried appliances and furniture. A few structures like dead branches extended from one corner; that was a metal coatrack, now mostly rust. Bai Bing copied part of the view and pasted it into another program, where he processed away the thick layer of sand on top, revealing a television and refrigerator rusted down to the bare frames, as well as a writing desk. A picture frame, long fallen over, lay on the desk. Bai Bing adjusted the viewing angle and zoomed in so that the small photo in the frame filled the screen.

It was a family portrait of three, but the three people in the photo were practically identical in appearance and dress. One could guess their gender only by the length of hair, and age only by height. They wore matching outfits similar to Mao suits, orderly and stiff, buttoned to the collar. When Song Cheng looked closer, he found that their features still displayed some variation. The effect of indistinguishability had come from their identical expressions, a sort of wooden serenity, a sort of dead graveness.

"Everyone in the photos and video fragments I could find had the same expression on their face. I haven't seen any other emotion, certainly not tears or laughter."

"How did it end up like this?" Song Cheng asked, horrified. "Can you look through the historical records they left?"

"I did. The course of history after us goes something like this: The age of the mirror will start in five years. During the first twenty years, digital mirrors will only be used by law enforcement, but they'll already be substantially affecting human society and causing structural changes. After that, digital mirrors will seep into every corner of life and society. History calls it the beginning of the Mirror Era. For the first five centuries of the new era, human society still gradually develops. The signs of total stagnation first appear in the mid-sixth century ME. Culture stagnates first, because human nature is now as pure as water, and there is nothing left to depict and express. Literature disappears, then all of the humanities. Science and technology will grind to a standstill after them. The stagnation of progress lasts thirty thousand years. History calls that protracted period the Middle Age of Light."

"What happens after?"

"The rest is straightforward. Earth runs out of resources, and all the arable land is lost to desertification. Meanwhile, humanity still doesn't have the technology to colonize space, or the power to excavate new resources. In those five thousand years, everything slowly winds down. . . . In the era

I showed you, there are still people living on all the continents, but there's really not much to see."

"Ah . . ." The sound Song Cheng made resembled the Senior Official's slow sigh. A long time passed before his shaking voice could ask, "Then . . . what do we do? Do we destroy the digital mirror right now?"

Bai Bing took out two cigarettes, handing one to Song Cheng. He lit his own and drew deeply, blowing the smoke at the three dead faces on the screen. "I'm definitely destroying the digital mirror. I only kept it around until now so you can see. But nothing we do now matters. That's one bit of consolation: everything that happens afterward has nothing to do with us."

"Someone else created a digital mirror too?"

"The theory and technology for it are both out there, and according to superstring theory, the number of viable initialization parameter sets is enormous, but still finite. If you keep going down the list, you'll eventually run into that one set. . . . More than thirty thousand years from now, till the last days of civilization, humanity will still be thanking and worshiping a guy named Nick Kristoff."

"Who is he?"

"According to the historical records: a devout Christian, physicist, and inventor of the digital mirror software."

MIRROR ERA

FIVE MONTHS LATER, AT THE PRINCETON UNIVERSITY
CENTER OF EXPERIMENTAL COSMOLOGY

When the radiant sea of stars appeared on one of the fifty display screens, all of the scientists and engineers present erupted into cheers. Five superstring computers stood here, each simulating ten virtual machines, for a total of fifty sets of big bang simulations running day and night. This newly created virtual universe was the 32,961st.

Only one middle-aged man remained unmoved. He was heavy-browed and alert-eyed, imposing in appearance, the silver cross at his breast all the more striking against his black sweater. He made the sign of the cross, and asked:

"Gravitational constant?"

"6.67 times 10^{-11}!"

"Speed of light in a vacuum?"

"2.998 times 10^5 kilometers per second!"

"Planck's constant?"

"6.626 times 10^{-34}!"

"Charge of electron?"

"1.602 times 10^{-19} coulombs!"

"One plus one?" He gravely kissed the cross at his chest.

"Equals two! This is our universe, Professor Kristoff!"

ODE TO JOY

An alternate history of the sophon

TRANSLATED BY JOEL MARTINSEN

THE CONCERT

The concert held to close the final session of the United Nations was a depressing one.

A utilitarian attitude toward the body, dating back to bad precedents set at the start of the century, had been on the rise; countries assumed the UN was a tool to achieve their interests, and interpreted its charter to their own benefit. Smaller nations challenged the authority of the permanent members, while each permanent member believed it deserved more authority within the organization, which lost all authority of its own as a result. A decade on, all efforts at a rescue had failed, and everyone agreed that the UN and the idealism it represented no longer applied to the real world. It was time to be rid of it.

All heads of state assembled for the final session, to observe a solemn funeral for the UN. The concert, held on the lawn outside the General Assembly building, was the final item on the program.

It was well after sunset. This was the most bewitching time of day, the handover from day to night when the cares of reality were masked by the growing dusk. The world was still visible under the last light from the setting sun, and on the lawn, the air was thick with the scent of budding flowers.

The secretary general was the last to arrive. On the lawn, she ran across

Richard Clayderman,* one of the evening's featured performers, and struck up a cheerful conversation.

"Your playing fascinates me," she told the prince of pianists with a smile.

Clayderman, dressed in his favorite snow-white suit, looked uncomfortable. "If that's genuine, then I'm overjoyed. But I've heard there have been complaints about my appearance at a concert like this."

Not merely complaints. The head of UNESCO, a noted art theorist, had publicly criticized Clayderman's playing as "busker-level," and his performances as "blasphemy against piano artistry."

The secretary general lifted a hand to stop him. "The UN can have none of classical music's arrogance. You've erected a bridge from classical music to the masses, and so must we bring humanity's highest ideals directly to the common people. That's why you were invited here tonight. Believe me, when I first heard your music under the sweltering sun in Africa, I had the feeling of standing in a ditch looking up at the stars. It was intoxicating."

Clayderman gestured toward the leaders on the lawn. "It feels more like a family gathering than a UN event."

The secretary general looked over the crowd. "On this lawn, for tonight at least, we have realized a utopia."

She crossed the lawn and reached the front row. It was a glorious evening. She had planned on switching off her political sixth sense and just relaxing for once, taking her place as an ordinary member of the audience, but this proved impossible. That sense had picked up a situation: The president of China, engaged in conversation with the president of the United States, looked up at the sky for a moment. The act itself was utterly unremarkable, but the secretary general noticed that it was a little on the long side, perhaps just an extra second or two, but she'd noticed it. When the secretary general sat down after shaking hands with the other world leaders in the front row, the Chinese president looked up at the sky again, confirming his perception. Where national leaders are concerned, apparently random actions are in fact

---

*The French musician's 1992 performance in China was the first by a major foreign pianist, and he has remained the most recognized classical musician in the decades since.

highly precise, and under normal circumstances, this act would not have been repeated. The US president also noticed it.

"The lights of New York wash out the stars. The sky's far brighter than this over DC," he said.

The Chinese president nodded but said nothing.

The US president went on, "I like looking at the stars, too. In the ever-changing course of history, our profession needs an immovable reference object."

"That object is an illusion," the Chinese president said.

"Why do you say that?"

Instead of responding directly, the Chinese president pointed at a cluster of stars that had just come out. "Look, that's the Southern Cross, and that's Canis Major."

The US president smiled. "You've proven they're immovable enough. Ten thousand years ago, primitive man would have seen the same Southern Cross and Canis Major as we do today. They may have even come up with those names."

"No, Mr. President. In fact, the sky might even have been different just yesterday." The Chinese president looked up for a third time. He remained calm, but the steel in his eyes made the other two nervous. They looked at the same placid sky they had seen so many times before; nothing seemed wrong. They looked questioningly at the Chinese president.

"The two constellations I just noted should only be visible from the southern hemisphere," he said without pointing them out or looking upward. He turned thoughtfully toward the horizon.

The secretary general and US president looked questioningly at him.

"We're looking at the sky from the other side of the Earth," he said.

The US president yelped, but then restrained himself and said in a voice even lower than before, "You've got to be kidding."

"Look, what's that?" the secretary general said, pointing at the sky with a hand raised only to eye level so as not to alarm the others.

"The moon, of course," the US president said after a brief glance overhead. But when the Chinese president slowly shook his head, he looked up a second time and was less certain. At first, the semicircular shape in the sky looked like the moon in first quarter, but it was bluish, as if a scrap of daytime sky had gotten stuck. The US president looked more closely at the blue semicircle. He held out a finger and measured the blue moon against it. "It's growing."

The three politicians stared up at the sky, not caring anymore if they'd startle the others. The heads of state in the surrounding seats noticed their movements, and more people looked upward. The orchestra on the outdoor stage abruptly stopped its warm-up.

By now, it was clear that the blue semicircle was not the moon, because its diameter had grown to twice that, and its darkness-shrouded other half was now visible in dim blue. In its brighter half, details could be made out; its surface was not a uniform blue but had patches of brown.

"God! Isn't that North America?" someone shouted. They were right. You could distinguish the familiar shape of the continent, which lay smack on the border between the light and dark halves. (It may have occurred to someone that was the very same position they occupied.) Then they found Asia, and the Arctic Ocean and the Bering Strait. . . .

"It's . . . Earth!"

The US president drew back his finger. The blue sphere in the sky was now growing at a rate visible without a reference object, and was now at least three times the diameter of the moon. At first, it looked like a balloon rapidly inflating in the sky, but then a shout from the crowd abruptly changed that impression:

"It's falling!"

The shout provided a reasonable interpretation of the scene before them. Regardless of its accuracy, they immediately had a new sense of what was happening: another Earth was crashing toward them in space! The approaching blue planet now occupied a third of the sky, and surface details could be made out: brown continents covered in mountain wrinkles, cloud coverage looking like unmelted snow, outlined in black from the shadows cast on the ground. There was white at the North Pole, parts of which glittered—ice, rather than clouds. On a blue ocean, a snow-white object spiraled lazily with the delicate beauty of a velvet flower in a blue crystal vase—a newborn hurricane. . . . But when the huge blue sphere grew to cover half the sky, their perception experienced an almost simultaneous transformation.

"God! We're falling!"

The feeling of inversion came in an instant. The sphere filling half the sky gave them a feeling of height, or that the ground beneath their feet had vanished and they were now falling toward the other Earth. Its surface was clearer now, and on the dark side, not far from the shadow line, those with keen eyes could see a faint glowing band: the lights of America's East Coast cities, their own location in New York a somewhat brighter spot within it. The other planet now filled two-thirds of the sky, and it seemed as if the two Earths would collide. There were screams from the crowd, and many of them shut their eyes.

Then all was still. The Earth overhead was no longer falling (or the ground they stood on was no longer falling toward it). The sphere hung motionless covering two-thirds of the sky, bathing the land in its blue glow.

Now sounds of chaos could be heard from the city, but the occupants of the lawn had the strongest nerves on the planet in unstable situations, so they held back their panic at the nightmarish scene and approached it more quietly.

"It's a hallucination," the secretary general said.

"Yes," the Chinese president said. "If it were real, we'd feel the gravity. And this close to the sea, we'd be drowned by the tide."

"It's more than just the tides," the Russian president said. "The two Earths would be torn to pieces by their mutual attraction."

"The laws of physics don't permit two Earths to remain motionless," the Japanese prime minister said, and, turning to the Chinese president, added, "When that Earth first appeared, you were saying that the stars of the southern hemisphere were in the sky above us. Could the two phenomena be connected?" It was a tacit admission of eavesdropping, but they were past caring at this point.

"Perhaps we're about to find out," the US president said. He spoke into a mobile phone; the secretary of state, at his elbow, informed the others that he was speaking with the International Space Station. And so they focused their anticipation on the president, who listened attentively to the phone but said only a few words. Silence reigned on the lawn, where in the blue light of that other Earth they looked like a throng of ghosts. After about two minutes, the president set down the phone, climbed onto a chair, and shouted to the expectant crowd:

"It's simple. A huge mirror has appeared next to the Earth!"

THE MIRROR

There was no way to describe it other than a huge mirror. Its surface perfectly reflected visual light as well as radar with no energy or image loss. Viewed from the right distance, the Earth would look like a stone on a go board ten billion square kilometers in area.

It shouldn't have been difficult for *Endeavor*'s astronauts to obtain preliminary data, since an astronomer and a space physicist were on board and had all the necessary equipment available and at their disposal, including the ISS, to conduct observations; however, their momentary panic had nearly sent the orbiter to its doom. The ISS was a fully-equipped observation platform, but its orbit was not conducive to observing an object situated 450 kilometers above the North Pole nearly perpendicular to the Earth's axis. *Endeavor*'s orbit sent it over the poles so it could carry out observations of the ozone holes; at a height of 280 kilometers, it was flying right between the Earth and the mirror.

Flying with an Earth on either side was nightmarish, like speeding along a canyon with blue cliffs towering above them. The pilot insisted it was a mirage, like the spatial disorientation he had experienced twice during his three thousand hours in a fighter jet, but the commander was convinced there really were two Earths. He ordered their orbit adjusted to compensate for the gravitational pull of the second one, but the astronomer stopped him in time. Once they got over their initial shock and learned from observations of the shuttle's orbit that one of the two Earths had no mass, they let out a sigh of relief: if they had made the compensational adjustments, *Endeavor* would be nothing more than a shooting star over the North Pole.

The astronauts carefully observed the massless Earth. Visual inspection indicated the orbiter was much farther away from it, but its North Pole seemed little different from that of the nearer Earth, if not entirely identical. They saw laser beams emitting from both North Poles, two long, dark red snakes twisting slowly in identical shapes at identical positions. Eventually they discovered one thing that the nearer Earth did not have: an object in flight above the massless Earth. Visually they judged it to be in an orbit roughly three hundred kilometers above its surface, but when they attempted to probe its orbit more precisely using shipboard radar, the radar seemed to bounce back from a solid wall a hundred-odd kilometers away. The massless Earth and the flying object were on the opposite side of that wall. Observing the object through the cockpit window using high-powered binoculars, the commander saw another space shuttle flying in low orbit over the frozen Arctic ice pack like a moth crawling along a blue striped wall. There was a figure behind that shuttle's cockpit window, looking through binoculars. The commander waved, and the figure waved at the same time.

And so they discovered the mirror.

They altered course to draw closer to the mirror. At a distance of three kilometers, the astronauts could see clearly *Endeavor*'s reflection six kilometers away, the glow of its aft engines lending it the form of a creeping firefly.

One astronaut took a spacewalk for humanity's first close encounter with the mirror. Thrusters on the suit spurted streams of white, speeding him across the distance. Carefully, he adjusted the jets to bring himself into position ten meters from the mirror. His reflection was remarkably clear, without any distortion. Since he was in orbit but the mirror was stationary with respect to the Earth, he had a relative speed of ten kilometers per second. He was racing past it, but no motion at all was visible. It was the smoothest, shiniest surface in the universe.

When the astronaut decelerated, his thruster jets had been aimed at the mirror for an extended period, and a white fog of benzene propellant had drifted toward it. During previous space walks, whenever the fog had come into contact with the shuttle or the outside wall of the ISS, it would leave a conspicuous smudge; he imagined it would be the same with the mirror, except that with the high relative velocity, the smudge would be a long stripe, like he used to draw with soap on the bathroom mirror as a child. But he saw nothing. The fog vanished upon contact with the mirror, whose surface remained bright as ever.

The shuttle's orbital trajectory gave them only a limited amount of time near the mirror, prompting the astronaut to act quickly. In an almost unconscious act the moment the fog disappeared, he took a wrench out of his tool bag and tossed it at the mirror, but once it left his hand, he and the astronauts aboard the shuttle were paralyzed with the realization that the relative velocity between it and the mirror gave it the force of a bomb. In terror they watched the wrench tumble toward the mirror and had a vision of the spiderweb fractures that in just moments would spread like lightning across the surface from the point of impact, and then the enormous mirror shattering into billions of glittering fragments, a sea of silver in the blackness of space. . . . But when the wrench touched the surface it vanished without a trace, and the mirror remained as smooth as before.

It actually wasn't hard to see that the mirror was massless, not a physical body, since floating motionless over Earth's North Pole would be impossible otherwise. (It might be more accurate to state, given their relative sizes, that the Earth was floating in the middle of the mirror.) Rather than a physical entity, the mirror was a field of some sort. Contact with the fog and the wrench proved that.

Delicately manipulating his thrusters and making continual microadjustments of the jets, the astronaut drew within half a meter of the mirror. He stared straight into his reflection, amazed once again at its fidelity: a perfect copy, one perhaps even more finely wrought than the original. He extended a hand toward it until he and his reflected hand were practically touching, separated by less than a centimeter. His earpiece was silent—the commander did not order him to stop—so he pushed forward, and his hand disappeared into the mirror. He and his image were joined at the wrist.

There had been no sensation of contact. He retracted his hand and looked at it carefully. The suit glove was perfectly unharmed. No marks whatsoever.

Below the astronaut, the shuttle was gradually drawing away from the mirror and had to constantly run its engines and thrusters to maintain proximity. However, due to its trajectory its drift was accelerating, and before long such adjustments would be impossible. A second encounter would require waiting an entire orbit, but would the mirror still be there? With this in mind, the astronaut made a decision. He switched on his thrusters and headed straight into the mirror.

His reflection loomed large, filling his field of vision with the quicksilver bubble of his helmet's one-way reflective faceplate. He fought to keep from closing his eyes as his head touched the mirror. At contact he felt nothing, but in that very moment everything vanished before his eyes, replaced by the darkness of space and the familiar Milky Way. He jerked around, and below him was the same view of the galaxy, with one addition: his own reflection receding into the distance, the maneuvering units he and his reflection wore linked by streams of thruster jet fog.

He had crossed the mirror, and the other side of it was a mirror, too.

His earpiece had been chirping with the commander's voice when he was approaching the mirror, but it had cut out. The mirror blocked radio waves. Worse, the Earth wasn't visible from this side. Surrounded entirely by stars gave the astronaut the feeling of being isolated in a different world, and he began to panic. He adjusted the jets and arrested his outward motion. He had passed through the first time with his body parallel to the mirror, but now he oriented himself perpendicular, as if diving headfirst into it. Just before contact, he cut his speed. Then the top of his head touched the top of his reflection, and then he passed through and saw with relief the blue Earth below him, and heard the commander's voice in his ear.

Once his upper torso was through he dropped his drift speed, leaving the remainder of his body on the other side. Then he reversed the direction of his jets and began to back up; fog from the jets on the opposite side of the mirror issued from the surface around him like steam rising from a lake in which he was partially submerged. When the surface reached his nose, he made another startling discovery: The mirror passed through his faceplate and filled the crescent space between it and his face. He looked downward and saw his frightened pupils reflected in the crescent. No doubt the mirror was passing through his entire head, but he felt nothing. He reduced his speed to the absolute minimum, no faster than the tick of a second hand, and advanced millimeter by millimeter until the mirror bisected his pupils and vanished.

Everything was back to normal: Earth's blue sphere on one side, the glittering Milky Way on the other. But that familiar world persisted only for a second or two. He couldn't reduce his speed to zero, so before long the mirror was above his eyes, and the Earth vanished, leaving only the Milky Way. Above him, the mirror blocking his view of Earth extending hundreds of thousands of kilometers into the distance. The angle of reflection distorted his view of the stars into a silver halo on the mirror's surface. He reversed thrusters and drifted back, and the mirror dropped down across his eyes, vanishing momentarily as it passed to reveal both Earth and Milky Way before the galaxy vanished and the halo turned blue on the mirror's surface. He moved slowly back and forth several times, and as his pupils oscillated on either side, he felt like he was passing across a membrane between two worlds. At last he managed a fairly lengthy pause with the mirror invisible at the center of his pupils. He opened his eyes wide for a glimpse of a line at its position, but he saw nothing.

"The thing's got no width!" he exclaimed.

"Maybe it's only a few atoms thick, so you just can't see it. Maybe it approached Earth edgewise and that's why it arrived undetected." That was the assessment of the shuttle crew, who were watching the images sent back.

The astonishing thing was that the mirror, perhaps just atoms thick but over a hundred Pacific Oceans in area, was so flat as to be invisible from a parallel vantage point; in classical geometry, it was an ideal plane.

Its absolute flatness explained its absolute smoothness. It was an ideal mirror.

A sense of isolation replaced the astronauts' shock and fear. The mirror made the universe strange and rendered them a group of newborn babes abandoned in a new, unfathomable world.

Then the mirror spoke.

THE MUSICIAN

"I am a musician," it said. "I am a musician."

The pleasing voice resounding through space was audible to all. In an instant, all sleepers on Earth awoke, and all those already awake froze like statues.

The mirror continued, "Below I see a concert whose audience members are capable of representing the planet's civilization. Do you wish to speak with me?"

The national leaders looked to the secretary general, who was momentarily at a loss for words.

"I have something to say," the mirror said.

"Can you hear us?" the secretary general ventured.

The mirror answered immediately, "Of course I can. I could distinguish the voice of every bacterium on the world below me, if I wanted to. I perceive things differently from you. I can observe the rotation of every atom simultaneously. My perception encompasses temporal dimensions: I can witness the entire history of a thing all at once. You only see cross sections, but I see all."

"How are we hearing your voice?" the US president asked.

"I am emitting superstring waves into your atmosphere."

"Superstring waves?"

"A strong interactive force released from an atomic nucleus. It excites your atmosphere like a giant hand beating a drum. That's how you hear me."

"Where do you come from?" the secretary general asked.

"I am a mirror drifting through the universe. I originate so far away in both time and space it is meaningless to speak of it."

"How did you learn English?"

"I said that I see all. I should note that I'm speaking English because most of the audience at this concert was conversing in that language, not because I believe any ethnic group on the world below is superior to any other. It's all I can do when there's no global common tongue."

"We do have a world language, but it is little used."

"Your world language? Less an effort toward world unity than a classic expression of chauvinism. Why should a world language be Latinate rather than based on some other language family?"

This caused a commotion among the world leaders, who whispered nervously to each other.

"We're surprised at your understanding of Earth culture," the secretary general said earnestly.

"I see all. Besides, a thorough understanding of a speck of dust isn't hard."

The US president looked up at the sky and said, "Are you referring to the Earth? You may be bigger, but on a cosmic scale you're on the same order as the Earth. You're a speck of dust, too."

"You're less than dust," the mirror said. "A long, long time ago I used to be dust, but now I'm just a mirror."

"Are you an individual or a collective?" the Chinese president asked.

"That question is meaningless. When a civilization travels far enough on the road of time, individual and collective both disappear."

"Is a mirror your intrinsic form, or one of your many expressions?" the UK prime minister asked.

The secretary general added, "In other words, are you deliberately exhibiting this form for our benefit?"

"This question is also meaningless. When a civilization travels far enough on the road of time, form and content both disappear."

"We don't understand your answers to the last two questions," the US president said.

The mirror said nothing.

Then the secretary general asked the key question: "Why have you come to the solar system?"

"I am a musician. A concert is being held here."

"Excellent," the secretary general said with a nod. "And humanity is the audience?"

"My audience is the entire universe, even if it will be a century before the nearest civilized world hears my playing."

"Playing? Where's your instrument?" Richard Clayderman asked from the stage.

They realized the reflected Earth covering most of the sky had begun to slip swiftly toward the east. The change was frightening, like the sky falling, and a few people on the lawn involuntarily buried their head in their hands. Soon the reflection's edge dipped below the horizon, but at practically the same time, everything turned hazy in a sudden bright light. When sight returned, they saw the sun sitting smack in the middle of the sky right where the reflected Earth had been. Brilliant sunlight illuminated their surroundings under a brilliant blue sky that had replaced the black night. The oceans of the reflected Earth blended with the blue of the sky so the land seemed like a patch of clouds. They stared in shock at the change, but then a word from the secretary general explained the change that had taken place.

"The mirror tilted."

Indeed, the huge mirror had tilted in space, drawing the sun into the reflection and casting its light onto the Earth's nighttime side.

"It rotates fast!" the Chinese president said.

The secretary general nodded. "Yes, and at that size, the edges must be nearing the speed of light!"

"No physical object can tolerate the stresses from that rotation. It's a field, like our astronaut demonstrated. Near-light-speed motion is entirely normal for a field," the US president said.

Then the mirror spoke: "This is my instrument. I am a star player. My instrument is the sun!"

These grand words silenced them all, and they stared mutely at the reflected sun for a long while before someone asked, their voice trembling with awe, how it was played.

"You're all aware that many of the instruments you play have a sound chamber whose thin walls reflect and confine sound waves, allowing them to resonate and produce pleasing sounds. In the case of EM waves, the chamber is a star—it may lack visible walls, but it has a transmission speed gradient that reflects and refracts the waves, confining them to produce EM resonance and play beautiful music."

"What does this instrument sound like?" Clayderman asked the sky.

"Nine minutes ago, I played tuning notes on the sun. The instrument's sound is now being transmitted at the speed of light. Of course, it's in EM form, but I can convert it to sound in your atmosphere through superstring waves. Listen. . . ."

They heard a few delicate, sustained notes, similar to those of a piano, but with a magic that held everyone momentarily under its spell.

"How does the sound make you feel?" the secretary general asked the Chinese president.

"Like the whole universe is a huge palace, one that's twenty billion light-years tall. And the sound fills it completely."

"Can you still deny the existence of God after hearing that?" the US president asked.

The Chinese president eyed him, and said, "The sound comes from the real world. If it can produce such a sound, then God is even less essential."

THE BEAT

"Is the performance about to start?" the secretary general asked.

"Yes. I'm waiting for the beat," the mirror replied.

"The beat?"

"The beat began four years ago and is being transmitted here at the speed of light."

Then there was a fearsome change in the sky. The reflected Earth and sun disappeared, replaced by dancing bright silver ripples that filled the sky, making them feel like Earth had been plunged into an enormous ocean and they were looking up at the blazing sun beyond the water's surface.

The mirror explained: "I'm blocking intense radiation from outer space. I can't totally reflect it, so what you're seeing is the small portion that gets through. The radiation comes from a star that went supernova four years ago."

"Four years ago? That's Centauri," someone said.

"That's right. Proxima Centauri."

"But that star has none of the necessary conditions for supernova," the Chinese president said.

"I created the conditions," the mirror said.

They realized that when the mirror had said it made preparations for this concert four years ago, it was referring to that event; after selecting the sun as its instrument, it had detonated Proxima Centauri. Judging from the audio test of the sun, it was evidently capable of acting through hyperspace and pulsing the sun 1 AU away. But whether it possessed the same ability for a star four light-years away remained unknown. The detonation of Proxima Centauri could have been accomplished in one of two ways: from the solar system via hyperspace, or by teleporting to its vicinity, detonating it, and then teleporting back. Both were godlike power, so far as humanity was concerned, and in any case the light from the supernova would still take four years to reach to the sun. The mirror said that music it played would be transmitted to the cosmos by EM, so was the speed of light for that hyper-civilization akin to the speed of sound for humans? And if light waves were their sound waves, what was light for them? Humanity would never know.

"Your ability to manipulate the physical world is alarming," the US president said.

"Stars are stones in the cosmic desert, the most commonplace of objects in my world. Sometimes I use stars as tools, other times as weapons, and other times as musical instruments. . . . I've turned Proxima Centauri into a metronome, basically the same as the stones used by your ancestors. We both take advantage of ordinary objects in our world to enlarge and extend our abilities."

But the occupants of the lawn could see no similarity between the two, and abandoned the attempt to discuss technology with the mirror. Humanity could no more comprehend it than an ant could understand the ISS.

Little by little the light in the sky began to dim, giving them the impression that it was moonlight shining on the ocean, not sunlight, and that the supernova was going out.

The secretary general said, "If the mirror hadn't blocked the energy from the supernova, the Earth would be a dead planet."

By this point the ripples in the sky were gone, and the Earth's enormous reflection again occupied most of the sky.

"Where's the beat?" Clayderman asked. He had left the stage and was sitting among the world leaders.

"Look to the east!" someone shouted, and they saw in the eastern sky a dividing line, ramrod straight, bisecting the heavens into two distinct images. The reflected Earth, partially cut off, remained on the western side, but in the east was a dazzling starfield that many of them knew was the correct one for the northern hemisphere rather than the reflected southern sky. The division line marched west, enlarging the starry sky and wiping out the reflected Earth.

"It's flying away!" shouted the secretary general. And they realized he was right: the mirror was leaving the space over Earth. Its edge soon vanished beneath the western horizon, leaving them standing beneath the stars of an ordinary sky. It did not reappear—perhaps it had flown off to the vicinity of its sun instrument.

It comforted them somewhat to see the familiar world, the stars and city lights as they had been, and to smell the blossoms wafting over the lawn.

Then came the beat.

Day arrived without warning with a sudden blue sky and blazing sunlight that flooded the land and lit up their surroundings with brilliant light. But daytime lasted but a second before extinguishing into renewed night as stars and city lights returned. And the night lasted only a second before day returned, only for a second, and then it was night again. Day, and then night, then day, then night . . . like a pulse, or as if the world were a projector switching back and forth between two slides.

A beat formed out of night and day.

They looked up and saw the flashing star, now just a blinding, dimensionless point of light in space. "A pulsar," said the Chinese president.

The remains of a supernova, a whirling neutron star, the naked hot spot on its dense surface turning it into a cosmic lighthouse, its revolution sweeping the beam emitted by its hot spot through space, and giving Earth a brief moment of daytime as it swept past the solar system.

"I seem to recall," the secretary general said, "that a pulsar's frequency is far faster than this. And it doesn't emit visible light."

Shielding his eyes with a hand and struggling to adjust to the crazy rhythm of the world, the US president said, "The high frequency is because the neutron star retains the former star's angular momentum. The mirror may be able to somehow drain that momentum. As for visible light . . . do you really think that's something the mirror can't do?"

"There's another thing," the Chinese president said. "There's no reason to believe that the pace of life for all beings in the universe is like that of humanity. The beat for their music might be on a completely different frequency. The mirror's normal beat, for example, may be faster than even our fastest computers."

"Yes," the US president said, nodding. "And there's no reason to believe that what they perceive as visible light is the same EM spectrum."

"So you're saying that the mirror's music is benchmarked to human senses?" the secretary general asked in surprise.

The Chinese president shook his head. "I don't know. But it's got to be based on something."

The pulsar's powerful beam swept across the empty sky like a four-trillion-kilometer-long baton, still growing at the speed of light. At this end, played on the sun by the mirror's invisible fingers and transmitted to the cosmos at the speed of light, the sun concert began.

SUN MUSIC

A rustle like radio jamming or the endless pounding of waves on sand occasionally offered up hints of a vast desolation within its more abundant chaos and disorder. The sound went on for more than ten minutes without changing.

The Russian president broke the silence: "Like I said, we can't understand their music."

"Listen!" Clayderman said, pointing at the sky, but it was a long moment before the rest of them heard the melody his trained ears had picked out at once. A simple structure of just two notes, reminiscent of a clock's tick-tock. The notes repeated, separated by lengthy gaps. Then another two-note section, and a third, and a fourth . . . paired tones emerging ceaselessly from the chaos like fireflies in the night.

Then a new melody emerged, four notes. Everyone turned toward Clayderman, who was listening attentively and seemed to have sensed something. The four-note phrases multiplied.

"Here," he said to the heads of state. "Let's each of us remember a two-note measure." And so they all listened carefully, and each found a two-note measure and then focused their energy on committing it to memory. After a while, Clayderman said, "Very well. Now concentrate on a four-note phrase. Quickly, though, or else the music will grow too complex for us to pick them out. . . . Yes, that one. Does anyone hear that?"

"The first half is the pair of notes I memorized!" called the head of Brazil.

"The second half is my pair!" said the head of Canada.

They realized that every four-note phrase was made up of two of the previous note pairs, and as the four-note phrases multiplied they seemed to be depleting the isolated pairs. Then came eight-note phrases, similarly formed out of sets of four-note phrases.

"What do you hear?" the secretary general asked the people around him.

"A primeval ocean lit by flashes of lightning and volcanoes, and small molecules combining into larger ones . . . of course, that's purely my own imagination," the Chinese president said.

"Don't constrain your imagination to the Earth," the US president said. "The clustering of these molecules may be taking place in a nebula glowing with starlight. Or maybe they're not molecules, but the nuclear vortices inside a star . . ."

Then came a high-pitched, multi-note phrase that repeated like a bright spark in the dim chaos. "It's like it's describing a fundamental transformation," the Chinese president said.

Then they heard a new instrument, a sustained violin-like string sound that repeated a gentle shadow of the standout melody.

"It's expressing a kind of duplication," the Russian president said.

Now came an uninterrupted melody from the violin voice, changing smoothly as if it were light in curvilinear motion. The UK prime minister said to the Chinese president, "To borrow your idea, that ocean has something swimming in it now."

At some point the background music, which they'd nearly forgotten about, had begun to change. From the sound of waves it had turned into an oscillating rush, like a storm assaulting the bare rock. Then it changed again, into wind-like bleakness. The US president said, "The swimmer has entered a new environment. The land, or perhaps the air."

Then all the instruments played in unison for a brief moment, a fearsomely loud sound like an enormous physical collapse, then they abruptly dropped out, leaving just the lonely sound of the surf. Then the simple note pairs started up again and turned gradually complex, and everything repeated. . . .

"I can say with certainty that a great extinction was just described, and now we're listening to the revival afterward."

After another long and arduous process, the ocean swimmer ventured again into other parts of the world. Slowly, the melody grew grander and more complicated, and interpretations diversified. Some people thought it was a river rushing downhill, others imagined the advance of a great army across a vast plain, others saw billowing nebulae in the darkness of space caught in the vortex of a black hole, but they all agreed that it was expressing some grand process, an evolutionary process. The movement was long, and an hour had passed before the theme at last began to change. The melody gradually split into two vying parts that smashed wildly into each other or tangled together. . . .

"The classic style of Beethoven," Clayderman declared, after a long stretch immersed in the grand music.

The secretary general said, "It's like a fleet smacking across huge waves on the sea."

"No," said the US president, shaking his head. "Not that. You can tell that the two forces are not essentially different. I think it's a battle that spans a world."

"Wait a moment," interrupted the Japanese prime minister, breaking a long silence. "Do you really imagine you can comprehend alien art? Your understanding of the music may be no better than a cow's appreciation for a lyre."

Clayderman said, "I think our understanding is basically correct. The common languages of the cosmos are mathematics and music."

The secretary general said, "Proving it won't be difficult. Can we predict the theme or style of the next movement?"

After a moment's thought, the Chinese president said, "I'd say next will be an expression of worship, and the melody will possess a strict architectural beauty."

"You mean like Bach?"

"Yes."

And so it was. The listeners seemed to hear a great imposing church and the echoes of their footsteps inside that magnificent space, and they were overcome by fear and awe of an all-encompassing power.

Then the complicated melody turned simple again. The background music vanished, and a series of short, clear beats appeared in the infinite stillness: one, then two, then three, then four . . . and then one, four, nine, and sixteen . . . and then increasingly complex series.

Someone asked, "Is this describing the emergence of mathematics and abstract thinking?"

Then it turned even stranger. Isolated two- and three-note phrases from the violin, each of identically pitched notes held for different durations; then glissandos, rising, falling, and then rising again. They listened intently, and when the president of Greece said, "It's . . . like a description of basic geometric shapes," they immediately had the sense they were watching triangles and rectangles shoot by through empty space. The glides conjured up images of round objects, ovals and perfect circles. . . . The melody changed slowly as single-note lines turned into glides, but the previous impression of floating geometric shapes remained, only now they were floating on water and distorted. . . .

"The discovery of the secrets of time," someone said.

The next movement began with a constant rhythm that repeated along a period resembling a pulsar's day-night beat. The music seemed to have stopped altogether but for the beat echoing in the silence, but it was soon joined by another constant rhythm, this one slightly faster. Then more rhythms at various frequencies were added, until finally a magnificent chorus emerged. But on the time axis the music was constant as a huge flat wall of sound.

Astonishingly, their interpretation of this movement was unanimous: "A giant machine at work."

Then came a delicate new melody, a tinkle of crystal, volatile and dreamlike, that contrasted with the thick wall beneath it like a silver fairy flitting over the enormous machine. This tiny drop of a powerful catalyst touched off a wondrous reaction in the iron world: the constant rhythm began to waver, and the machine's shafts and cogs turned soft and rubbery until the whole chorus turned as light and ethereal as the fairy melody.

They debated it: "The machine has intelligence!" "I think the machine is drawing closer to its creator."

The sun music progressed into a new movement, the most structurally complicated yet, and the hardest to understand. First the piano voice played a lonely tune, which was then taken up and extended by an increasingly complex group that turned it grander and more magnificent with every repetition.

After it had repeated several times, the Chinese president said, "Here's my interpretation: A thinker stands on an island in the sea contemplating the cosmos. As the camera pulls back, the thinker shrinks in the field of view, and when the frame encompasses the entire island, the thinker is no more visible than a grain of sand. The island shrinks as the camera pulls back beyond the atmosphere, and now the entire planet is in frame, with the island just a speck within it. As the camera pulls back into space, the entire planetary system is drawn into frame, but now only the star is visible, a lonely, shining billiard ball against the pitch-black sky, and the ocean planet has vanished like a speck. . . ."

Listening intently, the US president picked up the thought: ". . . The camera pulls back at light speed, and we discover that what from our scale is a vast and boundless cosmos is but glittering star dust, and when the entire galaxy comes into frame, the star and its planetary system vanish like specks. As the camera continues to cross unimaginable distances, a galaxy cluster is pulled into frame. We still see glittering dust, but the dust is formed not of stars but of galaxies . . ."

The secretary general said, ". . . And our galaxy has vanished. But where does it end?"

The audience once again immersed themselves in the music as it approached a climax. The musician's mind had propelled the cosmic camera outside the bounds of known space so its frame captured the entire universe, reducing the Milky Way's galaxy cluster to a speck of dust. They waited intently for the finale, but the grand chorus suddenly dropped out, leaving behind only a lonely piano-like sound, distant and empty.

"A return to the thinker on the island?" someone asked.

Clayderman shook his head. "No, it's a completely different melody."

Then the cosmic chorus struck up again, but after a brief moment gave way to the piano solo. The two melodies alternated like this for a long while.

Clayderman listened intently, and suddenly realized something: "The piano is playing an inversion of the chorus!"

The US president nodded. "Or maybe it's the mirror of the chorus. A cosmic mirror. That's what it is."

The music had clearly reached a denouement, and now the piano's inverted melody proceeded alongside the chorus, riding conspicuously on its back but gloriously harmonious.

The Chinese president said, "It reminds me of the Silvers style of mid-twentieth-century architecture, in which, in order to avoid impact on the surrounding environment, buildings were clad entirely in mirrors. Reflections were a way of putting them in harmony with their surroundings as well as self-expression."

"Yes," the secretary general answered thoughtfully. "When civilization reaches a certain level, it can express itself through its reflection of the cosmos."

The piano abruptly shifted to the uninverted theme, bringing it into unison with the chorus. The sun music had finished.

ODE TO JOY

"A perfect concert," the mirror said. "Thank you to all who enjoyed it. And now I will be going."

"Wait a moment!" shouted Clayderman. "We have one last request. Could you play a human song on the sun?"

"Yes. Which one?"

The heads of state glanced around at each other. "Beethoven's Fate Symphony?"* asked the German premier.

"No, not Fate," said the US president. "It's been proven that humanity is powerless to strangle fate. Our worth lies in that even knowing that fate can't be resisted and death will have the final victory, we still devote our limited life span to creating beautiful lives."

"Then 'Ode to Joy,'" said the Chinese president.

The mirror said, "You all sing. I'll use the sun to transmit the song out into the universe. It will be beautiful, I assure you."

More than two hundred voices joined in "Ode to Joy," their song passed by the mirror to the sun, which again began vibrating to send powerful EM waves into all reaches of space.

> *Joy, thou beauteous godly lightning,*
> *Daughter of Elysium,*

---

*Beethoven's Fifth Symphony is known as the Fate Symphony in Chinese.

Fire drunken we are ent'ring
Heavenly, thy holy home!
Thy enchantments bind together,
What did custom stern divide,
Every man becomes a brother,
*Where thy gentle wings abide."**

Five hours later, the song would exit the solar system. In four years, it would reach Proxima Centauri; in ten thousand, it would exit the galaxy; in two hundred thousand, it would reach the galaxy's nearest neighbor, the Large Magellanic Cloud. In six million years, their song would have reached the forty-odd galaxies in the cluster, and in a hundred million years, the fifty-odd clusters in the supercluster. In fifteen billion years, the song would have spread throughout the known universe and would continue onward, should the universe still be expanding.

"Joy commands the hardy mainspring
Of the universe eterne.
Joy, oh joy the wheel is driving
Which the worlds' great clock doth turn.
Flowers from the buds she coaxes,
Suns from out the hyaline,
Spheres she rotates through expanses,
Which the seer can't divine."

The song concluded, everyone fell silent on the concert lawn. World leaders were lost in thought.

"Maybe things aren't so hopeless just yet, and we ought to renew our efforts," the Chinese president said.

The US president nodded. "Yes. The world needs the UN."

---

* "Ode to Joy" by Friedrich Schiller.

"Concessions and sacrifices are insignificant compared to the future disasters they prevent," the Russian president said.

"What we're dealing with amounts to a grain of sand in the cosmos. It ought to be easy," the UK prime minister said, looking up at the stars.

The other leaders voiced their assent.

"So then, do we all agree to extend the present session of the UN?" the secretary general asked hopefully.

"This will of course require contacting our respective governments, but I believe that won't be a problem," the US president said with a smile.

"Then, my friends, today is a day to remember," the secretary general said, unable to hide his delight. "So let's join once more in song."

"Ode to Joy" started up again.

Speeding away from the sun at the speed of light, the mirror knew it would never return. In more than a billion years as a musician it had never held a repeat performance, just as a human shepherd will never toss the same stone twice. As it flew, it listened to the echoes of "Ode to Joy," and a barely perceptible ripple appeared on its smooth mirror surface.

"Oh, that's a good song."

FULL-SPECTRUM BARRAGE JAMMING

TRANSLATED BY CARMEN YILING YAN

*Dedicated with deep respect to the people of Russia, whose
literature has influenced me all my life.*

Liu Cixin (2000)

*On the subject of selecting a method of electromagnetic jamming for the
battlefield, this manual recommends the use of selective frequency-targeted
jamming rather than engaging in barrage jamming over a wide range of
simultaneous frequencies, as the latter will interfere with friendly electromagnetic communication and electronic support as well.*

—*U.S. Army Electronic Warfare Handbook*

JANUARY 5TH, SMOLENSK FRONT LINE

The fallen city had already disappeared from view. The front line had retreated forty kilometers in the span of a single night.

Under the light of the early-morning sky, the snowy plain appeared a cold,
dim blue. In the distance, black columns of smoke rose from destroyed targets. There was almost no wind; the smoke ascended straight and high, like
thin strands of black gauze tying heaven to earth. As Kalina's gaze followed
the smoke upward, she started: the brightening sky was clogged with a vast,
dense bramble of white, as if a demented giant had covered the sky in agitated
scrawls. They were the tangled fighter plane contrails left by the Russian and
NATO air forces in their fierce night battle for control over the airspace.

The aerial and long-range precision strikes had continued throughout the night, too. To a casual observer, the bombardment wouldn't have seemed particularly concentrated. The explosions sounded seconds, even minutes apart. But Kalina knew that nearly every explosion had signified some important target hit, sparking punctuation marks in the black pages of the previous night. By dawn, Kalina wasn't sure how much strength was left in the defensive lines, or even whether the defensive lines had survived at all. It seemed as if she were the last one standing against the onslaught.

Major Kalina's electronic-resistance platoon had been hit by six laser-guided missiles around midnight. She'd survived by pure luck. The BMP-2 armored tank carrying the radio-jamming equipment was still burning; the other electronic-warfare vehicles in the battery were now piles of blackened metal scattered around her. Residual heat was dissipating from the bomb crater Kalina was in, leaving her feeling the cold. She pushed herself to a sitting position with her hands. Her right hand touched something sticky and clammy. Covered in black ash, it looked like a lump of mud. She suddenly realized it was a piece of flesh. She didn't know what body part it came from, much less whose. A first lieutenant, two second lieutenants, and eight privates had died in last night's attack. Kalina vomited, though nothing came out but stomach acid. She shoved her hands in the snow, trying to wipe away the blood, but the smears of blackish red quickly congealed in the cold, as stark as before.

The suffocating stillness of the last half hour signified that a new round of ground assault was about to begin. Kalina turned up the volume dial on the walkie-talkie strapped to her shoulder, but heard only static. Suddenly, a few blurry sentences emerged through the receiver, like birds flitting through thick fog.

". . . Observation Station Six reporting! Position 1437 at twelve o'clock sees thirty-seven M1A2s averaging sixty meters apart, forty-one Bradley IFVs five hundred meters behind the M1A2s' vanguard; twenty-four M1A2s and eight Leclercs currently flanking Position 1633, already past the border of 1437. Positions 1437, 1633, and 1752, prepare to engage the enemy!"

Kalina forced back shivers from cold and fear, so that the horizon line steadied in her binoculars. She saw blurry masses of snow spray, edging the horizon with fuzzy trim.

That was when Kalina heard the rumble of engines behind her. A row of Russian tanks passed her position as they charged the enemy, more T-90 tanks leaving the highway behind them. Kalina heard a different rumble: enemy helicopters were appearing in the sky ahead in neat array, a black lattice in the ghastly white sky of dawn. The exhaust pipes of the tanks around Kalina kicked into action with low splutters, cloaking the battleground in white fog. Through its crevices she could also see Russian helicopters passing low overhead.

The tanks' 120 mm guns stormed and thundered, and the white fog became a wildly flashing pink light display. Almost simultaneously, the first enemy shells fell, the pink light replaced by the blue-white lightning of their explosion. Kalina, lying on her stomach at the bottom of the bomb crater, felt the ground reverberate with the intense percussion like a drumhead. Nearby dirt and rock flew into the air and landed all over her back. Amid the explosions, she could dimly hear the whinny of anti-tank missiles. Kalina felt as if her viscera were tearing apart in the cacophony, and all the universe, the pieces falling toward an endless abyss—

Just as her mind teetered on the breaking point, the tank battle ended. It had lasted only thirty seconds.

When the smoke cleared, Kalina saw that the snowy ground in front of her was scattered with destroyed Russian tanks, heaps of raging flames crowned with black smoke. She looked farther; even without binoculars, she could see a similar swath of destroyed NATO tanks in the distance, appearing as black smoking specks on the snow. But more enemy tanks were rushing past the wreckage, wreathed in the snow spray churned up by their treads. Now and then the Abramses' ferocious broad wedge heads emerged from the spray like snapping turtles launching themselves out of the waves, their smooth-bore muzzles flashing sporadically like eyes. Just above, the helicopters were still embroiled in their melee. Kalina saw an Apache explode in midair not far away. A Mi-28 wobbled low overhead, trailing fuel from a leak. It hit the ground a few dozen meters away and exploded into a fireball. Short-range air-to-air missiles slashed countless parallel white lines low in the air—

Kalina heard a bang behind her. She turned; not far away, a damaged and badly smoking T-90 dropped its rear hatch. No one got out, but she could see a hand hanging down from it. Kalina leapt from the bomb crater and rushed to the back of the tank. She grabbed hold of the hand and pulled. An explosion rumbled inside the tank. A blast of blazing air forced Kalina back several steps. Her hand held something soft and very hot: a piece of skin pulled loose from the tank crew member's hand, cooked through. Kalina raised her head and saw flames burst from the hatch. Through it, she could see that the tank interior was already an inferno in miniature. Among the flames, dimly red and transparent, she could clearly see the silhouette of the unmoving crewman, rippling as if in water.

She heard two new shrills. The artillery crew to her front and left fired its last two anti-tank missiles. The wire-guided Sagger missile successfully destroyed an Abrams; the other, radio-guided missile found its signal jammed and veered upward at an angle, missing its target. Meanwhile the six missile crewmen retreated from their bunker, running toward Kalina's bomb crater as a Comanche helicopter dove for them, its angular chassis resembling the profile of a savage alligator. Machine-gun bullets struck the ground in a long row, their impact abruptly standing snow and dirt up in a fence that just as quickly toppled. The fence crossed through the little squadron, felling four of them. Only a first lieutenant and a private made it over to the crater. There Kalina noticed that the lieutenant was wearing an antishock tank helmet, perhaps taken from a destroyed tank. The two of them held an RPG each.

The lieutenant jumped into the crater. He took a shot at the nearest enemy tank, hitting the M1A2 head-on, triggering its reactive armor, the sound of the rocket explosion and the armor explosion mingling peculiarly. The tank charged out of the cloud of smoke, scraps of reactive armor dangling from its front like a tattered shirt. The young private was still aiming, his RPG jittering with the tank's rise and fall, too uncertain to fire. Then the tank was just fifty, forty meters away, heading into a dip in the ground, and the private could only stand on the rim of the crater to aim downward.

His RPG and the Abrams's 120 mm gun sounded simultaneously.

The tank gunner had fired a nonexplosive depleted-uranium armor-piercing round in his desperation. With an initial velocity of eight hundred meters per second, it turned the soldier's upper body into a spray of gore upon impact. Kalina felt scraps of blood and meat strike her steel helmet, pitter-pattering. She opened her eyes. Just in front of her, at the edge of the crater, the private's legs were two black tree stumps, soundlessly rolling their way to the bottom of the crater next to her feet. The shattered remains of the rest of his body had spattered a radial pattern of red speckles in the snow.

The rocket had struck the Abrams, the focused jet of the explosion cutting through its armor. Thick smoke billowed from the chassis. But the steel monster was still charging toward them, trailing smoke. It was within twenty meters of them before an explosion from within stopped it in its tracks, hurling the top of its turret sky-high.

The NATO tank line went past them immediately after, the ground trembling under the heavy impact of treads, but these tanks took no interest in their bomb crater. Once the first wave of tanks was past, the lieutenant grabbed Kalina's hand and leapt from the crater, pulling her after him to the side of an already bullet-scarred jeep. Two hundred meters away, the second wave of armored assault was bearing down on them.

"Lie down and play dead!" the lieutenant said. So Kalina lay by the jeep's wheel and closed her eyes. "It looks more realistic with your eyes open!" the lieutenant added, and smeared a handful of somebody's blood on her face. He lay down, too, forming a right angle with Kalina, his head pressing against hers. His helmet had rolled to one side, and his coarse hair pricked at Kalina's temple. She opened her eyes wide, looking at the sky almost swallowed by smoke.

Two or three minutes later, a half-track Bradley infantry fighting vehicle stopped ten or so meters from them. A few American soldiers in blue-and-white snowy terrain camouflage jumped from the convoy. The bulk of them leveled their guns and advanced in a skirmish line. Only one walked toward the jeep. Kalina saw two snow-speckled paratrooper boots step next to her face; she could clearly make out the insignia of the Eighty-second Airborne

Division on the handle of the knife sheathed in his boot. The American crouched down to look at her. Their gazes met, and Kalina tried as hard as she could to make hers blank and lifeless across from that pair of startled blue eyes.

"*Oh, god!*" Kalina heard him exclaim. She didn't know if it was for the beauty of this woman with a major's star on her shoulder, or for the terrible sight of her bloody, dirty face; maybe it was both. He reached a hand to unfasten her collar. Goose bumps rose all over Kalina, and she nudged her hand a few centimeters closer to the pistol in her belt, but the American only tugged the dog tag from her neck.

They had to wait longer than expected. Enemy tanks and armored convoys thundered endlessly past them. Kalina could feel her body freezing almost solid on the snowy ground. It made her think of a couplet from an old army song, of all things. She'd read the words in an old book on Matrosov: "A soldier lies on the snowy ground / like they lie on white swan down." The day she received her Ph.D., she'd written the lines in her diary. That had been a snowy night, too. She'd stood in front of the window on the top floor of Moscow State University's Main Building; that night, the snow really did look like swan down, and through the haze of snow flickered the lights from the thousands of homes of the capital. She'd joined the army the next day.

A jeep stopped not far from them, three NATO officers smoking and conversing inside. But the area around Kalina and the lieutenant was clearing. The two finally rose. They jumped in their own jeep, the lieutenant turned the ignition, and they hurtled along the route planned out earlier. Submachine guns sounded behind them; bullets flew overhead, one shattering a rearview mirror. The jeep whipped into a turn, entering a burning residential area. The enemy hadn't pursued.

"Major, you have a doctorate, right?" the lieutenant said as he drove.

"Where do you know me from?"

"I've seen you with Marshal Levchenko's son."

After a silence, the lieutenant said, "Right now, his son is farther from the war than anyone else in the world."

"What are you implying? You know that—"

"Nothing, I was just saying," the lieutenant said neutrally. Neither of them had their mind on the conversation. They were still lingering on that last thread of hope.

Of the entire battlefront, this might be the only breach.

JANUARY 5TH, NEAR-SUN ORBIT,

ABOARD THE *VECHNYY BURAN*

Misha was experiencing the solitude of a lone inhabitant in an empty city.

The *Vechnyy Buran* really was the size of a small city. The modular space station had a volume equivalent to two supercarriers and could sustain five thousand residents in space at a time. When the complex was under centripetal force simulating gravity, it even contained a pool and a small flowing river. Compared to other space work environments of the day, it smacked of unparalleled extravagance. But in reality, the *Vechnyy Buran* was the product of the thrifty reasoning the Russian space program had demonstrated since Mir. The thinking behind its design went that, although combining all the functionality needed to explore the entire solar system into one structure might require a huge initial investment, it would prove absolutely economical in the long run. Western media jokingly called *Vechnyy Buran* the Swiss Army knife of space: It could serve as a space station orbiting at any height from Earth; it could relocate easily to moon orbit, or make exploratory flights to the other planets. *Vechnyy Buran* had already flown to Venus and Mars and probed the asteroid belt. With its huge capacity, it was like shipping an entire research center into space. In the field of space research, it had an advantage over the legion but dainty Western spaceships.

The war had broken out just as *Vechnyy Buran* was preparing for the three-year expedition to Jupiter. At that time, its over one hundred crew members, most of them air force officers, had left for Earth, leaving only Misha. The *Vechnyy Buran* had revealed a flaw: Militarily, it presented too big a target while possessing no defensive abilities. Failing to foresee the progressive militarization of space had been a mistake on the part of the designer.

Vechnyy Buran could only take avoidance measures. It couldn't depart for farther space, with numerous unmanned NATO satellites patrolling Jupiter's orbital path. They were small, but whether armed or unarmed, any one could pose a deadly threat to the *Vechnyy Buran*.

The only option was to draw near the sun. The automatic active-cooling heat-shielding system that was the pride of the *Vechnyy Buran* allowed it to go closer to the sun than any other man-made object yet. Now the *Vechnyy Buran* had reached Mercury's orbital path, five million kilometers from the sun and one hundred million kilometers from Earth.

Most of the *Vechnyy Buran*'s hold had been closed off, but the area left to Misha was still astonishingly enormous. Through the broad, clear dome ceiling, the sun looked three times larger than it looked on Earth. He could clearly see the sunspots and the singularly beautiful solar prominences emerging from the purple corona; sometimes, he could even see the granules formed by convection in the surface. The serenity here was an illusion. Outside, the sun pitched a raging storm of particles and electromagnetic radiation, and the *Vechnyy Buran* was just a tiny seed in a turbulent ocean.

A gossamer-thin thread of EM waves connected Misha to the Earth, and brought the troubles of that distant world to him as well. He had just been informed that the command center near Moscow had been destroyed by a cruise missile, and that the *Vechnyy Buran*'s control had passed to the secondary command center at Samara. He received the latest news of the war from Earth at five-hour intervals; at those times, each time, he would think of his father.

JANUARY 5TH, RUSSIAN ARMY GENERAL
STAFF HEADQUARTERS

Marshal Mikhail Semyonovich Levchenko felt as if he were face-to-face with a wall, though in reality, a holographic map of the Moscow theater of war lay in front of him. Conversely, when he turned toward the big paper map hanging on the wall, he could see breadth and depth, a sense of space.

No matter what, he preferred traditional maps. He didn't know how many times he'd sought a location on the very bottom of the map, forcing him and his strategists to get on hands and knees; the thought now made him smile a little. He also remembered spending the eve of military exercises in his battlefield tent, piecing together the newly received battle maps with clear tape. He always made a mess of it, but his son had done the taping neater than he ever did, that first time he came along to watch the exercises. . . .

Finding that his musings had returned to the subject of his son, the marshal vigilantly cut off his train of thought.

He and the commander of the Western Military District were the only people in the war room, the latter chain-smoking cigarettes as they watched the shifting clouds of smoke above the holographic map, their gaze as intent as if it were the grim battlefield itself.

The district commander said: "NATO has seventy-five divisions along the Smolensk front now. The battlefront is a hundred kilometers long. They've breached the line at multiple points."

"And the eastern front?" Marshal Levchenko asked.

"Most of our Eleventh Army defected to the Rightists too, as you know. The Rightist army is now twenty-four divisions strong, but their assaults on Yaroslavl remain exploratory in nature."

The earth shook with the faint vibrations of some ground explosion. The lights hanging from the ceiling cast swaying shadows around the war room.

"There's talk now of retreating to Moscow and using the barricades and fortifications for a street-to-street battle, like seventy-odd years ago."

"That's absurd! If we withdraw from the western front, NATO can swing north around us to join forces with the Rightists at Tver. Moscow would fall into panic without them lifting a finger. We have three options in our playbook right now: counterattack, counterattack, and counterattack."

The district commander sighed, looking wordlessly at the map.

Marshal Levchenko continued, "I know the western front isn't strong enough. I plan to relocate an army from the eastern front to strengthen it."

"What? But it's already going to be a challenge to defend Yaroslavl."

Marshal Levchenko chuckled. "Nowadays, the problem with many commanders is their tendency to only consider a problem from the military angle.

They can't see beyond the grim tactical situation. Looking at the current situation, do you think the Rightists lack the strength to take Yaroslavl?"

"I don't think so. The Fourteenth Army is an elite force with a high concentration of armored vehicles and low-altitude attack power. For them to advance less than fifteen kilometers a day while not having suffered serious setbacks seems like taking things slow on purpose."

"That's right, they're watching and waiting. They're watching the western front! And if we can take back the initiative in the western front, they'll keep on watching and waiting. They might even independently negotiate a cease-fire."

The district commander held his newest cigarette in his hand, but had forgotten all thoughts of lighting it.

"The defection of the armies on the eastern front really was a knife in our back, but some commanders have turned this into an excuse in their minds to steer us toward passive operational policies. That has to change! Of course, it must be said that our current strength in the Moscow region isn't enough for a total turnaround. Our hope lies in the relief forces from the Caucasus and Ural districts."

"The closer Caucasus forces will need at least a week to assemble and advance into place. If we account for possession of the airspace, it might take even longer."

JANUARY 5TH, MOSCOW

It was past three in the afternoon when Kalina and the first lieutenant entered the city in their jeep. The air raid alarm had just sounded, and the streets were empty.

"I miss my T-90 already, Major," sighed the lieutenant. "I finished armored-vehicle training right around the time I broke up with my girlfriend, but the moment I arrived at my unit and saw that tank, my heart soared right back up again. I put my hand on its armor, and it was smooth and warm, like touching a lover's hand. Ha, what was that relationship worth! Now I'd found a real love! But it took a Mistral missile this morning." He sighed again. "It might still be burning."

At that time they heard dense explosions from the northwest, a savage area bombing rare in modern aerial warfare.

The lieutenant was still wallowing in the morning's engagement. "Less than thirty seconds, and the whole tank company was gone."

"The enemy losses were heavy, too," Kalina said. "I observed the aftermath. There were about the same number of destroyed vehicles on each side."

"The ratio of destroyed tanks was about 1 to 1.2, I think. The helicopters were worse off, but it wouldn't have gone over 1 to 1.4."

"In that case, the battlefield initiative should have stayed on our side. We have a sizable advantage in numbers. How did the battle end up like this?"

The lieutenant turned to eye Kalina. "You're one of the electronic-warfare people. Don't you get it? All your toys—the fifth-generation C3I, the 3-D battle displays, the dynamic situation simulators, the attack-plan optimizer, whatever—looked great in the mock battles. But on the real battlefield, all the screen in front of me ever showed was 'COMMUNICATION ERROR' and 'COULD NOT LOG IN.' Take this morning, for example. I didn't have a clue what was happening in the front and flanks. I only got one order: 'Engage the enemy.' Ah, if we'd only had half our force again in reinforcements, the enemy wouldn't have broken through our position. It was probably the same way all down the line."

Kalina knew that in the battle that had just ended, the two sides had sent perhaps over ten thousand tanks into battle along the front, and half as many armed helicopters.

At that point they arrived at Arbat Street. The popular pedestrian boulevard of yesteryear was empty now, sandbags walling off the entrances to the antiques shops and artisans' places.

"My steel darling gave as good as she got." The lieutenant was still stuck on the morning's battle. "I'm sure I hit a Challenger tank. But most of all, I'd wanted to take down an Abrams, you know? An Abrams . . ."

Kalina pointed to the entrance of the antiques store they had just passed. "There. My grandfather died there."

"But I don't remember any bombs getting dropped here."

"I'm talking about twenty years ago—I was only four then. The winter that year was bitterly cold. The heating was cut off, and ice formed in the rooms. I wrapped myself around the TV for warmth, listening to the president promise the Russian people a gentle winter. I screamed and cried that I was cold, hungry.

"My grandfather looked at me silently, and finally he made up his mind. He took out his treasured military medal and took me here. This was a free market, where you could sell anything, from vodka to political views. An American wanted my grandfather's medal, but he was only willing to pay forty dollars. He said Order of the Red Star and Order of the Red Banner medals weren't worth anything, but he'd pay a hundred dollars for an Order of Bogdan Khmelnitsky, a hundred fifty for an Order of Glory, two hundred for an Order of Nakhimov, two hundred fifty for an Order of Ushakov. *Order of Victories are worth the most, but of course you wouldn't have one, those were only given to generals.* But Order of Suvorovs were worth a lot too, he'd pay four hundred fifty dollars for one. . . . My grandfather walked away then. We walked and walked along Arbat Street in the freezing cold. Then my grandfather couldn't walk anymore. The sky was almost dark. He sat heavily on the steps of that antiques store and told me to go home without him. The next day, they found him frozen to death there, his hand reaching into his jacket to clench the medal he'd earned with his own blood. His eyes were wide open, looking at the city he'd saved from Guderian's tanks fifty years ago. . . ."

JANUARY 5TH, RUSSIAN ARMY GENERAL

STAFF HEADQUARTERS

Marshal Levchenko left the underground war room for the first time in a week. He walked in the thick snowfall, searching for the sun, half set behind the snow-draped pinewoods. In his mind's eye, he saw a small black dot slowly moving against the orange setting sun: the *Vechnyy Burun*, with his son inside, farther than any other son from a father.

It had led to many ugly rumors within his homeland, and the enemy utilized it even more fully abroad. *The New York Times* had printed its headline in black type sized for shock: NO DESERTER HAS RUN FARTHER. Below was a photo of Misha, captioned "At a time when the communist regime is agitating three hundred million Russians for a bloodbath defense against the 'invaders,' the son of their marshal has fled the war aboard the nation's only massive-scale spacecraft. Sixty million miles from the battlefield, he is safer than any other of his fellow citizens."

But Marshal Levchenko didn't take it to heart. From secondary school to postgraduate studies, almost none of Misha's associates had known who his father was. The space program command center made its decision solely because Misha's field of study happened to be the mathematical modeling of stars. The *Vechnyy Buran* approaching the sun was a rare opportunity for his research, and the space complex couldn't be entirely piloted by remote control, requiring at least one person aboard. The general learned of Misha's background only later, from the Western news media.

On the other hand, whether Marshal Levchenko admitted it or not, deep down inside, he really did hope his son could stay away from the war. It wasn't solely a matter of blood ties; Marshal Levchenko had always felt that his son wasn't meant for war—perhaps he was the least meant for war of all the world's people. But he knew his notion was faulty: was anyone truly meant for war?

Besides, was Misha truly suited for the stars either? He liked stars, had devoted his life to their research, but he himself was the opposite of a star. He was more like Pluto, the silent and cold dwarf planet orbiting in its distant void, out of sight of the mortal realm. Misha was quiet and graceful. Solitude was his nourishment and air.

Misha was born in East Germany, and the day he was born was the darkest day in the marshal's life. He was only a major that evening in West Berlin, standing guard with his soldiers in front of the Soviet War Memorial in the Tiergarten, keeping vigil for the fallen for the last time in forty years. In front of them were a gaggle of grinning Western officers; and a few slovenly, shiftless German police officers trailing wolfhounds on leashes to replace them; and the skinhead neo-Nazis hollering "Red Army Go Home." Behind him were the tear-filled eyes of the senior company commander and soldiers. He couldn't help himself; he, too, let tears blur all this away.

He returned to the emptied barracks after dark. On this last night before he left for home, he was notified that Misha had been born, but that his wife had died of complications from childbirth.

His life after he returned was difficult, too. Like the 400,000 army men and 120,000 administrators withdrawn from Europe, he had no home to go to, and lived with Misha in a temporary shack of metal sheets, freezing in winter and broiling in summer. His old colleagues would do any work for a living, some becoming gun runners for the gangs, some reduced to strip dances at nightclubs. But he stuck to his honest soldier's life, and Misha quietly grew up amid the hardship. He wasn't like the other children; he seemed to have been born with an innate ability to endure, because he had a world of his own.

As early as primary school, Misha would quietly spend the entire night alone in his small room. Levchenko had thought he was reading at first, but by chance he discovered that his son was standing in front of the window, unmoving, watching the stars.

"Papa, I like the stars. I want to look at them all my life," he told his father.

On his eleventh birthday, Misha asked his father for a present for the first time: a telescope. He'd been using Levchenko's military binoculars to stargaze before then. Afterward, the telescope became Misha's only companion. He could stand on the balcony and watch the stars until the sky lightened in the east. A few times, father and son stargazed together. The marshal always turned the telescope toward the brightest-looking star, but his son would shake his head disapprovingly. "That one's not interesting, Papa. That's Venus. Venus is a planet, but I only like stars."

Misha didn't like any of the things that the other kids liked, either. The neighbor's boy, son of the old paratrooper chief of staff, snuck out his father's pistol to play with, and ended up shooting his own leg by accident. The general of the staff's children thought no reward better than their papa taking them to the company firing range and letting them take a shot. But that affinity seemed to have completely skipped over Misha.

Levchenko found his son's apathy for weapons unsettling, almost intolerable, to the point where he reacted in a way that embarrassed him to think of to this day: Once, he'd quietly set his Makarov semiautomatic on his son's writing desk. Not long after he returned from school, Misha came out of his room with the pistol. He held it like a child, his hand closed carefully around the barrel. He set the gun gently in front of his father and said, evenly, "Papa, be careful where you put it next time."

On the topic of Misha's future, the marshal was an understanding man. He wasn't like the other generals around him, determined that their sons and daughters would succeed them in the military. But Misha really was too distant from his father's work.

Marshal Levchenko wasn't a hot-tempered man, but as the commander in chief of the armies, he'd castigated more than one general in front of thousands of troops. He'd never lost his temper at Misha, though. Misha walked silently and steadily along his chosen path, giving his father little cause for concern. More importantly, Misha seemed to be born with an extraordinary aloofness from the world that at times elicited even Levchenko's reverence. It was as if he'd carelessly tossed a seed into a flowerpot only for a rare and exotic plant to sprout. He had watched this plant grow day by day, protecting it carefully, awaiting its flowering. His hopes had not fallen short. His son was now the most renowned astrophysicist in the world.

By this time, the sun had entirely set behind the pine forest, the white snow on the ground turning pale blue. Marshal Levchenko collected his thoughts and returned to the underground war room. All the personnel for the war meeting had arrived, including important commanders from the Western and Caucasus military districts.

Outnumbering them were the electronic-warfare commanders, all the ranks from captain to major general, most newly returned from the front. In the war room, a debate was raging between the Western Military District's ground- and electronic-warfare officers.

"We correctly determined the enemy assault's change in direction," Major

General Felitov of the Taman Division said. "Our tanks and close air support had no problems with maneuverability. But the communications system was jammed beyond belief. The C3I system was almost paralyzed! We expanded the electronic-warfare unit from a battalion to a division, from a division to a corps, and invested more money in them these two years than we invested in all the regular equipment. And we get this?!"

One of the lieutenant generals commanding electronic warfare in the region glanced at Kalina. Like all the other officers newly returned from the front line, her camo uniform was stained and scorched, and traces of blood still stuck to her face. "Major Kalina has done noteworthy work in electronic-warfare research, and was sent by the General Staff to observe the electronic battle. Perhaps her insights may better persuade you." Young Ph.D. officers like Kalina tended to be fearlessly outspoken toward superiors. They were often used as mouthpieces for tough words, and this was no exception.

Kalina stood. "General Felitov, that's hardly the case! Compared to NATO, the investment we've put into our C3I is nothing."

"What about electronic countermeasures?" the major general asked. "If the enemy can jam us, can't you jam them? Our C3I was useless, but NATO's worked like the wheels were greased. Just look at how quickly the enemy was able to change the direction of their attack this morning!"

Kalina gave a pained smile. "Speaking of jamming the enemy, General Felitov, don't forget that in your sector, your people forced their own electronic-warfare unit to turn off their jammers at gunpoint!"

"What happened out there?" Marshal Levchenko asked. Only then did the others notice his arrival and stand to bow.

"It was like this," the major general explained. "Their jamming was worse for our own communication and command system than NATO's! We could still maintain some wireless transmission through NATO's jamming. But once our forces turned on their own jammers, we were completely smothered!"

"But don't forget, the enemy would have been completely smothered too!" Kalina said. "Given our army's available electronic countermeasures, this was the only possible strategy. At this time, NATO has already widely adopted technologies like frequency hopping, direct-sequence spread spectrum, adaptive nulling systems, burst transmission, and frequency agility.* Our frequency-specific aimed jamming was completely useless. Full-spectrum barrage jamming was our only option."

A colonel from the Fifth Army spoke up. "Major, NATO exclusively uses frequency-specific aimed jamming too, with a fairly narrow range of frequencies. And our C3I system widely incorporates the technologies you mentioned as well. Why would their jamming be so effective against us?"

"That's easy. What systems are our C3I built upon? Unix, Linux, even Windows 2010, and our CPUs are made by Intel and AMD! We're using the dogs they raised to guard our own gate! Under these circumstances, the enemy can quickly figure out, say, the frequency-hopping patterns used for our intelligence reports, while using more numerous and more effective software attacks to strengthen the effects of their jamming. The Main Command suggested the widespread adoption of a Russian-made operating system in the past, but met heavy opposition from the ranks. Your division was the most stubborn holdout of all—"

"Yes, yes, we're here today to resolve precisely that problem and conflict," Marshal Levchenko interrupted. "I call this meeting to order!"

Once everyone was seated in front of the digital battle simulator, Marshal Levchenko called over a staff officer. The young major was tall and skinny, his eyes squinted into slits, as if they had trouble adjusting to the war room's brightness. "Let me introduce Major Bondarenko. His most obvious trait is his severe myopia. His glasses are different from other people's—their lenses rest inside the frame, while his stick out. Ha, they're as thick as the bottom of

---

* A simplified explanation of the electronic battle vocabulary:

Frequency hopping: The transmitter switches carrier frequencies according to a pattern possessed by the receiver.

Direct-sequence spread spectrum: The signal is distributed across a wide range of frequencies to make eavesdropping and jamming difficult.

Adaptive nulling system: An antenna array that nulls out signals coming from the direction of enemy jamming, allowing it to communicate with ally antennae in other directions.

Burst transmission: Transmitting data at a high rate over a short period of time using a wider-than-average frequency range.

Frequency agility: The signal is capable of rapidly and continuously changing frequency to avoid jamming.

a teacup! This morning they got smashed when the major's jeep was hit in an airstrike, which is why we don't see them now. I think he lost his contacts too?"

"Marshal, it was five days ago at Minsk. My eyes only became like this in the last half year. If it happened earlier, I wouldn't have been admitted into Frunze Military Academy," the major said stolidly.

No one knew why the marshal had chosen to introduce the major like this, though a few chuckled in the audience.

"Since the beginning of the war," the marshal continued, "events have shown that despite Russian losses on the battlefield, our aerial and ground weapons aren't far behind the enemy's. But in the field of electronic warfare, we've been unexpectedly left in the dust. Many events in the past contributed to this situation, but we're not here to point fingers. We're here to state this: In our situation, electronic warfare is the key to taking back the initiative in the war! We must first admit that the enemy has an advantage in this area, perhaps an overwhelming advantage. Then we must work within our army's hardware and software limitations to create an effective plan of battle. The goal of this plan is to even out our and NATO's electronic-warfare capabilities within a short period of time. Maybe you all think this is impossible—our military planning since the end of the last century has been based on the assumption of a limited-scope war. We really haven't done enough research for an invasion on all fronts by as powerful an enemy as the one we're facing right now. In our dire situation, we have to think in a completely new way. The central command's new electronic-warfare strategy, which I'm introducing next, will demonstrate the results of this mode of thinking."

The lights went out, the computer screens and digital battle simulator dimmed, and the heavy anti-radiation doors shut tightly. The war room was plunged into total darkness.

"I had the lights turned off." The marshal's voice came through the darkness.

A minute passed in dark and silence.

"How's everyone feeling?" Marshal Levchenko asked.

No one answered. The cloying darkness left the officers feeling as if they were at the bottom of a dark sea. It even felt hard to breathe.

"General Andreyev, tell it to us."

"Like it felt on the battlefield these few days," the commander of the Fifth Army said, eliciting a wave of quiet laughter from the darkness.

"Everyone else empathizes with him, I think," said the marshal. "Of course you do! Think of it—nothing but static in your headsets, solid white on your screens, not a clue as to your orders or the battlefield around you. That same feeling! The darkness presses down until you can't breathe!

"But not everyone feels like that. How are you, Major Bondarenko?" asked Marshal Levchenko.

Major Bondarenko's voice came from one corner of the room. "It's not so bad for me. Everything was a blur around me anyway back when the lights were on."

"Maybe you even feel an advantage?" asked Marshal Levchenko.

"Yes, sir. You may have heard the story of the New York blackout, where blind people led everyone out of the skyscrapers."

"But General Andreyev's sentiments are understandable. He's eagle-eyed, a legendary marksman—when he drinks, he uses his revolver to take the caps off his bottles at ten-odd meters. Wouldn't it be interesting to picture him having a gun duel with Major Bondarenko at this moment?"

The darkened war room once again sank into silence as the officers considered this.

The lights turned on. Everyone narrowed their eyes, less because of the discomfort of the sudden brightness, and more for the shock of what the marshal had just implied.

Marshal Levchenko stood up. "I think I've explained our army's new electronic-warfare strategy: large-scale, full-spectrum barrage jamming. With regard to EM communications, we're going to let both sides enjoy a blacked-out battlefield!"

"This will cause our own battlefield command system to completely break down!" someone said fearfully.

"NATO's will too! If we're going to be blind, let's both be blind. If we're going to be deaf, let's both be deaf. We can then reach equal footing with the enemy's electronic-warfare capabilities. This is the central tenet of our new strategy."

"But what are we supposed to do now, send messengers on motorcycles to transmit orders?"

"If the roads are bad, they'll have to ride horses," Marshal Levchenko said. "Our rough prediction shows that this kind of full-spectrum barrage jamming will cover at least seventy percent of NATO's battlefield communication network, meaning that their C3I system will suffer a complete breakdown. Simultaneously, we'll be leaving fifty to sixty percent of the enemy's long-range weapons useless. The best example is with the Tomahawk satellite-guided missile. Missile guidance has changed a lot since last century. Before, it primarily navigated using onboard TERCOM with a small-scale radar altimeter, but now these methods are only used in end-stage guidance, while most of the launch process relies on a GPS system. General Dynamics and McDonnell Douglas Corporation thought this change was a big step forward, but the Americans trust their EM wave guidance from space too well. Once we disrupt the GPS transmission, the Tomahawk will be blind. The dependency on GPS exists in most of NATO's long-range weapons. Under the battlefield conditions we've planned, we'll force the enemy into a traditional battle, allowing us to fully utilize our strengths."

"I'm still unsure about this," the commander of the Twelfth Army sent from the eastern front said anxiously. "Under these battlefield communication conditions, I'm not even sure my division can smoothly reach the western front from the east."

"Of course it will!" said Marshal Levchenko. "The distance was nothing even for Kutuzov, in Napoleon's time. I don't believe the Russian army needs wireless to do it today! The Americans should be the ones spoiled rotten by modern equipment, not us. I know that an EM blackout over all the battlefield will put fear in your hearts. But you have to remember, the enemy will feel ten times your fear!"

Watching Kalina disappear among the other camo-clad officers as they exited the war room, Marshal Levchenko felt apprehension rise in his heart. She was returning to the front, and her unit was stationed right in the middle of the enemy's most concentrated firepower. Yesterday, during his five minutes of communication with his son a hundred million miles away, the marshal had told him that Kalina was perfectly well. But she nearly hadn't come back from this morning's battle.

Misha and Kalina had met at one of the military exercises. The marshal had been eating dinner with his son one night, silently as usual, Misha's late mother looking on from her picture frame. Suddenly, Misha had said, "Papa, I recall that tomorrow is your fifty-first birthday. I should give you a gift. I thought of it when I saw the telescope; that was a wonderful present."

"How about you give me a few days of your time?"

Son quietly raised his head to look at father.

"You have your own work, and I'm happy for you. But surely it's not un-reasonable for a father to want his son to understand his life's work! How about you come with me to observe the military exercises?"

Misha smiled and nodded. He smiled very rarely.

It had been the largest Russian war game of the century. Misha showed little interest in the torrent of steel-armored vehicles rumbling past them on the highway that night before it started; the moment he was off the helicop-ter, he ducked into the tent to assemble the newly arrived battle maps with clear tape in his father's stead. The next day, Misha didn't show the slightest interest through all the exercises. Marshal Levchenko had expected that. But one incident gave him all the reassurance he could ever want.

The exercise scheduled for the morning was a tank division assaulting high ground; Misha sat with some local officials on the north side of the observation station. The station was safely out of range, but in order to sat-isfy the curiosity of the local officials, it had been placed much closer to the action than before.

Tu-22 bombers soared in formation above, heavy aerial bombs fell like rain, and the hilltop exploded into an erupting volcano. Only then did the officials understand the difference between movies and a real battle-field. As the ground quaked and the hill shook, they pressed themselves flat against the table and covered their heads with their arms, some even crawling under the table with shrieks. But the marshal saw that Misha alone sat with his back straight, the same cool expression on his face, calmly watching the terrible volcano as the light of the explosions flashed across his sunglasses. Warmth flooded into Levchenko's heart then. In the end, son, you have a soldier's blood in your veins!

That night, father and son walked along the practice field. In the distance, the headlamps of armored vehicles densely sprinkled the valleys and plains with stars. The faint smell of gunpowder smoke still lingered in the air.

"How much did it cost?" Misha asked.

"The direct cost was about three hundred million rubles."

Misha sighed. "Our task group wanted a third-generation evolving star model to work with. We couldn't get a grant of three hundred fifty thousand for expenses."

Marshal Levchenko at last said what he'd long wanted to tell his son. "Our two worlds are too far apart. Your stars are all four light-years away at the least, yes? They don't have any bearing on the armies and wars on Earth. I can't claim to know much about what you do, though I'm very proud of you all the same. But as an army man, I just want my son to appreciate my own profession. What father wouldn't feel the greatest happiness telling his son about his campaigns? But you've never cared for my work, when really, it's the foundation and safeguard for your own. Without an army strong enough and big enough to keep the country safe, fundamental science research like yours would be impossible."

"You've got it backward, Papa. If everyone were like us and spent all their life on exploring the universe, they'd understand its beauty, the beauty that lies behind its vastness and depth. And someone who truly understood the innate beauty of space and nature would never go to war."

"That thinking's as childish as you can get. If appreciation of beauty could prevent war, we'd never be short of peace!"

"Do you think it's easy for humanity to understand this kind of beauty?" Misha pointed at the night sky, a sea of shining stars. "Look at these stars. Everyone knows they're beautiful, but how many grasp the deepest nuances of their beauty? All these countless celestial bodies are so glorious in their metamorphosis from nebula to black hole, so vast and terrible in their explosive power. But do you know that a few elegant equations can accurately describe all of it? Mathematical models created from the equations can near perfectly predict everything a star does. Even mathematical models of our own planet's atmosphere are orders of magnitude less precise."

Marshal Levchenko nodded. "I can believe that. They say humanity knows more about the moon than the bottom of Earth's oceans. But the deeper beauty in space and nature you talk about still can't stop wars. No one could have understood that beauty more than Einstein, and didn't he advise the creation of the atomic bomb?"

"Einstein made little progress in his later research, largely because he became too involved in politics. I won't go down the same path as him. But, Papa, when it's necessary, I'll do my duty too."

Misha observed the exercise for five days. The marshal didn't know when his son first met Kalina; the first time he saw them together, they were already conversing on familiar terms. They were talking about stars, about which Kalina knew a considerable amount. Seeing an untried youngster like Kalina already wearing a major's star for her Ph.D. left the marshal feeling a little offended, but other than that, she'd made a fine first impression.

The second time Marshal Levchenko saw Misha and Kalina together, he discovered there was already a deep sense of closeness between them. Their topic of conversation surprised him: electronic warfare. They were standing by a tank parked not far from the marshal's jeep. Due to their topic of conversation, they didn't seem concerned with privacy.

The marshal heard Misha say: "Right now, your department has been focusing on only high-level pure software like the C3I, virus programs, the digital battlefield, and so on. But have you considered that this might leave you holding a wooden sword?" Seeing Kalina's surprise, Misha continued, "Have you put thought into the foundation they're built upon? The physical layer at the bottom of the seven layers of protocol defined by the Open Systems Interconnection model? Civilian networks can use fiber optics, fixed lasers, and the like for media and communication. But the terminals in a military-use C3I network are fast-moving and unpredictably located, so only EM waves can keep them in communication. And you know how EM waves are as fragile as thin ice under jamming. . . ."

The marshal was quite shocked. He'd never talked about these things with Misha, and his son would never have snuck a look at his classified documents, but here Misha had neatly and clearly laid out the same considerations that he'd come up with over the years!

Misha's words had an even greater impact on Kalina. She even shifted the direction of her own research to create an electromagnetic jamming unit code-named "Flood." It fit into an armored vehicle, and could simultaneously emit strong EM jamming waves ranging from three kilohertz to thirty gigahertz, drowning out all EM communication signals outside the millimeter radio range.

The first weapons test at one of the Siberian bases had sent a whole swarm of officials running over to protest. Flood had cut off all EM wave-based communication in the nearby city: cell phones found no reception, pagers fell silent, televisions and radios lost all signal. The impact on finance and stocks was disastrous; the local officials claimed astronomical losses.

Flood was inspired by a type of EMP bomb that utilized high explosives to create a powerful electromagnetic pulse within a one-use wire coil. As a result, Flood created shock waves like a rocket engine, shattering nearby windows in its trial. This meant that it could only be remotely operated, and its crew had to wear anti-microwave-radiation protective gear even though they were two or three kilometers away.

Flood had raised fierce debate in the armaments department and the electronic-warfare command. Many thought that it had no practical value; using it in a limited-scope battlefield would be like using a nuclear bomb in a street-to-street battle, devastating friend and foe alike. But under the marshal's insistence, two hundred Flood units had been mass-produced. Now, in the central command's new electronic-warfare strategy, it would take center stage.

That his son had fallen for a woman in the army had deeply surprised Marshal Levchenko. He assumed at the time that Misha's feelings for Kalina overlooked her occupation. But Misha later brought Kalina home on a few occasions. The first time, Kalina wore a pretty dress; when Marshal Levchenko walked close, he overheard Misha tell her, "You don't have to dress up for us. Wear your uniform next time, I know you feel more comfortable in it." That disproved the marshal's original theory. Now he understood that Misha fell for Kalina to some extent because she was a major in the army. He felt again what he felt that first morning of war training. The major's star on Kalina's shoulder now seemed incomparably beautiful.

JANUARY 6TH, MOSCOW THEATER OF OPERATIONS

Powerful electromagnetic waves gathered rapidly above the battlefield, at last becoming a mighty typhoon. After the war, people would reminisce: In the mountain villages far from the front line, they saw the animals fidget and stir, agitated; in the city with its enforced blackout, they saw induction trigger tiny sparks along the telephone wires.

As part of the Twelfth Army transferring from the eastern front to the west, the armored-car corps was advancing urgently. Their lieutenant general stood by his jeep parked at the roadside, watching his troops hasten through the snow and dust with satisfaction. The enemy's air raids had been far less intense than predicted, allowing his forces to travel by day.

Three Tomahawk missiles tore overhead, the low buzz of their jet engines crisp in the air. A moment later, three explosions sounded in the distance. The correspondent by the lieutenant general's side, his static-filled earpiece useless, turned to look in the direction of the explosion. He cried out in surprise. The general told him not to make a big deal out of nothing, but then a battalion commander beside him urged him to look, too. So he looked, and shook his head in confusion. Tomahawks weren't 100 percent accurate, but for three to land in an empty field, more than a kilometer from each other, really was a rare sight.

Two Su-27s flew five kilometers above the battlefield in an empty sky. They had belonged to a larger fighter squadron, but it had run into a skirmish with a NATO F-22 squadron above the sea, and the planes lost contact with the others in the turmoil of battle. Normally, regrouping would have been easy, but now the radio was down. The airspace that had seemed so small as to be cramped to a high-speed fighter plane now seemed as vast as outer space. Regrouping would be like finding a needle in a haystack. The lead pilot and his wingman were forced to fly wingtip-to-wingtip like stunt fliers to hear each other's wireless messages.

"Suspicious object to the upper left, azimuth 220, altitude 30!" the wingman reported. The lead pilot looked in that direction. The earlier snow had washed the winter sky clean and blue, and the visibility was excellent. The two planes ascended toward the target to investigate. It was flying in the same direction as them, but much slower, and it didn't take long to catch up.

Their first good look at the target was a bolt out of the blue.

That was a NATO E-4A early-warning aircraft. For a fighter-plane pilot to encounter one was like seeing the back of their own head. An E-4A could monitor up to one million square kilometers, completing a full sweep in just five seconds. It could locate targets two thousand kilometers from the defensive area, providing more than forty minutes of advance notice. It could separate out up to a thousand EM signals within one thousand to two thousand kilometers, and each scan could query and identify two thousand targets of any kind, land, sky, or sea. An early-warning aircraft didn't need the protection of escorts when its all-seeing eyes allowed it to easily avoid any threats.

That was why the lead pilot naturally assumed it was a trap. He and the wingman searched the surrounding sky carefully, but there was nothing in the cold, clear sky. The lead pilot decided to take a risk.

"Ball lightning, ball lightning, I'm going to attack. Guard azimuth 317, but be careful not to leave range of sight!"

Once his wingman flew in the direction he thought most likely for an ambush, he activated the afterburner and yanked at the controllers. Trailing black exhaust, the Su-27 lunged toward the early-warning aircraft above like a striking cobra. Now the E-4A discovered the approaching threat and turned to rush southeast in an escape maneuver. Magnesium heat pellets popped from its tail one after another to disrupt heat-seeking missiles, the trail of little fireballs looking like bits of its soul startled out of its mortal shell. An early-warning aircraft before a fighter plane was as helpless as a bicycle trying to outrun a motorbike. In that moment, the lead pilot decided that the order he'd given the wingman had turned out to be terribly selfish.

He followed the E-4A from above at a distance, admiring the prey he'd caught. The pale blue radar dome atop the E-4A was lovely in its curves, charming as a Christmas ornament; its broad white chassis was like a fat roast duck on its platter: so tempting, yet too lovely to violate with knife and fork. But instinct warned him not to drag this on any longer. He first fired a burst with the 20 mm cannon, shattering the radome, and watched scraps of the Westinghouse-made AN/ZPY-3 radar antenna scatter across the sky like silver Christmas confetti. He next severed a wing with the cannon, then at last lashed down the fatal blow with the 6,000 rpm double-barreled cannon, cutting the already tumbling and falling E-4A in two.

The Su-27 wheeled downward to follow the halves in their plunging descent. The pilot watched crew and equipment fall from the hold like chocolates from a box, a few parachutes blooming against the sky. He remembered the battle earlier, the sight of his comrade escaping from his hit plane: an F-22 had purposely flown low over the parachute, swooping past, three times, to knock it over. He'd watched as his comrade dropped like a stone, disappearing against the white backdrop of the ground.

He forced back the impulse to do something similar. Once he regrouped with his wingman, the pair abandoned the area at top speed.

They still suspected a trap.

The two weren't the only aircraft separated from their unit. A Comanche armed attack helicopter from the US Army First Cavalry Division flew with no target in sight, but its pilot, Lieutenant Walker, felt a rush of adrenaline all the same. He'd transferred from an Apache to the Comanche recently, and had yet to adjust to this sort of attack helicopter with troop-carrying capabilities, an innovation from the end of the previous century. He was unaccustomed to the Comanche's lack of foot pedals, and he thought the headset with its binocular helmet-mounted display wasn't as comfortable to use as the Apache's single sight. But most of all, he wasn't used to Captain Haney, the forward director sitting in front of him.

"You need to know your place, Lieutenant," Haney had told him the first time they met. "I'm the brain controlling this helicopter. You're a cogwheel in its machinery, and you're going to act like one!" And Walker hated nothing more than that.

He remembered the retired navy pilot who'd toured their base, a WWII vet pushing a hundred years old. He had shaken his head when he saw the Comanche's cockpit. "Oh, you kids. My P-51 Mustang back in the day had a simpler control panel than a microwave today, and that was the finest control panel I ever used!" He patted Walker's ass. "The difference between our generations of pilots is the difference between knights of the sky and computer operators."

Walker had wanted to be a knight of the sky. Here was his opportunity. Under the Russians' berserk jamming, the helicopter's combat mission integration system, the target analysis system, the auxiliary target examination and classification system, the RealSight situation imager, the resource burst system, whatever, they were all fucking fried! All that was left was the two 1,000-horsepower T800 engines, still loyally churning away. Haney normally earned his spot with his electronic gewgaws, but now his incessant orders had gone silent with them.

Haney's voice came through the internal mic system. "Attention, I've found a target. It seems to be to the left and front, maybe by that little hill. There's an armored-car unit that seems to be the enemy's. You . . . do what you can."

Walker nearly laughed aloud. Ha, that bastard. What he would have said in the past was, "I've found a target at azimuth 133. Seventeen 90-series tanks, twenty-one 89-series soldier convoys, moving toward azimuth 391 at an average speed of 43.5 klicks per hour and an average separation of 31.4 meters. Execute the AJ041 optimized attack plan and approach from azimuth 179 at a vertical angle of 37 degrees." And now? "It 'seems' to be an armored-car unit, 'maybe by' that little hill." *Who the hell needed you to say that? I saw it ages ago! Leave it to me, because you're useless now, Haney. This is*

my battle, and I'm going to use my ass for an accelerometer and be a knight! This
Comanche's gonna fight like its namesake in my hands.

The Comanche charged toward its open target and launched all sixty-two 27.5-inch Hornet missiles. Walker watched rapt as his swarm of fire-stingered little bees buzzed happily toward their target, swamping the enemy in a sea of fire. But when he turned to fly over the results of the encounter, he realized that something was wrong. The soldiers on the ground hadn't tried to conceal themselves. Instead, they stood in the snow, pointing at him. They seemed to be cussing him out.

Walker flew closer and clearly saw the destroyed armored car's insignia for himself: three concentric circles, blue at the center, white in the middle, red on the outside. Walker felt as if he'd dropped into hell. He started cussing, too.

"You son of a bitch, are you blind?!"

But he still had the wisdom to fly away in case the enraged French returned fire. "You son of a bitch, you're probably thinking of how to pin the blame on me in military court right this moment. I'm telling you here, you won't get away with this. You were the one in charge of identifying targets, are you clear?"

"Maybe . . . maybe we'll still have the chance to make up for our mistake," Haney said timidly. "I found another unit, right across—"

"Fuck you!" Walker said.

"They're definitely the enemy's this time! They're exchanging fire with the French!"

Walker perked up at that. He steered toward the new target and saw that the enemy force was primarily infantry without much armored-vehicle strength. This did support Haney's assessment. Walker launched his last four Hellfire missiles, then set his double-barreled Gatling gun to 1,500 rpm and started shooting. He felt the comfortable vibration of the machine gun through the chassis, watching as it scattered snow and powder like ground white pepper over the enemy skirmish line on the ground. But the intuition of a veteran armed helicopter pilot warned him of danger. He turned, only to see a soldier standing on a jeep fire a shoulder-mounted rocket launcher to his left.

Walker frantically shot off magnesium heat pellets as lures and swung backward for evasive maneuvers, but too late. The missile, trailing cobwebs of white smoke, had punched into the Comanche right under the nose.

When Walker woke from his brief explosion-induced concussion, he found that the helicopter had crashed in the snow. Walker scrambled desperately from the smoke-filled interior, bracing himself against a tree that had been severed neatly at waist height by the propeller. When he looked back, he could see the remains of Captain Haney in the front seat, blasted into a pulp by the explosion. When he looked forward, he saw a band of soldiers running toward him with submachine guns raised, their Slavic features clear.

Shaking, Walker dug out his handgun and set it on the snow in front of him. He dug out his Russian phrase book and began to clumsily read out his surrender.

"Y-ya postavil svoye oruzhiye. Ya voyennoplennym. V Zhenevskoy konventsii—"

Walker took a gun butt to the back of his head, then a boot to his belly. But as he collapsed into the snow, he was laughing. They might beat him half to death, but only half. He'd seen the eagle insignia of the Polish army on the soldiers' collars.

JANUARY 7TH, MINSK,
NATO COMBAT OPERATIONS CENTER

"Get that goddamn doctor over here!" General Tony Baker roared.

The gangly military doctor ran over.

"What the hell went wrong?" Baker demanded. "You've messed with my dentures twice and they're still buzzing!"

"I've never seen anything like it, General. Maybe it's your nervous system. How about I give you a shot of local anesthetic?"

"Give me the dentures, sir," said a major on the staff, walking over. "I know how to fix them." Baker took out his dentures and set them on the major's proffered paper towel.

According to the media, the general lost his two front teeth when his tank was hit during the Gulf War. Only Baker himself knew that this wasn't true. That time he'd broken his lower jaw; he'd lost the teeth earlier.

It had been at Clark Air Base in the Philippines, during the Mount Pinatubo eruption, when the world around seemed to be volcanic ash and nothing else. The sky was ash, the ground was ash, the air was ash, too. Even the C-130 Hercules that he and the last of the base personnel were about to board was coated with a thick layer of white. The dim red of magma glimmered intermittently in the gray distance.

Elena, the Filipina office worker he had been sleeping with, tracked him down after all this. The base was gone, she said, and she'd lost her job. Her house was buried under ash. How were she and the child in her belly supposed to live? She pulled at his hand and begged him to take her to America. He told her it was impossible. So she took off a high-heeled shoe and whacked him in the face, knocking out two of his teeth.

Where are you now, my child? Baker wondered, gazing at the gray ocean. *Are you living out your days with your mother in the slums of Manila? In a way, your father is fighting for your sake. Once the democratic government takes over in Russia after the war, NATO's vanguard will be at China's borders, and Subic Bay and Clark will once again become America's Pacific naval and air bases, even more prosperous than they were last century. You'll find work there! But most importantly, under NATO's pressure, those Chinese just might give you folks what you've wanted for so long: those beautiful islands in the South China Sea. I've seen them from the air: snow-white coral surrounding the brown sand, like eyes in the blue sea. Child, those are your father's eyes. . . .*

The major returned, cutting short the general's woolgathering. Baker accepted the dentures on the paper towel, put them in, and after a few seconds, looked at the major in astonishment. "How did you do that?"

"Sir, your dentures were buzzing because of electromagnetic resonance."

Baker stared at the major in clear disbelief.

"Sir, it's true! Maybe you've been exposed to strong EM waves before, for example near radar equipment, but the frequency of those waves must have been different from your dentures' resonant frequency. But now, the air is filled with powerful EM waves at all frequencies, which caused this condition.

I've modified the dentures to make their resonant frequency much higher. They're still vibrating, but you can't feel it anymore."

After the major left, General Baker's gaze fell onto the clock standing beside the digital battle map. Its base was a sculpture of Hannibal riding an elephant, engraved with the caption EVER VICTORIOUS. The clock had originally inhabited the Blue Room of the White House; when the president saw his gaze straying again and again in its direction, he'd personally picked up the clock from its century-old resting place and gifted it to him.

"God save America, General. You're God to us now!"

Baker pondered for a long time, then slowly said, "Tell all forces to halt the offensive. Use all our available airpower to find and destroy the source of the Russian jamming."

JANUARY 8TH, RUSSIAN ARMY GENERAL
STAFF HEADQUARTERS

"The enemy has disengaged, but you don't seem happy," Marshal Levchenko said to the commander of the Western Military District, newly returned from the front line.

"I don't have reason to be happy. NATO has concentrated all their airpower on destroying our jamming units. It's really proving an effective countertactic."

"It's no more than we expected," Marshal Levchenko said evenly. "Our strategy would catch the enemy unprepared at first, but they'd come up with a way to counter eventually. Barrage-type jammers emitting strong EM waves at all frequencies wouldn't be hard to find and destroy. But fortunately, we've managed to stall for a considerable length of time. All our hopes now rest on the reinforcement armies' swift arrival."

"The situation might be worse than we predicted," said the district commander. "We might not be able to give the Caucasus Army enough time to move into position before we lose the upper hand in the electronic battle."

After the district commander had left, Marshal Levchenko turned to the digital map display of the frontline terrain and thought of Kalina, right now under the enemy's massed fire, and as a result thought again of Misha.

That one day, Misha had returned home with his face bruised blue and purple. Marshal Levchenko had heard the gossip already: his son, the only anti-war factionist at the college, had been beaten up by students.

"I only said that we shouldn't speak of war lightly," Misha explained to his father. "Is it really impossible to reach a reasonable peace with the West?"

The marshal replied, his tone harsher than it had ever been toward his son, "You know your position. You can choose to stay silent, but you will not say things like that in the future."

Misha nodded.

Once they were through the door that night, Levchenko told Misha, "The Russian Communist Party has taken office."

Misha looked at his father. "Let's eat," he said, without inflection.

Later, the West declared the new Russian government unlawful. Tupolev assembled an extreme rightist alliance and instigated civil war. Marshal Levchenko didn't need to tell any of it to Misha. Every night, father and son silently ate dinner together as usual. Then one day, Misha received his order from the spaceflight base, packed his things, and left. Two days later, he boarded a spaceplane for the *Vechnyy Buran,* waiting in near-Earth orbit.

All-out war broke out a week later, an invasion by an unprecedentedly powerful enemy, from an unexpected direction, aiming to dismember Russia piece by piece.

JANUARY 9TH, NEAR-SUN ORBIT,
THE *VECHNYY BURAN* PASSES MERCURY

Due to the *Vechnyy Buran*'s high velocity, it couldn't settle into orbit around Mercury, only sweep past the sunward side. This was the first time humanity observed Mercury's surface at close range with the naked eye.

Misha saw cliffs two kilometers tall, winding hundreds of kilometers through plains covered with huge craters. He saw the Caloris Basin, too, thirteen hundred kilometers across, termed "Weird Terrain" by planetary

geologists. The weird part came from the similar-sized basin exactly opposite it on the other side of Mercury. It was hypothesized that a huge meteor
had struck Mercury, and that the powerful shock waves had passed right
through the planet, simultaneously creating nearly identical basins in both
hemispheres. Misha found new, thrilling things, too. The surface of Mercury was covered in shiny speckles, he saw. When he used the screen to
zoom in, the realization took his breath away.

Those were lakes of mercury on Mercury, each with a surface area of
thousands of square kilometers.

Misha imagined standing by the lake banks in the long Mercury days,
in the 1,800-degree-Celsius heat: what a sight it would be. Even in a
tempest, the mercury would lie calm and still. And Mercury didn't have
an atmosphere, or wind. The surface of the lakes would be like mirrored
plains, faithfully reflecting the light of the sun and Milky Way.

Once the *Vechnyy Buran* passed by Mercury, it was to continue approaching the sun until its insulation reached the absolute limit of what the fusion-
powered active-cooling system could sustain. The sun's heat was its best
protection; none of NATO's spacecraft could enter the inferno.

Gazing at the vastness of space, thinking of the war on his mother planet
a hundred million kilometers away, Misha once again sighed at the shortsightedness of humanity.

JANUARY 10TH, SMOLENSK FRONT LINE

As she watched the gradual encroachment of the enemy's skirmish line, Kalina understood why her location alone had survived where the surrounding
sources of jamming had been destroyed one by one. The enemy wanted to
capture a Flood unit intact.

The helicopter squadron, three Comanches and four Blackhawks, had
easily located this control unit. Due to Flood's massive EM radiation emis-
sions, it could only be remotely operated via fiber-optic cable. The enemy
had followed the cable to Kalina's control station three kilometers from the
Flood unit, a lone abandoned storehouse.

The four Blackhawks, carrying more than forty enemy infantry, had landed less than two hundred meters from the storehouse. At the time they arrived, there had still been a captain and a staff sergeant in the station with Kalina. Hearing the sound of an engine, the sergeant had gone to open the door; a sniper aboard the helicopter immediately shot off the top of his skull. Enemy fire was careful and restrained after that, fearful of damaging the precious equipment inside the storehouse, allowing Kalina and the captain to hold their ground for a while.

Now, to Kalina's left, the captain's submachine gun that had sounded her only comfort went silent. She saw the captain's unmoving body behind the tree stump he'd used for cover, a circle of bright red blood blooming in the snow around him.

Kalina was in front of the storehouse, behind the crude cover of a few piled sandbags. Eight submachine-gun cartridge clips lay at her feet, and the hot gun barrel hissed in the snow atop the sandbags. Every time Kalina opened fire, the enemy opposite her would crouch down, the bullets splattering snow in front of them, while the enemy on the other side of the semicircular encirclement would spring up and push a little closer. Now Kalina only had three cartridge clips left. She began to fire single shots, but this tactic only announced to the enemy that she was running out of ammunition. They began to push forward more boldly. The next time Kalina reloaded, she heard a sharp squeaking sound from the thick snow on top of the sandbags. Something flew out and struck her on the right, hard. There wasn't any pain, just a rapidly spreading numbness, and the heat of blood running down her right flank. She endured, firing the remnants of this clip wildly. When she reached for the last clip on the sandbags, a bullet cut through her forearm. The clip fell to the ground. Her forearm, connected by a last strip of skin, dangled in the air. Kalina got up and went for the storehouse door, a thin trail of blood following her steps. When she pulled open the door, another bullet pierced her left shoulder.

Captain Rhett Donaldson's SEAL team approached the storehouse cautiously. Donaldson and two marines stepped over the Russian sergeant's body, kicked open the door, and rushed in. They found a single young officer inside.

She was sitting beside their target, Flood's remote control equipment. One broken forearm hung uselessly from the control desk, the other hand was clenched in her hair. Her blood dripped down steadily, forming little puddles at her feet. She smiled at the American intruders and the row of gun barrels pointing at her, a greeting of sorts.

Donaldson exhaled, but wouldn't get the chance to inhale: he saw her turn her good hand from her hair to a dark green ovoid object resting on the remote control equipment. She picked it up, dangling it in midair. Donaldson instantly recognized it as a gas bomb, sized small for use on armed helicopters. It was triggered by a laser proximity signal and would explode twice at half a meter aboveground, first to disperse a gaseous explosive, second to trigger the vapor. He couldn't escape its range now if he were an arrow in flight.

He extended a placating hand. "Calm down, Major, calm down. Let's not get too hasty here." He gestured around him, and the marines lowered their guns. "Listen, things aren't as serious as you might think. You'll get the finest medical care. You'll be sent to the best hospitals in Germany and return in the first POW exchange."

The major smiled at him again, which encouraged him somewhat. "You don't have to do something so barbaric. This is a civilized war, you know. It would go like clockwork, I could tell already when we crossed the Russian border twenty days ago. Most of your firepower had been destroyed by then. That remaining little scatter of gunfire was just the perfect confetti to greet this glorious expedition. Everything will go like clockwork, you see? There's no need—"

"I know of an even more beautiful beginning," the major said in unaccented English. Her soft voice could have come from heaven, could have made flames extinguish and iron yield. "On a lovely beach, with palm trees, and welcome banners hanging overhead. There were beautiful girls with long, waist-length hair and silk trousers that rustled as they moved among the young soldiers and adorned them with red-and-pink leis, smiling shyly at the gawking boys. . . . Do you know of this landing?"

Donaldson shook his head, confused.

"March eighth, 1965, at nine A.M. It was the scene awaiting the first American marine forces landing at China Beach, the start of the Vietnam War."

Donaldson felt as if he'd been plunged into ice. His momentary calm vanished; his breathing sped and his voice started to shake. "No, Major, don't do this to us! We've hardly killed anyone, they're the ones who do all the killing," he said, pointing out the window to the helicopters hovering in midair. "Those pilots there, and the computer missile guidance gentlemen in the mother ships out in space. But they're all good people too. All their targets are just colored icons on their screen. They press a button or click a mouse, wait a bit, and the icon goes away. They're all civilized folks. They don't enjoy hurting people or anything, honest, they're not *evil*—are you listening?"

The major nodded, smiling. Who ever said that the god of death would be ugly and terrible?

"I have a girlfriend. She's working on her Ph.D. at the University of Maryland. She's beautiful like you, honest, and she attended the anti-war rally . . ." *I should have listened to her,* Donaldson thought. "Are you listening to me? Say something! Please, say something."

The major gave her foe one last radiant smile. "Captain, I do my duty."

A unit from the reinforcing Russian 104th Motorized Infantry Division was half a kilometer from the Flood operation station. They first heard a low explosion and saw the little storehouse in the broad, empty fields disappear in a cloud of white mist. Immediately after, a terrible cacophony a hundred times louder shook the ground. An enormous fireball emerged where the storehouse had been, the flames embroiled in black smoke rising high, transforming into a towering mushroom cloud, like a flower of lifeblood blooming in the expanse between heaven and earth.

JANUARY IITH, RUSSIAN ARMY GENERAL
STAFF HEADQUARTERS

"I know what you want. Don't waste words, spit it out!" Marshal Levchenko said to the commander of the Caucasus Army.

"I want the electromagnetic conditions on the battlefield for the last two days to last another four days."

"Surely you're aware that seventy percent of our battlefield jamming teams have been destroyed? I can't even give you another four hours!"

"In that case, our army won't be able to arrive in position on time. NATO airstrikes have greatly slowed the rate at which our forces can assemble."

"In that case, you might as well put a bullet in your head. The enemy is approaching Moscow. They've reached the position Guderian held seventy years ago."

As he exited the war room, the commander of the Caucasus Army said in his heart, *Moscow, endure!*

JANUARY 12TH, MOSCOW DEFENSIVE LINE

Major General Felitov of the Taman Division was fully aware that his line could endure at most one more assault.

The enemy's airstrikes and long-range strikes were slowly growing in intensity, while the Russian air cover was diminishing. The division had few tanks and armed helicopters left; this last stand would be borne on blood and flesh and little else.

The major general, dragging a leg broken by shrapnel, came out of the shelter using a rifle as a crutch. He saw that the new trenches were still shallow, unsurprising given that the majority of the soldiers here had been wounded in some way. But to his astonishment, neat breastworks about a half meter tall stood in front of the trenches.

What material could they have used to build a breastwork so quickly? He saw that a few branch-like shapes stuck out from the snow-covered breastwork. He came closer. They were pale, frozen human arms.

Rage boiled through him. He seized a colonel by the collar. "You bastard! Who told you to use the soldiers' corpses as building materials?"

"I did," the divisional chief of staff said evenly behind him. "We entered this new zone too quickly last night, and this is a crop field. We truly had nothing else to build with."

They looked at each other silently. The chief of staff's face was covered in rivulets of frozen blood, leaked from the bandage on his forehead.

A time passed. The two of them began to walk slowly along the trenches, along the breastworks made from youth, vitality, life. The general's left hand held the rifle he used as a crutch; his right hand straightened his helmet, then saluted the breastworks. They were inspecting their troops for the last time.

They passed by a private with both legs blown off. The blood from his leg stumps had mixed with the snow and dirt into a reddish black mud, and the mud was now crusted over with ice. He lay with an anti-tank grenade in his arms. Raising his bloodless face, he grinned at the general. "I'm gonna stuff this into an Abrams's treads."

The cold winds stirred up gusts of snow mist, howling like an ancient battle paean.

"If I die first, please use me in this wall too. There's no better place for me to end, truly," the general said.

"We won't be too long apart," said the chief of staff, with his characteristic calm.

JANUARY 12TH, RUSSIAN ARMY GENERAL
STAFF HEADQUARTERS

A staff officer came to inform Marshal Levchenko that the general director of the Russian Space Agency wanted to see him—the matter was urgent, involving Misha and the electronic battle.

Marshal Levchenko started at the sound of his son's name. He'd already heard that Kalina had been killed in action, but aside from that, he couldn't imagine what Misha had to do with the electronic battle a hundred million miles away. He couldn't imagine what Misha had to do with any part of Earth now.

The general director came in with his people behind him. Without preamble, he gave a three-inch laser disc to Marshal Levchenko. "Marshal, this is the reply we received from the *Vechnyy Buran* an hour ago. He added afterward that this isn't a private message, and that he hopes you'll play it in front of all relevant personnel."

Everyone in the war room heard the voice from a hundred million kilometers distant. "I've learned from the war news updates that if the electromagnetic jamming fails to last for another three to four days, we may lose the war. If this is true, Papa, I can give you that time.

"Before, you always thought that the stars I studied had nothing to do with the ways of the world, and I thought so too. But it looks like we were both wrong.

"I remember telling you that, although a star generates enormous power, it's fundamentally a relatively elegant and simple system. Take our sun, for example. It's composed of just the two simplest elements: hydrogen and helium; its behavior is the balance of just the two mechanisms of nuclear fission and gravity. As a result, it's easier to model its activity mathematically than our Earth. Research on the sun has given us an extremely accurate mathematical model by this time, work to which I've contributed. Using this model, we can accurately predict the sun's behavior. This would allow us to take advantage of a tiny disturbance to rapidly disrupt the equilibrium conditions inside the sun. The method is simple: use the *Vechnyy Buran* to make a precision strike on the surface of the sun.

"Perhaps you think it no more than tossing a pebble into the sea. But that's not the case, Papa. This is dropping a grain of sand into an eye.

"From the mathematical model, we know that the sun is in an extremely fine-tuned and sensitive state of energy equilibrium. If correctly placed, a small disturbance will create a chain reaction from the surface to a considerable distance down, spreading to disrupt the local equilibrium. There are recorded precedents: the latest incident was in early August of 1972, when a powerful but highly localized eruption created a massive EMP that heavily affected Earth. Compasses in planes and boats jumped wildly, long-distance wireless communications failed, the sky shone with dazzling red lights in high northern latitudes, electric lights flickered in villages as if they were in the center of a thunderstorm. The reactions continued for more than a week. A well-accepted theory nowadays is that a celestial body even smaller than the *Vechnyy Buran* collided with the surface of the sun at that time.

"These disruptions on the sun's surface certainly occurred many times, but most would have happened before humanity invented wireless equipment, and therefore went undetected. In addition, since these collisions were placed by random chance, the disturbances in equilibrium wouldn't have been optimal in strength and area.

"But the *Vechnyy Buran*'s impact location has been meticulously calculated, and the disturbance it will create will be orders of magnitude larger than the natural examples mentioned. This time, the sun will blast powerful electromagnetic radiation into space in every frequency, from the highest to the lowest. In addition, the powerful X-ray radiation generated by the sun will collide violently with Earth's ionosphere, blocking off short-wave radio communications, which are reliant on the layer.

"During the disturbance, the majority of wireless communications outside of the millimeter radio range will fail. The effect will weaken somewhat at night, but during the day, it will even exceed your jamming of the previous two days. Based on calculations, the disturbances will last a week.

"Papa, the two of us always did live in worlds far away from each other's. We could never interact much with each other. But now our worlds have come together. We're fighting for the same goal, for which I'm proud. Papa, like all your soldiers, I await your order."

"Everything Dr. Levchenko said is true," said the general director. "Last year, we sent a probe to enact a small-scale collision with the sun according to calculations based on the mathematical model. The experiment confirmed the model's predictions of the disturbance. Dr. Levchenko and his research group even hypothesized that this method could be used to alter Earth's climate in the future."

Marshal Levchenko walked into a side room and picked up the red telephone that was a direct line to the president. A little later, he walked back out.

The historical records give different accounts of this moment: some claim that he spoke immediately, while others recount that for a minute he was silent. But they concur on the words he said.

"Tell Misha to carry out his plan."

JANUARY 12TH, NEAR-SUN ORBIT,

ABOARD THE *VECHNYY BURAN*

The *Vechnyy Buran* fired all ten fission engines, jets of plasma hundreds of kilometers long erupting from every engine nozzle as it made final corrections to trajectory and orientation.

In front of the *Vechnyy Buran* was an enormous and lovely solar prominence, a current of superheated hydrogen wheeling upward from the sun's surface. Like long ribbons of gauze drifting high above the fiery sea of the sun, they shifted and changed like a dreamscape. Their ends anchored to the surface of the sun, forming a gigantic gateway.

The *Vechnyy Buran* passed slow and stately through the four-hundred-thousand-kilometer-tall triumphal arch. More solar prominences appeared in front, one end attached to the sun, but the other extending into the depths of space. The *Vechnyy Buran* with its blinking blue engine lights threaded through them like a firefly amid burning trees. Then the blue lights slowly dimmed. The engines stopped. The *Vechnyy Buran*'s trajectory had been meticulously established; the rest depended on the law of gravity.

As the spaceship entered the corona, the outermost layer of the sun's atmosphere, the black backdrop of space above turned a magenta all-pervading in its radiance. Below was a clear view of the sun's chromosphere, twinkling with countless needle-shaped structures: discovered in the nineteenth century, they were jets of incandescent gas emanating from the surface of the sun. They made the atmosphere of the sun look like a burning grassland, where each stalk of grass was thousands of kilometers tall. Underneath the burning plain was the sun's photosphere, a sea of endless fire.

From the last images relayed from the *Vechnyy Buran*, people saw Misha rise to his feet in front of the giant monitoring screen. He pressed a button to retract the protective cover outside the transparent dome, revealing the magnificent sea of fire before him. He wanted to see the world of his child-hood dreams with his own eyes. The view was distorting and rippling; that was the half-meter-thick insulation glass melting. Soon the glass barrier fell in a sheet of transparent liquid. Like someone who had never seen the sea facing the ocean wind in rapture, Misha spread his arms to greet the six-thousand-degree hurricane that roared toward him. In the last seconds of video before the camera and transmission equipment melted, one could see Misha's body catching alight, a slender torch melding into the sun's sea of fire. . . .

What sight would have followed could only be conjecture. The *Vechnyy Buran*'s solar panels and protruding structures would have melted first, surface tension making silver beads of fluid of them on the spaceship's surface. As the *Vechnyy Buran* traversed the boundary between the corona and chromosphere, its main body would begin to melt, fully liquefying at a depth of two thousand kilometers into the chromosphere. The beads of liquid metal would cohere into a huge silvery droplet, diving unerringly toward the target its now-melted computers had calculated. The effect of the sun's atmosphere would become apparent: a pale blue flame would emanate from the droplet, trailing hundreds of meters behind it, its color gradating from the pale blue, to yellow, to a gorgeous orange at the tail.

At last, this lovely phoenix would disappear into the endless sea of flames.

JANUARY 13TH, EARTH

Humanity returned to the world as it had been before Marconi.

As night fell, undulating auroras flooded the sky, even into the equatorial zones.

Facing television screens filled with white noise, most people could only guess and imagine at the situation in that vast land where war raged.

JANUARY 13TH, MOSCOW FRONT LINE

General Baker pushed aside the division commander of the Eighty-second Airborne and the assorted NATO frontline commanders attempting to drag him onto a helicopter. He raised his binoculars to continue surveilling the horizon, where the Russian front was rumbling in advance.

"Calibrate to four thousand meters! Load number-nine ammunition, delayed fuse, fire!"

From the sounds of artillery behind him, Baker could tell that no more than thirty of their 105 mm grenade launchers, last of the defensive heavy artillery, could still fire.

An hour ago, the German tank battalion that had been the last remaining armored-vehicle force in the position had launched an admirably courageous counterattack. They'd achieved outstanding results: eight kilometers away, they'd destroyed half again their number of Russian tanks. But under the crushing disadvantage in numbers, they had disappeared under the Russian army's roaring torrent of steel like dew under the noon sun.

"Calibrate to thirty-five hundred meters, fire!"

The explosive missiles hissed as they flew, and flung up a barrier of earth and fire in front of the Russian tank lines. But they were like a landslide before a flood, the earth a short-lived impediment against the implacable waters.

Once the earth blasted up by the explosions fell back to the ground, the Russian armored cars reappeared in view through the dense smoke. Baker saw that they were arranged as densely as if they were receiving inspection. Attacking in this formation would have been suicide a few days ago, but now, with almost all of NATO's aerial and long-distance firepower jammed, it was a perfectly feasible way to concentrate armored-vehicle strength as much as possible, ensuring a break in the enemy line.

Baker had expected that the defensive line would be poorly arranged. Under the electromagnetic conditions on the battlefield, it had been effectively impossible to quickly and accurately determine the direction the main enemy assault would take. As to how the defense would proceed, he didn't know. With the C3I system completely down, quickly adjusting the defensive dispositions would be enormously difficult.

"Calibrate to three thousand meters, fire!"

"General, you were looking for me?" The French commander Lieutenant General Rousselle came over. Beside him were only a French lieutenant colonel and a helicopter pilot. He wasn't wearing camouflage, and the medals on his chest and general's stars on his shoulders shone brightly polished, making the steel helmet he wore and the rifle he held seem incongruous.

"I hear that the French Foreign Legion is withdrawing from the fortifications on our left wing."

"Yes, General."

"General Rousselle, seven hundred thousand NATO troops are in the process of retreat behind us. Their successful breakthrough of the enemy encirclement depends on our steadfast defense!"

"Depends on your steadfast defense."

"Care to explain that comment?"

"You have plenty to explain yourself! You hid the real battle situation from us. You knew from the beginning that the Rightist allies would independently negotiate a cease-fire in the east!"

"As the commander in chief of the NATO forces, I had the right to do so. General, I think you're also clear on the duty placed on you and your troops to follow the orders given."

A silence.

"Calibrate to twenty-five hundred meters, fire!"

"I only obey the orders of the president of the French Republic."

"I do not believe you could have received orders to that effect right now."

"I received them months ago, at the National Day reception at Élysée Palace. The president personally informed me of how the French army should conduct itself under the present conditions."

Baker finally lost his temper. "You bastards haven't changed a bit since de Gaulle's time!"*

"Don't make it sound so unpleasant. If you won't leave, I will stay here without my retinue as well. We will fight and die honorably together on the snowy plain. Napoleon lost here too. It's nothing to be ashamed of," Rousselle said, gesturing with his French-made FAMAS rifle.

---

*In 1966, General de Gaulle withdrew all French armed forces from the NATO integrated military command, a serious blow to NATO's Cold War efforts at the time.

A silence.

"Calibrate to two thousand meters, fire!"

Baker turned slowly to face the frontline commanders in front of him. "Relay these words to the American soldiers defending these lines: We didn't start out as an army dependent on computers to fight our battles. We come from an army of farming men. Decades ago, on Okinawa, we fought the Japanese foxhole by foxhole through the jungle. At Khe Sanh, we deflected the North Vietnamese soldiers' grenades with shovels. Even longer ago, on that cold winter night, our great Washington himself led his barefoot soldiers across the icy Delaware to make history—"

"Calibrate to fifteen hundred meters, fire!"

"I order you, destroy all documents and excess supplies—"

"Calibrate to twelve hundred meters, fire!"

General Baker put on his helmet, strapped on his Kevlar vest, and clipped his 9 mm pistol to his left side. The grenade launchers went silent; the gunners were shoving the grenades into the barrels. Next sounded a mess of explosions.

"Troops," Baker said, looking at the Russian tanks spread in front of them like the veil of death. "Bayonets up!"

The sun faded in and out of the thick smoke of the battlefield, throwing shifting light and shadow onto the snowy plain as the battle raged.

SEA OF DREAMS

TRANSLATED BY JOHN CHU

FIRST HALF

The Low-Temperature Artist

It was the Ice and Snow Arts Festival that lured the low-temperature artist here. The idea was absurd, but once the oceans had dried, this was how Yan Dong always thought of it. No matter how many years passed by, the scene when the low-temperature artist arrived remained clear in her mind.

At the time, Yan Dong was standing in front of her own ice sculpture, which she'd just completed. Exquisitely carved ice sculptures surrounded her. In the distance, lofty ice structures towered over a snowfield. These sparkling and translucent skyscrapers and castles were steeped in the winter sun. They were short-lived works of art. Soon, this glittering world would become a pool of clear water in the spring breeze. People were sad to see them melt but the process embodied many of life's ineffable mysteries. This, perhaps, was the real reason why Yan Dong clung dearly to the ice and snow arts.

Yan Dong tore her gaze away from her own work, determined not to look at it again before the judges named the winners. She sighed, then glanced at the sky. It was at this moment that she saw the low-temperature artist for the first time.

Initially, she thought it was a plane dragging a white vapor trail behind it, but the flying object was much faster than a plane. It swept a great arc through the air. The vapor trail, like a giant piece of chalk, drew a hook in the blue sky. The flying object suddenly stopped high in the air right above Yan Dong. The vapor trail gradually disappeared from its tail to its head, as though the flying object were inhaling it back in.

Yan Dong studied the bit of the vapor trail that was the last to disappear. It was flickering oddly, and she decided it had to be from something reflecting the sunlight. She then saw what that *it* was—a small, ash-gray spheroid. Then quickly realized that the spheroid wasn't small—it looked small in the distance, but was now expanding rapidly. The spheroid was falling right toward her, it seemed, and from an incredibly high altitude. When the people around her realized, they fled in all directions. Yan Dong also ducked her head and ran, darting in and around the ice sculptures.

An enormous shadow hung over the area, and for a moment, Yan Dong's blood seemed to freeze. The expected impact never came, though. The artists and judges and festival spectators stopped running. They gazed upward, dumbstruck. She looked up, too. The massive gray spheroid floated a hundred meters over their heads. It wasn't wholly spheroid, as if the vapor expelled during its high-speed flight had warped its shape. The half in the direction of its flight was smooth, glossy, and round. The other half sprouted a large sheaf of hair, making it look like a comet whose tail had been trimmed. It was massive, well over one hundred meters in diameter, a mountain suspended in midair. Its presence felt oppressive to everyone beneath it.

After the spheroid halted, the air that had driven it charged the ground, sending up a rapidly expanding ring of dirt and snow. It's said that when people touched something they didn't expect to be as cold as an ice cube, it'd feel so hot that they'd shout as their hand recoiled. In the instant that the mass of air fell on her, that's how Yan Dong felt. Even someone from the bitterly cold Northeast would have felt the same way. Fortunately, the air diffused quickly, or else everyone on the ground would have frozen stiff. Even so, practically everyone with exposed skin suffered some frostbite.

Yan Dong's face was numb from the sudden cold. She looked up, transfixed by the spheroid's surface. It was made of a translucent ash-gray substance she recognized intimately: ice. This object suspended in the air was a giant ball of ice.

Once the air settled, large snowflakes were fluttering around the floating mountain of ice. An oddly pure white against the blue sky, they glittered in the sunlight. However, these snowflakes were only visible within a certain distance around the spheroid. When they floated farther away, they dissolved. They formed a snow ring with the spheroid as its center, as though the spheroid were a streetlamp lighting the snowflakes around it on a cold night.

"I am a low-temperature artist!" a clear, sharp voice emitted from the ball of ice. "I am a low-temperature artist!"

"This ball of ice is you?" Yan Dong shouted back.

"You can't see my true form. The ball of ice you see is formed by my freeze field from the moisture in the air," the low-temperature artist replied.

"What about those snowflakes?"

"They are crystals of the oxygen and nitrogen in the air. In addition, there's dry ice formed from the carbon dioxide."

"Wow. Your freeze field is so powerful!"

"Of course. It's like countless tiny hands holding countless tiny hearts tight. It forces all the molecules and atoms within its range to stop moving."

"It can also lift this gigantic ball of ice into the air?"

"That's a different kind of field, the antigravity field. The ice-sculpting tools you all use are so fascinating. You have small shovels and small chisels of every shape. Not to mention watering cans and blowtorches. Fascinating! To make low-temperature works of art, I also have a set of tiny tools. They are various types of force fields. Not as many tools as you have, but they work extremely well."

"You create ice sculptures, too?"

"Of course. I'm a low-temperature artist. Your world is extremely suitable for the ice- and snow-molding arts. I was shocked to discover they've long existed in this world. I'm thrilled to say that we're colleagues."

"Where do you come from?" the ice sculptor next to Yan Dong asked.

"I come from a faraway place, a world you have no way to understand. That world is not nearly as interesting as yours. Originally, I focused solely on the art. I didn't interact with other worlds. However, seeing exhibitions like this one, seeing so many colleagues, I found the desire to interact. But, frankly, very few of the low-temperature works below me deserve to be called works of art."

"Why?" someone asked.

"Excessively realistic, too reliant on form and detail. Besides space, there's nothing in the universe. The actual world is just a big pile of curved spaces. Once you understand this, you'll see how risible these works are. However, hm, this piece moves me a little."

Just as the voice faded away, a delicate thread extended from the snow-flakes around the ball of ice, as if it flowed down following an invisible funnel. The snowflake thread stretched from midair to the top of Yan Dong's ice sculpture before dissolving. Yan Dong stood on her tiptoes, and tentatively stretched a gloved hand toward the snowflake thread. As she neared it, her fingers felt that burning sensation again. She jerked her hand back, but it was already painfully cold inside the glove.

"Are you pointing to my work?" Yan Dong rubbed her frozen hand with the other. "I, I didn't use traditional methods. That is, carve it from ready-made blocks of ice. Instead, I built a structure composed of several large membranes. For a long time, steam produced from boiling water rose from the bottom of the structure. The steam froze to the membrane, forming a complex crystal. Once the crystal grew thick enough, I got rid of the membrane and the result is what you see here."

"Very good. So interesting. It so expresses the beauty of the cold. The inspiration for this work comes from . . ."

"Windowpanes! I don't know whether you will be able to understand my description: When you wake during a hard winter's night just before sunrise, your bleary gaze falls on the windowpane filled with crystals. They reflect the dark blue first light of early dawn, as though they were something you dreamed up overnight. . . ."

"Yes, yes, I understand!" The snowflakes around the low-temperature artist danced in a lively pattern. "I have been inspired. I want to create! I must create!"

"The Songhua River is that way. You can select a block of ice, or . . ."

"What? Your form of art is as pitiable as bacteria. Do you think my form of low-temperature art is anything like that? This place doesn't have the sort of ice I need."

The ice sculptors on the ground looked bewildered at the interstellar low-temperature artist. Yan Dong said, blankly, "Then, you want to go . . ."

"I want to go to the ocean!"

Collecting Ice

An immense fleet of airplanes flew at an altitude of five kilometers along the coastline. This was the most motley collection of airplanes in history. It was composed of all types, ranging from Boeing jumbo jets to mosquito-like light aircraft. Every major press service in the world had dispatched news planes. In addition, research organizations and governments had dispatched observation planes. This chaotic air armada trailed closely behind a short wake of thick white vapor, like a flock of sheep chasing after its shepherd. The wake was left by the low-temperature artist. It constantly urged the planes behind it to fly faster. To wait for them, it had to endure a rate of flight slower than crawling. (For someone who jumped through space-time at will, light speed was already crawling.) The whole way, it grumbled that this pace would kill its inspiration.

In the airplanes behind it, reporters rattled away, asking endless questions over the radio. The low-temperature artist had no desire to answer any of them. It was only interested in talking to Yan Dong, sitting in the Harbin Y-12 that China Central Television had rented. As a result, the reporters grew quiet. They listened carefully to the conversation between the two artists.

"Is your home within the Milky Way?" Yan Dong asked. The Harbin Y-12 was the plane closest to the low-temperature artist. She could see the flying ball of ice intermittently through the white vapor. This wake trailing it was formed from oxygen, nitrogen, and carbon dioxide in the atmosphere condensing in the ultralow temperatures around the ice ball. Sometimes, the plane would accidentally brush the wake's billows of white mist. A thick coat of frost would immediately coat the plane's windows.

"My home isn't part of any galaxy. It sits in the vast and empty void between galaxies."

"Your planet must be extremely cold."

"We don't have a planet. The low-temperature civilization developed in a cloud of dark matter. That realm is indeed extremely cold. With difficulty, life snatched a little heat from the near-absolute-zero environment. It sucked in every thread of radiation that came from distant stars. Once the low-temperature civilization learned how to leave, we couldn't wait to go to the closest warm planet in the Milky Way. On this world, we had to maintain a low-temperature environment to live, so we became that warm planet's low-temperature artists."

"The low-temperature art you're talking about is sculpting ice and snow?"

"Oh, no. No. Using a temperature far lower than a world's mean temperature to affect the world so as to produce artistic effects, this is all part of the low-temperature art. Sculpting ice and snow is just the low-temperature art that suits this world. The temperature of ice and snow is what this world considers a low temperature. For a dark-matter world, that would be a high temperature. For a stellar world, lava would be considered low-temperature material."

"We seem to overlap in what art we consider beautiful."

"That's not unusual. So-called warmth is just a brief effect of an equally brief spasm produced after the universe was born. It's gone in an instant like light after sunset. Energy dissipates. Only the cold is eternal. The beauty of the cold is the only enduring beauty."

"So you're saying the final fate of the universe is heat death?!" Yan Dong heard someone ask over her earpiece. Later, she learned the speaker was a theoretical physicist sitting in one of the planes following behind.

"No digressions. We will discuss only art," the low-temperature artist scolded.

"The ocean is below us!" Yan Dong happened to glance out the porthole. The crooked coastline passed below.

"Further ahead, we'll reach the deepest part of the ocean. That will be the most convenient place to collect ice."

"Where will there be ice?" Yan Dong asked, uncomprehending, as she looked at the vast, blue ocean.

"Wherever a low-temperature artist goes, there will be ice."

The low-temperature artist flew for another hour. Yan Dong stared out the window as they traveled. The view had long become a boundless surface of water. At that moment, the plane suddenly pulled up. She nearly blacked out from acceleration.

"We almost hit it!" the pilot shouted.

The low-temperature artist had stopped suddenly. Taken by surprise, the planes behind it scrambled to change direction.

"Damn it! The law of inertia doesn't apply to the fucker. Its speed seemed to drop to zero in an instant. By all rights, this sort of deceleration should have cracked the ball of ice into pieces," the pilot said to Yan Dong.

As he spoke, he steered the plane around. The other pilots did the same. The ball of ice, rotating majestically, lingered in midair. It produced oxygen and nitrogen snowflakes, but due to strong wind at the altitude, the snowflakes were all blown away. They seemed like white hair whirling in the wind around the ball of ice.

"I am about to create!" the low-temperature artist said. Without waiting for Yan Dong to respond, it suddenly dropped straight down as if the giant invisible hand that had held it suddenly let it go. It free-fell faster and faster until it disappeared into the blue backdrop that was the ocean, leaving only a faint thread of atoms stretching down from midair. A ring of white spray shot up from the sea surface. When it fell, a wave spread out in a circle on the water.

"This alien threw itself into the ocean and committed suicide," the pilot said to Yan Dong.

"Don't be ridiculous!" Yan Dong stretched out her Northeastern accent and glared at the pilot. "Fly a little lower. The ball of ice will float back up any moment now."

But the ball of ice didn't float back up. In its place, a white dot appeared on the ocean. It quickly expanded into a disk. The plane descended and Yan Dong could observe in detail.

The white disk was actually a white fog that covered the ocean. Soon, between its quick expansion and the airplane's continued descent, the only ocean she could see oozed a white fog from its surface. A noise from the sea covered the roaring of the plane's engine. It sounded both like rolling thunder and the cracking of the plains and mountains.

The airplane hovered close to sea level. Yan Dong peered at the surface of the ocean below the fog. The light the ocean reflected was mild, not like moments ago when glints of gold had slashed Yan Dong's eyes. The ocean grew deeper in color. Its rough waves grew level and smooth. What shocked her, though, was the next discovery: The waves became solid and motionless.

"Good heavens. The ocean froze!"

"Are you crazy?" The pilot turned his head to look at Yan Dong.

"See for yourself. . . . Hey! Why are you still descending? Do you want to land on the ice?!"

The pilot yanked the control stick. Once again, the world in front of Yan Dong grew black. She heard the pilot say, "Ah, no, fuck, how strange . . ." The pilot looked as though he were sleepwalking. "I wasn't descending. The ocean, no, the ice is rising by itself!"

At that moment, Yan Dong heard the low-temperature artist's voice: "Get your flying machine out of the way. Don't block the path of the rising ice. If there weren't a colleague in the flying machine, I would simply crash into you. I can't stand disruptions to my inspiration while I'm creating. Fly west, fly west, fly west. That direction is closer to the edge."

"Edge? The edge of what?" Yan Dong asked.

"The cube of ice I'm taking!"

Planes took off like a flock of startled birds, climbing into the sky and heading in the direction the low-temperature artist indicated. Below, because the white fog created by the temperature drop had dissipated, the dark blue ice field stretched to the horizon. Even though the plane was climbing, the ice field climbed even faster. As a result, the distance between the planes and the ice field continued to shrink.

"The Earth is chasing us!" the pilot screamed.

The plane now flew pressed against the ice field. Frozen dark blue waves roiled past the plane's wings.

The pilot yelled, "We have no choice but to land on the ice field. My god, climbing and landing at the same time. That's just too strange."

Just at that moment, the Harbin Y-12 reached the end of the ice. A straight edge swept past the fuselage. Below them, liquid sea reemerged, rippling and shimmering. It was like what a fighter jet saw the instant it leapt off the deck of an aircraft carrier, except the "aircraft carrier" was several kilometers tall.

Yan Dong snapped her head around. Behind them, an immense, dark blue cliff could be seen. The bottom of the massive block of ice had cleared the ocean.

As the chunk of ice continued to rise, Yan Dong finally understood what the low-temperature artist had meant: This was literally a giant block of ice. The dark blue cube occupied two-thirds of the sky. Afterward, radar observation indicated that the block of ice was sixty kilometers long, twenty kilometers wide, and five kilometers tall, a thin and flat cuboid. Its flat surface reflected the sunlight, like streaks of eye-piercing lightning high in the sky.

The giant block of ice kept rising, casting an unimaginably large shadow onto the sea. And when it shifted, it revealed the most terrifying sight since the dawn of history.

The planes were flying over a long, narrow basin, the empty space in the ocean that was left once the giant block of ice was removed. On each side was a mountain of seawater five kilometers high. Hundred-meter-high waves surged at the bottom of these liquid cliffs. At the top, the cliffs were collapsing, advancing as they did. Their surface rippled, but they remained perpendicular to the seafloor. As the seawater cliffs advanced, the basin shrank.

This was the reverse of Moses parting the Red Sea.

What startled Yan Dong the most was how slow the entire process seemed. This was, she assumed, due to the scale. She'd seen the Huangguoshu waterfalls. The water had seemed to fall slowly there, too. And these cliffs of seawater before her were magnitudes larger than those waterfalls. Watching them felt like an endless moment of unparalleled wonder.

The shadow cast by the block of ice had completely disappeared. Yan Dong looked up. The block of ice was now just the size of two full moons.

As the two seawater cliffs advanced, the basin shrank into a canyon. Then the two seawater cliffs, tens of kilometers long, five thousand meters high, crashed into each other. An incredible roar echoed between the sea and sky. The space in the ocean the ice block left was gone.

"We aren't dreaming, are we?" Yan Dong said to herself.

"If this were a dream, everything would be fine. Look!"

The pilot pointed below. Where the two cliffs had crashed into each other, the sea hadn't yet settled. Two waves as long as those cliffs rose, as if they were the reincarnation of those two seawater cliffs on the sea's surface. They parted, heading in opposite directions. From high above, the waves weren't that impressive, but careful measurements showed they were over two hundred meters tall. Viewed from up close, they'd seem like two moving mountain ranges.

"Tidal waves?" Yan Dong asked.

"Yes. Could be the largest ever. The coast is in for a disaster."

Yan Dong looked up. She could no longer see the frozen block in the blue sky. According to radar, it had become an ice satellite of Earth.

For the rest of the day, the low-temperature artist removed, in the same way, hundreds of blocks of ice of the same size from the Pacific Ocean. It sent them into orbit around the Earth.

By nightfall, a cluster of twinkling points could be seen flying across the sky every couple of hours. You could distinguish them from the usual stars because, on careful inspection, someone could make out the shape of each point. They were each a small cuboid. They all, in their own orientations, spun on their own axes. As a result, they reflected the sunlight and twinkled at different rates.

People thought for a long time, but were never quite able to adequately describe these small objects in space. Finally, a reporter came up with an analogy that got some traction.

"They're like a handful of crystalline dominoes scattered by a space giant."

A Dialogue Between Two Artists

"We ought to have a chat," Yan Dong said.

"I asked you to come just to do that, but only about art," the low-temperature artist said.

Yan Dong stood on a giant block of ice suspended five thousand meters in the air. The low-temperature artist had invited her here. The helicopter that had brought her had landed and now waited to the side. Its rotors were still spinning, ready to take off at any moment.

Ice fields stretched to the horizon on all sides. The ice surface reflected the dazzling sunlight. The layer of blue ice below her seemed bottomless. At this altitude, the sky was clear and boundless. The wind blew stiffly.

This was one of the five thousand giant blocks of ice the low-temperature artist had taken from the oceans. Over the past five days, it had taken, on average, one thousand blocks a day from the oceans and sent them into orbit. All across the Pacific and Atlantic oceans, giant blocks of ice were being frozen and then carried into the air to become one of an increasing number of glittering "space dominoes." Tidal waves assaulted every major city along the world's coasts. Over time, though, these disasters became less frequent. The reason was simple: The sea level had dropped.

Earth's oceans had become blocks of ice revolving around it.

Yan Dong stamped her feet on the hard ice surface. "Such a large block of ice, how did you freeze it in an instant? How did you do it in one piece without it cracking? What force are you using to send it into orbit? All of this is beyond our understanding and imagination."

The low-temperature artist said, "This is nothing. In the course of creation, we've often destroyed stars! Didn't we agree to discuss only art? I, creating art in this way, you, using small knives and shovels to carve ice sculptures, from the view from the perspective of art, aren't all that different."

"When those ice blocks orbiting in space are exposed to intense sunlight, why don't they melt?"

"I covered every ice block with a layer of extremely thin, transparent, light-filtering membrane. It only allows cold light, whose frequencies don't generate heat, to get into the block of ice. The frequencies that do generate heat are all reflected. As a result, the block of ice doesn't melt. This is the last time I'll answer this sort of question. I didn't stop work to discuss these trivial things. From now on, we'll discuss only art, or else you might as well leave. We'll no longer be colleagues and friends."

"In that case, how much ice do you ultimately plan to take from the oceans? This is surely relevant to the creation of art!"

"Of course, I'll only take as much as there is. I've talked to you before about my design. I'd like to realize it perfectly. Initially, I planned to take ice from Jupiter's satellites if it had turned out that Earth's oceans aren't enough, but it seems there's enough to make do."

The wind mussed Yan Dong's hair. She smoothed it back into place. The cold at this altitude made her shiver. "Is art important to you?"

"It's everything."

"But . . . there are other things in life. For example, we still need to work to survive. I'm an engineer at the Changchun Institute of Optics. I can only make art in my spare time."

The low-temperature artist's voice rumbled from the depths of the ice. The vibrating ice surface tickled Yan Dong's feet. "Survival. Ha! It's just the diaper of a civilization's infancy that needs to be changed. Later, that's as easy as breathing. You'll forget there ever was a time when it took effort to survive."

"What about societal and political matters?"

"The existence of individuals is also a troublesome part of infant civilizations. Later, individuals melt into the whole. There's no society or politics as such."

"What about science? There must be science, right? Doesn't a civilization need to understand the universe?"

"That is also a course of study infant civilizations take. Once exploration has carried out to the proper extent, everything down to the slightest will be revealed. You will discover that the universe is so simple, even science is unnecessary."

"So that just leaves art?"

"Yes. Art is the only reason for a civilization to exist."

"But we have other reasons. We want to survive. The several billion people on this planet below us and even more of other species want to survive. You want to dry our oceans, to make this living planet a doomed desert, to make us all die of thirst."

A wave of laughter propagated from the depths of the ice. Again, it tickled Yan Dong's feet.

"Colleague, look, once the violent surge of creative inspiration had passed, I talked to you about art. But, every time, you gossip with me about trivialities. It disappoints me greatly. You ought to be ashamed. Go. I'm going to work."

Yan Dong finally lost her patience. "Fuck your ancestors!" she shouted, then continued to swear in a Northeastern dialect of Chinese.

"Are those obscenities?" the low-temperature artist asked placidly. "Our species is one where the same body matures as it evolves. No ancestors. As for treating your colleague like this . . ." It laughed. "I understand. You're jealous of me. You don't have my ability. You can only make art at the level of bacteria."

"But, you just said that our art requires different tools but there's no essential difference."

"I've just now changed my perspective. At first, I thought I'd run into a real artist, but, as it turns out, you're a mediocre, pitiful creature who chatters on about the oceans drying, ecological collapse, and other inconsequential things that have nothing to do with art. Too trivial, too trivial, I tell you. Artists cannot be like this."

"Fuck your ancestors anyway."

"Yes, well. I'm working. Go."

For a moment, Yan Dong felt heavy. She fell ass-first onto the slick ice as a gust of wind swept down from above. The ice block was rising again. She scrambled into the helicopter, which, with difficulty, took off from the nearest edge of the block of ice, nearly crashing in the tornado produced as the block of ice rose.

Communication between humanity and the low-temperature artist had failed.

Sea of Dreams

Yan Dong stood in a white world. The ground below her feet and the surrounding mountains were covered in a silvery white cloak. The mountains were steep and treacherous. She felt as though she were in the snow-covered Himalayas. But in fact, it was the opposite; she was at the lowest place on Earth. The Marianas Trench. Once the deepest part of the Pacific Ocean. The white material that covered everything was not snow but the minerals that had once made the water salty. After the seawater froze, these minerals separated out and were deposited on the seafloor. At the thickest, these deposits were as much as one hundred meters deep.

In the past two hundred days, the oceans of the Earth were exhausted by the low-temperature artist. Even the glaciers of Greenland and Antarctica were completely pillaged.

Now, the low-temperature artist invited Yan Dong to participate in its work's final rite of completion.

In the ravine ahead lay a surface of blue water. The blue was pure and deep. It seemed all the more touching among so many snow-white mountain peaks.

This was the last ocean on Earth. It was about the area of Dianchi Lake in Yunnan. Its great waves had long ceased. Only gentle ripples swayed on the water, as though it were a secluded lake deep in the mountains. Three rivers converged into this final ocean. These were great rivers that had survived by luck, trudging through the vast, dehydrated seafloor. They were the longest rivers on Earth. By the time they'd arrived here, they'd become slender rivulets.

Yan Dong walked to the oceanfront. Standing on the white beach, she dipped her hand into the lightly rippling sea. Because the water was so saturated with salt, its waves seemed sluggish. A gentle breeze blew Yan Dong's hand dry, leaving a layer of white salt.

The sharp sound that Yan Dong knew so well pierced the air. It tore through the air whenever the low-temperature artist slid toward the ground. Yan Dong spotted it in the sky as it approached.

The low-temperature artist didn't greet Yan Dong. The ball of ice fell into the middle of this last ocean, causing a tall column of water to spout. Afterward, once again, a familiar scene emerged: A disk of white fog oozed out from the point where the low-temperature artist hit the water. Rapidly, the white fog covered the entire ocean. The water quickly froze with a loud cracking sound. Once again, the fog dissipating revealed a frozen ocean surface. Unlike before, this time, the entire body of water was frozen. There wasn't a drop of liquid water left. The ocean surface also didn't have frozen waves. It was as smooth as a mirror. Throughout the freezing process, Yan Dong felt a cold draft on her face.

The now-frozen final ocean was lifted off the ground. At first, it was lifted only several careful centimeters off the ground. A long black fissure emerged from the edge of the ice field between the ice and white salt beach. Air, forming a strong wind low to the ground, rushed into the long fissure, filling the newly created space. It blew the salt around, so that it now buried Yan Dong's feet. The rate the lake was rising at increased. In the blink of an eye, the final ocean was in midair. So much volume rising so quickly produced violent, chaotic winds. A gust swirled up the salt into a white column in the ravine. Yan Dong spit out the salt that flew into her mouth. It wasn't salty like she'd imagined. It tasted bitter in a way that was hard to express, like the reality that humanity was up against.

The final ocean wasn't a cuboid. Its bottom was an exact impression of the contours of the seafloor. Yan Dong watched it rise until it became a small point of light that dissolved into the mighty ring of ice.

The ring of ice was about as wide as the Milky Way in the sky. Unlike the rings of Uranus and Neptune, the surface of the ring of ice was neither perpendicular nor parallel to the surface of the Earth. It was like a broad belt of light in space. A broad belt composed of two hundred thousand blocks of ice completely surrounding the Earth. From the ground, one could clearly make out every block of ice. Some of them rotated while others seemed static. Throughout the day, the ring of ice varied with dramatic changes in brightness and color. The two hundred thousand points of light, some twinkling, some not, formed a majestic, heavenly river that flowed solemnly across the Earth's sky.

Its colors were the most dramatic at dawn and dusk. The ring of ice changed gradually from the orange-red of the horizon to a dark red and then to dark green and dark blue, like a rainbow in space.

During the daytime, the ring of ice assumed a dazzling silver color against the blue sky, like a great river of diamonds flowing across a blue plain. The daytime ring of ice looked most spectacular during an eclipse, when it blocked the sun. Massive blocks of ice refracted the sunlight. Like a strange and magnificent fireworks show in the sky.

How long the sun was blocked by the ice ring depended on whether it was an intersecting eclipse or a parallel eclipse. What was known as a parallel eclipse was when the sun followed the ring of ice for some distance. Every year, there was one total parallel eclipse. For a day, the sun, from sunrise to sunset, followed the path of the ice ring for its entire journey. On this day, the ring of ice seemed like a belt of silver gunpowder set loose on the sky. Ignited at sunrise, the dazzling fireball burned wildly across the sky. When it set in the west, the sight was magnificent, too difficult to put into words. Some people proclaimed, "Today, God strolled across the sky."

Even so, the ring of ice's most enchanting moment was at night. It was twice as bright as a full moon. Its silver light filled the Earth. It was as though every star in the universe had lined up to march solemnly across the night sky. Unlike the Milky Way, in this mighty river of stars, one could clearly make out every cuboid star. Of these thickly clustered stars, half of them glittered. Those hundred thousand twinkling stars formed a ripple that surged, as though driven by a gale. It transformed the river of stars into an intelligent whole. . . .

With a sharp squeal, the low-temperature artist returned from space for the last time. The ball of ice was suspended over Yan Dong. A ring of snowflakes appeared and wrapped itself tightly around it.

"I've completed it. What you do think?" it asked.

Yan Dong stayed silent for a long time, then said only one short phrase: "I give up."

She had truly given up. Once, she'd stared up at the ring of ice for three consecutive days and three nights, without food or drink, until she collapsed. Once she could get out of bed again, she went back outside to stare at the ice ring again. She felt she as if she could gaze at it forever and it wouldn't be enough. Beneath the ring of ice, she was sometimes dazed, sometimes steeped in an indescribable happiness. This was the happiness of when an artist found ultimate beauty. She was completely conquered by this immense beauty. Her entire soul was dissolved in it.

"As an artist, now that you're able to see such work, are you still striving for it?" the low-temperature artist asked.

"Truly, I'm not," Yan Dong answered sincerely.

"However, you're merely looking. Certainly, you can't create such beauty. You're too trivial."

"Yes. I'm too trivial. We're too trivial. How can we? We have to support ourselves and our children."

Yan Dong sat on the saline soil. Steeped in sorrow, she buried her head in her hands. This was the deep sorrow that arose when an artist saw beauty she could never produce, when she realized she would never be able to transcend her limitations.

"So, how about we name this work together? Call it—*Ring of Dreams,* perhaps?"

Yan Dong considered this. Slowly, she shook her head. "No, it came from the sea or, rather, was sublimated from the sea. Not even in our dreams could we conceive that the sea possessed this form of beauty. It should be called—*Sea of Dreams*."

"*Sea of Dreams* . . . very good, very good. We'll call it that, *Sea of Dreams*."

Then, Yan Dong remembered her mission. "I'd like to ask, before you leave, can you return *Sea of Dreams* to become our actual seas?"

"Have me personally destroy my own work? Ridiculous!"

"Then, after you leave, can we restore the seas ourselves?"

"Of course you can. Just return these blocks of ice and everything should be fine, right?"

"How do we do that?" Yan Dong asked, her head raised. All of humanity strained to hear the answer.

"How should I know?" the low-temperature artist said indifferently.

"One final question: As colleagues, we all know that works of art made from ice and snow are short-lived. So *Sea of Dreams* . . ."

"*Sea of Dreams* is also short-lived. A block of ice's light-filtering membrane will age. It'll no longer be able to block heat. But they will dissolve differently than your ice sculptures. The process will be more violent and magnificent. Blocks of ice will vaporize. The pressure will cause the membrane to burst. Every block of ice will turn into a small comet. The entire ring of ice will blur into a silver fog. Then *Sea of Dreams* will disappear into that silver fog. Then the silver fog will scatter and disappear into space. The universe can only look forward to my next work on some other distant world."

"How long until this happens?" Yan Dong's voice quavered.

"The light-filtering membrane will become ineffective, as you reckon time, hm, in about twenty years. Oh, why are we talking about things other than art again? Trivial, trivial! Okay, colleague. Goodbye. Enjoy the beauty I have left you!"

The ball of ice shot into the air, disappearing into the sky. According to the measurements of every major astronomical organization in the world, the ball of ice flew rapidly along a perpendicular to the ecliptic plane. Once it had accelerated to half the speed of light, it abruptly disappeared thirteen astronomical units away from the sun, as if it'd squeezed into an invisible hole. It never returned.

SECOND HALF

Monument and Waveguide

The drought had already lasted for five years.

Withered ground swept past the car window. It was midsummer and there was not a bit of green anywhere on the ground. The trees were all withered. Cracks like black spiderwebs covered the ground. Frequent dry, hot winds kicked up sand that concealed everything. Quite a few times, Yan Dong thought she saw the corpses of people who had died of thirst along the railroad tracks, but they might have just been fallen, dry tree branches, nothing to be afraid of. This harsh, arid world contrasted sharply with the silver *Sea of Dreams* in the sky.

Yan Dong licked her parched lips. She couldn't bring herself to drink from her water flask. That was four days' rations for her entire family. Her husband had forced it on her at the train station. Yesterday, her workmates had protested, demanding to be paid in water. In the market, nonrationed water grew scarcer and scarcer. Even the rich weren't able to buy any. . . . Someone touched her shoulder. It was the person in the seat beside her.

"You're that alien's colleague, aren't you?"

Since she'd become the low-temperature artist's messenger, Yan Dong had also become a celebrity. At first, she was considered a role model and a hero. However, after the low-temperature artist left, the situation changed. One way of looking at things is, it was her work that had inspired the low-temperature artist at the Ice and Snow Arts Festival. Without that, none of this would have happened. Most people understood that this was utter nonsense, but having a scapegoat was a good thing. So, in people's eyes she was eventually seen as the low-temperature artist's conspirator. But fortunately, after the artist had left, there were bigger issues to worry about. People gradually forgot about Yan Dong. However, this time, even though she was wearing sunglasses, she had been recognized.

"Ask me to drink some water!" the man beside her said, his voice rasping. Two flakes of dry skin fell from his lips.

"What are you doing? Are you robbing me?"

"Be smart, or else I'll scream!"

Yan Dong felt obliged to hand over her water flask. The man drained the flask in one swallow. The people around them watched this with shock on their faces. Even the train attendant who had been passing by stopped in the aisle and stared at him, stupefied. That anyone could be so wasteful was nearly beyond belief. It was like back in the Oceaned Days (what people called the age before the arrival of the low-temperature artist), watching a rich person eat a sumptuous dinner that cost one hundred thousand yuan.

The man returned the empty flask to Yan Dong. Patting Yan Dong's shoulder again, the man said in a low voice, "It doesn't matter. Soon, it'll all be over."

Yan Dong understood what the man meant.

The capital seldom had cars on its streets anymore. The rare few had all been retrofitted to be air-cooled. Using a conventional liquid-cooled car was strictly prohibited. Fortunately, the Chinese branch of the World Crisis Organization had sent a car to pick her up. Otherwise, she'd absolutely have had no way to reach their offices. On the way, she saw that sandstorms had covered all the roads with yellow sand. She didn't see many pedestrians. For anyone dehydrated, walking around in the hot, dry wind was too dangerous.

The world was like a fish out of water, already begging for a breath.

When she arrived at the World Crisis Organization, Yan Dong reported to the bureau chief. The bureau chief brought her to a large office and introduced her to the group she would be working with. Yan Dong looked at the office door. Unlike the other ones, this one had no nameplate. The bureau chief said:

"This is a secret group. Everything done here is strictly confidential. In order to avoid social unrest, we call this group the Monument Division."

Entering the office, Yan Dong realized the people here were all somewhat eccentric: Some had hair that was too long. Some had no hair at all. Some were immaculately dressed, as if the world weren't falling apart around them. Some wore only shorts. Some seemed dejected, others abnormally excited. Many oddly shaped models sat on a long table in the middle of the office. Yan Dong couldn't guess what they might be for.

"Welcome, Ice Sculptor." The head of the Monument Division enthusiastically shook Yan Dong's hand after the bureau chief's introduction. "You'll finally have the opportunity to elaborate on the inspiration you received from the alien. Of course, this time, you can't use ice. What we want to build is a work that must last forever."

"What for?"

The division head looked at the bureau chief, then back at Yan Dong. "You still don't know? We want to establish a monument to humanity!"

Yan Dong felt even more at a loss with this explanation.

"It's humanity's tombstone," an artist to her side said. This person had long hair and tattered clothes, and gave the impression of decadence. One hand held a bottle of sorghum liquor that he'd drunk until he was somewhat tipsy. The liquor was left over from the Oceaned Days and now much cheaper than water.

Yan Dong looked all around, then said, "But . . . we're not dead yet."

"If we wait until we're dead, it'll be too late," the bureau chief said. "We ought to plan for the worst case. The time to think about this is now."

The division head nodded. "This is humanity's final work of art, and also its greatest work of art. For an artist, what can be more profound than to join in its creation?"

"Fucking, actually. . . . Much more," the long-haired artist said, waving the bottle. "Tombstones are for your descendants to pay homage to. We'll have no descendants, but we'll still erect a fucking tomb?"

"Pay attention to the name. It's a monument," the division head corrected solemnly. Laughing, he said to Yan Dong, "However, the idea he put forth is very good: He proposed that everyone in the world donate a tooth. Those teeth can be used to create a gigantic tablet. Carving a word on each tooth is sufficient to engrave the most detailed history of human civilization on the tablet." He pointed at a model that looked like a white pyramid.

"This is blasphemy against humanity," a bald-headed artist shouted. "The worth of humanity lies in its brains, but he wants to commemorate us with our teeth!"

The long-haired artist took another swig from his bottle. "Teeth. . . . Teeth are easy to preserve."

"The vast majority of people are still alive!" Yan Dong repeated solemnly.

"But for how long?" the long-haired artist said. As he asked this question, his enunciation suddenly became precise. "Water no longer falls from the sky. The rivers have dried. Our crops have utterly failed for three years now. Ninety percent of the factories have stopped production. The remaining food and water, how long can that sustain us?"

"You heap of waste." The bald-headed artist pointed at the bureau chief. "Bustling around for five years and you still can't bring even one block of ice back from space."

The bureau chief laughed off the bald-headed artist's criticism. "It's not that simple. Given current technology, forcing down one block of ice from orbit isn't hard. Forcing down one hundred, up to one thousand blocks of ice is doable. But forcing back all two hundred thousand blocks of ice orbiting the Earth, that's another matter completely. If we use conventional techniques, a rocket engine could slow a block of ice enough that it would fall back into the atmosphere. That would mean building a large number of reusable high-power engines, then sending them into space. That's a massive-scale engineering project. Given our current technology level and what resources we've stockpiled, there are many insurmountable obstacles. For example, in order to save the Earth's ecosystem, if we start now, we'd need to force down half the blocks of ice within four years, an average of twenty-five thousand per year. The weight of rocket fuel required would be greater than the amount of gasoline humanity used in one year during the Oceaned Days! Except it isn't gasoline. It's liquid hydrogen, liquid oxygen, dinitrogen tetroxide, unsymmetrical dimethylhydrazine, and so on. They need over a hundred times more energy and natural resources to produce than gasoline. Just this one thing makes the entire plan impossible."

The long-haired artist nodded. "In other words, doomsday is not far away."

The bureau chief said, "No, not necessarily. We can still adopt some non-conventional techniques. There is still hope. While we're working on this, though, we must still plan for the worst."

"This is exactly why I came," Yan Dong said.

"To plan for the worst?" the long-haired artist asked.

"No, because there's still hope." She turned to the bureau chief. "It doesn't matter why you brought me here. I came for my own purpose." She pointed to her bulky travel bag. "Please take me to the Ocean Recovery Division."

"What can you do in the Ocean Recovery Division? They're all scientists and engineers there," the bald-headed artist wondered.

"I'm a research fellow in applied optics." Yan Dong's gaze swept past the artists. "Besides daydreaming along with you, I can also do some practical things."

After Yan Dong insisted, the bureau chief brought her to the Ocean Recovery Division. The mood here was completely different from the Monument Division. Everyone was tense, working on their computers. A drinking fountain stood in the middle of the office. They could take a drink whenever they wanted. This was treatment worthy of kings. But considering that the hope of the world rested on the people in this room, it wasn't so surprising.

When Yan Dong saw the Ocean Recovery Division's lead engineer, she told her, "I've brought a plan for reclaiming the ice blocks."

As she spoke, she opened her travel bag. She took out a white tube about as thick as an arm, followed by a cylinder about a meter long. Yan Dong walked to a window that faced the sun. She stuck the cylinder out the window, then shook it back and forth. The cylinder opened like an umbrella. Its concave side was plated with a mirror coating. That turned it into something like a parabolic reflector for a solar stove. Next, Yan Dong pushed the tube through a small hole at the bottom of the paraboloid, then adjusted the reflector so that it focused sunlight at the end of the tube. Immediately, the other end of the tube cast an eye-stabbing point of light on the floor. Because the tube lay flat on the floor, the point was an exaggerated oval.

Yan Dong said, "This uses the latest optical fiber to create a waveguide. There's very little attenuation. Naturally, an actual system would be much larger than this. In space, a parabolic reflector only about twenty meters in diameter can create a point of light at the other end of the waveguide with a temperature of over three thousand degrees."

Yan Dong looked around. Her demonstration hadn't produced the reaction she'd expected. The engineers took a look, then returned to their computer screens, paying her no mind. It wasn't until a stream of dark smoke rose from the point of light on the antistatic floor that the nearest person came over and said, "What did you do? I doubt it's hot."

At the same time, the person nudged back the waveguide, moving the light coming through the window away from the focal length of the parabolic reflector. Although the point was still on the floor, it immediately darkened and lost heat. Yan Dong was surprised at how adept the person was at adjusting the thing.

The lead engineer pointed at the waveguide. "Pack up your gear and drink some water. I heard you took the train. The one to here from Changchun is still running? You must be extremely thirsty."

Yan Dong desperately wanted to explain her invention, but she truly was thirsty. Her throat burned and it was painful to speak.

"Very good. This is a really practical plan." The lead engineer handed Yan Dong a glass of water.

Yan Dong drained the glass of water in one gulp. She looked blankly at the lead engineer. "Are you saying that someone has already thought of this?"

The lead engineer laughed. "Spending time with aliens has made you underestimate human intellect. In fact, from the moment the low-temperature artist sent the first block of ice into space, many people have come up with this plan. Afterward, there were lots of variants. For example, some used solar panels instead of reflectors. Some used wires and electric heating elements instead of waveguides. The advantage is that the equipment is easy to manufacture and transport. The disadvantage is the efficiency is not as high as waveguides. We've been researching this for five years now. The technology is already mature. The equipment we need has mostly been manufactured."

"Then why haven't you carried the plan out?"

An engineer next to them said, "With this plan, the Earth will lose twenty-one percent of its water. Either during propulsion as vaporized steam or during reentry from high-temperature dissociation."

The lead engineer turned to that engineer. "We don't know that yet. The latest American simulations show, below the ionosphere, the hydrogen produced by high-temperature dissociation during reentry will immediately recombine with the surrounding oxygen into water. We overestimated the high-temperature-dissociation loss. The total loss estimate is around eighteen percent." She turned back to Yan Dong. "But this percentage is high enough."

"Then do you have a plan to bring back all of the water from space?"

The lead engineer shook her head. "The only possibility is to use a nuclear fusion engine. But, right now, on Earth, controlled nuclear fusion isn't within our capabilities."

"Then why aren't you acting more quickly? You know, if you dither around, the Earth will lose one hundred percent of its water."

The lead engineer nodded. "So, after a long time of hesitation, we've decided to act. Soon, the Earth will be in for the fight of its life."

Reclaiming the Oceans

Yan Dong joined the Ocean Recovery Division, in charge of receiving and checking the waveguides that had been produced. Although this wasn't a core posting, she found it fulfilling.

One month after Yan Dong arrived at the capital, humanity's project to reclaim the oceans started.

Within one short week, eight hundred large-scale carrier rockets shot into the sky from every launch site in the world, sending fifty thousand tons of freight into Earth orbit. Then, from the North American launch site, twenty space shuttles ferried three hundred astronauts into space. Because launches generally followed the same route, the skies above the launch sites all had a single rocket contrail that never dispersed. Viewed from orbit, it seemed like threads of spider silk stretching up from every continent into space.

These launches increased human space activity by an order of magnitude, but the technology used was still twentieth-century technology. People realized, under existing conditions, if the entire world worked together and risked everything on one attempt, it could do anything.

On live television, Yan Dong and everyone else witnessed the first time a deceleration propulsion system was installed on a block of ice.

To make things less difficult, the first blocks of ice they forced back weren't the ones that rotated about their own axes. Three astronauts landed on a block of ice. They brought with them the following equipment: an artillery-shell-shaped vehicle that could drill a hole into the block of ice, three waveguides, one expeller tube, and three folded-up parabolic reflectors. It was only now that anyone could get the sense of the immense size of a block of ice. The three people seemed to land on a tiny crystalline world. Under intense sunlight in space, the giant field of ice under their feet seemed unfathomable.

Near and far, innumerable similar crystalline worlds hung in the black sky. Some of them still rotated about their own axes. The surrounding rotating and nonrotating blocks of ice reflected and refracted the sunlight. On the ice the three astronauts stood on, they cast a dazzling pattern of ever-changing light and shadow. In the distance, the blocks of ice in the ring looked smaller and smaller, but gathered closer and closer together, gradually shrinking into a delicate, silver belt twisting toward the other side of the Earth. The closest block of ice was only three thousand meters away from this one. Because it rotated about its minor axis, in their eyes, such a rotation had a breathtaking momentum, as though they were three tiny ants watching a crystalline skyscraper collapsing over and over again. Due to gravity, these two ice blocks would eventually crash into each other. The light-filtering membranes would rupture and the blocks of ice would disintegrate. The smashed blocks of ice would quickly evaporate in the sunlight and disappear. Such collisions had already happened twice in the ring of ice. This was also why this block was the first block of ice to be forced back.

First, an astronaut started the driller vehicle. As the drill head spun, crumbs of ice flew out in a cone-shaped spray, twinkling in the sunlight. The driller vehicle broke through the invisible light-filtering membrane. Like a twisting screw, it dug into the ice, leaving a round hole in its wake. Along with the hole that stretched into the depths of the ice, a faint white line could be seen in the ice itself. Once the hole reached the prescribed depth, the vehicle headed out toward another part of the ice. It then bored another hole. At last, it drilled four holes in total. They all intersected at one point deep in the ice.

The astronauts inserted the three waveguides into three of the holes, then inserted the expeller into the wider fourth hole. The expeller tube's mouth was pointed in the direction of the motion of the block of ice. After that, the astronauts used a thin tube to caulk the gap the three waveguides and the expeller tube left against their holes' walls with a fast-sealing liquid to create a good seal. Finally, they opened the parabolic reflectors. If the initial phase of ocean reclamation employed the latest technology, it was these parabolic reflectors. They were a miracle created by nanotechnology. Folded up, each was only a cubic meter. Unfolded, each formed a giant reflector five hundred meters in diameter. These three reflectors were like three silver lotus leaves that grew on the block of ice. The astronauts adjusted each waveguide so that its receiver coincided with the focal point of its reflector.

A bright point of light appeared where the three holes intersected deep in the ice. It seemed like a tiny sun, illuminating within the block of ice spectacular sights of mythic proportions: a school of silver fish, dancing seaweed drifting with the waves . . . Everything retained its lifelike appearance at the instant it was frozen. Even the strings of bubbles spat from fishes' mouths were clear and distinct. Over one hundred kilometers away, inside another ice block being reclaimed, the sunlight that the waveguides led into the ice revealed a giant black shadow. It was a blue whale over twenty meters long! This had to be the Earth's seas of old.

Deep in the ice, steam soon blurred the point of light. As the steam dispersed, the point changed into a bright white ball. It swelled in size as the ice melted. Once the pressure had built up to a predetermined level, the expeller mouth cover was broken open. A violent gush of turbulent steam exploded out. Because there were no obstructions, it formed a sharp cone that scattered in the distance. Finally, it disappeared in the sunlight. Some portion of the steam entered another ice block's shadow and condensed into ice crystals that seemed like a swarm of flickering fireflies.

The deceleration propulsion system in the first batch of one hundred blocks of ice activated. Because the blocks of ice were so massive, the thrust the system produced was, relatively speaking, very small. As a result, they needed to orbit fifteen days to a month before they could slow the blocks of ice down enough for them to fall into the atmosphere. Later, reclaiming ice blocks that rotated was much more complicated. The propulsion system had to stop the rotation first, then slow down the block of ice.

Before the blocks of ice entered the atmosphere, astronauts would land on them again to recover the waveguides and reflectors. If they wanted to force all two hundred thousand blocks down, this equipment had to be reused as much as possible.

Ice Meteors

Yan Dong and members of the Crisis Committee arrived together at the flatlands in the middle of the Pacific Ocean to watch the first batch of ice meteors fall.

The ocean bed of former days looked like a snowy white plain, reflecting the intense sunlight—no one could open their eyes unless they were wearing sunglasses. But the white plain before them didn't make Yan Dong think of the snowfields of her native Northeast because, here, it was as hot as hell. The temperature was near fifty degrees Celsius. Hot winds kicked up salty dirt, which hurt when it hit her face. A hundred-thousand-ton oil tanker was in the distance. The gigantic hull lay tilted on the ground. Its propeller, several stories tall, and rudder completely covered the salt bed. An unbroken chain of white mountains stood even farther in the distance. That was a mountain range on the seafloor humanity had never seen until now. A two-sentence poem came to Yan Dong's mind: *The open sea is a boat's land. Night is love's day.*

She laughed bitterly then. She'd experienced this tragedy, yet she still couldn't shake off thinking like an artist.

Cheers erupted. Yan Dong raised her head and looked to where everyone was pointing. In the distance, a bright red point had appeared in the silver ring of ice that traversed the sky. The point of light drifted out of the ring. It swelled into a fireball. A white contrail dragged behind the fireball. This contrail of steam grew ever longer and thicker. Its color became even denser, even whiter. Soon, the fireball split into ten pieces. Each piece continued to split. A long white contrail dragged behind every small piece. This field of white contrails filled half the sky, as though it were a white Christmas tree and a small, bright lamp hung on the tip of every branch. . . .

Even more ice meteors appeared. Their sonic booms shook the earth like rumbles of spring thunder. As old contrails gradually dissipated, new contrails appeared to replace them. They covered the sky in a complex white net. Several trillion tons of water now belonged to the Earth again.

Most of the ice meteors broke apart and vaporized in the air, but one large fragment of ice fell to the ground about forty kilometers from Yan Dong. The loud crash shook the flatlands. A colossal mushroom cloud rose from somewhere in the distant mountain range. The water vapor shone a dazzling white in the sunlight. Gradually, it dispersed in the wind and became the sky's first cloud layer. The clouds multiplied and, for the first time, blocked the sun that had been scorching the earth for five years. They covered the entire sky. For a while, Yan Dong felt a pleasant coolness that oozed into her heart and lungs.

The cloud layer grew thick and dark. Red light flickered within it. Maybe it was lightning or the light from the continuous waves of ice meteors falling toward the earth.

It rained! This was a downpour so heavy it would have been rare even in the Oceaned Days. Yan Dong and everyone else there ran around screaming wildly in the storm. They felt their souls dissolve in the rain. Then they retreated into their cars and helicopters because, right now, people would suffocate in the rain.

The rain fell nonstop until dusk. Waterlogged depressions appeared on the seafloor flatlands. A crack in the clouds revealed the golden, flickering rays of the setting sun, as though the Earth had just opened its eyes.

Yan Dong followed the crowd, stepping through the thick salty mud. They ran to the nearest depression. She cupped some water in her hands, then splashed that thick brine on her face. As it fell, mixed with her tears, she said, choking with sobs:

"The ocean, our ocean . . ."

Epilogue

TEN YEARS LATER

Yan Dong walked onto the frozen-over Songhua River. She was wrapped in a tattered overcoat. Her travel bag held the tools that she'd kept for fifteen years: several knives and shovels of various shapes, a hammer, and a watering can. She stamped her feet to make sure that the river had truly frozen. The Songhua River had water as early as five years ago, but this was the first time it had frozen, and during the summer, no less.

Due to the arid conditions and, at the same time, the potential energy of the many ice meteors converting into thermal energy in the atmosphere, the global climate had stayed hotter than ever. But in the final stage of ocean reclamation, the largest blocks of ice were forced down. These blocks of ice broke into larger fragments. Most of them crashed onto the ground. This not only destroyed a few cities but also kicked up dust that blocked the sun's heat. Temperatures fell rapidly all over the world. Earth entered a new ice age.

Yan Dong looked at the night sky. This was the starscape of her childhood.

The ring of ice had disappeared. She could only make out the vestiges of the remaining small blocks of ice from their rapid motion against the background of stars. *Sea of Dreams* had turned back into actual seas again. This magnificent work of art, its cruel beauty as well as nightmare, would forever be inscribed in the collective memory of humanity.

Although the ocean-reclamation effort had been a success, Earth's climate would be a harsh one from now on. The ecosystem would take a long time to recover. For the foreseeable future, humanity's existence would be extremely difficult. Nevertheless, at least existence was possible. Most people felt content with that. Indeed, the Ring of Ice Era made humanity learn contentment, and also something even more important.

The World Crisis Organization would change its name to the Space Water Retrieval Organization. They were considering another great engineering project: Humanity intended to fly to distant Jupiter, then take water from Jupiter's moons and the rings of Saturn back to Earth in order to make up for the 18 percent lost in the course of the Ocean Reclamation Project.

At first, people intended to use the technology for propelling blocks of ice that they'd already mastered to drive blocks of ice from the rings of Saturn to Earth. Of course, that far away, the sunlight was too weak. Only using nuclear fusion to vaporize the cores of the blocks of ice could provide the necessary thrust. As for the water from Jupiter's moons, that required even larger and more complex technology to acquire. Some people had already proposed pulling the whole of Europa out of Jupiter's deep gravity well, pushing it to Earth, and making it Earth's second moon. This way, Earth would receive much more water than 18 percent. It could turn Earth's ecosystem into a glorious paradise. Naturally, this was a matter for the far future. No one alive hoped to see it during their lifetime. However, this hope made people in their hard lives feel a happiness they'd never felt before. This was the most valuable thing humanity received from the Ring of Ice Era: Reclaiming *Sea of Dreams* made humanity see its own strength, taught it to dream what it had never before dared to dream.

Yan Dong saw in the distance a group of people gathered on the ice. She walked to them, gliding with each step. When they spotted her, they began to run toward her. Some slipped and fell, then picked themselves up and raced to catch up with the others.

"Our old friend! Hello!" The first one to reach Yan Dong wrapped her in a warm hug. Yan Dong recognized him. He was one of the ice sculpture judges from so many ice and snow festivals before the Ring of Ice Era.

As they neared, she recognized the others, most of them ice sculptors from before the Ring of Ice Era. Like everyone else of this era, they wore tattered clothes. Suffering and time had dyed the hair on their temples white. Yan Dong felt as though she'd come home after years of wandering.

"I heard that the Ice and Snow Arts Festival has started back up again?" she asked.

"Of course. Otherwise, what are we all doing here?"

"I've been thinking. Times are so hard . . ."

Yan Dong wrapped her large overcoat tighter around herself. She shivered in the cold wind, constantly stamping her numb feet against the ice. Everyone else did the same, shivering, stamping their feet, like a group of begging refugees.

"So what if times are hard? Even in hard times, you can't not make art, right?" an old ice sculptor said through chattering teeth.

"Art is the only reason for a civilization to exist!" someone else said.

"Fuck that, I have plenty of reasons to go on," Yan Dong said loudly.

Everyone laughed, then fell silent as they thought back on ten years of hard times. One by one, they counted their reasons to go on. Finally, they changed themselves from survivors of a disaster back to artists again.

Yan Dong took a bottle of sorghum liquor from her bag. They warmed up as each one took a swig then passed it on to the next. They built a fire on the vast riverbank and heated up a chainsaw until it would start in the bitter cold. They all stepped onto the river, and the chainsaw growled as it cut into the ice. White crumbs of ice fell around them. Soon, they pulled their first block of glittering, translucent ice from the Songhua River.

CLOUD OF POEMS

TRANSLATED BY CARMEN YILING YAN

A yacht bore Yi Yi and his two companions across the South Pacific on a voyage dedicated to poetry. Their destination was the South Pole. Upon a successful arrival in a few days, they would climb through the Earth's crust to view the Cloud of Poems.

Today, the sky and seas were clear. For the purposes of poem making, the workings of the world seemed to be laid out in glass. Looking up, one could see the North American continent in rare clarity in the sky. On the vast world-encompassing dome as seen from the eastern hemisphere, the continent looked like a patch of missing plaster on a wall.

Oh, yes, humanity lived inside the Earth nowadays. To be more accurate, humanity lived inside the Air, for the Earth had become a gas balloon. The Earth had been hollowed out, leaving only a thin shell about a hundred kilometers thick. The continents and oceans remained in their old places, only they had all migrated to the inside of the shell. The atmosphere also remained, moved inside as well. So now the Earth was a balloon, with the oceans and continents clinging to its inner surface. The hollow Earth still rotated, but the significance of the rotation was much different than before: It now produced gravity. The attractional force generated by the bit of mass forming Earth's crust was so weak as to be insignificant, so now the Earth's "gravity" had to come from the centrifugal force of rotation. But this kind of "gravity" was unevenly distributed across the regions of the world.

It was strongest at the equator, being about 1.5 times Earth's original gravity. With increase of latitude came a gradual decrease in gravity—the two poles experienced weightlessness. The yacht was currently at the exact latitude that experienced 1.0 gees as per the old scale, but Yi Yi nonetheless found it difficult to recall the sensation of standing on the old, solid Earth.

At the heart of the hollow Earth hovered a tiny sun, which currently illuminated the world with the light of noon. The sun's luminosity changed continuously in a twenty-four-hour cycle, from its maximum to total darkness, providing the hollow Earth with alternating day and night. On suitable nights, it even gave off cold moonlight. But the light came from a single point; there was no round, full moon to be seen.

Of the three people on the yacht, two of them were not, in fact, people. One was a dinosaur named Bigtooth. The yacht swayed and tilted with every shift of his ten-meter-tall body, to the annoyance of the one reciting poetry at the boat's prow. This was a thin, wiry old man, garbed in the loose, archaic robes of the Tang Dynasty, whose snow-white hair and snow-white whiskers flowed in the wind as one. He resembled a bold calligraphy character splashed in the space between sea and sky.

This was the creator of the new world, the great poet Li Bai.

THE GIFT

The matter began ten years ago, when the Devouring Empire completed its two-century-long pillage of the solar system. The dinosaurs from Earth's ancient past departed for Cygnus in their ring-shaped world fifty thousand kilometers in diameter, leaving the sun behind them. The Devouring Empire took 1.2 billion humans with them as well, to be raised as livestock. But as the ring world approached the orbit of Saturn, it suddenly began to decelerate, before, incredibly, returning along its earlier route to the inner reaches of the solar system.

One ring-world week after the Devouring Empire began its return, the emissary Bigtooth piloted away from the ring in his spaceship shaped like an old boiler, a human named Yi Yi in his pocket.

"You're going to be a present!" Bigtooth told Yi Yi, eyes on the black void outside the window port. His booming voice rattled Yi Yi's bones.

"For whom?" Yi Yi threw his head back and shouted from the pocket. From the opening, he could see the dinosaur's lower jaw, like a boulder jutting out from the top of a giant cliff.

"You'll be given to a god! A god came to the solar system. That's why the Empire is returning."

"A real god?"

"Their kind controls unimaginable technology. They've transformed into beings of pure energy, and can instantaneously jump from one side of the Milky Way to the other. They're gods, all right. If we can get just a hundredth of their ultra-advanced technology, the Devouring Empire will have a bright future ahead. We're entering the final step of this important mission. You need to get the god to like you!"

"Why did you pick me? My meat is very low-grade," said Yi Yi. He was in his thirties. Next to the tender, pale-fleshed humans cultivated with so much care by the Devouring Empire, he appeared rather old and world-worn.

"The god doesn't eat bug-bugs, just collects them. I heard from the breeder that you're really special. Apparently you have many students?"

"I'm a poet. I currently teach Classic literature to the livestock humans on the feedlot." Yi Yi struggled to pronounce "poet" and "literature," rarely used words in the Devourer language.

"Boring, useless knowledge. Your breeder turns a blind eye to your classes because their spiritual effects improve the bug-bugs' meat quality. . . . From what I've observed, you think highly of yourself and give little notice to others. They must be very interesting traits for a head of livestock to have."

"All poets are like this!" Yi Yi stood tall in the pocket. Even though he knew that Bigtooth couldn't see, he raised his head proudly.

"Did your ancestors participate in the Earth Defense War?"

Yi Yi shook his head. "My ancestors from that era were also poets."

"The most useless kind of bug-bug. Your kind was already rare on Earth back then."

"They lived in the world of their innermost selves, untouched by changes to the outside world."

"Shameless . . . ha, we're almost there."

Hearing this, Yi Yi stuck his head out of the pocket. Through the huge window port, he could see the two white, glowing objects ahead of the ship: a square and a sphere, floating in space. When the spaceship reached the level of the square, the latter briefly disappeared against the backdrop of the stars, revealing that it had virtually zero thickness. The perfect sphere hovered directly above the plane. Both shone with soft, white light, so evenly distributed that no features could be distinguished on their surfaces. They looked like objects taken from a computer database, two concise yet abstract concepts in a disorderly universe.

"Where's the god?" Yi Yi asked.

"He's the two geometric objects, of course. Gods like to keep it nice and simple."

As they approached, Yi Yi saw that the plane was the size of a soccer field. The spaceship descended upon the plane thruster side down, but the flames left no marks on the surface, as if the plane were nothing but an illusion. Yet Yi Yi felt gravity, and the jarring sensation when the spaceship touched down proved that the plane was real.

Bigtooth must have come here before; he opened the hatch without hesitation and walked out. Yi Yi's heart seized up when he saw that Bigtooth had simultaneously opened the hatches on both side of the airlock, but the air inside the chamber didn't howl outward. As Bigtooth walked out of the ship, Yi Yi smelled fresh air from inside his pocket. When he poked his head out, a soft, cool breeze caressed his face. This was ultra-advanced technology beyond the comprehension of either humans or dinosaurs. Its comfortable, casual application astounded Yi Yi, in a way that pierced the soul more deeply than what humanity must have felt in its first encounter with Devourers. He looked up. The sphere floated overhead against the backdrop of the radiant Milky Way.

"What little gift have you brought me this time, Emissary?" asked the god in the language of the Devourers. His voice was not loud, seeming to come from a boundless distance away, from the deep void of outer space.

It was the first time Yi Yi had found the crude language of the dinosaurs pleasing to the ear.

Bigtooth extended a claw into his pocket, caught Yi Yi, and set him down on the plane. Yi Yi could feel the elasticity of the plane through the soles of his feet.

"Esteemed god," Bigtooth said. "I heard you like to collect small organisms from different star systems, so I brought you this very entertaining little thing: a human from Earth."

"I only like *perfect* organisms. Why did you bring me such a filthy insect?" said the god. The sphere and the plane flickered twice, perhaps to express disgust.

"You know about this species?" Bigtooth raised his head in astonishment.

"Not intimately, but I've heard about them from certain visitors to this arm of the galaxy. They made frequent visits to Earth in the brief course of these organisms' evolution, and were revolted at the vulgarness of their thoughts, the lowliness of their actions, the disorder and filth of their history. Not a single visitor would deign to establish contact with them up to the destruction of Earth. Hurry and throw it away."

Bigtooth seized Yi Yi, rotating his massive head to look for a place to throw him. "The trash incinerator is behind you," said the god. Bigtooth turned and saw that a small, round opening had appeared in the plane behind him. Inside shimmered a faint blue light. . . .

"Don't dismiss us like that! Humanity created a magnificent civilization!" Yi Yi shouted with all his might in the language of the Devourers.

The sphere and plane again flickered twice. The god gave two cold laughs. "Civilization? Emissary, tell this insect what civilization is."

Bigtooth lifted Yi Yi to his eye level; Yi Yi could even hear the *gululu* of the dinosaur's giant eyeballs turning in their sockets. "Bug-bug, in this universe, the standard measure of any race's level of civilization is the number of dimensions it can access. The basic requirement for joining civilization at large is six or more. Our esteemed god's race can already access the eleventh dimension. The Devouring Empire can access the fourth dimension in small-scale laboratory environments, and only qualifies as a primitive, uncivilized tribe in the Milky Way. You, in the eyes of a god, are in the same category as weeds and lichen."

"Throw it away already, it's disgusting," the god urged impatiently.

Having finished speaking, Bigtooth headed for the incinerator's aperture. Yi Yi struggled frantically. Numerous pieces of white paper fluttered loose from his clothing. The sphere shot out a needle-thin beam of light, hitting one of the sheets, which froze unmoving in midair. The beam scanned rapidly over its surface.

"Oh my, wait, what's this?"

Bigtooth allowed Yi Yi to dangle over the incinerator's aperture as he turned to look at the sphere.

"That's . . . my students' homework!" Yi Yi managed laboriously, struggling in the dinosaur's giant claw.

"These squarish symbols are very interesting, and the little arrays they form are quite amusing too," said the god. The sphere's beam of light rapidly scanned over the other sheets of paper, which had since landed on the plane.

"They're Ch-Chinese characters. These are poems in Classical Chinese!"

"Poems?" the god exclaimed, retracting its beam of light. "I trust you understand the language of these insects, Emissary?"

"Of course, esteemed god. Before the Devouring Empire ate Earth, we spent a long time living on their world." Bigtooth set Yi Yi down on the plane next to the incinerator, bent over, and picked up a sheet of paper. He held it just in front of his eyes, trying with effort to distinguish the small characters on it. "More or less, it says—"

"Forget it, you'll distort the meaning!" Yi Yi waved a hand to interrupt Bigtooth.

"How so?" asked the god interestedly.

"Because this is a form of art that can only be expressed in Classical Chinese. Even translating these poems into other human languages alters them until they lose much of their meaning and beauty."

"Emissary, do you have this language in your computer database? Send me the relevant data, as well as all the information you have on Earth history. Just use the communications channel we established during our last meeting."

Bigtooth hurried back to the spaceship and banged around on the computer inside for a while, muttering, "We don't have the Classical Chinese portion here, so we'll have to upload it from the Empire's network. There might be some delay." Through the open hatchway, Yi Yi saw the morphing colors of the computer screen reflected off the dinosaur's huge eyeballs.

By the time Bigtooth got off the ship, the god could already read the poem on one sheet of paper with perfect modern Chinese pronunciation.

> "*Bai ri yi shan jin,*
> *Huang he ru hai liu,*
> *Yu qiong qian li mu,*
> *Geng shang yi ceng lou.*"

"You're a fast learner!" Yi Yi exclaimed.

The god ignored him, silent.

Bigtooth explained, "It means, the star has set behind the orbiting planet's mountains. A liquid river called the Yellow River is flowing in the direction of the ocean. Oh, the river and the ocean are both made of the chemical compound consisting of one oxygen atom and two hydrogen atoms. If you want to see further, you must climb further up the edifice."

The god remained silent.

"Esteemed god, you visited the Devouring Empire not long ago. The scenery there is almost identical to that of the world known to this poem's author bug-bug, with mountains, rivers, and seas, so . . ."

"So I understand the meaning of the poem," said the god. The sphere suddenly moved so it was right above Bigtooth's head. Yi Yi thought it looked like a giant pupilless eye staring at Bigtooth. "But, didn't you feel something?"

Bigtooth shook his head, confused.

"That is to say, something hidden behind the outward meaning of that simple, elegant array of square symbols?"

Bigtooth looked even more confused, so the god recited another Classical poem:

> *"Qian bu jian gu ren,*
> *Hou bu jian lai zhe,*
> *Nian tian di zhi you,*
> *Du cang ran er ti xia."*

Bigtooth hurried eagerly to explain. "This poem means, looking in front of you, you can't see all the bug-bugs who lived on the planet in the distant past. Looking behind you, you can't see all the bug-bugs who will live on the planet in the future. So you feel how time and space are just too big and end up crying."

The god brooded.

"Ha, crying is one way for Earth bug-bugs to express their grief. So at that point their visual organs—"

"Do you still feel nothing?" the god interrupted Bigtooth. The sphere descended further, nearly touching Bigtooth's snout.

Bigtooth shook his head firmly this time. "Esteemed god, I don't think there's anything inside. It's just a simple little poem."

Next, the god recited several more poems, one after the other. They were all short and simple, yet imbued with a spirit that transcended their topics. They included Li Bai's "Downriver to Jiangling," "Still Night Thoughts," and "Bidding Meng Haoran Farewell at Yellow Crane Tower"; Liu Zongyuan's "River Snow"; Cui Hao's "Yellow Crane Tower"; Meng Haoran's "Spring Dawn"; and so forth.

Bigtooth said, "The Devouring Empire has many historical epic poems with millions of lines. We would happily present them all to you, esteemed god! In comparison, the poems of human bug-bugs are so puny and simple, like their technology—"

The sphere suddenly departed its position above Bigtooth's head, drifting in unthinking arcs in midair. "Emissary, I know your people's greatest hope is that I'll answer the question 'The Devouring Empire has existed for eight million years, so why is its technology still stalled in the Atomic Age?' Now I know the answer."

Bigtooth gazed at the sphere passionately. "Esteemed god, the answer is crucial to us! Please—"

"Esteemed god," Yi Yi called out, raising a hand. "I have a question too. May I speak?"

Bigtooth glared resentfully at Yi Yi, as if he wanted to swallow him in one bite. But the god said, "Though I continue to despise Earth insects, those little arrays have won you the right."

"Is art common throughout the universe?"

The sphere vibrated faintly in midair, as if nodding. "Yes—I'm an intergalactic art collector and researcher myself, in fact. In my travels, I've encountered the various arts of numerous civilizations. Most are ponderous, unintelligible setups. But using so few symbols, in so small and clever an array, to encompass such rich sensory layers and subtle meaning, all the while operating under such sadistically exacting formal rules and rhyme schemes? I have to say, I've never seen anything like it. . . . Emissary, you may now throw away this insect."

Once again, Bigtooth seized Yi Yi with his claw. "That's right, we ought to throw it away. Esteemed god, we have fairly abundant resources on human civilization stored in the Devouring Empire's central networks. All those resources are now in your memory, while this bug-bug probably doesn't know any more than a couple of the little poems." He carried Yi Yi toward the incinerator as he spoke.

"Throw away those pieces of paper too," the god said. Bigtooth hurriedly returned and used his other claw to collect the papers. At this point, Yi Yi hollered from between the massive claws.

"O god, save these papers with the ancient poems of humanity, as a memento! You've discovered an unsurpassable art. You can spread it throughout the universe!"

"Wait." The god once again stopped Bigtooth. Yi Yi was already hanging above the incinerator aperture, feeling the heat of the blue flames below him. The sphere floated over, coming to a stop a few centimeters from Yi Yi's forehead. Yi Yi, like Bigtooth earlier, felt the force of the enormous pupilless eye's gaze.

"Unsurpassable?"

Bigtooth laughed, holding up Yi Yi. "Can you believe the pitiable bug-bug, saying these things in front of a magnificent god? Hilarious! What remains to humanity? You've lost everything on Earth. Even the scientific knowledge you've managed to bring with you has been largely forgotten. One time at dinner, I asked the human I was about to eat, what were the atomic bombs used by the humans in the Earth Defense War made of? He told me they were made of atoms!"

"Hahahaha . . ." The god joined Bigtooth in laughter, the sphere vibrating so hard it became an ellipsoid. "It's certainly the most accurate answer of them all, hahaha . . ."

"Esteemed god, all these dirty bug-bugs have left are a couple of those little poems! Hahaha—"

"But they cannot be surpassed!" Yi Yi said solemnly in the middle of the claw, puffing out his chest.

The sphere stopped vibrating. It said, in an almost intimate whisper, "Technology can surpass anything."

"It has nothing to do with technology. They are the quintessence of the human spiritual realm. They cannot be surpassed!"

"Only because you haven't witnessed the power of technology in its ultimate stage, little insect. Little, little insect. You haven't seen." The god's tone of voice became as gentle as a father's, but Yi Yi shivered at the icy killing edge hidden deep within. The god said, "Look at the sun."

Yi Yi obeyed. They were in the vacuum between the orbits of Earth and Mars. The sun's radiance made him squint.

"What's your favorite color?" asked the god.

"Green."

The word had barely left his lips before the sun turned green. It was a bewitching shade; the sun resembled a cat's eye floating in the void of space. Under its gaze, the whole universe looked strange and sinister.

Bigtooth's claw trembled, dropping Yi Yi onto the plane. When their reason returned, they realized a fact even more unnerving than the sun turning green: the light should have taken more than ten minutes to travel here from the sun, but the change had occurred instantaneously!

Half a minute later, the sun returned to its previous condition, emitting brilliant white light once more.

"See? This is technology. This is the force that allowed my race to ascend from slugs in ocean mud to gods. Technology itself is the true God, in fact. We all worship it devotedly."

Yi Yi blinked his dazzled eyes. "But that god can't surpass this art. We have gods too, in our minds. We worship them, but we don't believe they can write poems like Li Bai and Du Fu."

The god laughed coldly. "What an extraordinarily stubborn insect," it said to Yi Yi. "It makes you even more loathsome. But, for the sake of killing time, let me surpass your array-art."

Yi Yi laughed back. "It's impossible. First of all, you aren't human, so you can't feel with a human's soul. Human art to you is only a flower on a stone slab. Technology can't help you surmount this obstacle."

"Technology can surmount this obstacle as easily as snapping your fingers. Give me your DNA!"

Yi Yi was confused. "Give the god one of your hairs!" Bigtooth prompted him. Yi Yi reached up and plucked out a hair; an invisible suction force drew the hair into the sphere. A while later, the hair fell from the sphere, drifting to the plane. The god had only extracted a bit of skin from its root.

The sphere roiled with white light, then gradually became clear. It was now filled with transparent liquid in which strings of bubbles rose. Next, Yi Yi spotted a ball the size of an egg yolk inside the liquid, made pale red by the sunlight shining through, as if it were luminous in and of itself. The ball soon grew. Yi Yi realized that it was a curled-up embryo, its bulging eyes squeezed shut, its oversized head crisscrossed with red blood vessels. The embryo continued to mature. The tiny body finally uncurled and swam frog-like in the sphere of liquid. The liquid gradually became cloudy, so that the sunlight coming through the sphere revealed only a blurry silhouette that continued to rapidly mature until it became that of a swimming grown man. At this point, the sphere reverted to its original opaque, glowing state, and a naked human fell out of it and onto the plane.

Yi Yi's clone stood up unsteadily, the sunlight glistening off his wet form. He was long-haired and long-bearded, but one could tell that he was only in his thirties or forties. Aside from the wiry thinness, he didn't look at all like the original Yi Yi.

The clone stood stiffly, gazing dully into the infinite distance, as if completely oblivious to the universe he'd just joined. Above him, the sphere's white light dimmed, before extinguishing altogether. The sphere itself disappeared as if evaporating. But just then, Yi Yi thought he saw something else light up, and realized that it was the clone's eyes. The dullness had been replaced with the divine gleam of wisdom. In this moment, Yi Yi would learn, the god had transferred all his memories to the clone body.

"Cold . . . so this is cold?" A breeze had blown past. The clone had wrapped his arms around his slick shoulders, shivering, but his voice was full of delighted surprise. "This is cold! This is pain, immaculate, impeccable pain, the sensation I scoured the stars for, as piercing as the ten-dimensional string through time and space, as crystalline as a diamond of pure energy at the heart of a star, ah . . ." He spread his emaciated arms and beheld the Milky Way. "*Qian bu jian gu ren, hou bu jian lai zhe, nian yu zhou zhi—*" A spate of shivers left the clone's teeth chattering. He hurriedly stopped commemorating his birth and ran over to warm himself over the incinerator.

The clone extended his hands over the blue flames inside the aperture, shivering as he said to Yi Yi, "Really, this is something I do all the time. When researching and collecting a civilization's art, I always lodge my consciousness inside a member organism of that civilization, to ensure my complete understanding of the art."

The flames inside the incinerator's aperture suddenly flared. The plane surrounding it roiled with multicolored light as well, so that Yi Yi felt as if the entire plane were a sheet of frosted glass floating on a sea of fire.

"The incinerator has turned into a fabricator," Bigtooth whispered to Yi Yi. "The god is performing energy-matter exchange." Seeing Yi Yi's continued puzzlement, he explained again, "Idiot, he's making objects out of pure energy, the handicraft of a god!"

Suddenly, a white mass burst from the fabricator, unfurling in midair as it fell—clothing, which the clone caught and put on. Yi Yi saw that it was a loose, flowing Tang Dynasty robe, made of snow-white silk and trimmed with a wide band of black. The clone, who had appeared so pitiable earlier, looked like an ethereal sage with it on. Yi Yi couldn't imagine how it had been made from the blue flames.

The fabricator completed another object. Something black flew from the aperture and thudded onto the plane like a rock. Yi Yi ran over and picked it up. He might not trust his eyes, but his hand clearly registered a heavy inkstone, icy cold at that. Something else smacked onto the plane; Yi Yi picked up a black rod. No doubt about it—it was an inkstick! Next came several brush pens, a brush holder, a sheet of snow-white mulberry paper (paper, out of the flames!), and several little decorative antiques. The last object out was also the largest: an old-fashioned writing desk! Yi Yi and Bigtooth hurriedly righted the desk and arranged the other objects on top of it.

"The amount of energy he converted into these objects could have pulverized a planet," Bigtooth whispered to Yi Yi, his voice shaking slightly.

The clone walked over to the desk, nodding in satisfaction when he saw the arrangement on it. One hand stroked his newly dry beard. He said, "I, Li Bai."

Yi Yi examined the clone. "Do you mean you want to become Li Bai, or do you really think you're Li Bai?"

"I'm Li Bai, pure and simple. A Li Bai to surpass Li Bai!"

Yi Yi laughed and shook his head.

"What, do you question me even now?"

Yi Yi nodded. "I concede that your technology far exceeds my understanding. It's indistinguishable from human ideas of magic and acts of God. Even in the fields of art and poetry, you've astonished me. Despite such an enormous cultural, spatial, and temporal gap, you've managed to sense the hidden nuances of Classical Chinese poetry. . . . But understanding Li Bai is one matter, and exceeding him is another. I continue to believe that you face an unsurpassable body of art."

A mysterious amusement appeared on the clone's—Li Bai's—face, only to quickly vanish. He pointed at the desk. "Grind ink!" he bellowed to Yi Yi, before striding away. He was nearly at the edge of the plane before he stopped, stroking his whiskers, gazing toward the distant Milky Way, descending into thought.

Yi Yi took the Yixing clay pot on the desk and poured a trickle of clear water into the depression in the inkstone. Then he began to grind the inkstick against the stone. It was the first time he'd done this; he clumsily angled the stick to scrape at its corners. As he watched the liquid thicken and darken, Yi Yi thought of himself, 1.5 astronomical units away from the sun, perched on this infinitely thin plane in the vastness of outer space. (Even while it was making things out of pure energy, a distant viewer would have perceived zero thickness.) It was a stage floating in the void of the universe, on which a dinosaur, a human raised as dinosaur livestock, and a technological god in period dress planning to surpass Li Bai were performing bizarre live theater. With that thought, Yi Yi shook his head and laughed wanly.

Once he thought the ink was ready, Yi Yi stood and waited next to Bigtooth. The breeze on the plane had ceased by this time; the sun and Milky Way shone calmly, as if the whole universe were waiting in anticipation.

Li Bai stood steadily at the edge of the plane. The layer of air above the plane created almost no scattering effect, so that the sunlight cast him in crispest light and shadow. Aside from the movements of his hand when he smoothed his beard now and then, he was practically a statue hewn from stone.

Yi Yi and Bigtooth waited and waited. Time flowed past silently. The brush on the desk, plump with ink, began to dry. The position of the sun changed unnoticed in the sky; they, the desk, and the spaceship cast long shadows, while the white paper that was spread out on the desk appeared as if it had become part of the plane.

Finally, Li Bai turned and slowly stepped over to the desk. Yi Yi hurriedly re-dipped the brush in ink and offered it with both hands, but Li Bai held up a hand in refusal. He only stared at the blank paper on the desk in continued deep thought, something new in his gaze.

Yi Yi, with glee, saw that it was perplexity and unease.

"I need to make some more things. They're all . . . fragile goods. Be sure to catch them." Li Bai pointed at the fabricator; the flames within, which had dimmed, grew bright once more. Just as Yi Yi and Bigtooth ran over, a tongue of blue flame pushed out a round object. Bigtooth caught it agilely. Upon closer inspection, it was a large earthen jar. Next, three large bowls sprang out of the blue flames. Yi Yi caught two of them, but the third fell and shattered. Bigtooth carried the jar to the desk and carefully unsealed it. The powerful fragrance of wine emerged. Bigtooth and Yi Yi exchanged astonished looks.

"There wasn't much documentation on human winemaking in the Earth-related data I received from the Devouring Empire, so I'm not sure I fabricated this correctly," said Li Bai, pointing to the jar of wine to indicate that Yi Yi should taste it.

Yi Yi took a bowl, scooped a little from the jar, and took a sip. Fiery heat ran past his throat down into his belly. He nodded. "It's wine, albeit much too strong compared to the kind we drink to improve our meat quality."

Li Bai pointed to the other bowl on the desk. "Fill it up." He waited for Bigtooth to pour a bowlful of the strong wine, then picked it up and glugged the whole thing down. Then he turned and once again walked off into the distance, weaving a stagger here and there along the way. Once he reached the edge of the plane, he stood there and resumed his pondering in the direction of the stars, only this time his body swayed rhythmically left and right, as if to some unheard melody. Li Bai didn't ponder for long before returning to the desk once more, and on the walk back he staggered every step. He grabbed the brush being proffered by Yi Yi and threw it into the distance.

"Fill it up," Li Bai said, eyes fixed on the empty bowl. . . .

An hour later, Bigtooth's two immense claws carefully lowered a passed-out Li Bai onto the cleared desk, only for him to roll over and fall right off, muttering something in a language incomprehensible to dinosaur and human alike. He'd already vomited a particolored pile (although no one knew when he'd had the occasion to eat in the first place), some of it staining his flowing robes. With the white light of the plane passing through, the vomit formed some sort of abstract image. Li Bai's mouth was black with ink: after finishing his fourth bowl, he'd tried to write something on the paper, but had ended up merely stabbing his ink-plump brush heavily upon the table. After that, he'd tried to smooth the brush with his mouth, like a child at his first calligraphy lesson. . . .

"Esteemed god?" Bigtooth bent down and asked carefully.

"Wayakaaaaa . . . kaaaayiaiwa," said Li Bai, tongue lolling.

Bigtooth straightened, shook his head, and sighed. He said to Yi Yi, "Let's go."

THE SECOND PATH

Yi Yi's feedlot was located on the Devourers' equator. While the planet had lain within the inner reaches of the solar system, this had been a beautiful prairie between two rivers. When the Devourers left the orbit of Jupiter, a harsh winter had descended, the prairie disappearing and the rivers freezing. The humans raised there had all been relocated to an underground city. After the Devourers received the summons from the god and returned, spring had come back to the land with the approach of the sun. The two rivers quickly defrosted, and the prairie began to turn green as well.

In times of good weather, Yi Yi lived alone in the crude grass hut he'd built himself by the riverside, tilling the land and amusing himself. A normal human wouldn't have been allowed, but as Yi Yi's feedlot lectures on ancient literature had edifying properties, imparting a unique flavor to the flesh of his students, the dinosaur breeder didn't stop him.

It was dusk, two months after Yi Yi had first met Li Bai, the sun just tipping over the perfectly straight horizon line of the Devouring Empire. The two rivers reflected the sunset, meeting at the edge of the sky. In the riverside hut, a breeze carried faint, distant sounds of song and celebration over the prairie. Yi Yi was alone, playing weiqi with himself.

He looked up and saw Li Bai and Bigtooth walking along the riverbank toward him. Li Bai was much changed from before: his hair was unkempt, his beard even longer, his face sun-browned. He had a rough cloth pack slung over his left shoulder and a large bottle-gourd in his right hand. His robes had been reduced to rags; his woven-straw shoes were mangled with wear. But Yi Yi thought that he now seemed more like a human being.

Li Bai walked over to the weiqi table. Like the last few times, he slammed the gourd down without looking at Yi Yi and said, "Bowl!" When Yi Yi had brought over the two wooden bowls, Li Bai uncorked the gourd and filled them with wine, then took a paper package from his pack. Yi Yi opened it to discover cooked meat, already sliced, its aroma greeting his nose enthusiastically. He couldn't help but grab a piece and start chewing.

Bigtooth only stood, a few meters away, watching them silently. He knew from before that the two of them were going to discuss poetry again, a topic in which he had no interest and no ability.

"Delicious," Yi Yi said, nodding approvingly. "Is the beef made directly from energy too?"

"No, I've gone natural for a long while now. You might not know, but there's a pasture a long distance away from here where they raise Earth cows. I cooked the beef myself in the Shanxi Pingyao style. There's a trick to it. When you stew the meat, you have to add . . ." Li Bai whispered mysteriously into Yi Yi's ear, "Urea."

Yi Yi looked at him uncomprehendingly.

"Oh, that's what you get when you take human urine, let it evaporate, and extract the white stuff. It makes the cooked meat red and juicy with a tender texture, while keeping the fatty parts from being cloying and the lean parts from being leathery."

"The urea . . . it's made from pure energy, right?" Yi Yi asked, horrified.

"I told you, I've gone natural! It took me a lot of work to collect the urea from several human feedlots. This is a very traditional folk cuisine technique, faded from use long before the destruction of Earth."

Yi Yi had already swallowed his bite of beef. He picked up the wine bowl to prevent himself from vomiting.

Li Bai pointed at the gourd. "Under my direction, the Devouring Empire has built a number of distilleries, already capable of producing many of the wines famous on Earth. This is bona-fide zhuyeqing, made by steeping bamboo leaves in sorghum liquor."

Yi Yi only now discovered that the wine in his bowl was different from what Li Bai had brought previously. It was emerald green, with a sweet aftertaste of herbs.

"Looks like you've really mastered human culture," Yi Yi said feelingly to Li Bai.

"That's not all. I've also spent a lot of time on personal enrichment. As you know, the scenery of many parts of the Devouring Empire is near identical to what Li Bai saw on Earth. In these two months, I've wandered the mountains and waters, feasting my eyes on picturesque landscapes, drinking wine under moonlight, declaiming poetry on mountain summits, even having a few romantic encounters in the human feedlots everywhere . . ."

"Then, you should be ready to show me your works of poetry."

Li Bai exhaled and set down his wine bowl. He stood and paced uneasily. "I've composed some poems, yes, and I'm certain you'd be astonished at them. You'd find that I'm already a remarkable poet, even more remarkable than you and your great-grandfather. But I don't want you to see the poems, because I'm equally certain you'd think they fail to surpass Li Bai's. And I . . ." He looked up and far away, at the residual radiance of the setting sun, his gaze dazed and pained. "I think so too."

On the distant prairie, the dances had ended. People were happily turning to their abundant dinner. A group of girls ran to the riverbank to splash in the shallows near shore. Circlets of flowers adorned their heads, and light gauze like mist draped over their bodies, forming an intoxicating scene in the lighting of dusk. Yi Yi pointed at one girl near the hut. "Is she beautiful?"

"Of course," Li Bai said, looking uncomprehendingly at Yi Yi.

"Imagine cutting her open with a sharp knife, removing her every organ, plucking out her eyes, scooping out her brain, picking out all her bones, slicing apart her muscles and fat according to position and function, gathering her blood vessels and nerves into two bundles. Finally, imagine laying out a big white cloth and arranging all those pieces, classified according to anatomical principles. Would you still think her beautiful?"

"How do you think of such a thing while drinking? Disgusting," Li Bai said, wrinkling his brow.

"How is it disgusting? Is this not the technology you worship?"

"What are you trying to say?"

"Li Bai saw nature like you see the girls down by the riverside. But in technology's eyes, nature is its components, perfectly arrayed and dripping blood on a white cloth. Therefore, technology is antithetical to poetry."

"Then you have a suggestion for me?" Li Bai said thoughtfully, stroking his beard.

"I still don't think you stand a chance at surpassing Li Bai, but I can point your energies in the correct direction. Technology has clouded your eyes, blinding you to the beauty of nature. Therefore, you must first forget all your ultra-advanced technological knowledge. If you can transplant all your memories into your current brain, you can certainly delete some of them."

Li Bai exchanged looks with Bigtooth. Both burst into laughter. "Esteemed god, I told you from the start, these are tricky bug-bugs," said Bigtooth. "A moment of carelessness and you'll fall into one of their traps."

"Hahahaha, tricky indeed, but entertaining as well," Li Bai said to Bigtooth, before turning toward Yi Yi with cold amusement. "Did you really think I came here to admit defeat?"

"You could not surpass the pinnacle of human poetry. That's a fact."

Abruptly, Li Bai raised a finger and pointed to the river. "How many ways are there to walk to the riverbank?"

Yi Yi looked uncomprehendingly at Li Bai for a few seconds. "It seems . . . there's only one."

"No, there's two. I can also walk in this direction," Li Bai indicated the direction opposite from the river, "and keep going, all the way around the

Devouring Empire, crossing the river from the other side to reach this bank. I can even make a full circuit around the Milky Way and return here. With our technology, it's just as easy. Technology can surpass anything! I am now forced to take the second path!"

Yi Yi pondered this for a long time before shaking his head in bewilderment. "Even if you have the technology of a god, I can't think of a second path to surpassing Li Bai."

Li Bai stood. "It's simple. There are two ways to surpass Li Bai. The first is to write poems that surpass his. The other is to write every poem!"

Yi Yi looked even more confused, but Bigtooth beside him seemed to have had an epiphany.

"I will write every five-character-line and seven-character-line poem possible. They were Li Bai's specialty. In addition, I'm going to write down every possible lyrical poem for the common line formats! How do you not understand? I'm going to try every possible permutation of Chinese characters that fits the format rules!"

"Ah, magnificent! What a magnificent undertaking!" Bigtooth crowed, forgetting all dignity.

"Is this hard?" Yi Yi asked ignorantly.

"Of course, incredibly so! The largest computer in the Devouring Empire might not be able to finish the calculations before the death of the universe!"

"Surely not," Yi Yi said, skeptical.

"Of course yes!" Li Bai nodded with satisfaction. "But by using quantum computing, which you're still a long way from mastering, we can complete the calculations in an acceptable length of time. Then I'll have written every single poem, including everything that's been written in the past, and, much more importantly, everything that may be written someday in the future! This will naturally include poems that surpass Li Bai's best works. In fact, I've ended the art of poetry. Every poet from now on to the destruction of the universe, no matter how great, will be no more than a plagiarist. Their works will turn up in a search of my enormous storage device."

Bigtooth suddenly gave a guttural cry, his gaze on Li Bai changing from excitement to shock. "An enormous . . . storage device? Esteemed god, do you mean to say, you're going to . . . *save* all the poems the quantum computer writes?"

"What's the fun in deleting everything right after I write it? Of course I'm going to save them! It will be a monument to the artistic contributions my race has made to this universe!"

Bigtooth's expression changed from shock to horror. He extended his bulky claws and bent his legs, as if trying to kneel to Li Bai. "You mustn't, esteemed god," he cried. "You mustn't!"

"What's got you so scared?" Yi Yi regarded Bigtooth with astonishment.

"You idiot! Don't you know that atomic bombs are made of atoms? The storage device will be made of atoms too, and its storage precision can't possibly exceed the atomic level! Do you know what atomic-level storage is? It means that all of humanity's books can be stored in an area the size of the point of a needle! Not the couple of books you have left, but all the books that existed before we ate Earth!"

"Ah, that sounds plausible. I've heard that a glass of water contains more atoms than the Earth's oceans contained cups of water. Then, he can just write down those poems and take the needle with him," Yi Yi said, pointing at Li Bai.

Bigtooth nearly burst with outrage. He had to rapidly pace a few steps to summon a little more patience. "Okay, okay, tell me, if the god writes all those five-character- and seven-character-line poems, and the common lyrical poetry formats, one time each, how many characters would that be?"

"Not many, no more than two or three thousand, right? Classical poetry is the most concise art form there is."

"Fine, you idiot bug-bug, let me show you how concise it really is!" Bigtooth strode to the table and pointed at the game board with one claw. "What is it you call this stupid game . . . ah yes, weiqi. How many grid intersections are on the board?"

"There are nineteen lines in both the vertical and horizontal directions, for a total of three hundred and sixty-one points."

"Very good, each intersection can be occupied by a black piece, a white piece, or no piece, a total of three states in all. So you can think of each game state as using three characters to write a poem of nineteen lines and three hundred and sixty-one characters."

"That's a clever comparison."

"Now, if we exhaust all the possible permutations of these three characters in this poem format, how many poems can we write? Let me tell you: 3^{361}, or, let me think, 10^{172}!"

"Is . . . is that a lot?"

"Idiot!" Bigtooth spat the word at him for the third time. "In all the universe, there are only . . . grargh!" He was too infuriated to speak.

"How many?" Yi Yi still wore a befuddled expression.

"10^{80} atoms! You idiot bug-bug—"

Only now did Yi Yi show any sign of astonishment. "You mean to say, if we could save one poem in every atom, we might use up every atom in the universe and still not be able to fit all of his quantum computer's poems?"

"Far from it! Off by a factor of 10^{92}! Besides, how can one atom store a whole poem? The memory devices of human bug-bugs would have needed more atoms to store one poem than your population. As for us, ai, technology to store one bit per atom is still in the laboratory stage. . . ."

"Here you display your shortsightedness and lack of imagination, Emissary, one of the reasons behind the laggardly advancement of Devouring Empire technology," Li Bai said, laughing. "Using quantum storage devices based on the quantum superposition principle, the poems can be stored in very little matter. Of course, quantum storage is none too stable. To preserve the poems forever, it needs to be used in tandem with more traditional storage techniques. Nonetheless, the amount of matter required is minuscule."

"How much?" Bigtooth asked, looking as if his heart were in his throat.

"Approximately 10^{57} atoms, a pittance really."

"That's . . . that's exactly the amount of matter in the solar system!"

"Correct, including all the planets orbiting the sun, and of course including the Devouring Empire."

Li Bai said this last sentence easily and naturally, but it struck Yi Yi like a bolt out of the blue. Bigtooth, on the other hand, seemed to have calmed down. After the long torment of sensing disaster on the horizon, the actual onslaught only left a sense of relief.

"Can't you convert pure energy into matter?" asked Bigtooth.

"You should know how much energy it would take to create such an enormous amount of matter. The prospect is unimaginable even to us. We'll go with ready-made."

"His Majesty's concerns weren't unjustified," Bigtooth murmured to himself.

"Yes, yes," Li Bai said happily. "I informed the Emperor of the Devourers the day before yesterday. This great ring-world empire shall be used for an even greater goal. The dinosaurs should feel honored."

"Esteemed god, you'll see how the Devouring Empire feels," Bigtooth said darkly. "I also have one more concern. Compared to the sun, the amount of matter in the Devouring Empire is insignificantly minuscule. Is it really necessary to destroy a civilization millions of years of evolution in the making, just to obtain a few scraps?"

"I fully understand your reservations. But you must know, extinguishing, cooling, and disassembling the sun will take a long time. The quantum calculations should begin before then, and we need to save the resulting poems elsewhere so that the computer can clear its internal storage and continue work. Therefore the planets and the Devouring Empire, which can immediately provide matter for manufacturing storage devices, are crucial."

"I understand, esteemed god. I have one last question: Is it necessary to store all the results? Why can't you add an analytical program at the end, to delete all the poems that don't warrant saving? From what I know, Classical Chinese poetry has to follow a strict structure. If we delete all the poems that violate the formal rules, we'll greatly decrease the volume of the results."

"Formal rules? Ha." Li Bai shook his head contemptuously. "Shackles upon inspiration, and nothing more. Classical Chinese poetry wasn't bound by these rules before the Northern and Southern Dynasties. Even after the

Tang Dynasty, which popularized the strict jintishi form, many master poets ignored the rules to write some extraordinary biantishi works. That's
why, for this ultimate poetry composition, I won't take formal rules into
consideration."

"But, you should still consider the poem's content, right? Ninety-nine
percent of the results are obviously going to be rubbish. What's the point of
storing a bunch of randomly generated character arrays?"

"Rubbish?" Li Bai shrugged. "Emissary, you are not the one who decides
whether a poem is meaningful. Neither am I, nor any other person. Time
decides. Many poems once considered worthless at the time of their writing
were later lauded as masterpieces. Many of the masterpieces of today and
tomorrow would have been considered worthless in the distant past. I'm going to write all the poems there are. Trillions of years from now, who knows
which of them mighty Time will choose as the finest?"

"That's absurd!" Bigtooth bellowed, startling several birds hidden in
the distant grass into flight. "If we go by the human bug-bugs' preexisting
Chinese character database, the first poem your quantum computer writes
should be:

"*a a a a a*

a a a a a

a a a a a

a a a a ai

"Might I ask, would mighty Time choose *this* as a masterpiece?!"

Yi Yi broke his silence to cheer. "Wow! Who needs mighty Time to
choose? It's a masterpiece right now! The first three lines and the first
four characters of the fourth are the exclamations—*ah!*—of living beings
witnessing the majestic grandeur of the universe. The last character is the
clincher, where the poet, having witnessed the vastness of the universe, expresses the insignificance of life in the infinity of time and space with a
single sigh of inevitability."

"Hahahaha . . ." Li Bai stroked his whiskers, unable to stop smiling. "A fine poem, my bug-bug Yi Yi, a fine poem indeed, hahaha . . ." He took up the gourd and poured Yi Yi wine.

Bigtooth raised his massive claws and flung Yi Yi into the distance with one swat. "Nasty bug-bug, I know you're happy now. But don't forget, once the Devouring Empire is destroyed, your kind won't survive either!"

Yi Yi rolled all the way to the riverbank. It took a long time before he could crawl back up. A grin cracked across his dirt-covered face; he was laughing despite his pain, truly happy. "This is great! This universe is mother-fucking incredible!" he yelled with no thought to dignity.

"Any other questions, Emissary?" asked Li Bai. Bigtooth shook his head. "Then I'll leave tomorrow. The day after the next, the quantum computer will execute its poetry-writing software, commencing the ultimate poetry composition. At the same time, the work to extinguish the sun and disman-tle the planets and the Devouring Empire shall commence."

Bigtooth straightened. "Esteemed god, the Devouring Empire will com-plete preparations for battle tonight!" he said solemnly.

"Good, very good, the coming days will be interesting. But before all else, let us finish this gourd." Li Bai nodded happily as he took up the gourd and poured the remaining wine. He looked at the river, now shrouded in night, and continued to savor those words: "A fine poem indeed, the first, haha, the first and already so fine."

THE ULTIMATE POETRY COMPOSITION

The poetry-composition software was in fact very simple. Represented in humanity's C language, it would be no more than two thousand lines of code, with an additional database of modest size appended storing the Chinese characters. Once the software was uploaded onto the quantum computer in the orbit of Neptune, an enormous transparent cone floating in the vacuum, the ultimate poetry composition began.

Only now did the Devouring Empire learn that the god version of Li Bai was merely one individual member of his ultra-advanced civilization. The dinosaurs had previously assumed that any society that had advanced to this level of technology would have melded their consciousness into one being long ago; all five of the ultra-advanced civilizations they'd met in the past ten million years had done so. That Li Bai's race had preserved their individual existences also somewhat explained their extraordinary ability to grasp art. When the poetry composition began, more individuals from Li Bai's race jumped into the solar system from various places in distant space and began construction on the storage device.

The humans living in the Devouring Empire couldn't see the quantum computer in space, or the new arrivals from the race of gods. To them, the process of the ultimate poetry composition was simply the increase and decrease of the number of suns in space.

One week after the poetry software began execution, the gods successfully extinguished the sun, reducing the sun count to zero. But the cessation of nuclear fission inside the sun caused the star's outer layer to lose support, and it quickly collapsed into a new star that illuminated the darkness once more. However, this sun's luminosity was a hundred times greater than before; smoke rose from the grass and trees on the surface of the Devouring Empire. The new star was once again extinguished, but a while later it burst alight again. So it went on, lighting only to be extinguished, extinguishing only to light once more, as if the sun were a cat with nine lives, struggling stubbornly. But the gods were highly practiced at killing stars. They patiently extinguished the new star again and again, until its matter had, as much as possible, fused into the heavier elements needed in the construction of the storage device. Only after the eleventh star dimmed was the sun snuffed out for good.

At this point, the ultimate poetry composition had run for three Earth months. Long before then, during the appearance of the third new star, other suns had appeared in space. These suns rose and fell in succession throughout space, brightening and dimming. At one point, there were nine new suns in the sky. They were releases of energy as the gods dismantled the planets.

With the star-sized sun diminishing in brightness later on, people could no longer tell the suns apart.

The dismantlement of the Devouring Empire commenced the fifth week after the start of the poetry composition. Before it, Li Bai had made a suggestion to the Empire: The gods could jump all the dinosaurs to a world on the other side of the Milky Way. The civilization there was much less advanced than the gods', its members being unable to convert themselves into pure energy, but still much more advanced than the Devourers' civilization. There, the dinosaurs would be raised as a form of livestock and live happy lives with all their needs taken care of. But the dinosaurs would rather break than bend, and angrily refused this suggestion.

Next, Li Bai made another request: that humanity be allowed to return to their mother planet. To be sure, Earth had been dismantled, and most of it went toward the storage device. But the gods saved a small amount of matter to construct a hollow Earth, about the same size as the original, but with only a hundredth of its mass. To say that the hollow Earth was Earth hollowed-out would be incorrect, because the layer of brittle rock that originally covered the Earth could hardly be used to make the spherical shell. The shell material was perhaps taken from the Earth's core. In addition, razor-thin but extremely strong reinforcing hoops crisscrossed the shell, like lines of latitude and longitude, made from the neutronium produced in the collapse of the sun.

Movingly, the Devouring Empire not only immediately agreed to Li Bai's request, allowing all humans to leave the great ring world, but also returned the seawater and air they'd taken from Earth in their entirety. The gods used them to restore all of Earth's original continents, oceans, and atmosphere inside the hollow Earth.

Next, the terrible battle to defend the great ring began. The Devouring Empire launched barrages of nuclear missiles and gamma rays at the gods in space, but these were useless against their foe. The gods launched a powerful, invisible force that pushed at the Devourers' ring, spinning it faster and faster, until it finally fell apart under the centrifugal forces of such rapid rotation. At this time, Yi Yi was en route to the hollow Earth. From twelve million kilometers away, he witnessed the complete course of the Devouring Empire's destruction:

> The ring came apart very slowly, dreamlike. Against the pitch-black backdrop of space, this immense world dispersed like a piece of milk foam on coffee, the fragments at its edges slowly sinking into darkness, as if being dissolved by space. Only by the flashes of sporadic explosions would they reappear.
>
> Excerpt from Devourer

The great, fierce civilization from ancient Earth was thus destroyed, to Yi Yi's deepest lament. Only a few dinosaurs survived, returning to Earth with humanity, including the emissary Bigtooth.

On the return journey to Earth, the humans were largely in low spirits, but for different reasons than Yi Yi: Once they were back on Earth, they'd have to farm and plow if they wanted to eat. To humans accustomed to having every need provided for in their long captivity, grown indolent and ignorant of labor, it really did seem like a nightmare.

But Yi Yi believed in Earth's future. No matter how many challenges lay ahead, humans were going to become people once more.

THE CLOUD OF POEMS

The poetry voyage arrived on the shores of Antarctica.

The gravity here was already weak; the waves cycled slowly in a dreamlike dance. Under the low gravity, the impact of waves upon shore sent spray dozens of meters into the air, where the seawater contracted under surface tension into countless spheres, some as large as soccer balls, some as small as raindrops, which fell so slowly that one could draw rings around them with one's hand. They refracted the rays of the little sun, so that when Yi Yi, Li Bai, and Bigtooth disembarked, they were surrounded by crystalline brilliance.

Due to the forces of rotation, the Earth was slightly stretched at the North and South Poles, causing the hollow Earth's pole regions to maintain their old chilly state. Low-gravity snow was a wonder, loose and foamy, waist-high in the shallow parts and deep enough at others that even Bigtooth disappeared beneath it. But having disappeared, they could still breathe normally inside the snow! The entire Antarctic continent was buried underneath this snow-foam, creating an undulating landscape of white.

Yi Yi and company rode a snowmobile toward the South Pole. The snowmobile skimmed across the snow-foam like a speedboat, throwing waves of white to either side.

The next day, they arrived at the South Pole, marked by a towering pyramid of crystal, a memorial dedicated to the Earth Defense War of two centuries ago. Neither writing nor images marked its surface. There was just the crystal form in the snow-foam at the apex of the Earth, silently refracting the sunlight.

From here, one could gaze upon the entire world. Continents and oceans surrounded the radiant little sun, so that it looked as if it had floated up from the waters of the Arctic Sea.

"Will that little sun really be able to shine forever?" Yi Yi asked Li Bai.

"At the very least, it will last until the new Earth civilization is advanced enough to create a new sun. It is a miniature white hole."

"White hole? Is that the inverse of a black hole?" asked Bigtooth.

"Yes, it's connected through a wormhole to a black hole orbiting a star, two million light-years away. The black hole sucks in the star's light, which is released here. Think of the sun as one end of a fiber-optic cable running through hyperspace."

The apex of the monument was the southern starting point of the Lagrangian axis, the thirteen-thousand-kilometer line of zero gravity between the North and South Poles of the hollow Earth, named after the zero-gravity Lagrangian point that had existed between the Earth and moon before the war. In the future, people were certain to launch various satellites onto the Lagrangian axis. Compared to the process on Earth before the war, this would be easy: one would only have to ship the satellite to the North or South Pole, by donkey if one wanted to, and give it a good kick up with one's foot.

As the party viewed the memorial, another, larger snowmobile ferried over a crowd of young human tourists. After disembarking, the tourists bent their legs and jumped straight into the air, flying high along the Lagrangian axis, turning themselves into satellites. From here, one could see many small, black specks in the air, marking out the position of the axis: tourists and vehicles drifting in zero gravity. They would have been able to fly directly to the North Pole if it weren't for the sun, placed at the midpoint of the Lagrangian axis. In the past, some tourists flying along the axis had discovered their handheld miniature air-jet thrusters broken, been unable to decelerate, and flown straight into the sun. Well, in truth, they vaporized a considerable distance from it.

In the hollow Earth, entering space was also easy. One only needed to jump into one of the five deep wells on the equator (called Earthgates) and fall (fly?) a hundred kilometers through the shell, then be flung by the centrifugal forces of the hollow Earth's rotation into space.

Yi Yi and company also needed to pass through the shell to see the Cloud of Poems, but they were heading through the Antarctic Earthgate. Here, there were no centrifugal forces, so instead of being flung into space, they would only reach the outer surface of the hollow Earth. Once they'd put on lightweight space suits at the Antarctic control station, they entered the one-hundred-kilometer well—although, without gravity, it was better termed a tunnel. Being weightless here, they used the thrusters on their space suits to move forward. This was much slower than the free fall on the equator; it took them half an hour to arrive on the outside.

The outer surface of the hollow Earth was completely barren. There were only the crisscrossing reinforcing hoops of neutronium, which divided the outside by latitude and longitude into a grid. The South Pole was indeed where all the longitudinal hoops met. When Yi Yi and company walked out of the Earthgate, they saw that they were located on a modestly sized plateau. The hoops that reinforced Earth resembled many long mountain ranges, radiating in every direction from the plateau.

Looking up, they saw the Cloud of Poems.

In place of the solar system was the Cloud of Poems, a spiral galaxy a hundred astronomical units across, shaped much like the Milky Way. The hollow Earth was situated at the edge of the Cloud, much as the sun had been in the actual Milky Way. The difference was that Earth's position was not coplanar with the Cloud of Poems, which allowed one to see one face of the Cloud head-on, instead of only edge-on as with the Milky Way. But Earth wasn't nearly far enough from the plane to allow people here to observe the full form of the Cloud of Poems. Instead, the Cloud blanketed the entire sky of the southern hemisphere.

The Cloud of Poems emitted a silvery radiance bright enough to cast shadows on the ground. It wasn't that the Cloud itself was made to glow, apparently, but rather that cosmic rays would excite it into silver luminescence. Due to the uneven spatial distribution of the cosmic rays, glowing masses frequently rippled through the Cloud of Poems, their varicolored light rolling across the sky like luminescent whales diving through the Cloud. Rarely, with spikes in the cosmic radiation, the Cloud of Poems emitted dapples of light that made the Cloud look utterly unlike a cloud. Instead, the entire sky seemed to be the surface of a moonlit sea seen from below.

Earth and the Cloud did not move in sync, so sometimes Earth lay in the gaps between the spiral arms. Through the gap, one could see the night sky and the stars, and most thrillingly, a cross-sectional view of the Cloud of Poems. Immense structures resembling Earthly cumulonimbuses rose from the spiraling plane, shimmering with silvery light, morphing through magnificent forms that inspired the human imagination, as if they belonged to the dreamscape of some super-advanced consciousness.

Yi Yi tore his gaze from the Cloud of Poems and picked up a crystal chip off the ground. These chips were scattered around them, sparkling like shards of ice in winter. Yi Yi raised the chip against a sky thick with the Cloud of Poems. The chip was very thin, and half the size of his palm. It appeared transparent from the front, but if he tilted it slightly, he could see the bright light of the Cloud of Poems reflect off its surface in rainbow halos. This was a quantum memory chip. All the written information created in human history would take up less than a millionth of a percent of one chip. The Cloud of Poems was composed of 10^{40} of these storage devices, and contained all the results of the ultimate poem composition. It was manufactured using all the matter in the sun and its nine major planets, of course including the Devouring Empire.

"What a magnificent work of art!" Bigtooth sighed sincerely.

"Yes, it's beautiful in its significance: a nebula fifteen billion kilometers across, encompassing every poem possible. It's too spectacular!" Yi Yi said, gazing at the nebula. "Even I'm starting to worship technology."

Li Bai gave a long sigh. He had been in a low mood all this time. "*Ai*, it seems like we've both come around to the other person's viewpoint. I witnessed the limits of technology in art. I—" He began to sob. "I've failed. . . ."

"How can you say that?" Yi Yi pointed at the Cloud of Poems overhead. "This holds all the possible poems, so of course it holds the poems that surpass Li Bai's!"

"But I can't get to them!" Li Bai stomped his foot, which shot him meters into the air. He curled into a ball in midair, miserably burying his face between his knees in a fetal position; he slowly descended under the weak gravitational pull of the Earth's shell. "At the start of the poetry composition, I immediately set out to program software that could analyze poetry. At that point, technology once again met that unsurpassable obstacle in the pursuit of art. Even now, I'm still unable to write software that can judge and appreciate poetry." He pointed up at the Cloud of Poems. "Yes, with the help of mighty technology, I've written the ultimate works of poetry. But I can't find them amid the Cloud of Poems, *ai* . . ."

"Is the soul and essence of intelligent life truly untouchable by technology?" Bigtooth loudly asked the Cloud of Poems above. He'd become increasingly philosophical after all he'd endured.

"Since the Cloud of Poems encompasses all possible poems, then naturally some portion of those poems describes all of our pasts and all of our futures, possible and impossible. The bug-bug Yi Yi would certainly find a poem that describes how he felt one night thirty years ago while clipping his fingernails, or a menu from a lunch twelve years in his future. Emissary

Bigtooth, too, might find a poem that describes the color of a particular scale on his leg five years from now. . . ."

Li Bai had touched down once more on the ground; as he spoke, he took out two chips, shimmering under the light of the Cloud of Poems. "These are my parting gifts for you two. The quantum computer used your names as keywords to search through the Cloud of Poems, and found several quadrillion poems that describe your various possible future lives. Of course, these are only a tiny portion of the poems with you as subject in the Cloud of Poems. I've only read a couple dozen of these. My favorite is a seven-character-line poem about Yi Yi describing a romantic riverbank scene between him and a beautiful woman from a faraway village. . . .

"After I leave, I hope humanity and the remaining dinosaurs can get along with each other, and that humanity can get along with itself even better. If someone nukes a hole into the shell of the hollow Earth, it's going to be a real problem. . . . The good poems in the Cloud of Poems don't belong to anyone yet. Hopefully humans will be able to write some of them."

"What happened to me and the woman, afterward?" Yi Yi asked.

Under the silver light of the Cloud of Poems, Li Bai chuckled. "Together, you lived happily ever after."

THE THINKER

TRANSLATED BY JOHN CHU

THE SUN

He still remembered how he felt the first time he saw the Mount Siyun Astronomical Observatory thirty-four years ago. After his ambulance crossed the mountain ridge, Mount Siyun's highest peak emerged in the distance. Its observatories' spherical roofs reflected the golden light of the setting sun like pearls inlaid into the mountain peak.

At the time, he'd just graduated from medical school. A brain-surgery intern assisting the chief of surgery, he'd been rushed here to save a visiting research scholar from England who'd fallen on a hike. The scholar had injured his head too seriously to be moved. Once the ambulance arrived, they drilled a hole in the patient's skull, then drained some blood out to reduce brain swelling. Once the patient had been stabilized enough to move, the ambulance took him to the hospital for surgery.

It was late at night by the time they could leave. Out of curiosity, while others carried the patient into the ambulance, he examined the several spherical observatories that surrounded him. How they were laid out seemed to imply some sort of hidden message, like a Stonehenge in the moonlight. Spurred on by some mystical force that he still didn't understand even after a lifetime of contemplation, he walked to the nearest observatory, opened its door, then walked inside.

The lights inside were off except for numerous small signal lamps. He felt as though he'd walked from a moonlit starry sky to a moonless starry sky.

The only moonlight was a sliver that penetrated the crack in the spherical roof. It fell on the giant astronomical telescope, partially sketching out its contours in silver lines. The telescope looked like a piece of abstract art in a town square at night.

He stepped silently to the bottom of the telescope. In the weak light, he saw a large pile of machinery. It was more complex than he'd imagined. He searched for an eyepiece. A soft voice came from the door:

"This is a solar telescope. It doesn't have an eyepiece."

A figure wearing white work clothes walked through the door, as though a feather had drifted in from the moonlight. The woman walked over to him, bringing a light breeze along with her.

"A traditional solar telescope casts an image onto a screen. Nowadays, we usually use a monitor. . . . Doctor, you seem to be very interested in this."

He nodded. "An observatory is such a sublime and rarefied place. I like how it makes me feel."

"Then why did you go into medicine? Oh, that was very rude of me."

"Medicine isn't just some trivial skill. Sometimes, it, too, is sublime, like my specialty of brain medicine, for example."

"Oh? When you use a scalpel to open up the brain, you can see thoughts?" she said.

Her smiling face in the weak light made him think of something he'd never seen before, the sun cast onto a screen. Once the violent flares disappeared, the magnificence that remained couldn't help but make his heart skip a beat. He smiled, too, hoping she could see his smile.

"Oh, we can look at the brain all we want," he said, "but consider this: Say a mushroom-shaped thing you can hold in one hand turns out to be a rich and varied universe. From a certain philosophical viewpoint, this universe is even grander than the one you observe. Even though your universe is tens of billions of light-years wide, it's been established that it's finite. My universe is infinite because thought is infinite."

"Ah, not everybody's thoughts are infinite but, Doctor, yours seem to be. As for astronomy, it's not as rarefied as you think. Several thousand years ago on the banks of the Nile and several hundred years ago on a long sea voyage, it was a practical skill. An astronomer of the time often spent years marking the positions of thousands of stars on star charts. A census of the stars consumed their lives. Nowadays, the actual work of astronomical research is dull and meaningless. For example, I study the twinkling of stars. I make endless observations, take notes, then make more observations and take more notes. It's definitely not sublime as well as not rarefied."

His eyebrows rose in surprise. "The twinkling of stars? Like the kind we can see?" When he saw her laugh, he laughed, too, shaking his head. "Oh, I know, of course, that's atmospheric refraction."

"However, as a visual metaphor, it's pretty accurate. Get rid of the constant terms, just show the fluctuations in their energy output, and stars really do look like they're twinkling."

"Is it because of sunspots?"

She stopped smiling. "No, this is the fluctuation of a star's total energy. It's like how when a lamp flickers, it's not because of the moths surrounding it, but because of fluctuations in voltage. Of course, the fluctuations of a twinkling star are minuscule, detectable only by the most precise measurements. Otherwise, we'd have been burned by the twinkling of the sun long ago. Researching this sort of twinkling is one way of understanding the deep structure of stars."

"What have you discovered so far?"

"It'll be a while before we discover anything. For now, we've only observed the twinkling of the star that's the easiest to observe—the sun. We can do this for years while we gradually expand out to the rest of the stars. . . . You know, we could spend ten, twenty years taking measurements of the universe before we make any discoveries and come to some conclusion. This is my dissertation topic, but I think I'll be working on this for a long while, perhaps my whole life."

"So you don't think astronomy is dull, after all."

"I think what I'm working on is beautiful. Entering the world of stars is like entering an infinitely vast garden. No two flowers are alike. . . . You have to think that's a weird analogy, but it's exactly how I feel."

As she spoke, seemingly without realizing it, she gestured at the wall. A

painting hung there, very abstract, just a thick line undulating from one end
to the other. When she noticed what he was looking at, she took it down,
then handed it to him. The thick, undulating line was a mosaic of colorful
pebbles from the area.

"It's lovely, but what does it represent? The local mountain range?"

"Our most recent measurements of the sun twinkling, it was so intense
and we'd rarely ever seen it fluctuate like that this year. This is a picture of
the curve of the energy radiated as it twinkled. Oh, when I hike, I like to
collect pebbles, so . . ."

The scientist was only partially visible in the surrounding shadow. She
looked like an elegant ink line a brilliant artist drew on a piece of fine,
white calligraphy paper. The curve's intelligence of spirit filled that perfect white paper immediately with vitality and intention. . . . In the city he
lived in outside the mountains, at any given moment, more than a million
young women, like a large group of particles in Brownian motion, chased
the showy and vain, without even a moment of reflection. But who could
imagine that on this mountain in the middle of nowhere, there was a gentle
and quiet woman who stared for long stretches at the stars. . . .

"You can reveal this kind of beauty from the universe. That's truly rare
and also very fortunate." He realized he was staring and looked away. He
returned the painting to her but, lightly, she pushed it back to him.

"Keep it as a souvenir, Doctor. Professor Wilson is my advisor. Thank
you for saving his life."

After ten minutes, the ambulance left under the moonlight. Slowly, he
realized what he'd left on the mountain.

FIRST TIME

Once he married, he abandoned his effort to fight against time. One day,
he moved his things out of his apartment to the one he now shared with
his wife. Those things that two people shouldn't share, he brought to his
office at the hospital. As he riffled through them, he found a mosaic made

of colorful pebbles. Seeing the multicolored curve, he suddenly realized that the trip to Mount Siyun was ten years ago.

ALPHA CENTAURI A

The hospital's young employees' group had a spring outing. He cherished this outing particularly, because it was getting less and less likely they'd invite him again. This time, the trip organizer was deliberately mysterious, pulling down the blinds on all the coach windows and having everyone guess where they were once they arrived. The first one to guess correctly won a prize. He knew where they were the instant he stepped off the coach, but he kept quiet.

The highest peak of Mount Siyun stood before him. The pearl-like spherical roofs on its summit glittered in the sunlight.

After someone guessed where they were, he told the trip organizer that he wanted to go to the observatory to visit an acquaintance. He left on foot, following the meandering road up the mountain.

He hadn't lied, but the woman whose name he didn't even know wasn't part of the observatory staff. After ten years, she probably wasn't here any-more. He didn't actually want to go inside, just to look around at the place where, ten years ago, his soul, hot, dry, and as bright as the sun, spilled into a thread of moonlight.

One hour later, he reached the mountaintop and the observatory's white railings. Its paint had cracked and faded. Silently, he took in the individual observatories. The place hadn't changed much. He quickly located the domed building that he'd once entered. He sat on a stone block on the grass, lit a cigarette, then studied the building's iron door, spellbound. The scene he'd long cherished replayed from the depths of his memory: with the iron door half open, in the midst of a ray of moonlight like water, a feather drifted in. . . .

He was so completely steeped in that long-gone dream that when the miracle happened, he wasn't surprised: the observatory's iron door opened for real. The feather that once had emerged from the moonlight drifted into

322   CIXIN LIU

the sunlight. She left in a hurry to go into another observatory. This couldn't have taken more twenty seconds, but he knew he wasn't mistaken.

Five minutes later, they reunited.

This was the first time he'd seen her with adequate light. She was exactly as he'd imagined. He wasn't surprised. It'd been ten years, though. She shouldn't have looked exactly like the woman barely lit by a few signal lamps and the moon. He was puzzled.

She was pleasantly surprised to see him, but no more than that. "Doctor, I make a round of every observatory for my project. In a given year, I'm only here for half a month. To run into you again, it must be fate!"

That last sentence, tossed off lightly, confirmed his initial impression: She didn't feel anything more about seeing him again besides surprise. However, she still recognized him after ten years. He took a shred of comfort in that.

They exchanged a few words about what had happened to the visiting English scholar who'd suffered the brain injury. Finally, he asked, "Are you still researching the twinkling of stars?"

"Yes. After observing the sun's twinkling for two years, I moved on to other stars. As I'm sure you understand, the techniques necessary to observe other stars are completely different from those to observe the sun. The project didn't have new funding. It halted for many years. We just started it back up three years ago. Right now, we are only observing twenty-five stars. The number and scope are still growing."

"Then you must have produced more mosaics."

The moonlit smile that had surfaced so many times from the depths of memory over the past ten years now emerged in the sunlight. "Ah, you still remember! Yes, every time I come to Mount Siyun, I collect pretty pebbles. Come, I'll show you!"

She took him into the observatory where they'd first met. A giant telescope confronted him. He didn't know whether it was the same telescope from ten years ago, but the computers that surrounded it were practically new. Familiar things hung on a tall curved wall: mosaics of all different sizes. Each one was of an undulating curve. They were all of different lengths. Some were as gentle as the sea. Others were violent, like a row of tall towers strung together at random.

One by one, she told him which waves came from which stars. "These twinklings, we call type A twinklings. They don't occur as much as other types. The difference between type A twinklings and those of other types, besides that their energy fluctuations are orders of magnitude larger, is that the mathematics of their curves is even more elegant."

He shook his head, puzzled. "You scientists doing basic research are always talking about the elegance of mathematics. I guess that's your prerogative. For example, you all think that Maxwell's equations are incredibly elegant. I understood them once, but I couldn't see where the elegance was. . . ."

Just like ten years ago, she suddenly grew serious. "They're elegant like crystals, very hard, very pure, and very transparent."

Unexpectedly, he recognized one of the mosaics. "Oh, you re-created one?" Seeing her uncomprehending expression, he continued. "That's the waveform of the sun twinkling in the mosaic you gave me ten years ago."

"But . . . that's the waveform from a type A twinkling from Alpha Centauri A. We observed it, um, last October."

He trusted that she was genuinely puzzled, but he trusted his own judgment as well. He knew that waveform too well. Moreover, he could even recall the color and shape of every stone that made up the curve. He didn't want her to know that, until he got married last year, that mosaic had always hung on his wall. There were a few nights every month when moonlight would seep in after he'd turned out the lights, and he could make out the mosaic from his bed. That was when he'd silently count the pebbles that made up the curve. His gaze crawled along the curve like a beetle. Usually, by the time he'd crawled along the entire curve and gone halfway back, he'd fallen asleep. In his dreams, he continued to stroll along this curve that came from the sun, like stepping from colorful stone to colorful stone to cross a river whose banks he'd never see. . . .

"Can you look up the curve of the sun twinkling from ten years ago? The date was April twenty-third."

"Of course."

She gave him an odd look, obviously startled that he remembered that date so easily. At the computer, she pulled up that waveform of the sun twinkling followed by the waveform of Alpha Centauri A twinkling that was on the wall. She stared at the screen, dumbfounded.

The two waveforms overlapped perfectly.

When her long silence grew unbearable, he suggested, "Maybe these two stars have the same structure, so they also twinkle the same way. You said before that type A twinkling reflects the star's deep structure."

"They are both on the main sequence and they both have spectral type G2, but their structures are not identical. The crux, though, is that even for two stars with the same structure, we still wouldn't see this. It's like banyan trees. Have you ever seen two that were absolutely identical? For such complex waveforms to actually overlap perfectly, that's like having two large banyan trees where even their outermost branches were exactly the same."

"Perhaps there really are two large banyan trees that are exactly the same," he consoled, knowing his words were meaningless.

She shook her head lightly. Suddenly, she thought of something and leapt to stand. Fear joined the surprise already in her gaze.

"My god," she said.

"What?"

"You . . . Have you ever thought about time?"

He quickly caught on to what she was thinking. "As far as I know, Alpha Centauri A is our closest star. It's only about . . . four light-years away."

"1.3 parsecs is 4.25 light-years." She was still in the grip of astonishment. It was as if she couldn't believe the things she herself was saying.

Now it was all clear: The two identical twinklings occurred eight years and six months apart, just long enough for light to make a round trip between the two stars. After 4.25 years, when the light of the sun's twinkling reached Alpha Centauri A, the latter twinkled in the same way, and after the same amount of time, the light of Alpha Centauri's twinkling was observed here.

She hunched over her computer, making calculations and talking to herself. "Even if we take into account the several years where the two stars regressed from each other, the result still fits."

"I hope what I said doesn't cause you too much worry. There's ultimately nothing we can do to confirm this, right? It's just a theory."

"Nothing we can do to confirm this? Don't be so sure. That light from the sun twinkling was broadcast into space. Perhaps that'll lead to another star twinkling in the same way."

"After Alpha Centauri, the next closest star is . . ."

"Barnard's Star, 1.81 parsecs away, but it's too dim. There's no way to measure it. The next star out, Wolf 359, 2.35 parsecs away, is just as dim. Can't measure it. Yet farther out, Lalande 21185, 2.52 parsecs away, is also too dim. . . . That leaves Sirius."

"That seems like a star bright enough to see. How far is it?"

"2.65 parsecs away, just 8.6 light-years."

"The light from the sun twinkling has already traveled for ten years. It's already reached there. Perhaps Sirius has already twinkled back."

"But the light from it twinkling won't arrive for another seven years." She seemed to wake all of a sudden from a dream, then laughed. "Oh, dear, what am I thinking? It's too ridiculous!"

"So you're saying, as an astronomer, the idea is ridiculous?"

She studied him earnestly. "What else can it be? As a brain surgeon, how do you feel when someone discusses with you where thought comes from, the brain or the heart?"

He had nothing to say. She glanced at her watch, so he started to leave. She didn't urge him to stay, but she accompanied him quite a distance along the road that led down the mountain. He stopped himself from asking for her number because he knew, in her eyes, he was just some stranger who bumped into her again by chance ten years later.

After they said goodbye, she walked up toward the observatory. Her white lab coat swayed in the mountain breeze. Unexpectedly, it stirred up in him how it had felt when they'd said goodbye ten years ago. The sunlight seemed to change into moonlight. That feather disappeared in the distance . . . like a straw of rice, sinking into the water, that someone desperately tries to grab. He decided he wanted to maintain that cobweb-like connection between them. Almost instinctively, he shouted at her back:

"If, seven years from now, you see Sirius actually twinkles like that . . ."

She stopped walking and turned toward him. With a smile, she answered, "Then we'll meet here!"

SECOND TIME

With marriage, he entered a completely different life, but what changed his life thoroughly was a child. After the child was born, the train of life suddenly changed from the local to the express. It rushed past stop after stop in its never-ending journey onward. He grew numb from the journey. His eyes shut, he no longer paid attention to the unchanging scenery. Weary, he went to sleep. However, as with so many others sleeping on the train, a tiny clock deep in his heart still ticked. He woke the minute he reached his destination.

One night, his wife and child slept soundly but he couldn't sleep. On some mysterious impulse, he threw on his clothes, then went to the balcony. Overhead, the fog of city lights dimmed the many stars in the sky. He was searching for something, but what? It was a good while before his heart answered him: He was looking for Sirius. He couldn't help but shiver at that.

Seven years had passed. The time left before the appointment he'd made with her: two days.

SIRIUS

The first snow of the year had fallen the day before, and the roads were slippery. The taxi couldn't make it up the last stretch to the mountain's peak. He had to go, once again, on foot, clambering to the peak of Mount Siyun.

On the road, more than once, he wondered whether he was thinking straight. The probability she'd keep the appointment was zero. The reason was simple: Sirius couldn't twinkle like the sun had seventeen years earlier. In the past seven years, he had skimmed a lot of astronomy and astrophysics. That he'd said something so ridiculous seven years ago filled him with shame. He was grateful that she hadn't laughed at him there and then. Thinking about it now, he realized she had merely been polite when she seemed to take it seriously. In the intervening seven years, he'd pondered the promise she'd made as they left each other many, many times. The more he did, the more it seemed to take on a mocking tone. . . .

Astronomical observations had shifted to telescopes in Earth orbit. Mount Siyun Observatory had shut down four years ago. The buildings there became vacation villas. No one was around in the off-season. What was he going to do there? He stopped. The seven years that'd passed had taken their toll. He couldn't climb up the mountain as easily anymore. He hesitated for a moment, but ultimately abandoned the idea of turning back. He continued upward.

He'd waited so long, why not finally chase a dream just this once?

When he saw the white figure, he thought it was a hallucination. The figure wearing the white windbreaker in front of the former observatory blended into the backdrop of the snow-packed mountain. It was difficult to make out at first, but when she saw him, she ran to him. She looked like a feather flying over the snowfield. He could only stand dumbstruck, and wait for her to reach him. She gasped for air, unable to speak. Except that her long hair was now short, she hadn't changed much. Seven years wasn't long. Compared to the lifetimes of stars, it didn't even count as an instant, and she studied stars.

She looked him in the eyes. "Doctor, at first, I didn't have much hope of seeing you. I came only to carry out a promise or perhaps to fulfill a wish."

"Me too."

"I almost let the observation date slip by, but I never truly forgot it, just stowed it in the deepest recesses of my memory. A few nights ago, I suddenly thought of it. . . ."

"Me too."

Neither of them spoke. They just listened to the gusts of wind that blew through the trees reverberate among the mountains.

"Did Sirius actually twinkle like that?" he asked finally, his voice trembling a little.

"The waveform of its twinkling overlaps precisely the sun's from seventeen years ago and Alpha Centauri A's from seven years ago. It also arrived exactly on time. The space telescope Confucius 3 observed it. There's no way it can be wrong."

They fell again into another long stretch of silence. The rumble of wind through the trees rose and fell. The sound spiraled among the mountains, filling the space between earth and sky. It seemed as though some sort of force throughout the universe thrummed like a deep and mystical chorus. . . . He couldn't help but shiver. She, evidently feeling the same way, broke the silence, as though to cast off her fears.

"But this situation, this strange phenomenon, goes beyond our current theories. It requires many more observations and much more evidence in order for the scientific community to deal with it."

"I know. The next possible observable star is . . ."

"It would have been Procyon, in Canis Minor, but five years ago, it rapidly grew too dark to be worth measuring. Maybe it drifted into a nearby cloud of interstellar dust. So, the next measurable star is Altair, in the constellation Aquila."

"How far is it?"

"5.1 parsecs, 16.6 light-years. The sun's twinkling from seventeen years ago has just reached it."

"So we have to wait another seventeen years?"

"People's lives are bitter and short."

Her last sentence touched something deep in his heart. His eyes, blown dry by the winter wind, suddenly teared. "Indeed. People's lives are bitter and short."

"But at least we'll still be around to keep this sort of appointment again."

He stared at her dumbly. Did she really want to part ways again for seventeen years?!

"Excuse me. This is all a bit overwhelming," he said. "I need some time to think."

The wind had blown her hair onto her forehead. She brushed it away. She saw into his heart, then laughed sympathetically. "Of course. I'll give you my number and email address. If you're willing, we'll keep in touch."

He let out a long breath, as if a riverboat on the misty ocean finally saw the lighthouse on the shore. His heart filled with a happiness he was too embarrassed to admit to.

"But . . . Why don't I escort you down the mountain."

Laughing, she shook her head and pointed to the domed vacation villa behind her. "I'm going to stay here awhile. Don't worry. There's electricity and good company. They live here, forest rangers . . . I really need some peace and quiet, a long time of peace and quiet."

They made their quick goodbyes. He followed the snow-packed road down the mountain. She stood at Mount Siyun's peak for a long while watching him leave. They both prepared for a seventeen-year wait.

THIRD TIME

After the third time he returned from Mount Siyun, he was suddenly aware of the end of his life. Neither of them had more than seventeen years left. The vast and desolate universe made light as slow as a snail. Life was as worth mentioning as dirt.

They kept in touch for the first five of the seventeen years. They exchanged emails, occasionally called each other, but they never met. She lived in another city, far away. Later, they each walked toward the summit of their own lives. He became a celebrated brain-medicine expert and the head of a major hospital. She became a member of an international academy of science. They had more and more to worry about. At the same time, he understood that, with the most prominent astronomer in academic circles, it was inappropriate to discuss too much this myth-like thing that linked them together. So, they gradually grew further and further apart. Halfway through their seventeen years, they stopped contacting each other entirely.

However, he wasn't worried. He knew that, between them, they had an unbreakable bond, the light from Altair rushing through vast and desolate space to Earth. They both waited silently for it to arrive.

ALTAIR

They met at the peak of Mount Siyun in the dark of night. Both of them wanted to show up early to avoid making the other wait. So around three in the morning, they both clambered up the mountain. Their flying cars could have easily reached the peak, but they both parked at the foot of the mountain and then walked up, as if they wanted to re-create the past.

Mount Siyun was designated as a nature preserve ten years ago, and it had become one of the few wild places left on Earth. The observatory and vacation villas of old became vine-covered ruins. It was among these ruins that they met under the starlight. He'd recently seen her on TV, so he knew the marks that time had left on her. Even though there was no moon tonight, no matter what he imagined, he felt that the woman before him was still the one who stood under the moonlight thirty-four years ago. Her eyes reflected starlight, making his heart melt in his feelings of the past.

She said, "Let's not start by talking about Altair, okay? These past few years, I've been in charge of a research project, precisely to measure the transmission of type A twinkling between stars."

"Oh, wow. I hadn't let myself hope that anything might actually come from all this."

"How could it not? We have to face up to the truth that it exists. In the universe that classical relativity and quantum physics describes, its oddity is already inconceivable. . . . We discovered in these few years of observation that transmitting type A twinkling between stars is a universal phenomenon. At any given moment, innumerable stars are originating type A twinklings. Surrounding stars propagate them. Any star can initiate a twinkling or propagate the twinkling of other stars. The whole of space seems to be a pool flooded with ripples in the midst of rain. . . . What? Aren't you excited?"

"I guess I don't understand: Observing the transmission of twinkling through four stars took over thirty years. How can you . . ."

"You're a smart person. You ought to be able to think of a way."

"I think . . . Is it like this: Search for some stars near each other to observe. For example, star A and star B, they're ten thousand light-years from Earth, but they're only five light-years from each other. This way, you only need five years to observe the twinkle they transmitted ten thousand years ago."

"You really are a smart man! The Milky Way has hundreds of billions of stars. We can find plenty of stars like those."

He laughed. Just like thirty-four years ago, he wished she could see him laugh in the night.

"I brought you a present."

As he spoke, he opened a traveling bag, then took out an odd thing about the size of a soccer ball. At first glance, it seemed like a haphazardly balled-up fishing net. Bits of starlight pierced through its small holes. He turned on his flashlight. The thing was made of an uncountably large number of tiny globes, each about the size of a grain of rice. Attached to each globe was a different number of sticks so slender they were almost invisible. They connected one globe to another. Together, they formed an extremely complex netlike system.

He turned off the flashlight. In the dark, he pressed a switch at the base of the structure. A dazzling burst of quickly moving bright dots filled the structure, as though tens of thousands of fireflies had been loaded into the tiny, hollow, glass globes. One globe lit, then its light propagated to surrounding globes. At any given moment, some portion of the tiny globes produced an initial point of light or propagated the light another globe produced. Vividly, she saw her own analogy: a pond in the midst of rain.

"Is this a model of the propagation of twinkling among the stars? Oh, so beautiful. Can it be . . . you'd already predicted everything?!"

"I'd guessed that propagating the twinkling among the stars was a universal phenomenon. Of course, it was just intuition. However, this isn't a model of the propagation of stellar twinkling. Our campus has a brainscience research project that uses three-dimensional holographic-microscopy molecular-positioning technology to study the propagation of signals between neurons in the brain. This is just the model of signal propagation in the right brain cortex, albeit a really small part of it."

She stared, captivated by the sphere with the dancing lights. "Is this consciousness?"

"Yes. Just as a computer's ability to operate is a product of a tremendous amount of zeros and ones, consciousness is also just a product of a tremendous amount of simple connections between neurons. In other words, consciousness is what happens when there is a tremendous amount of signal propagation between nodes."

Silently, they stared at this star-filled model of the brain. In the universal abyss that surrounded them, hundreds of billions of stars floating in the Milky Way and hundreds of billions of stars outside the Milky Way were propagating innumerable type A twinklings between each other.

She said lightly, "It's almost light. Let's wait for sunrise."

They sat together on a broken wall, looking at the model of the brain in front of them. The flicker light had a hypnotic effect. Gradually, she fell asleep.

THINKER

She flew against a great, boundless gray river. This was the river of time. She was flying toward time's source. Galaxies like frigid moraines floated in space. She flew fast. One flutter of her wings and she crossed over a hundred million years. The universe shrank. Galaxies clustered together. Background radiation shot up. After one billion years had passed, moraines of galaxies began to melt in a sea of energy, quickly scattering into unconstrained particles. Afterward, the particles transformed into pure energy. Space began to give off light, dark red at first. She seemed to slink in a bloodred energy sea. The light rapidly grew in intensity, changing from the dark red to orange, then again to an eye-piercing pure blue. She seemed to fly within a giant tube of neon light. Particles of matter had already melted in the energy sea. Shining through this dazzling space, she saw the borders of the universe bend into a spherical surface, like the closing of a giant palm. The universe shrank down to the size of a large parlor. She was suspended in its center waiting for a strange particle to arrive. Finally, everything fell into pitch darkness. She knew she was already within a strange particle.

After a blast of cold, she found herself standing on a broad white plain. Above her was a limitless black void. The ground was pure white, covered by a layer of smooth, transparent, sticky liquid. She walked ahead to the side of a bright red river. A transparent membrane covered the river surface. The red river water surged under the membrane. She left the ground, soaring into the sky. Not far away, the blood river branched into many tributaries, forming a complex network of waterways. She soared even higher. The blood rivers grew slender, mere traces against the white ground, which still stretched to the horizon. She flew forward. A black sea appeared. Once she flew over the sea, she realized it wasn't black. It seemed so because it was deep and completely transparent. The mountain ranges on the vast seafloor came into view. These crystalline mountain ranges stretched radially from the center of the sea to the shore. . . . She pushed herself up even higher and didn't look down again until who knows how long. Now, she saw the entire universe at once.

The universe was a giant eye calmly looking at her.

She woke suddenly. Her forehead was wet. She wasn't sure if it was sweat or dew. He hadn't slept, always at her side silently looking at her. Sitting on the grass in front of them, the model of the brain had exhausted its battery. The starlight that pierced it had extinguished.

Above them, those stars hovered as before.

"What are 'they' thinking?" she asked, breaking the silence.

"Now?"

"In these thirty-four years."

"The twinkling the sun originated could just be a primitive neural impulse. Those happen all the time. Most of them are like mosquitoes causing tiny ripples on a pond, insubstantial. Only those impulses that spread through the whole universe can become an actual experience."

"We used up a lifetime, and saw of 'him' just one twinkling impulse that 'he' couldn't even feel?" she said hazily, as though still in the middle of a dream.

"Use an entire human civilization's life span, and we still might not see one of 'his' actual experiences."

"People's lives are bitter and short."

"Yes. People's lives are bitter and short. . . ."

"A truly insightful, solitary person."

"What?" He looked at her, uncomprehending.

"Oh, I said 'he,' apart from completeness, is nothingness. 'He' is everything. Still thinking, or maybe dreaming. But dreaming about what . . ."

"Let's not try to be philosophers!" He waved his hand as though he were shooing something away.

Out of the blue, something occurred to her. She got off of the broken wall. "According to the big bang theory of modern cosmology, while the universe is expanding, the light emitted from a given point can never spread widely across the universe."

"In other words, 'he' can never have even one actual experience."

Her eyes focused infinitely far away. She stayed silent for a long time, before speaking. "Do we?"

Her question sank him into his recollection of the past. Meanwhile, the woods of Mount Siyun heard its first birdcall. A ray of light appeared on the eastern horizon.

"I have," he answered confidently.

Yes, he had. It was thirty-four years ago during a peaceful moonlit night on this mountain peak. A feather-like figure in the moonlight, a pair of eyes looking up at the stars . . . A twinkling in his brain quickly propagated through the entire universe of his mind. From then on, that twinkling never disappeared. That universe contained in his brain was more magnificent than the star-filled exterior universe that had already expanded for about fourteen billion years. Although the external universe was vast, the evidence ultimately showed it was finite. Thought, however, was infinite.

The eastern sky grew brighter and brighter, starting to hide its sea of stars. Mount Siyun revealed its rough contours. On its highest peak, at the vine-covered ruins of the observatory, these two nearly sixty-year-old people gazed eastward expectantly, waiting for that dazzling brain cell to rise over the horizon.